P9-DIW-777

THE X-FILES™

GOBLINS

WHIRLWIND

THE X-FILES™

GOBLINS
WHIRLWIND

Charles Grant

Based on the characters created
by Chris Carter

HarperPrism
An Imprint of HarperPaperbacks

The X-Files is a trademark of the Twentieth Century Fox Film Corporation.

If you purchased this book without a cover, you should be aware that this book is stolen property. It was reported as "unsold and destroyed" to the publisher and neither the author nor the publisher has received any payment for this "stripped book."

This is a work of fiction. The characters, incidents, and dialogues are products of the author's imagination and are not to be construed as real. Any resemblance to actual events or persons, living or dead, is entirely coincidental.

HarperPaperbacks *A Division of* HarperCollins*Publishers*
10 East 53rd Street, New York, N.Y. 10022

Goblins. Copyright © 1994 by the Twentieth Century Fox Film Corporation.
Whirlwind. Copyright © 1995 by the Twentieth Century Fox Film Corporation.

Copyright © 1996 by the Twentieth Century Fox Film Corporation. All rights reserved. No part of this book may be used or reproduced in any manner whatsoever without written permission of the publisher, except in the case of brief quotations embodied in critical articles and reviews. For information address HarperCollins*Publishers,* 10 East 53rd Street, New York, N.Y. 10022.

HarperPaperbacks may be purchased for educational, business, or sales promotional use. For information, please write: Special Markets Department, HarperCollins*Publishers,* 10 East 53rd Street, New York, N.Y. 10022-5299.

Library of Congress Cataloging-in-Publication data is on file with the publisher.

First HarperPrism printing: August 1996

Printed in the United States of America

HarperPrism is an imprint of HarperPaperbacks. HarperPaperbacks, HarperPrism, and colophon are trademarks of HarperCollins*Publishers*

97 98 99 ❖ 10 9 8 7 6 5 4 3

GOBLINS

This is for Chris Carter, no question about it.

Because, quite literally, without his wonderful
and addictive show, this book wouldn't exist,
and I wouldn't have anything to do on
Friday nights but work.

ACKNOWLEDGMENTS

Many, many thanks, for reasons that would probably bore you to tears, to:

John Silbersack, editor and keeper of the editorial whip, for extreme patience under fire, and helping me keep mine;

Howard Morhaim, fastest and best damn agent in the West;

The Jersey Conspiracy, whose enthusiastic support kept me sane, and whose invaluable assistance steered me away from making too many stupid mistakes—it isn't their fault if I made them anyway;

T. Liam McDonald, for the inside scoop;

Ms. Carolee Nisbet, Public Affairs Office, Fort Dix, New Jersey, who was always gracious and helpful, especially when blathered memories of basic training kept getting in the way of intelligent discussion—if you don't recognize some of the post as described here, the changes were made for story reasons only, not because Ms. Nisbet steered me wrong.

And last, but never least, to Ashley McConnell, who called one night and ordered me to watch the show, sent me information I couldn't do without, and still hasn't said, "I told you so." Yet.

ONE

The tavern was filled with ghosts that night.

Grady Pierce could feel them, but he didn't much care as long as the bartender kept pouring the drinks.

They were ghosts of the old days, when recruits, mostly draftees, were bused almost daily into Fort Dix for basic training, scared or strutting, and hustled out of their seats by drill instructors with hard faces and hard eyes who never spoke in less than a yell. The scared became terrified, and the strutters soon lost that smug look they wore—it was apparent from the moment they were shorn of their hair that this wasn't going to be a Technicolor, wide-screen John Wayne movie.

This was real.

This was the real Army.

And there was a damn good chance they were going someplace to die.

Grady ought to know; he had trained enough of them himself.

But that was the old days.

This was now, and what the hell—if the ghosts of the boys

who never came back wanted to stand behind him and demand he teach them again and this time do it right, well, hell, that was what they did, no skin off his nose.

What he did these days was drink, and damned good at it he was.

He sat on his stool, bony shoulders hunched, hands clasped on the bar before him as if he were saying grace before taking up the glass. His face under the mostly gray brush cut was all angles, sharp and dark with shadows; he wore worn and stained fatigues loose at the waist, a too-large field jacket torn at one shoulder, scuffed hiking boots so thin he could feel pebbles beneath the soles.

From where he sat at the bar's far end, he could see the dozen scarred darkwood tables, the half-dozen dark booths along the side wall, the twenty or so customers bent over their drinks. Usually the place was close to bedlam with top-of-the-voice, not always good-natured arguments about the Giants, the Phillies, the 76ers, the government. Waylon would be howling on the jukebox, a game on the TV hanging on the wall, and beneath it all the comforting clatter of balls over at the pool table, floating green in the light of the single lamp above it. There might even be a few working girls hanging out, joining in, not always looking for business.

Good thing, too, he thought with a quick grin; most of the gals these days were a little long in the tooth and short in the looks.

Tonight, however, was pretty damn miserable.

Rain all day, changing to a hard mist at sundown. The temperature had risen, too, slipping pockets of shifting fog into the alleys and gutters.

It was April, nearly May, but it felt a whole lot like November.

He glanced at his watch—just a few minutes past midnight—and rubbed his eyes with bony knuckles. Time he was having one for the road, then getting on that road while he could still find it.

He reached for the glass, one ice cube and Jack Daniel's

halfway to the rim. He frowned and pulled his hand back. He could have sworn that that glass had been full a second ago.

Man, I'm worse than I thought.

He reached for it again.

"You sure about that?" Aaron Noel, who was more muscle than any man had a right to own and still be able to move, flipped a drying towel over his shoulder and leaned back against the shelf fronting the smoke-fogged mirror. His white T-shirt was tight, the sleeves cut off to give his upper arms some room. He was a younger man who looked as if he had lived one lifetime too many. "Not that I'm complaining, Grady, but I ain't taking you home tonight again, no offense."

Grady grinned. "You my old lady now?"

"Nope. But the weather sucks, right? And every time the weather sucks, you get the miseries, drink too much and pass out, and then I gotta lug your sorry ass to that sorry hole you call a house." He shook his head. "No way. Not tonight." He waggled his eyebrows. "Got a meeting when I'm done."

Grady glanced at the window by the exit. Past the neon he could see the mist, the dark street, the empty storefronts on the other side.

"So?" the bartender said, nodding toward the unfinished glass.

Grady straightened, yanked on an earlobe, and pinched his cheeks. It was an old trick to see if he was numb enough yet to go home and sleep without having those damn dreams. He wasn't, but he wasn't drunk enough to defy a man who could break his back with his pinky, either.

If the truth be known, Noel was good for him. More than once over the past fifteen years, he had stopped Grady from getting into fights that would have easily turned him into one of his own ghosts. He didn't know why the guy cared; it had just turned out that way.

He considered the glass carefully, grimaced at the way his

stomach lurched with acid, and said with a resigned sigh, "Ah, the hell with it."

Aaron approved.

Grady slipped off the stool and held onto the bar with his left hand while he waited for his balance to get it right. When he figured he could walk without looking like he was on a steamer in a hurricane, he saluted the bartender and dropped a bill beside the glass. "Catch you around," he said.

"Whatever," the bartender said. "Just get the hell home and get some sleep."

Grady reached into his hip pocket and pulled out a Yankees cap, snapped it open and jammed it onto his head, and made his way toward the door.

When he checked over his shoulder, Aaron was already talking with another guy at the bar.

"Good night, gentlemen," he said loudly, and stepped outside, laughing at the way some of them snapped their heads up, eyes wide, as if he'd just shaken them out of a nap.

As soon as the door closed behind him, the laughter twisted into a spasm of coughing, forcing him to lean against the brick wall until it passed.

"Jesus," he muttered, wiping his mouth with the back of a hand. "Quit drinking, quit smoking, you old fart, before they find you in the damn gutter."

He paused at the curb, then crossed over and moved on up the street, keeping close to the closed shops, the empty shops with plywood for windows, and decided as he did that he'd finally had it with this burg. As the government kept chipping away at Dix's assignments, folks up and left, and nobody came in to take their place.

Hell, if he was going to drink himself to death, he might as well do it somewhere pretty, Florida or something, where at least it stays warm most of the damn year.

He hiccuped, spat on the sidewalk, and belched loudly.

On the other hand, he decided the same thing every damn night, and hadn't moved yet.

Goddamn army.

Too old, pal, we don't need you anymore. Take your pension and split, you old fart.

He belched again, spat again, and seriously considered going back to Barney's to have a farewell drink. That would shake them up, no question about it.

Half a block later he stopped, scowling at himself, and squinted down the street. The tarmac was a black mirror, streetlight and neon twisted and shimmering in the puddles. Nothing there but small shops and offices, a distant traffic light winking amber.

He looked behind him.

The street was deserted there, too.

Nothing moved but small patches of fog.

You're spooking yourself, bud; knock it off.

He rolled his shoulders, straightened his spine, and crossed to the other side. Two more blocks, a left, a right, and he'd be at the worn-down apartment complex where he had spent most of the years since his discharge.

He could find the damn thing blindfolded.

He glanced back again, thinking someone from the bar was following him.

The end of the block, and he turned around.

Damnit, there was someone back there. It wasn't so much the sound of footsteps as it was a presence. A feeling. The certainty that he wasn't alone. He knew that feeling well—it had almost driven him around the bend, over there in the jungle, knowing they were in the trees, watching, waiting, fingers on triggers.

"Hey!" he called, glad for the sound of his voice, wishing it didn't echo so much.

Nothing there.

Yes, there was.

Screw it, he thought, turning with a disgusted wave of his hand; I don't need the aggravation.

If it was another drunk, he didn't care; if it was some kid looking for a quick mugging, he didn't care about that either because he didn't have anything worth taking.

But by the end of the block he couldn't help it; he had to look.

Nothing.

Nothing at all.

A sudden breeze made him narrow his eyes as it sifted mist against his face, and when he did, he saw something move at the mouth of a narrow alley about thirty feet back.

"Hey, damnit!"

No one answered.

And that pissed him off.

Bad enough the army had fucked him over, and bad enough he hadn't been able to leave this damn place and leave the ghosts behind, but he was not about to let some goddamn punk mess with his head.

He pulled his hands out of his pockets and marched back, breathing slowly, deeply, letting his anger build by degrees instead of exploding.

"Hey, you son of a bitch!"

No one answered.

Nothing moved.

By the time he reached the alley, he was in full-bore fighting mode, and he stood at the mouth, feet slightly apart, fists on his hips.

"You want to come outta there, buddy?"

A sigh; maybe the breeze, maybe not.

He couldn't see more than five feet in—three stories of brick on either side, a pair of dented trash cans on the left, scraps of paper on the ground, fluttering weakly as the breeze blew again.

He wasn't sure, but he thought the alley was a dead end, which meant the sucker wasn't going anywhere as long as he stood here. The question was, how far was he going to push this thing? How drunk was he?

He took one step in, and heard the breathing.

Slow, measured; someone was trying very hard not to be heard.

This didn't make sense. If whoever it was had hidden himself back there, Grady would have heard him moving around. Had to. There was too much crap on the ground, too much water. His own single step had sounded like a gunshot.

And the breathing sounded close.

"I ain't got time for this," he muttered, and turned.

And saw the arm reach out of the brick wall on his right.

The arm, and the hand with the blade.

He knew what it was; God knows he had used it himself dozens of times.

He also knew how sharp it was.

He almost didn't feel it sweep across his throat.

And he almost managed to make it to the street before his knees gave out and he fell against the wall, staring at the arm, at the hand, at the bayonet as he slid down, legs stretched out before him.

"Goddamn ghost," he whispered.

"Not quite," someone answered. "Not quite, old man."

That's when Grady felt the fire around his neck, and the warmth flowing over his chest, and the garbage beneath him, and the fog settling on his face.

That's when he saw the face of the thing that had killed him.

TWO

The afternoon was pleasantly warm, the sky a sharp and cloudless blue. The sounds of Thursday traffic were muted by the trees carrying their new leaves, although the cherry trees hadn't yet sprung all their blossoms. The tourists were few at the Jefferson Memorial, mostly older people with cameras around their necks or camcorders in their hands, moving slowly, taking their time. A handful of joggers followed the Tidal Basin rim; two paddleboats glided over the water, seemingly in a clumsy, not very earnest race.

That's why Fox Mulder preferred this place over the others when he wanted time to think. He could sit undisturbed on the steps, off to one side, without having to listen to terminally bored tour guides chattering like robots, or schoolkids laughing and horsing around, or any of the rest of the circus that Old Abe or the Washington Monument managed to attract.

His dark blue suit jacket was folded on the marble step beside him. His tie was pulled down and his collar unbuttoned. He looked much younger than his years, his face as yet unlined, his brown hair unruly in the light breeze that slipped over the water. Those who bothered to look in his direction figured, he supposed, that he was some kind of academic.

That was all right with him.

His sandwich was almost done, a plastic cup of soda just about empty, when he saw a tall man in a dark brown suit moving around the edge of the Basin, staring at those he passed as if expecting to discover someone he knew. Mulder looked quickly from side to side, but there was no way he could duck around the building or into the trees without being seen.

"Hey!" the man called, catching sight of him and waving.

Mulder smiled politely, but he didn't stand.

This was not what he needed on a great day like this. What he needed was his sandwich, his soda—although he'd prefer a cold beer in a bottle, preferably sitting in a booth at Ripley's, in Alexandria—and maybe that short brunette over there, taking slow tight circles on a pair of inline skates, earphones attached to a Walkman at her waist. He supposed maintaining balance was a lot like being on ice skates; it seemed to be the same principle. Not that he was all that good when roller skates had wheels at the corners, spending, as he had done, more time on his rump than attaining great speeds.

The skater shifted suddenly, and he blinked, realizing for the first time how tan she was, and how snug her red satin shorts and red T-shirt were.

Then a shadow blocked his view.

It was the redhead.

"Mulder," the man said, standing two steps below him, grinning like an idiot, "where the hell have you been?"

"Right here, Hank."

Special Agent Hank Webber stared over Mulder's head at the daylit figure of Thomas Jefferson standing tall beneath the dome. A puzzled frown came and went. "Never did see this place, you know what I mean?" He shook his head, scratched through his dark red hair. "What do you want to come to a place like this for?"

Mulder shrugged. "It's nice. It's quiet." He deepened his voice. "It's not the office."

Webber didn't take the hint. "So, did you hear what came in?"

Mulder just looked at him.

"Oh." The younger man grinned sheepishly. "Sorry. Of course you wouldn't hear. You were here."

"Hank, your powers of deduction have never failed to give me a shiver." He smiled when the younger man sputtered, telling him with a gesture that it was only a stupid joke. Hank was a good man, but there were times when Mulder thought him dense as a post. "Hear what?"

"Helevito."

He sat up slowly, lunch momentarily forgotten. "What about him?"

"They got him."

He didn't know whether to laugh, cheer, shock the kid with a victory dance, or play it the Bureau way by simply nodding, as if the outcome of a three-month manhunt for a kidnapper had never been in doubt, especially since the kidnapped child had already been recovered safely. What he decided to do was take another bite of his sandwich.

Webber hooked a thumb in his belt. "Yep. Not two hours ago. You figured it right, Mulder. They staked out his cousin's place in Biloxi, and sure enough, he comes strolling in this morning all by his lonesome. Spent most of the night on one of those new riverboats, pissing away half the ransom money at roulette. Most of the rest evidently went to some blonde." He laughed and shook his head. "I heard the first thing he said was, 'I knew I should've played thirty-six and red.'"

He nodded.

Mulder took another bite, another sip, and waited.

"So." Webber squinted as he checked out the memorial again.

A quartet of nuns chattered past, smiling at him, smiling at Mulder.

The skater left, not even a glance in their direction.

Webber sniffed, and fussed with his tie. "So."

"Hank, I am eating my lunch. I am enjoying the fresh air, the sunshine . . . and I am especially enjoying the peace and quiet that comes with not being at the Bureau for a while. I'm not sure what you want me to say."

The younger man seemed bewildered. "But . . . but if it hadn't been for you, they never would've gotten him, right? I mean, nobody else figured out his gambling problem, right? Nobody else knew about that cousin. So . . ." He spread his hands. "So aren't you glad?"

"Overjoyed," he answered flatly.

And instantly regretted it when Webber's expression sagged into youthful disappointment. He knew the kid believed that every bust was righteous, every arrest an occasion for celebration, every crook large or small put behind bars a reason to dance. What he hadn't figured on was, between the first bust and the fourth and the fiftieth and the millionth, the exhilaration was always there. Always. And the feeling that finally one of the bad guys lost.

But the good agents, the best ones, never forgot that on the far side of that exhilaration there was always someone else waiting in line.

It never ended.

It just never ended.

That fact alone sometimes turned a perfectly good agent into a cynic who made mistakes. And it sometimes got him killed.

Mulder didn't want that to happen to him.

He had too much to do.

He had too much yet left undone.

On the other hand, he also hadn't finished his lunch, and

there were still five other folders waiting on his desk in varying stages of investigation. He wasn't the primary agent on any of them, but he had been asked to take a look, to see if he could spot something the others had missed.

It was what he was good at; very good, if you paid attention to some of the talk around the office. Although he really didn't see it that way. It was, simply, what he did, and he had never really bothered to analyze it.

When the younger man finally looked as if he were either going to cry or scream, Mulder swallowed, touched his chin with a finger, and pointed. "If I remember, Hank, you were the one who came up with the Biloxi connection. We all missed it. You got it."

Webber blushed.

He couldn't believe it—the kid actually blushed, ducked his head, scuffed his shoe on the step. Mulder decided that if he said, "Aw, shucks," he would have to be killed.

"Thanks," he said instead, fighting hard not to grin. "That . . . well, that means a lot." He gestured vaguely. "I didn't mean to interrupt but . . ." He gestured again. "I thought you'd want to know."

"I did. Honestly. Thanks."

"So." Webber backed away, and almost toppled off the step. He laughed self-consciously, his right arm flapping. "So, I guess I'll get back, okay?"

"Sure."

"You'll be—"

Mulder held up what was left of the sandwich.

"Right. Sure." He waved, reached into his jacket pocket, pulled out a pair of sunglasses, and slipped them on.

Suddenly he wasn't a kid named Hank Webber anymore.

Suddenly he was a man in a suit too dark for the weather, wearing sunglasses too dark for the sun. Suddenly he wasn't a part of the scene anymore. If he had painted a sign on his back, he couldn't have said FBI any better.

Mulder smiled to himself as Webber walked off, practically marching, and washed the last of his lunch down with the soda. Then he glanced around, not really seeing anything, before hooking his jacket with a forefinger, draping it over his shoulder, and moving into the memorial itself.

He liked it in here, especially now, when there was no one else around. It didn't feel like a cathedral, the way Old Abe's place did, yet he was in awe just the same of the man who rose above him. Jefferson wasn't a god. He had his faults. But those faults only made his accomplishments all the more remarkable.

This was where he liked to work puzzles out, following crooked mental paths to see where they led, maybe hoping some of the third president's genius would rub off on him.

In here he couldn't hear the traffic, the tourists, nothing but the sound of his shoes on the polished marble floor.

What he had to consider today was a case in Louisiana that involved at least one brutal murder, one daylight robbery of $25,000, and witnesses who swore on every Bible handed to them that the person who had done it had vanished into thin air. In the middle of a circus tent. While wearing the costume of a hobo clown.

His instincts were usually pretty reliable. This time they suggested this had nothing to do with an X-File, those cases he specialized in, that had about them an air of the bizarre, the inexplicable.

The paranormal.

The kind of cases the Bureau officially frowned upon, but couldn't always ignore.

Which was why he had been shown this one. This kind of thing, whether the upper echelon liked it or not—and they usually didn't—was his specialty.

Louisiana just didn't have that X-File scent.

Still, there was always a chance he was wrong. It wouldn't

be the first time. His usual partner, Dana Scully, had told him that so often, he had finally suggested she print up cards: *Mulder, this is an ordinary case, only with weird stuff; aliens, monsters, and UFOs need not apply.* Whenever he began to think that X the unknown was actually something they should look into, she was supposed to hand him a card, or staple it to his forehead, and get on with it.

She hadn't thought that very funny.

Except for the stapling part.

Still, he had been right often enough in the past, even if she was too stubborn to admit it.

What he was afraid of now, what always kept him alert, was that every case with supposed "weird stuff" in it would make him jump before he thought, and thus bring down the wrath of his superiors, forcing the X-File Section closed.

It had already happened once.

He didn't want it to happen again.

Especially when he had been so close to final proof that the Earth wasn't alone . . . so close . . .

Too close for some.

Others would call that paranoia; he called it simply watching his back. Not for the knife. For the razor.

The fact that he tended to elaborate on or improvise on the Bureau's standard operating procedures also hadn't made him many friends in high places.

That the section had been reinstated was a stroke of good fortune, but he never gloated.

He did his job.

Looking.

Always looking.

Following the crooked path.

He wandered around to the back of the statue, tracing his fingers along the marble base.

What he wanted to do now was make sure that this Louisiana thing was weird stuff, nothing more.

He had to be sure that he wasn't so desperate that he saw only what he wanted to see, not what was really there.

Not so easy to do these days, when he had been so close.

So damn close.

He stepped back as he slipped into his jacket and looked up at the president, dark bronze and gleaming, towering above him.

"So what do you think?" he said quietly. "You bought the stupid place, is there anything out there?"

A hand gripped his shoulder.

When he tried to turn, the grip tightened, ordering him to stay where he was.

His throat dried instantly, but he did as he was bidden. He wasn't afraid, just wary.

He lowered his head slowly to keep his neck from cramping.

The hand didn't move, nor did it relax its grip.

"Well?" he asked mildly.

Mint; he smelled an aftershave or cologne with a faint touch of mint, and the warmth of the sun on someone's clothes, as if he'd walked a long way to reach him. The hand was strong, but he couldn't see it without turning his head.

"Mr. Mulder." A smooth voice, not very deep.

He nodded. He was patient. Not often, however; both his temper and his temperament never had liked short leashes. He tried to adjust his shoulder, but the fingers wouldn't let him.

"Louisiana," the voice said, fading slightly, telling him the man had turned his head. "It's not what you hope, but you shouldn't ignore it."

"Mind if I ask who you are?" Still mild, still calm.

"Yes."

"Mind if I ask if—"

"Yes."

The grip tightened, pinching a nerve that made Mulder's eyes close briefly. He nodded, once. He understood—*keep your mouth shut, ask no questions, pay attention.*

Voices approached outside—children, for a change sounding respectful, not rowdy.

A car's horn blared.

"The fact, Mr. Mulder, that your section has been reactivated does not mean there still aren't those who would like to make sure you stay out of their way. Permanently." A shift of cloth, and the voice was closer, a harsh whisper in his left ear. "You're still not protected, Mr. Mulder, but you're not in chains, either. Remember that. You'll have to."

The grip tightened again, abruptly, just as the voices entered the memorial and turned to echoes. His eyes instantly filled with tears, and his knees buckled as he cried out softly. A lunge with his arm couldn't prevent his forehead from slamming against the pedestal as he went down. By the time his vision cleared, no more than a few seconds, he was kneeling, head down, and when he looked to his right, grimacing, the only person he saw was a little girl with an ice cream cone, braids, and a vivid blue jumper.

"Are you okay, mister?" she asked, licking at the cone.

He touched his shoulder gingerly, swallowed a curse, and managed a nod while taking several deep breaths.

A woman appeared behind the girl, gently easing her away. "Sir, do you need help?"

He looked up at her and smiled. "Just felt a little dizzy, that's all." Bracing one hand against the pedestal got him to his feet. The woman and the girl, and about a dozen others, backed away warily as he moved. "Thanks," he said to the woman.

She nodded politely.

He stepped outside.

The breeze attacked his forelock, and he swiped at it absently as he slipped into his jacket. His shoulder stung, but he barely noticed it. What he did notice was the breath of ice across the back of his neck.

Whoever the man was, there had been no threats, but there had been no promises either.

And for the first time in a long time, he felt that tiny rush of excitement that told him the hunt was on again.

Not the hunt for the bad guys.

The hunt for the truth.

THREE

Corporal Frank Ulman was tired of lying in bed. His back was sore, his ass was sore, his legs were sore. The only thing that wasn't sore was his head, and he figured that would fall off if he had to count the holes in the ceiling one more time.

It was, no question about it, a lousy way to spend a Saturday night.

What made it worse was the fact that he was here because he had been stupid. Really stupid. All he had wanted last night was a quiet drink, pick up someone for the evening because his regular girl had to work, and wake up the next day without a hangover. No big deal. So he had wrangled a pass from the sarge, no sweat, put on his civies, and hitched a ride into Marville with a couple of half-bald warrant officers who spent the whole time bitching about the way the DoD couldn't make up its mind whether to close Dix down or not.

They had dropped him off at Barney's Tavern.

He went in and had his drink, passed a few words with the muscle-bound bartender, watched a couple of innings of Phillies baseball on the TV, and listened while the curiously noisy crowd gabbed about old Grady getting his throat slashed the weekend before.

It was a shame. He had kind of liked the old fart, had bought him a drink now and then, and enjoyed listening to his stories. Grady had called him "Sal," because, he said, Frankie looked like some old actor or something named Sal Mineo. After the first couple of times, Frankie hadn't bothered to correct him. If the old guy thought he looked like a movie star, it was no skin off his nose.

Now that Grady was dead, so was Sal.

Too bad.

Another drink, another inning, and he made his first mistake: He tried to pick up a woman sitting by herself at a table near the back. Not bad looking in the tavern's twilight, but he wasn't about to be fussy. Angie wasn't here, and he was. Just like always. It was a mistake because the bitch didn't want to be picked up, said so loudly when he persisted, and finally suggested that he perform a certain number of mind-boggling, and definitely unnatural, sexual acts upon himself on his way home to his momma.

His second mistake was dropping a twenty on the table in front of her and telling her to either put up or shut up, and don't forget the change.

His third mistake was not listening to that muscle-bound bartender, who told him to get his sorry ass out of his bar before the roof fell in.

Corporal Ulman, with too many boilermakers and a hell of an attitude under his belt, called the bartender a fag.

The next thing he knew he was in Walson, the air force hospital on post, getting stitched under the chin, getting a cast on his left arm, and getting a faceful of the sarge, who had been waiting for him when the cops brought him in.

Bed rest was the order, take these pills, stay out of trouble, don't come back.

All day he stared at the barracks ceiling, his left arm throb-bing in a sling, his face a road map of yellow and purple bruises.

Nobody felt sorry for him.

The sarge had told him that when he got up the next day, he was going to be busted. Again.

So he figured he didn't have a whole hell of a lot to lose when he swung his legs over the side of the bed and waited for the dizziness to pass. He had to get out. Walk around a little. Get some fresh air. Maybe find a card game and tell a few stories of his own. Anything but count those damn holes again.

Clumsily he dressed in boots and fatigues, made it as far as the door before he felt the first ache, deep in his jawbone. It almost sent him back, but now it was a matter of pride. A busted arm, a few bruises, what kind of a soldier would he be if he let something like that keep him on his back?

He checked the second floor corridor and saw no one, heard nothing. Why should he? Everyone else was having a good time, bumping around Marville, Browns Mills, drinking themselves blind, getting laid, catching a flick.

The thought made him angry.

One goddamn lucky punch, one lousy mistake, and here he was, practically a cripple. And he wouldn't put it past one of the guys to call Angie and tell her everything.

Son of a bitch.

What he needed, he decided then, wasn't a card game, it was a drink. Something to calm him down, something to ease the pain.

He knew just where to get it.

Five minutes later, after slipping a cheap and slim flashlight into his hip pocket and dry-swallowing one of the pain pills the doc had given him, he was in and out of Howie Jacker's room, two pints of Southern Comfort tucked into his shirt. The jerk never learned to lock his locker, his loss, Frankie's gain.

Five minutes after that he was outside. Behind the brick barracks the woods began, and he slipped into them quickly, making his way along a well-worn path toward a clearing half a mile in. He'd been invited there last summer, a place reserved for those who wanted to drink, or whatever, alone, without the hassle of officially leaving the post.

Actually, the clearing was beyond the post's boundary, which meant that its users were technically AWOL.

Not that anybody cared.

One part of these damn woods was the same as another.

He took the first sip almost before the barracks lights were blocked by the trees, gasping at the hundred-proof sweetness, smacking his lips as the throbbing began to fade. This was a great idea, and beat counting holes all to hell and gone. He took another drink, tucked the pint into the sling, and pulled out the flash. The beam was narrow, but he only needed it to warn him of pine boughs and oak branches. The trail itself had been used so often, it was practically a ditch.

He moved quickly, glancing up now and then in hopes of seeing the stars or the moon. It wasn't that he was afraid of the woods. Not really. For a city boy, he had learned to take them or leave them.

What he didn't like was the voice the trees had.

When the breeze blew, there were whispers, like old men talking about him behind their hands; when the air was still, the leaves still moved, nudged by night things who stayed just out of reach of the narrow white beam.

He drank again.

The woods talked to him.

He stopped once and checked behind him, slashing the beam up the trail, seeing nothing but gray trunks and colorless underbrush.

He drank, walked, and cursed when he realized the first pint was already empty. He tossed the bottle aside angrily, took out the second one, and slipped it into the sling. Later; that one was for later.

The breeze kicked into a gust of strong wind, damp and cool.

The branches danced and whispered.

Okay, he thought, so maybe not such a hot idea after all. Maybe he should just go back, lay down, drink himself into a stupor, and let the sarge do his worst in the morning.

His head ached, his arm ached, his jaw ached.

"Jesus," he muttered.

Another gust shoved him off the trail, the beam blurring across the ground, sparkling as it passed through pockets of mist.

Something moved, out there in the dark.

Something large.

Frankie swayed, wishing he hadn't drunk so much, wishing he hadn't taken those pills first. His stomach felt on fire, and sweat had broken out across his brow and down his spine.

It wasn't warm at all.

The wind had turned cold.

He heard it again, something moving toward him, not bothering to mask its approach.

His first thought was *Jersey Devil,* and he giggled. Right. A real live monster in the middle of New Jersey. Right. Tell me another.

His stomach lurched.

He swallowed hard and hurried on, swerving around a bush whose thorns clawed at his legs. His broken arm burned now, too, and he cradled it with his free hand, sending the beam sideways, poking at the black without pushing it away.

When he collided with a sapling that threw him to the ground, he cried out, cursed, kicked himself awkwardly to his feet, and demanded to know who the hell was out there, he was a sick man, he was lost, goddamnit, and he didn't need this shit.

The wind tugged at his hair, plucked at his shirt.

A drop of rain splattered on the tip of nose.

"Oh great," he muttered. "That's just fucking great."

Something in the trees overhead.

Something in the dark just behind.

He wiped his face with a forearm, used the flashlight like a lance as he found a clear path and broke into a slow trot. It wasn't the right trail, but it had to lead somewhere, and right now somewhere other than here was exactly where he wanted to be.

Stupid; he was stupid.

The sarge was going to kill him, Angie was going to kill him, and Howie would definitely kill him when he found his stash gone.

Something behind.

Something above.

Light rain slipped between the leaves, between the branches.

God, he thought, get me outta here.

He swerved easily around a gnarled oak, dodged the grasp of a cage of white birch. He couldn't hear anything but his own breathing now, and the wind, and the patter of the rain, but he couldn't stop running. Every step exploded in his arm, but he couldn't stop running, following the sweep and dart of the beam until he rounded a thicket and the ground was gone.

He yelled as he tumbled into a ditch, screamed when he landed on his arm, and blacked out until the pain brought him back.

Rain on his face, like the touch of spider legs.

He rolled onto his knees and hand, and threw up until his throat burned. Then he rocked back on his heels, amazed that the flashlight was still in his grip. He used it to check the ditch, saw it was barely three feet deep.

And there was a road.

"All right!"

Dizzy, swallowing rapidly, he staggered to his feet and looked back at the woods.

No way. No way. He would hike until someone found him, or he found a way back to the post. If it was an MP patrol, who cared? Anything was better than this. Even the sarge.

He slipped-crawled up the other side and onto the tarmac, took a deep breath, and began walking.

The ditch ended a few yards later, the trees closing in, not even leaving a shoulder.

It didn't take long before the pain finally reasserted itself and he had to stop, lean against a dead pine whose branches had been stripped off all the way to the top. There were several of them here, and he figured it was lightning, a quick fire; there was a lot of patches like this here in the Barrens.

"Okay," he said. "Okay, move your butt."

Maybe a drink.

One drink.

The rain was cold and the wind was cold and he was too cold for a spring night like this. He reached into the sling, and laughed when he pulled out the second pint, intact.

He unscrewed the cap and lifted the bottle in a toast to the sky.

He drank and licked his lips.

He lowered his head and saw the outline of a covered Jeep not fifty yards ahead, parked on the left.

He grinned, waved the flashlight, and started up the road, every few feet bracing himself against one of the trees. It wasn't the MPs, thank God. Probably somebody out to get a little with a townie. He laughed. A Jeep, while it was possible, was hardly the best way in the world.

He drank and waved the flashlight again.

The passenger door swung open, and he saw a woman's face.

"Hey!" he called. Hiccuped. "Give a guy a lift?"

The woman's face disappeared.

He drank and grinned, stumbled, and reached out to catch himself on a trunk.

The wood was soft.

Too soft.

He yelped and jumped back, the bottle dropping from his hand.

He aimed the flashlight unsteadily, and saw the arm reach out of the bark.

He saw the blade.

He heard himself scream.

But he could only scream once.

FOUR

Mulder freely admitted to anyone who asked that his office, such as it was, seldom complied, strictly or otherwise, with regulations. While he knew where everything was, usually, it wasn't always where Bureau section heads decreed it ought to be. Controlled tornado was how one of his friends had put it; a hell of a mess was how he described it. Usually with a shrug. Always without apology. Nevertheless, despite the fact that it was in the basement of the J. Edgar Hoover Building, it served its purpose; and the fact that he still had it after all the waves he had made over previous X-File cases was, to more than a few, a minor miracle.

He sat there now, chair tilted back as he wadded up blank sheets of paper and tossed them toward a metal wastebasket set in front of a pair of brown metal file cabinets. "Toward" was the right word. "Into" would have been nicer, but that rarely happened.

Like visiting with Jefferson, it helped him think.

Today, it also helped him kill time while waiting to be summoned to his appointment with his new immediate superior,

Arlen Douglas. The word on the floor was, the man, even though he was only in the slot temporarily, wasn't pleased with the success rate of his agents, and he was hunting for scalps.

Which was why the floor in front of his filing cabinets looked like a snowfield when Carl Barelli walked in, visitor's pass clipped to his sports jacket's breast pocket.

Mulder tossed, missed, swiveled his chair around, and said, "Michael Jordan is safe for another season."

"Jordan retired last year."

Mulder rolled his eyes. "That's the trouble with you, Carl. You pay too much attention to details. It's the big picture you have to consider."

To his surprise, his old friend didn't respond. Instead, he wandered around the room, fingers drifting but touching nothing, glancing at without really seeing the charts and Most Wanted sheets, the notes and NASA posters taped and tacked to the wall.

He was a swarthy man with thick black hair and a classic Italian profile dented and scarred just enough to prevent him from being pretty. He was also a former semi-pro footballer who had all the heart and few of the major skills to make it in the NFL or Canada. Luckily, he had recognized the shortcomings before it was too late; now he wrote about the sport for the revitalized *New Jersey Chronicle,* and once every six weeks or so came down to Washington to check out the Redskins, or to see what Congress was up to with a recent flurry of sports safety legislation. While he was here, he always dropped in, looking for a free meal, or a long night of pub-crawling.

Mulder never asked how his friend always managed to get a pass without calling ahead; he had a feeling he didn't need to know the answer.

"So," Barelli said, finally lighting on a chair, kicking aside the paper balls as he stretched out his legs. He glanced through the doorway to the quiet flow of agents outside, then back at the walls.

"So," Mulder echoed.

"So where's Scully?"

"She took some time off. She went West someplace, to see friends, I think. She's too cheap to send me a postcard." A shrug with his eyebrows. "Today's Wednesday, the fifth, right? She'll be back on Monday."

"Too bad. I could've saved her."

Mulder smiled, but it wasn't wide, merely polite. Carl had been trying to get Scully out of the Bureau and into his love life, not necessarily in that order, ever since he had met her just over a year ago. Scully, although she claimed to be flattered by the attention, didn't think this was the guy who would, as she put it, light up her life.

Neither did Mulder.

While he liked Carl a lot, and they had good times together, the man was incorrigible and unrepentant when it came to chasing women. As far as Mulder was concerned, Scully was permanently out of bounds.

Barelli folded his hands over his stomach, pursed his lips, licked them, blew out a silent whistle.

"What?" Mulder was puzzled. No handshake, no raucous invitation to debauchery, no futile attempt to show him exactly how to shoot a basket. The established routine had been abandoned, and he didn't care for the way the man refused to meet his gaze.

The reporter shook himself elaborately, forced a smile, crossed his legs. "Sorry, pal. To be honest, I've had a pretty shitty week, all in all, and it sure ain't getting any better sitting in this place. When the hell are you going to get a room with a view?"

"I like it here. It's quiet."

"It's like a tomb is what it is."

Mulder didn't take the bait. "What's the problem, Carl?"

The man hesitated before clearing his throat. "You remember Frank Ulman?"

Mulder wadded up another sheet. "No, I don't think so. Should I?"

"He was at my sister's a couple of Christmases ago. Skinny kid? Regular army? He kept hitting on my cousin Angie, she kept shooting him down, and you decided to show him how to do it right."

Suddenly, as he threw the paper ball, he remembered the night, and the memory brought a smile. The kid, and he wasn't much more than that, had paraded around the Barellis' suburban North Jersey house in his dress uniform, desperately trying to find a woman who would be impressed by his bearing and ribbons. He was so eager, he was laughable, and Mulder had finally taken pity on him. Unfortunately, the heart-to-heart they had had in the rec room didn't take. Barelli's cousin's brother had had to be physically restrained from punching the guy into the new year.

"Yeah," he said, nodding. "Yeah."

The ball went in.

"Well, a couple, three months ago, he and Angie got together. Kind of serious, actually. I heard they were talking marriage and stuff."

Mulder's eyes widened. "Your cousin and that guy? Really? Why didn't her brother kill him?"

Barelli winced and looked away.

Oh shit, Mulder thought; open mouth, insert foot.

He abandoned his slouch for a posture more attentive. "Tell me."

"He was killed last weekend."

"Damn. Hey, I'm sorry, Carl. I didn't mean—"

Barelli waved him silent. "It's okay, don't sweat it, you couldn't have known." His smile was bitter. "Not exactly national news, you know?" Then he inhaled slowly. "The thing is, Mulder, he was stationed at Fort Dix, some kind of pissant clerical job, even though he thought he should have been something else. You know, glamorous? Green Berets, something like that. Anyway, he got himself into a fight at a bar in a nearby town, they call it Marville—"

"Over a woman, I'll bet."

"Yeah. Something like that. Anyway, he ended up at the base hospital Friday night, busted up some, and was supposed to stay in bed until Sunday. Frankie didn't want to stay in bed, apparently. He was found on a road just south of the post, on Sunday morning."

"How?"

Barelli swiped at something invisible on his shirtfront. "Somebody cut his throat."

Mulder closed his eyes briefly, both in sympathy and at the image. "Have they caught the one who did it?"

"No."

"Witnesses?"

The man snorted. "Oh yeah, right. In the middle of the night out in the middle of nowhere? Jesus, Mulder, gimme a break." Then he shrugged. "Yeah. Actually, there was one. A woman." He leaned forward, bracing his arms on his legs. "But Jesus, Mulder, she was hysterical and drunk and maybe doped up. You know what she said? She said the damn tree grew an arm and killed him."

Arlen Douglas could have been anywhere from his early forties to early sixties. His perpetually tanned face was finely lined, his hair an aristocratic mix of brown and silver, and his figure one of someone who was in close to perfect shape. He sat behind his desk and took a single swipe at his tie before closing the manila folder that lay before him on the leather-trim blotter.

It hadn't taken him long to make the office his—framed photographs of his family on the desk, framed photographs of him and three presidents, a handful of movie stars, and a dozen senators on the walls. An American flag in a brass stand to the right. Behind him, a large window whose view of the city was cut off by pale beige blinds.

When his intercom buzzed, he touched a button, said, "Send him in, Miss Cort," and checked his tie again.

Special Agent Webber opened the door hesitantly, smiled, and stepped across the threshold. Another hesitation before he closed the door and marched to the desk.

Douglas prayed that the kid wouldn't salute him.

"You sent for me, sir?"

"Indeed I did, Hank." He tapped the folder. "A fine job your team did on that Helevito case. A very nice job indeed."

Webber beamed. "Thank you, sir. But it wasn't really my team, it was Agent Mulder's."

Douglas smiled without showing any teeth. "Of course. But it seems you came up with a vital piece of the puzzle, and exhibited some very fine investigative techniques."

He waited while the young man did his best to contain his pleasure. This, he thought, was going to be a piece of cake.

"Tell me something, Hank, how did you like working with Fox Mulder?"

"Oh, boy," Webber said enthusiastically. "It was great. I mean, they teach you all that stuff at Quantico, but it doesn't really have anything to do with . . ." He stopped himself and frowned briefly. "What I mean, sir, isn't that Quantico doesn't do its job. Not at all. I mean—"

"I know what you mean," Douglas said, still smiling, hands now flat on the folder. "It doesn't come alive, does it, until you actually see it all in action."

"Yes, sir. Exactly."

Well, of course, it doesn't, you idiot, he thought. Someone was going to owe him big time for this. Real big time.

"And you found working with Mulder instructive?"

"Absolutely."

"By the book, everything in its place, nothing for anyone to be ashamed of?"

He knew the young man would falter, and he did, torn between his liking for Mulder and his loyalty to the Bureau. Douglas was well aware that Mulder used the book when he had to, and his own, rather unique experience when necessary. The problem was, that experience. Half the time, it seemed like nothing but hunches; the other half consisted of such wild speculation that Douglas was amazed the man had any arrest record at all.

He waved a dismissive hand. "Never mind, Hank. It's not really important." He slid his hands off the folder. "As I said, this is fine work. Thanks to you, we should have no trouble in court putting Helevito away for most of the rest of his life." The smile faded to an expression that was both an invitation to the inner circle and a warning against betrayed confidences. "But before you decide to make Mulder your hero, there's something you should know."

Webber frowned his puzzlement.

"And something I'd like you to do for me." The smile returned, this time with teeth. "A personal favor. One, I think, which will not hinder your advancement in the Bureau one iota."

Mulder wasn't sure what he was supposed to say next. He had already explained to Barelli as carefully as he could that he couldn't take on the case without authorization, or without a request from the local law enforcement agency, but the reporter refused to accept it. He kept insisting this was Mulder's kind of thing, right up his alley.

Weird stuff, Mulder thought sourly; famous throughout the whole damn world for weird stuff.

"It doesn't matter," he said, making sure Carl heard and saw the regret. "You said yourself the woman had been drinking. And was hysterical. As anyone very well might be who had witnessed something sudden and gruesome like that. Which is why, believe it or not, eyewitnesses aren't always the best way to pursue a case. Get three people at the scene of a violent crime like this, and I'll guarantee three different versions of what happened."

"Look, Fox, I know—"

Mulder held up a palm. "What I'm saying is, Carl, that this woman was obviously severely shaken up. Like I said, anyone would be, and—"

"Speak for yourself," a dry voice said from the doorway.

Barelli instantly leapt to his feet, a great, wolfish smile cracking his solemnity. "Dana! Darlin'!"

Mulder merely looked to the door. "You're back early."

Dana Scully made a face, tossed her purse at him, and shrugged out of her light topcoat. "I got back last night. I got tired of looking at interstates. After a few days they're all the same—boring. And very exhausting."

She didn't look exhausted to him. Her light auburn hair was in place, her slightly rounded face clear of any hint of weariness, and her clothes—a ruffled blouse and wine-colored jacket with matching skirt—were impeccable.

As practically always.

"You look perfect," Barelli said, crossing the room and engulfing her in a hug.

"Hi, Carl." She accepted the hug for only a few seconds, then slipped out of it so deftly Mulder wanted to applaud.

He nodded toward his friend instead. "Carl has a problem, but I'm afraid we can't help him."

"Bullshit." Barelli laughed heartily. "You just need some convincing, that's all. And this is just the little lady who can do it."

Scully avoided another hug by catching the purse Mulder tossed back to her and, at the same time, preempting the other chair.

"So how was the trip?"

She took her time answering. "Nice. Very relaxing."

"You should have stayed the whole time."

"What, are you kidding?" Barelli folded his arms and leaned against the jamb. "You don't know that little lady very well, Mulder. Can't keep her mind off business for more than two hours at a time." His smile was seductive, he knew it, and he used it. "Which makes me glad to see you, Dana. Maybe you can talk this guy into giving a friend a hand."

Scully quickly glared at Mulder, who had already raised his hands to offer mock applause. Instead the right hand shot to scratch at the back of his head, while the left answered the perfectly timed ringing phone beside him.

He listened.

He watched Dana watching him.

He hung up and said, "Carl, I'm sorry, but I have to see the boss" as he rose and reached for his suit jacket. "Let Dana know where you're staying and I'll call you later."

"Mulder?" Dana frowned.

"No, don't worry, I'm not in trouble." He paused at the door. "I don't think I'm in trouble." He stepped over the threshold and looked over his shoulder. "How can I be in trouble? We just closed a big case."

FIVE

Diamond Street was barely wide enough for two lanes of traffic on its easy downward slope toward the Potomac River. Richly crowned hickory and maple lined the worn curbs, hiding for most of its length old and small, brick and clapboard homes with front lawns scarcely large enough for the name. At the top of the slope were a handful of businesses, spillovers from South Washington Street. On the west side was Ripley's, flanked on the left by a corner grocery, and on the right by a narrow three-story Victorian converted to a dress shop on the ground floor, law offices above. The bar's simple brick facade was deliberately no advertisement; all there was was a dark green padded door over which hung a scripted sign in red. No window large or small. It was a neighborhood bar, no outsiders or the outside need apply.

Mulder stepped in and immediately stripped off his coat, sighing a little, pushing a weary hand through his hair. To his left were a half-dozen small tables, already taken; to his right, a wall covered above dark wood wainscoting with film and old radio show posters framed in polished wood. As soon as his vision adjusted to the dim lighting, all except for the bar itself from short candles in amber chimneys on the tables and sconces on the walls, he moved slowly toward the back, down a narrow aisle created where the mahogany bar began. That was filled too, but the noise level was low.

Conversation, quiet laughter, a few nods and smiles in his direction.

When the bar ended, the room opened up into a large square, with more tables and high-backed booths settled against the walls. There was no TV, no jukebox; the background music piped through hidden speakers was barely loud enough to register. Sometimes it was country, sometimes jazz, sometimes themes from films and Broadway shows. It all depended on the mood Stuff Felstead was in when he opened for lunch.

It didn't take Mulder long to recognize the soundtrack from *Alien*. Stuff had apparently seen him coming.

With a grin he swung left and dropped into the booth nearest the end of the bar, shifted, and sat with his back against the wall, one leg stretched out on the padded seat, his topcoat dumped on the other seat. Within seconds, a tall woman stood in front of him in loose black slacks, puff-sleeved white blouse. Black Irish from head to toe—hair, eyes, fair skin, a faint suggestion of freckles across her upturned nose.

"Are you dead or drinking?"

He rolled his eyes and groaned. "Both, I think."

"Beer?"

He nodded.

She winked and drifted away.

He covered his eyes with his left hand, elbow propped on the table, and wondered if maybe he had slipped into some alternate time zone, some parallel universe.

All the signs were there: Arlen Douglas hadn't kept him waiting, but had personally ushered him into his office. Congratulations on the Helevito case were suspiciously effusive, as was praise for taking such good care of Hank Webber. Mulder hadn't had a chance to say a word save a murmur of thanks before the section head asked him what he thought about the disappearing clown.

"A trick, obviously."

"What makes you think so?"

"He's not the Invisible Man, sir. Nobody can snap his fingers and vanish."

"Intriguing, though, don't you think?"

He heard the warning bells immediately and did his best to avoid what he feared was coming, pointing out suspect witnesses, the very backdrop of the circus, incomplete preliminary reports from the local sheriff . . .

It didn't work.

He had one day to finish the Helevito paperwork, and then he was off to Louisiana over the weekend.

"Just up your alley, wouldn't you say, Agent Mulder?"

Mulder had wanted to say, "Up your alley, too. Sir." But a sudden attack of restraint kept him silent as he was handed a blue-tabbed case folder and ushered back out before he had a chance to continue his objections.

It wasn't until he'd returned to his empty office and flipped through the pages that he realized Scully wouldn't be going with him. Hank Webber would.

This wasn't right. Not that he didn't mind shepherding the younger man through the minefields of Bureau investigations; that was the least of his problems, and Webber was a personable, if somewhat overenthusiastic man.

What wasn't right was the smell of it. Right up his alley, the man had said. Weird stuff. But this wasn't weird at all; it was just nuts, and he wondered exactly who had asked for the FBI to join in what looked to be an obvious local matter.

Plus, let's not forget the man at the memorial. Invisible as well, and all too real.

Not protected, but not chained.

Alice was right—curiouser and curiouser.

Parallel universe; it had to be.

"If it's that bad, maybe I'll bring hemlock for a chaser."

He opened his eyes and kept his expression bland as the waitress set a bottle of beer on the table, along with a plate filled with french fries. He pointed. "I didn't order those, Trudy."

"You haven't eaten."

Their aroma made his stomach growl, and she laughed silently when he reached for one and popped it into his mouth, hissing as it burned his tongue. Reluctantly, stiffly, he swung his leg back under the table and saw that a thick, all-the-trimmings hamburger had been buried beneath the fries. He looked at her sideways, and she winked again before heading across the room at a customer's call.

He didn't hide his interest. She was an attractive woman, a law student now at Georgetown, and they had dated a couple of times, nothing fancy, nothing hot. He enjoyed her and her company, although he couldn't always take her mothering. Tonight, however, it was right on target, and he ate as if he hadn't done so in a week, ordering a second burger before he'd finished the first. Taking his time. No hurry at all.

Because it was the middle of the week, the room didn't fill. The booths were taken first, and a handful of tables changed occupants once or twice as he watched them. Mostly younger people back here; the old-timers stuck to the stools where they were closer to what mattered.

A couple of times women seated close by would glance at him, glance away, glance back, but he didn't acknowledge them and so lost their interest. Two men in golf caps and cardigans argued quietly at a table with someone in a booth he couldn't see.

A married couple dressed more for the theater than Ripley's fussed unhappily with kaiser roll sandwiches. A quartet of college kids tried to pick Trudy and the other two waitresses up.

A normal night.

In a parallel universe.

Oh, brother, he thought; maybe it's time I took a vacation.

A room whose walls weren't all the same color, mostly shadow now, mostly dark.

On the right-hand wall a dark-framed print, Gainesborough's *The Blue Boy*, fronted with nonreflective glass.

Against the left-hand wall, a bunk with a thin mattress, blanket, and sheet drawn taut and folded in the military style. A footlocker at the head, closed, chipped and scarred.

A metal desk set perpendicular to the rear wall. On it two piles of paperback books, a stackable stereo system, a handful of compact discs. A yellow legal pad, with a ballpoint pen just off-center. A green-shaded lamp, softly lit. A swivel chair whose seat and back were comfortably padded.

In the far corner a club chair, with a standing brass lamp behind it, an end table beside it with a seashell ashtray.

The floor was concrete, uncarpeted save for a remnant throw in front of the chair.

A man in a long lab coat wandered around the room, poking at the books, the CDs, scowling at the legal pad whose top sheet was blank, picking up the pen, stabbing the page lightly before dropping it again. Although he was only in his mid-forties, he had more scalp than hair, his face sharp angles without seeming harsh. When he straightened, he was tall, broad at the shoulders and chest, and broad at his stomach. He glanced around, his nose wrinkling at the faint stench of cigarette smoke and mildew, sweat and blood, and finally, with a satisfied nod, strode to a padded door in the wall. He opened it without hesitation and stepped up into a corridor whose ceiling lighting was contrast enough to force a squint as he checked through the round judas window before turning right and stepping up into the next room, itself dimly lighted.

"Ready?" A woman in white sat at a wall-long shelf on which was a series of monitors and keyboards, space for notebooks and pads, and two Styrofoam cups of steaming coffee.

The shelf was set just beneath a window that looked through the ghost of the *Blue Boy*, down into the other room.

"Leonard, I asked if you were ready." Long blond hair pulled back and held back by a rubber band, feathered bangs on a high forehead.

Leonard Tymons, when he had first met her, thought Rosemary Elkhart quite attractive in a hard sort of way. After four years he hadn't changed his mind, but he had changed his plans for seduction and a brief affair. She indeed did have fair hair and fair skin, pale lips and pale blue eyes, but when he was alone he called her a black widow.

"Leonard, damnit."

He dropped into a wheeled chair beside her. "You saw."

She nodded toward a microphone attached to one of the computers. "For the record, okay? Let's remember the record."

He nodded. "For the record, everything is fine. Nothing has changed since last time. Jesus, can't we get anyone to clean that place right? It smells like a . . . a . . ." He shook his head in disgust. "Just get someone to scrub it down before next time."

"I will."

There was silence then as they worked at their keyboards, setting programs in motion, for the moment paying little attention to the diagrams and numbers that flashed across the screens.

Then Tymons reached out and flicked off the mike.

Rosemary looked at him oddly.

"We blew it, didn't we," he said matter-of-factly. A tilt of his head toward the glass. "We're not going to bring it off, are we?"

Her face hardened as if she were about to lose her temper, and for several seconds she refused to answer.

"Rosemary."

She sagged, and whispered, "Damn."

The soft hum of fans, the creak of his chair's wheels as he pushed away from the shelf desk and rubbed his face with both hands.

"Maybe," she said, "there's a way."

"Maybe," he answered, "there's a Santa Claus."

Her face hardened again, and she gestured him back to his position. "Santa Claus or not," she told him, "we will find a way." She glanced at him sideways. "If not, we'll just get another."

The music had changed to the muted soundtrack from *Damn Yankees* when Trudy Gaines slipped into the seat opposite Mulder, lit a cigarette, and brushed a strand of damp hair from her brow as she blew smoke at the ceiling. "One day, he's going to find everyone in here puddled on his precious floor."

Mulder raised an eyebrow. "You're warm?" He hadn't noticed.

She nodded, and even in the gloom he could see the lines, the shadows, that made her more her age. "I think I'm getting the flu or something."

He finished the last burger, picked up his second beer. "So take a day off."

"You pay my rent?"

"You give me that autographed *Thing From Another World* poster?"

"In your dreams, G-man. In your dreams."

The Golf Caps' argument grew louder.

"Jesus," she muttered.

"What's up?" The person in the booth was still in shadow; all he could see was one arm, in a tweed, elbow-patched sleeve.

"The Redskins," she said in disgust.

He couldn't help a laugh. "What? May's just started, for God's sake."

She looked at him with one eye open. "It's always autumn when you're a Redskins fan, Mulder, don't you know that?"

One of the Golf Caps stood, his chair scraping back. Before anyone could move, a man in shirtsleeves, a white apron tied around his waist, appeared by the table. He was, Mulder thought, the perfect walking cadaver. Only the badly arthritic hands spoiled the image. Evidently the Golf Cap didn't think Stuff Felstead could do anything but glower. He was wrong. Ripley's owner said something so low only the other man could hear. It was enough. He sputtered, gestured placatingly, and by his expression suggested to his companion that they leave.

It was over in less than ten seconds.

"Magic," Trudy said, catching him staring.

"Probably. After all this time, I still don't see how he does it."

"Keep it that way," she advised him. "Believe me, you don't want to know." She set her palms flat on the table. "Well, break's over. Gotta finish up."

"Nice visiting with you, too," he said, sweeping up the last of the ketchup with the last french fry. "So what's the problem?"

She froze halfway out of the booth, avoiding his gaze, staring at the seatback behind him.

He waited.

Finally, she slumped back and shook her head. "It's silly."

"Probably."

"I feel like a jerk."

He reached out his hand and waggled it until she handed him his coat. "You're off in ten minutes, you've had another fight with your boyfriend, you have a tort quiz tomorrow, and you want a walk home in case he tries to hassle you."

She didn't blink. "You know, Mulder, sometimes you're damn weird."

He shrugged. "So they tell me."

"Fifteen minutes?"

"Sure. No problem."

A quick smile was her thanks as she returned to work, and fifteen minutes later she was back, heavy sweater over her arm. He paid at the register at the end of the bar and followed her to the street. His own apartment was a couple of blocks past King Street, closer to the Potomac; she lived the same distance in the opposite direction. He didn't mind. It was a nice night, a comfortable breeze, and Trudy spent most of the time complaining about her landlady in a way that, at one point, had him laughing so hard he tripped over a raised section of sidewalk.

He didn't fall. A quick, exaggerated turn kept his balance.

But not so quick that he didn't see the man in the tweed jacket strolling behind them a block away.

It didn't register at first because they had already reached her place, a renovated colonial divided into a half-dozen apartments, hidden beneath a clutch of oaks. She kissed his cheek quickly for thanks and hurried up the walk, fussing in her purse for the keys.

He didn't leave until the front door was open and she was inside.

Then he turned around and headed back the way they had come, hands in his pockets, whistling softly. His footsteps were loud. Traffic didn't exist. A dog raced silently across a sloped lawn to check him out, tail wagging, fangs bared. Mulder gave the animal a smile and walked on.

Checking the shadows for a shadow that didn't belong.

By the time he had crossed King Street again, he had begun to scold himself. After all, people had to live someplace, some of them actually lived in the same area he did, and the Tweed Man was probably one of them.

His own building was on a quiet residential street. Well-kept dark brick with a slight arch over the recessed entrance. Hedges that made the tiny lawn seem even smaller. As he slipped his keys out of his pocket, he began making a list of things he'd have to do in the morning, not the least of which would be to try to change Douglas's mind.

A disappearing murderous clown was not his idea of a good reason to see Louisiana.

By the time he reached the door he was already in bed; all he had to do was get his body settled in the same place.

He turned the lock and absently glanced over his shoulder.

The Tweed Man strolled by on the other side of the street, cigarette in one hand tracing orange in the dark, face hidden by a felt hat pulled low.

Weariness slowed Mulder's reaction. In the few seconds it took to convince himself he wasn't imagining it, the man was gone, lost in the shifting shadows between widely spaced streetlamps.

SIX

X Dana Scully stood amid the clutter of Mulder's office and flapped her arms hopelessly. There were times when she admired the way he could find needles in haystacks and times like this, when she wanted nothing more than to put a match to it and force him to start from scratch. Which, she knew, wouldn't change a thing. Two days later it would look just the same.

Hefting her briefcase in one hand, she turned with a resigned sigh to the woman standing in the doorway and said, "Sorry, Bette, but I don't think it's here."

"Sure it is," the secretary said brightly. She crossed the room to a waist-high shelf built out of the wall, shoved a pile of papers aside, and held up a blue-tagged folder. "I can smell 'em a mile away."

A cheery smile, and she was gone, leaving Scully open-mouthed and slightly annoyed. She didn't mind cases being targeted to other teams; that was part of the game, and part of the procedure. And that particular case was, by FBI standards, so perfectly ordinary she was surprised Mulder hadn't pushed it on

49

himself. What she did mind was the new section head's near imperious refusal to give his reasons. If he wasn't happy with the way things were going, he simply changed teams. Fresh minds and fresh bodies was his only explanation.

"Hey."

Mulder came through the door, dropped his coat onto the back of his chair. "Listen, I've been thinking about that Louisiana thing."

Dana shook her head. "Mulder—"

He dropped into his chair, swiveled it around to face her, and tented his fingers beneath his chin. "Not that I think it's really going to be as bizarre as the mighty Douglas thinks it is, but I've been looking through the folder, see . . ." He reached over to the shelf without looking. "I think what they've got there is a—"

"Mulder—"

He frowned, kicked the chair around, and began slapping papers aside. "Damn, I swore I left it here last night. Maybe Webber took it. That guy's so gung-ho, he makes me nervous."

Dana closed her eyes briefly to summon patience, then tapped him on the shoulder. Hard. "Mulder, pay attention."

"What? What?" He didn't look around. "Maybe I filed it." He shuddered. "God, what a thought."

"It doesn't matter."

"Of course it matters. Do you think I'd actually . . ." He fell silent and slowly turned to look at her. "You have news."

With a look to the ceiling, she thought *thank you* before pushing a hand absently at her hair. "In the first place, I do not appreciate your leaving me alone with that human octopus. I swear to God he has hands growing out of his ears."

At least he had the grace to look contrite. "Sorry. Douglas had the appointment already set up. I had no choice."

When she heard what the section head had to say, she told him she had already been briefed. The man had caught her in the hall on the way to Mulder's office.

"But that doesn't make any difference right now."

He was startled. "What do you mean?"

"Table that for a minute. What I want from you now is your word that you'll never, ever leave me alone with that reporter again." She shuddered to prove her point. "I am a doctor, Mulder. I know secret doctor things. If I'm forced to, if he lays one more paw on me, I swear I'm going to make sure he never touches another woman again."

Mulder held up a hand. "Okay, okay. I didn't think he'd be that bad. Honest." He frowned. "I guess this thing about his cousin's boyfriend shook him up more than I thought."

Angrily she told him that was no excuse. It was perhaps understandable, but it was still no excuse. When he apologized again, she allowed herself a moment to calm down, then took the other chair and hauled her briefcase onto her lap.

"What's the other news?" he wanted to know, eyeing the case suspiciously.

"Good news and bad news, actually."

He stared at her for so long, she thought he hadn't heard. Then he slumped a little in resignation and gave her his full attention.

"The good news is, you don't have to go to Louisiana. You can't find the file because Bette took it back just a few minutes ago."

He barely reacted, little more than a blink.

"The other good news is, you're still stuck with me."

A lopsided smile flared and vanished. "The bad news is," he said dryly, "we're going to North Dakota, no bathrooms, and we have to live in a tent."

"Not quite." If it wasn't so infuriating, this whole thing would have been laughable. "Actually, it's New Jersey."

"What?"

She looked up without raising her head. "New Jersey."

He frowned his puzzlement. "Why New Jersey? What—" His

eyes widened in dismay. "Oh, God, Scully, please, not the Invisible Man."

She unsnapped the briefcase flaps and pulled out a folder marked with a red tab, set the case on the floor and the folder on her lap. She flipped it open and picked up the top sheet. Only then did she nod, and waited patiently until he had stopped muttering to himself and grunted for her to continue.

"The—"

"Hold it," he said. "Wait a minute. What changed the mighty Douglas's mind? Yesterday it was disappearing clowns, today it's Claude Rains. I don't get it. Does he really think this is an X-File?"

Scully smiled. "I don't know. But it seems your friend has a friend."

"Carl? The sports reporter Carl?" He didn't believe it. "Carl Barelli has friends in high places?" He shook his head slowly; wonders never ceased.

"Not quite," she admitted. "Angie Tonero, his cousin, has a brother. The one who tried to dismember her soon-to-be boyfriend, remember? The brother's name is Major Joseph Tonero. Air force. Temporarily attached to Medical. You'll never guess where he's currently stationed."

Mulder didn't bother. His expression was enough; he knew that McGuire Air Force Base was adjacent to Fort Dix. "And Major Tonero is . . . ?"

"Apparently, a very good, dear, close personal friend of the Garden State's junior United States senator, John Carmen."

Mulder clearly couldn't decide whether to be amused or angry, and at the moment she wasn't inclined to give him a hand. She only nodded when he said, "Whose office just happened to call the director, right? Probably in the middle of the night. Probably causing the director to be not all that happy, which means that when he called the mighty Douglas, our supposedly temporary section head lost a lot of sleep. Which, I suppose, means he's really pissed off."

"To put it mildly." She fussed with her skirt, her hair again. "Now, granted, we're not supposed to be at the beck and call of individual members of Congress, but there are budgets and there are appropriations. And the senator is a ranking member of a couple of pretty important committees."

"I love this town," Mulder groused.

She handed over the paper. "This is the report on Frank Ulman."

He took it; he didn't look at it until she stared him into it. When he was finished, no more than a cursory glance at best, she handed him the second one.

"So what's this?" he asked, barely giving it a glance as well. "A second opinion or something?"

"No. And if you'd just look instead of griping . . ."

He did as he was told as he gave her his best martyr's sigh, and she only just managed not to laugh when he sat up so quickly he nearly slid off the chair. "Scully . . ." He read the papers carefully, one hand pushing through his hair.

"Right," she said. "Two killings. One week apart. Saturday night, early Sunday morning. Each victim with a slashed throat, no other injuries, no indication of robbery or sexual assault. That wouldn't necessarily make them connected, except for the fact that now it seems there was a witness to the first murder, too."

Mulder's lips moved as he read the second sheet more carefully. "Another Invisible Man?"

"Could be."

"Or the same one."

"Could be."

"This first guy"—he checked the report—"Pierce, he was drunk. So was the witness."

"No question."

He compared the reports again. "And the second witness, to Frank's murder, she was drunk, too. And . . . drugs?"

"That's right. Heroin."

She saw the look, saw the slight quickening of his movements.

"So . . ." He closed one eye, and his lips twitched into a faint smile. "So . . . maybe."

"Could be."

"Scully," he said, "I give up, all right? You've made your point about Barelli. Several times, in fact." He reached for the folder.

She shook her head. "Not yet."

The frown returned. "What is this? I'm being tortured because I wouldn't look at the slides of your trip? You want me to personally break Carl's arms?"

"No. It's just that there's . . . well . . . a tad more bad news."

"Tad?" He leaned forward. "You just said tad?"

"Hank, actually."

It took him a moment to figure it out, and dismiss it with a *no big deal, we can live with it* wave.

"And company," she added.

Someone knocked on the doorframe.

"What the hell does that mean, 'and company'?" he snapped. "Scully, what's going on, huh?"

She stood, pointed to the door, and said, "Fox Mulder, meet the company."

"Hi," said the tall blonde entering the office as Mulder stumbled to his feet. "I'm Licia Andrews. I'm really glad to meet you, Agent Mulder. Hank's told me so much about you."

"Hank?" Mulder echoed dumbly as he shook her hand.

Licia glanced at Dana. "Why, yes. Hank Webber. Didn't he tell you? We're partners. Sort of. We're going to New Jersey with you. Right, Agent Scully?"

"Oh, yes," Dana said, enjoying herself immensely, and not the least bit ashamed of it. "Absolutely."

•　•　•

The view from the apex of the Delaware Memorial Bridge was probably spectacular—the Delaware Bay below, wooded shoreline upriver, the ocean to the right, the factories and plants that lined the banks on both sides. It probably was, but Barelli never saw it. He hated the height, hated the seagulls gloating at him from eye level, and his knuckles bled white every time he crossed it. Still, it was better than flying by a factor of ten.

And once on the north side, he aimed his battered yellow Taurus straight for the Turnpike, not wasting any time. Despite the call he had made even before he had seen Mulder, and despite the senator's reassurances that the family matter would be expedited, he didn't quite believe it.

Especially after what Dana had said.

After refusing, again, to succumb to his charms, she had coldly walked him to the hushed, vast lobby and had, for God's sake, patted his goddamn arm as if he were a kid.

"Stick to sports, Carl," she'd said. "I'm sorry about the corporal, but use your head, okay?"

He'd been so mad, he'd barely been able to kiss and hug her good-bye.

Stick to sports.

Who the hell did she think she was, Sherlock Holmes in a skirt?

Besides, he was not a sports reporter. He was a reporter whose interests happened to lie in sports. There was a difference, and he was going to prove it.

Fifteen minutes later he was speeding north on the Turnpike, through a speckled twilight rapidly slipping into dusk, ignoring the press of the forest on either side, or the late-hunting hawks that drifted patiently above the dense scrub oak and twisted pine that made up the Pine Barrens. He ignored the speed limit as well, keeping to the left of the two lanes, pushing seventy. The Yankees on the radio. Wind from the open passenger window stirring scraps of paper and crumpled tissues on the back seat and floor. A cigarette in his left hand.

Goddamn bitch. He wondered why he wasted his time, and smiled mirthlessly at the all too obvious answer—she wouldn't give in. He admired that. Hell, he admired her. And one of these days she would learn to admire him.

Soon.

It would be soon.

Although he wasn't exactly a national figure, his byline in this state carried with it no little recognition. He figured he could trade on that once he reached Marville, wherever the hell that was. It sounded like, and most likely was, a two-bit town that leeched off Fort Dix and McGuire. A celebrity like him should find loose tongues easily. A few drinks, a few questions, a few slaps on the back and a couple of knowing winks, and effing Fox Mulder could kiss this reporter's ass.

Besides which, Ulman had practically been family. The last time he had seen Angie, her eyes had been so puffed from crying she could barely see.

Nobody, but nobody, did that to his people.

In fact, with a little luck, he might catch the creep alone, the one who did Frankie in.

He smiled again as he switched on his headlamps.

The smile didn't last.

He couldn't hold it.

All he could hold was the steering wheel, and the idea that Carl Barelli wasn't going to be deterred by some freak with a knife. He knew others saw him as soft, too long at the desk. Too often for them, those others found out different.

Don't worry, Angie, he promised to the early night; *you hang in there, kid, Cousin Carl is on the job.*

•   •   •

Dana had never liked the way moonlight and headlight bleached the land of its color. There was never any real white, only black and shades of grey, and the things that moved between them.

Graveyard time.

She reached for her left ear and pinched the lobe, just sharply enough to hurt and wake her up. She had thought, had hoped, she would be done with long-distance driving for a while, but Mulder had insisted there was no sense waiting until tomorrow. They might as well get their act together and the show on the road so they'd be ready to work first thing Friday morning.

That wasn't so bad, actually. He had volunteered to do all the driving, brought the coffee and some sandwiches, and had some-how convinced Webber that he ought to drive on alone with Andrews, get to know her, let her get to know him. Partners, he had lectured solemnly and truthfully, had to be able to predict each other's reactions so backs could be guarded and missteps minimized when the action got hot. What he had failed to tell them was that the action hardly ever got hot, except in the movies.

Unless, of course, the partner was Fox Mulder.

Licia hadn't minded; Webber, to Scully's amazement, had actually seemed flustered.

Now she figured them to be fifteen minutes ahead, their first assignment to book rooms in a motel called the Royal Baron, a recommendation Mulder had picked up from a visiting agent stationed in Philadelphia.

There was no question it would be as horrid as it sounded. Mulder was an expert at picking such places. He called it a knack; she knew it was a curse.

"You okay?" He glanced over. "You can sleep if you want."

"Mulder, it isn't even nine. If I sleep now, I'll be awake at dawn." She watched him for a moment, then reached over and turned down the heater. The night was chilly, but it wasn't that cold. "What's the matter?"

He shrugged. "Nothing."

"This breaking into pairs isn't your style."

"Maybe, but four agents driving into a place called Marville would be like a parade, don't you think?"

"And two cars with agents isn't?"

He said nothing.

A mile passed, black and grey, before she repeated her earlier question. "And don't jive me, Mulder, I'm not in the mood."

He laughed silently. "Good lord. First 'tad,' now 'jive.' What the hell did you do on that vacation?"

"I didn't change the subject every time I was asked a question."

He drove on, thumb tapping lightly on the wheel. "I had a visitor the other day."

She listened as he told her about the man at the Jefferson Memorial, not saying a word. At one point she pulled her coat closer across her neck; when he had finished she had folded her arms across her stomach. She didn't doubt that the meeting had occurred, but she had never been able to fully accept his absolute belief in extraterrestrial life, or his notion that there were those in the government, and those seemingly beyond the government's reach, who were just as convinced, and were as dangerous to him as any murderer they had ever sought.

Add to that the equally bizarre idea that among those Shadow People, as he called them, there were also a handful who were actually on his side, and in any other human being she would see a full-blown case of whatever lay beyond extreme paranoia.

In Mulder, however, it almost seemed plausible.

All right, she admitted; maybe more than "almost."

The Tweed Man, on the other hand, was more likely a coincidence, nothing more, and when she said so, he only grunted. Not entirely convinced, but with no solid reason to think otherwise.

"So what does this case mean to . . . whoever?" she said, staring out at the dark by her shoulder. "And what does it have to do with Louisiana?"

"Beats me. I'm not a psychic."

She shifted. "Mulder, weird stuff, remember?"

He tapped his forehead. "Got it stapled right here."

She caught the grin and held her silence until the silence made her sleepy. Then: "So what does it mean to you?"

"I don't know. Well, yes, I do. It means we have two people dead, and there'll probably be more." A glance, a quick smile. "That's all, Scully, that's all."

She nodded her approval, even though she knew there was no question he was lying.

SEVEN

The Royal Baron Motel was a long, white and red, two-story stucco building facing the two-lane county road that led into Marville. On the west side was the office, whose spotlighted top was supposedly a bejeweled gold crown; on the east was a restaurant; between them were two dozen rooms, twelve up and twelve down, with a red iron stairway in the center and at each end.

Behind it, and across the road, there was nothing but dense forest.

The restaurant—booths along the windows, round tables at the far end, and a long counter—was called the Queen's Inn.

Exhausted, Mulder slumped by the window in a red leatherette booth, still feeling as if he were on something that moved and had no intention of stopping. His head throbbed, his vision blurred now and then, and all he really wanted was to crawl into bed and forget the world existed for a while. Webber and Andrews, however, had been waiting in the office, rooms already booked, just as he and Scully had pulled up. Despite his protestations, he was dragged off for something to eat.

They were the only customers in the room; the young waitress spent her time dusting gleaming tables and whispering to the cook through the serving gap in the back wall.

He didn't order anything—the very thought of food made his stomach lurch—but when the orders arrived, he had to admit that the plate of silver dollar pancakes Webber had in front of him actually smelled pretty good.

"That bacon's going to kill you," Scully said dryly, nodding to the double side order beside Webber's plate.

"My guilty pleasure," Webber told her with a boyish grin, and poured what Mulder figured was at least a gallon of syrup over the heavily buttered stack.

Scully watched in amazement. "Never mind."

Andrews had contented herself with a cup of soup, her lean face etched with weariness, her topcoat buttoned all the way to her chin.

Outside the window, a breeze danced with a handful of dead leaves, guiding them onto the road where they were scattered by a passing car.

"So are we going to check it out tonight?" Webber wanted to know.

Mulder looked at him blankly. "What?"

The agent pointed over Mulder's shoulder with his loaded fork, then yanked it back when syrup began to drip on the table. "Marville. Are we going to check it out tonight?"

He shook his head. "Not until morning. Then the first thing we have to do is introduce ourselves to the local chief, let him know we're here."

Webber nodded. "Hawks."

Mulder blinked.

"Hawks," Webber repeated. "Todd Hawks. The chief of police. That's who he is."

"Ah."

Webber glanced at his partner, but her attention was on the empty road, and stifling a fierce yawn with her hand. "Didn't you read the file? I mean, it's all in there. About him. Hawks, I mean."

A gust shimmered the window.

Andrews shivered, but she didn't look away.

"Fox?"

"Mulder." He pushed a hand back through his hair. "Don't call me Fox. Mulder is fine."

Webber nodded once, correction noted and filed, it won't happen again.

This kid, Mulder thought wearily, is going to drive me up the wall.

And since he knows the drill full well, he must either be too excited, too eager, or he's scared. That wouldn't be surprising. So far, the young man's field work had been primarily confined to the immediate D.C. area. Now he was out here, no convenient home office to run to, working with a guy supposed to be more than a little off-center.

That almost, but not quite, made him feel better.

Andrews finished her soup, yawned, and stretched her arms stiffly over her head, clasping her hands and popping her knuckles. "God," she said huskily. "God." The topcoat did nothing to mask her figure.

Mulder felt Scully's shoe poke his ankle, so he figured he must have been staring, even though nothing had registered. That more than anything convinced him it was time to stop being sociable and make his good nights. What he hadn't counted on, however, was Webber trying to save the Bureau a buck by booking only two rooms, one for the ladies, one for the men.

As he unlocked the door and staggered in, tossing his small suitcase on the nearest bed, he said, "If you snore, Hank, I'm going to have to shoot you."

Webber laughed nervously, swore he slept like a baby, and laughed again while he unpacked, toiletries neatly arranged in the bathroom, fresh suit hung on the clothes rack by the bathroom door, the rest put away in the second drawer of a low dresser that stretched halfway along the left-hand wall.

Mulder was too tired to watch the ritual; he'd take care of his own things in the morning. He washed, he undressed, he was in bed and sleeping within ten minutes, ignoring the soft voice of the news on the TV.

He dreamed.

of a room not quite fully dark, outlines of bedroom furniture, outline of a window where the moon crept around the curtains;

a cool night and all the voices that go with it, from soft whispering leaves to the call of tree frogs and crickets;

a faint rumbling, but he knew he didn't live near the tracks, knew it wasn't a train;

louder, and the light around the curtains brightened to a glare, spearing suddenly into the room, shifting, slants and darts stabbing across the walls, the bed and the figure that lay on it, the ceiling, as if its source was spinning slowly outside the window;

frightened

he was frightened, standing by the door, slowly dropping into a crouch;

too frightened to move when the light became too bright and the rumbling too loud and the figure on the bed rose and tossed the coverlet aside, her young face colorless, her young eyes wide not with fear but with intent;

he wanted to stop her, but he couldn't stop dropping, couldn't stop himself from trying to push backward through the wall to get away from the light that exploded into the room, making him scream as the girl child was taken and swallowed by the white.

making him scream.

Making him gasp and sit up, crushing his pillow against his chest, blinking sweat from his eyes, sheet and blanket kicked away from his legs.

When he thought he could move without falling over, he sat on the edge of the mattress and put the pillow against the head-board. A forced shudder, a hard swallow, and he pushed himself to his feet, padding around a cheap table beneath its hanging lamp to the thin drapes on the room's only window. He parted them and looked out, and saw nothing but the road and the trees ranged beyond.

He couldn't see the stars, but he knew they were there.

Behind him, Webber snored lightly.

Oh, boy, he thought; oh, brother.

He wiped his face with a forearm and moved quietly into the bathroom, closed the door, but didn't turn on the light. He knew what he could see—a man forever haunted by the disappearance of his sister, Samantha, when both of them had been children. The dream tried to tell him how. Maybe it was true, maybe it wasn't. It didn't make any difference.

Dream or not, it was what kept him going.

He splashed water on his face to sluice away the tears he hadn't noticed before, dried himself, and returned to bed.

He didn't look at his watch, but he didn't think it was much beyond midnight.

A truck rumbled by.

When he slept this time, he didn't think he dreamed.

•   •   •

"Dana?"

Scully grunted to tell Licia she was awake, and to tell her she was also trying her best to get to sleep, whatever it was, it could wait until morning.

"Is there something . . . is there something wrong with Mulder I should know about?"

The voice out of the dark was naturally husky, almost masculine; she had already seen its effect on Webber and Mulder, and wondered how well Licia knew how to use it. It could be a devastating weapon, no question about it. She smiled at the ceiling—*when used for Good, not Evil.*

"Dana?"

She sighed loudly and rolled onto her side. "No. He's fine."

"He sure seemed out of it."

"It's the beginning."

"The what?"

Scully wasn't sure how to explain; after all this time, she barely understood it herself.

"At the start of every case that really catches his attention, he gets . . . hyper. Charged up." To say the least, she added silently. "Then, unfortunately, he has to get where the case is. He doesn't like that, the traveling. In fact, he hates it. It's valuable time wasted when he . . . we could be doing our job. So whenever he gets there, all that initial energy has been expended on the trip. So he crashes."

Silence for a moment before: "Will he be all right in the morning?"

She frowned her puzzlement. Concern was understandable for someone who hadn't worked with Mulder before, but she thought she detected something more in the woman's voice. Her eyes closed, half in a prayer that Andrews wasn't going to screw things up by developing a crush.

"He'll be fine," she answered at last.

"Good."

She said nothing.

The woman's voice faded as she rolled over. "I'd hate to have my first real case screwed all to hell."

Scully almost sat up to demand an explanation and, in the process, an apology. It was natural for someone like Andrews to want to shine first time out. God knows, she had prayed for it herself a hundred times before that first one. In fact, it had made her a nervous wreck. But not only didn't Andrews seem nervous, she seemed almost too calm, too ready. And that could be just as bad.

Or, she thought, I could be overreacting because I'm so damn tired.

A truck growled by.

She yawned, and tucked the covers up under her chin.

"Dana?"

This time Licia's voice sounded very small, very young.

"I'm listening."

"Do you think I'll have to use my gun?"

The corner of her mouth pulled back. "Hardly ever, Licia, believe me."

"Really?"

"Yes." She paused. "The government's too cheap to buy us all that ammunition."

Silence again, while she thought, dear Lord, I'm starting to sound like Mulder.

Then Andrews giggled, laughed, and said, "I guess I've been watching too many movies." The rustle of sheets was followed by, "Good night. And thanks."

"You're welcome, and good night."

Another truck drove by, this one in the opposite direction. Scully listened to the engine until she couldn't hear it anymore, using the fading grumble to pull her into sleep.

Her last thought was of Mulder.

She hoped he wasn't dreaming.

EIGHT

X The blue of the previous day turned to thickening overcast shortly after Friday's dawn. By the time Mulder and his team were on the road, Webber driving, a chill easterly wind had begun to coast down the road, sweeping leaves and brown pine needles in front of the car.

Mulder didn't like it; it looked too much like late autumn.

Marville itself began a quarter of a mile from the motel, with a handful of houses squatting in clearings hacked out of the Barrens on either side of the road. Sandy, pebbled soil served as shoulders, and showed as bare spots on lawns looking as tired as the houses themselves.

He sensed right away the little town was dying.

The commercial district was five short blocks long, some of the businesses spilling around the corners. None of the buildings were more than three stories tall, mostly wood, a few with weather-stained stone or brick facades. He counted six that were for rent, and far too many whose display windows had been boarded up with plywood or painted a dead white. A narrow banner sagged over Main Street, announcing the community's 150th anniversary, which made him wonder, as he often did, what had caused this place to attract settlers in the beginning. There was no river, the trees weren't lumber quality, and Fort Dix hadn't been established until 1917, neighboring McGuire Air Force Base some time later.

Webber snapped his fingers and jerked a thumb to his left. "Barney's Tavern."

Mulder spotted the corner bar, one of several still operating on the street, and supposed that, whatever the reason for Marville's founding, its eventual life support must have been traffic from the post and air force base. And solid support as well, from the looks of things. He could see, behind the faded paint and needed repairs, a town that had done quite well for the time that it had had, especially considering what must have been the fierce competition from other towns around it.

A stolid granite bank anchored the next corner, on the left. The shops here were still very much in business, or as much as they were going to get with the economy the way it was, and the army post drastically cut back over the past several years.

"This is depressing," Andrews said from the back seat. "How could anyone live here?"

"Cheap housing, for one thing," Webber supposed, slowing to allow a trio of old women to make their way across the street. "It's not near very much. I remember the map, but I don't think you can commute all the way to Philadelphia from here easily. Not and make any money."

Inertia, Mulder suspected, was the rest of the answer. No place to go when you can barely afford to live here. Anyone asked would probably give a different answer, but it no doubt boiled down to, "Why bother?"

"There," Scully said, the first time she'd spoken since breakfast.

A single-story, long white clapboard building took a third of the block on the right. A new, gold-lettered sign in front marked it as the police station; an American flag drooped from a flagpole next to the double-door entrance.

Webber pulled into a space in front, rubbed his hands eagerly, and fairly leapt from the car, hustling around to open the rear door for Andrews.

Mulder moved more deliberately, waiting until Scully joined him. They didn't speak, just exchanged quick *are you ready* glances and started up the concrete walk. Andrews wanted to know why they had to start here since the senator's connections were with Fort Dix and the air force.

Scully averted her face from a mild gust. "Let's just say it's usually a little easier dealing with civilians."

"Their loss," said Webber brightly.

Mulder looked at him, looked at Scully, and pulled open the door, allowing the others to precede him into an open room that took up the entire front third of the building. A waist-high wood rail stretched from wall to wall, and just left of its center gate a uniformed dispatcher sat at her radio, scribbling in a logbook; behind her were three metal desks, none of which were occupied.

To the gate's right a fourth, much larger desk faced the entrance. Behind it was a policeman whose uniform, Mulder reckoned, had been tailored for him ten years and twenty pounds ago. His face belonged to a man who spent most of his time outdoors, and a lot of that time drinking. His hair was brush-cut, and at one time had been red.

Mulder took out his wallet and held up his ID. "FBI, Sergeant, good morning." He spoke politely, with well-practiced due deference. He introduced the others quickly. "We're here to see Chief Hawks."

Sergeant Nilssen wasn't visibly impressed. He said nothing, just pushed away from his work and took his time walking to an unmarked door in the rear wall. Mulder saw the puzzlement in Webber's expression, the outrage in Andrews's. "It's their turf," he reminded them quietly. "They didn't ask for us, remember?"

"Still," Webber answered.

Mulder had neither the time nor the inclination for a quick lesson on the politics of competing law enforcement agencies. He kept his attention on the sergeant, who stood in the open doorway, one hand on a cocked hip, the other trying to scratch the small of his back, then his nape. Beefy, maybe, but not very soft. A glance at the dispatcher, who stared back at him without apology. She was in her late twenties, evidently enamored of heavy makeup and the way her wavy brown hair puffed down to her shoulders.

When she finally nodded a greeting, he nodded politely back.

"Slow day?" Scully asked her, looking around the empty room.

She shrugged—her name tag read *Vincent*—and waved one hand. "Guys are on the road." A faint smile. "Rush hour, you know?"

Scully chuckled as the woman coughed lightly into a fist.

"Poison ivy?" Mulder said, nodding at the blotches of white lotion on the back of her hand. "I hate that stuff."

Vincent made a face in agreement. "Yeah, I got it—"

"Hey."

The sergeant beckoned with a crooked finger.

Webber stiffened, but Scully touched his arm as Mulder led the way through the gate, smiling, always smiling, thanking the sergeant as he stepped aside to let the others precede him.

Nilssen didn't smile back. After an expressionless, just shy of openly rude once-over, he returned to his desk, leaving Mulder to make the introductions again, this time to Todd Hawks.

• • •

The Marville chief was younger than Mulder expected, not much older than his mid-forties, thick black hair brushed straight back from a widow's peak that pointed at where his heavy eyebrows nearly met across the bridge of a slightly hooked nose. He did not wear a uniform, nor did he wear a tie. White shirt and black trousers, their matching jacket on an antler coat rack in the corner.

His desk was battleship gray, just like the others, the only personal touch a silver-frame triptych Mulder noted held pictures of what must be his wife and three children.

Hawks rose and shook their hands, waving Scully and Andrews to the only other chairs in the room. Webber chose to lean against the wall near the door, arms folded casually across his chest.

The chief picked up a sheet of paper, glanced at it, and frowned. "I have to tell you, Agent Mulder, this fax your man Webber sent kind of took me by surprise. I wasn't expecting any feds to get involved." He let the paper drop, glanced at the closed door, and fingered a pen in his breast pocket. "To tell you the truth, though, I think I'm glad to see you. This shit's a little deep for me and my people, and those—" He stopped, lowered himself back into his chair, and picked up a pencil he rapped on the desktop. "The gentlemen from Dix aren't really much on letting us hick boys in on much of anything, even though the corporal wasn't killed on post." He used the eraser to scratch at his temple. "Technically, the Ulman murder is ours. Try to tell them that, though."

Mulder gave him the perfect *us against them* smile. "That's what we're here for, Chief. We're going to need all the assistance we can get, and we'd definitely appreciate all you can tell us."

"No problem." Hawks, like his sergeant, wasn't awed, but not for the same reasons. "You just let me know what you need, I'll do what I can." The pencil tapped as his expression darkened. "The thing is, I didn't know that corporal at all. Grady Pierce, though, he was a royal pain in the ass, but I could think of a couple dozen guys I'd rather see take it the way he did. The poor son of a bitch."

"Friend of yours?" Webber asked from the back of the room.

Hawks looked around Mulder at him, shaking his head. "Not really, no. Just known him a long time. Retired drill instructor, wife left him right after the service forced him out." He looked back at Mulder. "He had no skills to speak of except bending his elbow, and AC."

Andrews, who had been sitting stiffly in her chair, distaste clear in the set of her lips, said, "AC?"

"Atlantic City, Agent Andrews," the man explained.

"Oh." Distaste became disdain. "Gambling."

Hawks didn't blink; he only nodded.

"So you think it was a gambling debt or something?" Webber asked, dropping his arms, eagerness creeping into his voice. "Pierce, I mean?"

"Not hardly. When he went, he mostly won." He grinned. "Nicely supplemented his retirement pay, which wasn't a hell of a lot." He opened the center drawer and pulled out a folder. "This is pretty much what we've got on both men, Agent Mulder." He handed it over. "You can see it isn't much, even after two weeks with Grady." He shook his head and shrugged. "The trail's probably dead, if you'll excuse the expression. You're welcome to it, though."

Mulder nodded his thanks and handed it to Scully, who flipped through it and frowned. "I don't see any body diagrams in this autopsy report. Just photographs, and not much commentary."

Hawks scowled. "You'll have to ask them on the post about that. It seems they cared as much about old Grady as we did."

Well, well, Mulder thought. No love lost between Marville and Fort Dix. He wondered if that extended to the merchants as well.

Scully held a sheet of paper closer to her eyes, frowning in confusion. "What's this say here in the margins? Gablin? Goblin?"

Mulder looked at her quickly. "Goblin?"

"Go see Sam Junis," the chief suggested as she slapped the folder shut. "He's the local doc, did the work on both men. He scribbles a lot, half the time nobody can read it but him. He lives in the first house west of where you're staying. He knows you'll be dropping in."

"How did you know where we were staying?" Andrews demanded.

Mulder didn't turn, but he hoped the chief wouldn't take offense.

"Miss," Hawks answered with a lazy smile, "you maybe have noticed we're not exactly the metropolitan Washington area around here. And this time of year, Babs out there at the motel doesn't get hardly any business except on weekends, and not much even then. Hell, if you want, I'll even tell you what you had for breakfast."

"What?" Webber asked, as if the chief were a magician about to reveal an ancient secret.

Hawks looked at Mulder—Is this one for real?—and stood. "You're the redhead, so you had more pancakes than you ought to, gonna need a new notch on that belt, son, before long. Agent Scully had toast and coffee, bran cereal, orange juice. Agent Andrews had tea, toast, corn flakes. And you, Agent Mulder, had toast, bacon, two eggs over medium, coffee, orange juice, and blueberry jam."

Mulder grinned his appreciation as the chief came around the desk and ushered them to the door.

"And I suppose you know what side of the bed I slept on?" Andrews asked coldly.

"Beats the shit out of me, Miss," he said. "Damn drapes were closed too tight."

Mulder couldn't help it; he turned away and laughed as the chief asked them to wait outside while he cleared a couple of things up before taking them down to the first crime scene. Although it looked as if Andrews was about to object, Mulder agreed immediately and shook the man's hand, thanking him again for his cooperation. Then he herded the team into the outer office, nodded to the sergeant—the dispatcher was gone, replaced by a man who stared at them, bewildered—and didn't stop again until he was on the front walk, but unfortunately, not before Andrews made a deliberately loud comment to Hank about the "insufferable hicks in this damn burg." Mulder, hands in his open topcoat pockets, looked up the street, seeking patience and inspiration, and a way to heed Scully's silent warning not to lose his temper.

"Look," he finally told them, "we have to work with these people, you understand? We need them on our side so we can do our job and get back to Washington as quickly as we can. I don't care what you think of them personally," he said to Licia, "but you keep your comments to yourself from now on, understood?"

She hesitated before nodding, and he made a note to have Scully Dutch uncle her later.

Webber, chastened even though he hadn't been the one scolded, cleared his throat. "Uh, Mulder? Who's Babs?"

Mulder nodded toward the far end of town. "Babs Radnor. She's the owner of the motel."

Webber frowned. "How did you know that?"

Without looking at Scully, he said, "Spooky, Hank. I'm just damn spooky," turned, and pointed to a brick-faced diner across the street. "We'll meet there about one for lunch, okay?" He told Hank and Andrews to canvass the area around Barney's, talk to everyone they could find about the dead men, the bar's reputation, the night of the murder, anything at all that might yield them information the reports hadn't told them.

Webber almost saluted as he led his partner off, leaning close, whispering urgently.

"Hello," Mulder said quietly as Scully came up beside him. "My name is Agent Webber, FBI. Tell me all you know or I'll smile you to death."

She slapped his arm lightly. "Give him a break, Mulder, okay? He's not all that bad."

He agreed. "But it's not him I'm worried about."

He looked at the sky, at the lowering clouds, and smelled the first hint of rain as the wind strengthened, snapping the tired banner, scattering debris in the gutters. At that moment, nothing moved on the street.

No pedestrians, no cars, not even a stray dog or cat.

"Ghost town," Scully said.

"Graveyard," he answered.

NINE

They walked east along Main Street, Mulder on the outside. The deserted moment had passed, and shoppers, not many, drifted in and out of stores, while automobiles and pickups made their way between the traffic lights. Few bothered to look at him and Scully, and those who did smiled faintly and moved on.

A breeze drifted down the sidewalk, picking up strength, flapping his open topcoat against his legs, slipping an unpleasant chill inside his suit.

Scully followed the meandering progress of a mongrel along the curb. "Did you notice how he changed? Hawks, I mean?"

He nodded. "Cop for us, hick for Licia. The man's no dope. I'm actually a little surprised he didn't ask for help right away. As far as I can tell, when they need a detective, he's it. And what's with Andrews, anyway?"

She shrugged. "First case jitters?"

He supposed it could be, but he didn't like it. Like the assignment of this case, it just didn't feel right. He didn't doubt she was

76

competent; she wouldn't have gotten this far otherwise. Something, however, would have to be done about that superior attitude she had taken in the station. Behavior like that would shut Hawks up faster than a judge's order.

As Barney's slipped by them on the far side, he glanced over and saw, as before, nothing special. A tired bar in a tired town. Pick it up and put it down in Michigan or Oregon, it wouldn't change. And immediately he thought it, he realized he had probably made a big mistake, letting her go with Webber. The man had a knack for getting people to talk to him. That face, that grin, that shock of red hair was disarming. He hoped it would be enough to offset Licia Andrews.

The morning light dimmed.

The scent of rain grew stronger.

From the corner of his vision he watched Scully tracing the probable path Grady Pierce had taken, leaving the bar, making his way at some point across the street, maybe weaving, maybe not. An empty street. Light rain.

"He didn't see anybody," he said as they approached the alley. It was set between a pair of three-story brick buildings, clothing stores on the ground floor in both, what looked to be apartments above.

Scully didn't question him. "Or he didn't notice."

"That late, in this town? On a Saturday night? It may not be very healthy, but it isn't dead yet. He would have noticed. Especially if it was raining."

Again Scully didn't argue. She only said, "Unless he knew him."

A sideways glance: "Sexist comment, Scully. I am offended."

"Impersonal pronoun, Mulder. I am unbiased. So far."

Just as they reached their destination, a gleaming white patrol car pulled in at the curb, facing in the wrong direction. Chief Hawks slid out, jacket and tie in place, hair barely touched by the breeze now a wind. As he came around the trunk, he was greeted by several pedestrians, and he responded in kind, calling each by name. He slipped a hand into a pocket as he joined them, pushing the suit jacket behind his arm.

Mulder saw the shoulder holster.

The chief shivered, rolling his shoulders against the damp. "Are you sure about this?"

"I know it's old," Mulder answered, "but it's always better than reading about it in a report."

"Visualization," Scully added.

Hawks nodded understanding. "So . . . ?"

The alley was a few inches wider than six feet, extending another twenty yards to a twelve-foot-high, weather-stained stockade fence. Although there were no garbage cans or a Dumpster, there were small fluttering islands of wind-deposited trash against the base of the walls. There were no windows. There were no fire escapes. The yellow crime scene ribbon had long since been taken down.

They stood on the sidewalk, forcing what foot traffic there was to walk behind them.

The stores on either side had SALE signs in their windows, but the one on the right was dark, nothing on display. Above, the windows were all curtained or blind with shades.

Somebody died here, Mulder thought; some poor guy bled to death here.

It was time to walk the crooked path.

Hawks pointed: "Grady was found there, a couple of feet in, sitting against the wall. Even with the rain, it looked like he took a shower in his own blood."

Mulder took a single step in and hunkered down, looking at the spot, looking over and up at the wall. He saw no evidence of the dying, but he could sense it here just the same.

Scully stood behind him. "He was killed where?"

Hawks walked around them and stood about a yard from Mulder. "The way the blood trail was—and again, remember it was raining—it looked like he was cut here, took a step or two, maybe trying to get to the street, and ended up there, where Agent Mulder is." He moved aside when Scully took his place. "The thing is, those streetlights don't reach in very far. A couple of feet at most, and I'll bet he wasn't seeing all that clearly."

"Mulder?"

He rose slowly, watching her turn until her back was against the right-hand wall.

"The killer was standing about here."

Hawks frowned. "How do you know that?"

"The autopsy report," she said, gaze constantly shifting, examining the ground, the opposite wall, the ground again. "If your Doc Junis is right, he'd have to be. Can I borrow your pen?"

The chief, looking for and not getting a reaction from Mulder, handed her a ballpoint, which she held in her right hand as if it were a knife, not for stabbing but for cutting.

"The photographs weren't all that clear," she continued, almost as though she were talking to herself. "But look . . ." She gestured until Hawks stood with his back to the street, then stood in front of him and, before he could move, whipped the pen through the air at his throat.

He jumped.

Her apology was a sardonic smile. "No blood on the walls. It was a single slash, very strong, cutting jugular and carotid. There wouldn't have been a gusher, so to speak, but some significant blood would have hit the walls if he'd been facing in or out." She handed the pen back. "There was none." She pointed in. "And there wasn't any back there, either."

"Rain," the chief reminded her. "And it was at least an hour before he was found."

She nodded. "But the trail, even after all that time, seemed pretty clear, at least from the pictures." She looked up, squinting, using her chin to show the chief the opposing roofs' slight overhang, bulging with sagging copper gutters; it may have been raining, but only a downpour and strong wind would have made the alley as soaked as the street. Then she looked at Mulder. "He was facing the wall."

And that, Mulder knew, was a hell of a thing.

If Scully was right, Grady Pierce would have had to have been damn near blind not to see his attacker.

Unless the attacker was invisible.

"No," she said to the look on his face. "There's another explanation, Mulder."

He didn't respond. He walked carefully, slowly, to the back and poked a finger at the fence. The wood was spongy with rot, and there were no marks on or in it to indicate anyone had climbed over. Or had tried to.

So the killer had left the way he had come in.

"Pierce must have known him," Scully said as he rejoined them.

Hawks agreed. "The way it looks, there's no other reasonable explanation." He sniffed, laughed, hitched at his belt. "Unless you believe Elly."

"The witness," Mulder said.

"If you want to call her that. I wouldn't bet my life on it, though." He led them back to the sidewalk. "See, Elly is what we call in our small town, scientific jargon, a fruitcake." He laughed again, shaking his head. "She's a dear, Elly Lang is, but she has this theory."

"Which is?"

"Oh, no. I'm not going to spoil it. This is something you have to hear firsthand."

The first floor apartment was nearly as dark as the approaching storm.

A single lamp with a saffron chimney on a tilted end table lit only that part of the love seat where Elly Lang sat. Hawks stood in the living room entrance, his back to the tiny foyer; he leaned casually against the wall, hands loose in his pockets. Scully sat in a Queen Ann wingback that smelled of must and mildew. Mulder was on a padded footstool, leaning forward, hands clasped on his knees.

A small room, a Pullman kitchenette at the end of a short hall, a bathroom, a bedroom barely large enough for the single bed and a dresser missing two of its five drawers. Framed prints on the papered walls; a false fireplace with no logs; a jumbled collection of plastic and ceramic horses on the mantel; a fringed carpet worn through in places, only the ghosts of its original colors left behind. The bay window was covered with yellowed flocked curtains tattered along the edges and at the bottom. No television; only a small, portable clock radio on the end table beneath the lamp.

Elly Lang wore discolored, thick-soled nurse's shoes, argyle socks rolled down to midshin, and a simple brown dress without a belt or trim. There was no telling how old she was. In the lamplight she could have been ancient—no lower teeth, collapsed cheeks, strings of dirty white hair untrapped by a hair net. No makeup at all. She kept her hands primly folded in her lap, no rings or watch.

But Mulder watched her eyes. They weren't old at all, and of an odd pale gray that made them appear almost transparent.

"Goblin," she said with a sharp nod, and a *don't you dare contradict me* glare at the chief.

Mulder nodded. "Okay."

She closed one eye partway as she regarded him suspiciously. "I said goblin."

He nodded again. "Okay."

"They live in the woods, you know." Her voice was low, harsh, the rasp of a childhood Halloween witch. "Came when the army did, back in '16, '17, I don't remember, just before I was born." She straightened her spine, and she faded, leaving only the shine of her eyes, the bloodless line of her lips. "Things happen sometimes, and they don't like it."

"What things?" he asked patiently.

"I wouldn't know. I ain't a goblin."

He smiled, just barely, and just barely, she smiled back.

"Miss Lang—"

"Ms.," she instructed. "I ain't blind. I read the papers."

"I'm sorry. *Ms.* Lang. What my partner and I need to know is what you saw that night. The night Grady Pierce died."

"Profanity," she answered without hesitation.

He waited, head tilted, watching her eyes, watching her lips.

"A profane man was Grady Pierce. Every other word out of his mouth a profanity. Especially when he was drinking. Which"—her lips pursed in disapproval—"he was most of the time. Always going on about his ghosts, his stupid ghosts. Like he was the only one in the world who saw them." A slow disapproving shake of her head. "He never listened to me, you know. I told him once, I told him a hundred times to stay home when the goblins were out, but he never listened. Never."

Quietly, respectfully: "You were out?"

"Of course. My obligations, you know."

Mulder questioned her with a look.

"I mark them," she explained. "The goblins. When I see them, I mark them, so this so-called policeman can lock them away until they burn up in the sun. But he never does, you know." The head turned, and Mulder sensed another glare. "He could have saved that old coot's life if he had picked up the marked ones."

"I have a feeling that will change, Ms. Lang," Scully said.

"Damn right it will," the old woman snapped.

"What you saw," Mulder prompted softly.

She shifted, pushing back into the love seat. Her fingers began an endless weaving.

"I was heading home."

"From?"

"The Company G."

Mulder kept his expression neutral. "And that's . . . a bar?"

"A cocktail lounge and restaurant, young man, use the brains God gave you. I do not go to bars. Never have, never will."

"Sorry. Of course."

"It's east of that hideous place Grady always went to, whores and old men, that's all that's there. Around the corner, on Marchant Street. A very nice establishment." The lips smiled. "I know the owner personally."

He heard the chief shift impatiently, heard a faint rustle as Scully shifted in her chair.

Elly cleared her throat to recapture his attention. "I saw Grady up ahead, going into that alley between McConnell's and The Orion Shop. The Orion Shop is closed, you know. They cheated on your change. And the clothes they sold weren't fit for a cow. The goblins drove them away. They do that sometimes, drive the robbers away."

The fingers weaving.

The patter of light rain against the windows.

"I didn't care, of course. About Grady, I mean. He called me names all the time, drunk and sober, so I didn't care at all when he went into the alley. I kept on walking, didn't dare stop, it isn't safe for a woman on the streets at night these days, you know." She looked over to Scully, who nodded her agreement. "I heard a voice."

"From across the street?"

"He was yelling, young man. Grady Pierce always yelled. The army did that to him, made him deaf, I think, so he was always yelling even when he wasn't, if you know what I mean."

83

Mulder looked at the carpet. "Did you hear what he said?"

She sniffed. "I don't pay attention to things that don't concern me. He was yelling, that's all. I just kept walking."

Fingers weaving, then abruptly still.

He watched her left heel rise and fall, silently tapping.

"I looked over. Natural curiosity, to see what a drunk was yelling at in an alley."

He watched her hands clasp, in a grip so tight he thought the bones might snap. He wanted to cover them, calm them, but he didn't dare move.

"I couldn't see him, except one leg kind of sticking into the light. I saw the goblin, though."

"You did."

The heel stopped; the fingers unwound.

"You don't have to humor me, Mr. Mulder. I don't like being humored. The goblin stepped out of the wall, kicked that old man's leg, and ran up the street."

"Did you call the police?"

She snorted. "Of course not. I knew what they would say. Don't need to be locked up again, not at my age. I'm going to die right here in this house, not in any damn cell."

He gave her that smile again. "But you did call later, didn't you?"

She leaned farther back, all her face now in shadow. "Yes. Yes, I did. Damn conscience wouldn't leave me be until I did, even though I knew they wouldn't do anything about the goblin."

"Ms. Lang?" It was Scully.

Mulder sat up carefully.

"Ms. Lang, what did the goblin look like?"

"It was black, child," Elly said.

"You mean—"

"No, not a Negro, that's not what I mean. I mean just what I said. It was black. All black. It had no color at all."

•　　•　　•

They stood on the sidewalk outside the building. A handful of children played noisy baseball in a small park diagonally across the street. The brief rain had stopped, leaving behind the clouds, and the smell of wet tarmac.

Hawks seemed embarrassed. "She drinks," he said quietly. "Like a fish. That's all she does when she's not marking her goblins." The laugh he uttered was partly embarrassment, partly mirth. "Orange spray paint, if you can believe it. Most of the time she sits over there in the park, watches the kids play ball. That bench there on the grass by the third base line, that's hers. But every so often she goes off on a tear, I have no idea what triggers it. She starts walking around town, zapping people with orange spray paint. Then she comes to the station and tells me to lock the goblins up."

He waited until they were in the patrol car before he jammed a toothpick into his mouth and pulled away from the curb. "Just about everyone knows her, see, so we don't arrest her or anything. We pay for the clothes or whatever she wrecks, and that's usually the end of it. No real harm done." He grinned around the toothpick. "What you might call local color."

"So you don't think she saw anything?" Mulder asked from the back seat.

"I wish I knew, I really do. We looked, of course, but we didn't find a thing. Myself, I think she saw shadows, that's all. It was raining, there was wind . . . that's all."

No one spoke as he headed back to the station. "But what," Scully asked, "if she did see something?"

The toothpick flipped from one corner of his mouth to the other. "A black goblin, Agent Scully? What the hell am I supposed to do with that?" He didn't wait for an answer. "Like I said, she was drunk, like always, and it was shadows."

Maybe, Mulder thought; but wherever there's a shadow, there's always something to make it.

Then Scully said, "Is she the only one, Chief?"

Mulder saw him twitch.

"Only one what?"

"Is she the only one who's seen the goblin?"

They passed another small park where a pick-up baseball game had drawn a small crowd.

"No," he admitted quietly. "No, damnit, there've been others."

TEN

Major Joseph Tonero loved his sister, even if she did have appalling taste in men. With their father gone and their mother an invalid, he had automatically assumed the role of head of the family. He didn't mind at all. It was not unlike his role in the service, mediating crises between people who were grown up enough to know better, issuing orders carefully couched as strong suggestion, and laying plans for the time when he could trade his uniform for a well-tailored suit that would fit right in on Capitol Hill.

So he wasn't all that concerned with the fit Rosemary Elkhart threw in his office in Walson Hospital. He simply sat back, folded his hands in his lap, and let her rant, pacing the oak-paneled room until she finally dropped into an armchair. Her lab coat fell away when she crossed her legs, and he made no effort not to stare.

It wasn't as if he hadn't seen those thighs before.

"So what you're saying," he told her mildly, "is that you're annoyed."

She glowered, but couldn't hold it, finally laughing and shaking her head. "You amaze me, Joseph. You absolutely amaze me."

"Why?"

She sputtered, blinked, slapped in frustration at her bangs. "All that's at stake, and you, of all people, actually call in the FBI. Leonard's thinking about running to Brazil."

The smile he gave her carried no artifice. It wasn't necessary here; she knew all the tricks of his trade, and had taught him a few new ones herself. "I didn't exactly call them personally."

Close enough, her expression told him.

He waved her objection away. "I'm not worried about the feds, Rosie, and neither should you be. They come in, they read the reports, they look at a crime scene that's been cold for a week—"

"And what about Kuyser? She's a witness."

"Oh, really?"

Rosemary shrugged a minor concession. "Okay, not much of one, granted." She toyed with the edge of her coat, just above the knee. "But what about Leonard?"

His expression hardened. "We need him. I don't like it, you don't like it, but the Project needs him." He rose and walked around the desk, stood behind her and stared blindly at the wall while he massaged her shoulders. "Once this little problem—"

She barked a laugh.

"—is settled, once you're back in the groove, then we'll see about Dr. Tymons."

She tilted her head and kissed his hand. "I can do it, you know, Joseph. It's not hopeless."

"I have every faith in you, Rosie."

"A small adjustment, that's all."

"As I knew it would be."

She turned to look up at him. "A week, perhaps two."

His gaze shifted to her face, that back of his left hand to her cheek, gliding down across her chin. "And . . . confinement?"

She leaned into the hand, eyes partly closed. If she had been a cat, he thought, she'd be purring.

"None."

The hand stopped.

"We can't, Joseph," she said, easing out of the chair. "We have to trust Leonard's judgment on this."

"We already have. Twice."

"If we confine, we lose."

He sighed without a sound. He knew that, yet it was so untidy, so uncontrolled. But if the Project was to work, if the Department of Defense was to be convinced, it wouldn't do to have a psychotic subject. He had little choice. Tymons would continue to be the control until perfection was achieved.

Unless . . .

He took her hand and led her to the door. "Rosie, if there's another failure, I don't think I'll be able to protect him."

Her smile was genuine as well, and he suppressed a shudder when he saw it. "You won't have to, Joseph."

She kissed him quickly and left, the smell of her, the taste of her, lingering in the office. He savored it for a few seconds before striding back to his desk. The problem with Tymons and the Project was the least of his worries right now. He didn't much care if the subject wiped out half the goddamn state; with the right slant, a well-chosen word, it would only prove the Project's ultimate worth. And he had been telling Rosie the truth—his concern over the FBI was minimal as well.

The real problem was that asshole Carl Barelli. The idiot had already called him twice this morning, demanding an appointment, and the major knew well that kind of man—if no appointment was forthcoming, he'd show up on the post anyway and make enough noise to wake the dead.

Not to mention alerting those whose need to know did not, by any stretch of the regulations or imagination, extend to the Tymons Project.

You don't turn on a spotlight when you're working in the dark.

That was the problem with goddamn reporters these days— they thought they owned the goddamn Constitution. Barelli would have to be mollified. Having the FBI around would help. So would assurances that he himself was personally monitoring the situation, maintaining constant contact with the CID and the civil authorities. He'd do that anyway; he wasn't a fool. The fact that he had thought Ulman was a class-A jerk shouldn't deter him from extending what comfort he could to his sister.

Still, if Angie took up with a serviceman again, he would personally see to it the jerk was transferred to South Korea.

He took his chair and reached for the telephone, his free hand drumming thoughtfully on the desk. He would get hold of Carl, meet him for a late lunch, take him on the two-bit tour, pat him on the back, shed a tear with him for the loss of Angie's love, and get the sonofabitch the hell off his post. Let him go back to writing about hockey or basketball or whatever the hell it was he wrote about in April.

Hell's bells, he was only a cousin, for Christ's sake.

It wasn't like he was real family.

Goblins, Elly thought nervously; the goblins are back.

She stood in the kitchenette, squinting myopically at a calendar hanging on the refrigerator door. She knew those government people hadn't believed her, nobody did, but tomorrow was Saturday again, and the goblins would be back.

She was tired of being the only one who saw them.

That young man, though, he might be persuaded. He had the

look about him. The believing look. The wanting look. All she had to do was mark one and show it to him.

That's all it would take.

Once he knew, the others would come around.

She licked her lips and turned to the cupboard under a rust-stained sink. From it she pulled a brand new can of marking magic, shook it, took off the rounded top, and tested it in the sink.

It worked.

She cackled.

Her pale eyes hardened to steel gray.

"So when he took off for California," said Babs Radnor, a distinct Tennessee drawl in her voice, "I got a lawyer, emptied the bank account, took over the motel, and have become, as you can see, a lady of leisure."

She sat in her king-size four-poster, two pillows fluffed behind her back. She bordered on the painfully thin, with short black hair brushed behind her ears, hard black eyes, and a voice that husked with too much liquor, too many cigarettes. Her right hand held a floral sheet modestly over her breasts, while her left hand held a tumbler of bourbon and ice.

"I am not a lush, though," she insisted, waving the glass from side to side. "Like the French, I always have a little something with every meal. It's supposed to be good for the heart and circulation."

Carl stood at the low, twelve-drawer dresser and watched his reflection trying to make sense of his tie. "That's wine, Babs. Wine."

She shrugged. "Who gives a damn. It's working, right? So who cares?"

He didn't argue. Not even twenty-four hours, and he already knew she did not take lightly to contradiction or correction. Nor did she exaggerate when she had suggested without being coy or cute that he would have a much more pleasant evening in her company than the company of a TV, even if it did have free HBO.

It beat all to hell paying for a room.

It also afforded him a way to keep tabs on Mulder and his team. Babs, as she had already proven, knew everything about every blessed person who stayed in her motel. And if she didn't know, she found out. There wasn't, she had confessed, a whole lot else to do around here.

"So anyway, I'm figuring one more year, maybe two, sell out and get my buns to someplace like Phoenix, Tucson, someplace like that. Have you ever been to Arizona, sugar?"

He shook his head, damned his tie, and yanked it off. He didn't figure the major would take him anyplace fancy anyway. There was, as the saying goes, no love lost between them, and it didn't bother him a bit. Tonero was an ambitious little toad, and Carl's skin crawled each time they met. He didn't know how Angie could be from the same mother. Still, the guy had been sincere enough when they finally connected, and this lunch thing would give him a chance to see where Frankie had died.

Once he had done that, gotten the lay of the land, he could take the next step.

Whatever that might be.

"On the other hand, San Diego is supposed to have perfect weather, you know?" She laughed hoarsely. "The trouble is, it's in California. They hate it when you drink, smoke, and eat a decent meal, a steak and all. I don't know if I could stand it. I'm not too thrilled about those earthquakes, either."

He turned and spread his arms. "So? Do I look good enough to see a major?"

She waggled her heavy eyebrows. "Good enough to eat, if you ask me."

He laughed and sat on the edge of the bed, taking the hand that held the sheet in both of his. The sheet began to slide. "When I'm done, how about I take you out to dinner?"

"Yeah, right."

"Really, Babs, I'd like to. Is there a place around here, some-place nice?"

She looked at him carefully.

The sheet made it to her waist.

"If you don't mind driving a little . . . ?"

His eyes widened comically, showing her his struggle not to look at her chest. "A little?"

"An hour?"

"What's an hour?"

"Atlantic City. There's some really nice places at Resorts and the Taj." Then she stuck her tongue out and laughed, pulled his hands to her breast, and stuck her tongue out again. "Just so you don't forget."

He kissed her then, long and soft. "Like I would," he whispered.

"Liar."

"Maybe." He slipped away and stood. "But I'm damn cute, right?"

She didn't laugh, didn't smile.

He leaned over and kissed her again, quickly but just as earnestly. "See you later."

"I'll be here, sugar. No place else to go."

He blew her a kiss from the door, closed it behind him, and hurried down the long gold and royal blue corridor. Her apart-ment was above the office, tucked behind the crown facade, and he used the outside back stairs to get to his car, hastily parked there when he had spotted that redheaded agent pull up not long after he himself had arrived. He figured he would run into Mul-der sooner or later, but right now he preferred it to be later. The way he figured it, the agents wouldn't be here more than a couple of days, not on a case that was as cold as this one, and they'd probably eat at least one meal at the Inn.

They would talk while they ate.

Whatever they said, he would know less than an hour after they were done.

It was so perfect, he crossed his fingers to ward off the feeling that it just might be too perfect.

But he wasn't going to run from it, either. Hell, he got a free room, a free woman, and a chance to sneak up on Dana again. What the hell more could he ask for?

The killer, he answered as he pulled slowly around the side of the building; I want the killer, that's what I want.

He had another feeling, and he leaned forward, looked up, and saw her standing at her bedroom window. He gave her the smile, and the wave, and when she waved back he blew her a kiss before speeding out onto the road.

What a day this was going to be. Lunch with a uniformed toad who thinks his cousin is a jerk, a little investigative work around town, dinner in Atlantic City, a roll in the hay in a bed so big he could build a house on it.

Life, he decided, just doesn't get any better.

Leonard stood at the end of the basement corridor, listening.

He didn't know what he expected to hear. There was never any noise save for the faint grumble of the machines that gave the building its power.

Nevertheless he listened, and wished there were more lights.

A single bulb over the entrance, one down at the far end. Nothing more. No need for more. He and Rosemary were the only ones who used it; Major Tonero was the only one who visited.

Still, he couldn't help thinking there should be some sound other than the rasp of his breathing.

You're making yourself jumpy, he scolded as he started toward the Project office. Not that he shouldn't be. So much had gone right, and so much had gone wrong, that half the time he didn't know whether he should shout or cry. Rosemary didn't help either, nagging at him constantly, pushing him, reminding him unnecessarily that this had to be the right one or all support would vanish as if it had never been.

And, he feared, him with it.

Ten yards down he reached the first of three doors on the right—there were none on the left at all.

The first was his private office. No markings, just dull steel. The second door was the same, the Project center within. He glanced through the wire-mesh window and saw that it was empty. Rosemary must still be at lunch.

The third door was closed.

He glanced at it nervously, checked back toward the exit, and decided he had to know.

With one hand in his pocket to stop his keys from jangling, he hurried to it and looked through the reinforced glass judas window.

No one sat in the armchair, or at the desk now stripped of everything but the pen and legal pad. He couldn't see the bed.

He flipped a switch by the jamb and rapped lightly on the window with a knuckle, and jumped back with a stifled cry when a face suddenly grinned at him from the other side.

"Jesus," he said, eyes closing briefly. "You scared me to death."

Above the door was a microphone embedded in the concrete, a speaker grille beside it.

"Sorry." The voice was distorted, asexual. "I'm on break. I thought I'd drop in. Sorry."

It wasn't sorry at all.

"How do you feel?" He approached the door again, warily, as if the face belonged to a superhuman monster that could, at the slightest provocation, smash through the steel. The stupid thing was, the door wasn't locked. He could walk right in if he wanted to. If he had the nerve.

"How do you think I feel?"

Tymons refused the bait, the invitation to guilt. That sort of emotion had died the first time he had skinned a subject capuchin alive. He hadn't liked it, of course, but there had been no other way.

Guilt, for the Project, was too damn expensive.

"When do I get to see the results?" It wasn't a plea, it was barely a question.

"Later," he promised. Below the level of the window, he crossed his fingers. Just in case.

"I feel pretty good."

"You're looking good."

He returned the smile.

"I've almost got it, too."

Tymons nodded. He heard that every week, every month. "You'd better. They're . . ." He couldn't help a grin. "They're a little annoyed."

"It wasn't *my* fault. You're the doctor."

He had heard that one, too. Every week. Every month.

"But I'll take care of it."

Tymons glared and pointed. "You'll do no such thing, you understand? You let me handle everything."

The face didn't change expression, but Tymons looked away from the contempt.

"I'd like my books back, please."

He shook his head. "That didn't work, and you know it. The books, the music, the TV. Too many distractions. You need to concentrate on your concentration." He chuckled. "As it were."

"I *can* concentrate, damnit. I concentrate so much my brain is falling out."

Tymons nodded sympathetically. "I know, I know, and I'll talk to you about it later. Right now I have work to do."

Even through the distortion, the sarcasm was clear: "Another little adjustment?"

Tymons didn't answer. He switched off the communication unit, waved vaguely, and hurried to his office. Once inside, he locked the door behind him and dropped behind his desk, switched on his computer, leaned back, and closed his eyes.

This was wrong.

Things weren't getting better, and no goddamn adjustments were ever going to work.

He sighed and checked his watch—he had almost two hours before Rosemary arrived. Plenty of time to complete copying his files. Plenty of time to take the army-issue .45 Tonero had given him and go back next door. And use it.

Plenty of time to vanish.

After all, he thought with a hollow laugh, he was the expert at things like that.

Then he glanced through *The Blue Boy*, and started.

The room was empty.

"Damn." He flicked a switch beneath the shelf, activating the lights embedded in the room's ceiling. All color vanished, all shadows.

Still empty.

The bastard had already left.

Like a ghost, he thought, glancing nervously at the door; the damn thing moves like a ghost.

After all this time, he couldn't bring himself to think of it as human.

ELEVEN

X   The overcast thickened, splotches of shifting cloud from gray to black bulging and spreading, using the wind to warn that the rain that had fallen before would be nothing like the rain to come.

Dana stood uneasily in the middle of a narrow paved road, not at all caring for the way the woodland pressed around her, not liking the faint hint of ozone that promised lightning when the storm broke again.

They had eaten in the diner as planned, but neither she nor Mulder had been either surprised or pleased with what they had heard: Webber and Andrews had learned nothing that hadn't been recorded or implied in the reports already. No one had seen anything, no one had heard anything; many of the shopkeepers knew Grady, most of them not kindly; a couple recognized Ulman's picture, but there was nothing more than that. He was from the post. Big deal.

No miracles.

No one had mentioned goblins, either.

Hawks had explained that, over the past couple of months,

some kids and a couple of adults had reported seeing . . . something drifting around the town. They called it a goblin because everyone knew of Elly Lang's obsession.

"But it doesn't mean anything," he had insisted calmly. "A story like that, it kind of feeds on itself."

By two, the afternoon light had worsened, shifting closer to false twilight. Mulder decided to check the site of the corporal's murder before the storm broke. Andrews, on a hunch, volunteered to return to the motel to interview the owner; it was possible, she said, Ulman had used the out-of-the-way place for weekend escapes. Maybe he had provoked the wrath of someone's husband. Chief Hawks quickly volunteered to drive and introduce her.

"And keep her out of trouble," Mulder had said later, in the car.

Scully hadn't liked the idea then, and she didn't like it now. Webber, on the trip out, had already told them that Andrews, her attitude unchanged, had made the interviews, brief as they were, "kind of difficult." Except, predictably, when the subjects were men.

Webber stood now some fifty yards up the road, hands in his pockets, playing the part of the Jeep the Ulman witness had been in. He looked miserable as the wind slapped his hair and coat around; about as miserable as she felt.

Mulder was on his third circle of the tree from which the arm and weapon had allegedly appeared. It had been easy to find—there was still a ragged piece of yellow crime scene ribbon wrapped around its thick trunk.

She glanced up; the sky was lower.

Nothing moved in the woods but leaves and bare branches. And the slow-strengthening wind.

Behind her, their car shuddered when a gust slammed it broadside.

She turned in a slow circle, shaking her head. The corporal had been drinking; he had, for some reason, come out of the woods down there by the ditch, staggered up here . . . and had been killed.

Mulder joined her, waving Webber to them. "You see it?" he asked.

The road was a flattened loop that left the county highway just west of Marville, skirted the post boundary here, and met the highway again a mile farther on. While it was possible Grady had been a random victim, there was no way she would believe Ulman had simply been in the wrong place at the wrong time.

The killer had followed him through the woods.

"He was meant to die," she said.

He nodded. "I think so, yes."

Webber trotted up. "So is it hollow or what?"

She frowned. "What? The tree?"

"Sure. That woman saw—"

Scully took his arm gently and turned him around, pointing to the place he'd just left. "There are no lights, there was no moon, and all she saw, from way back there, was whatever the corporal's flashlight showed her."

She waited.

"Okay." He nodded. "Okay. But what was she doing out here?"

Mulder didn't answer. He grunted, and headed back for the tree.

"Well," she said, watching Mulder circle the tree again, squeezing between it and the caged white birch on either side, "she could be an accomplice. She could have been waiting for the killer."

Webber disagreed, as she knew he would. "That would mean they both knew Ulman would be here, at that time. And they didn't, right?"

"Right."

"So it was what? Her bad luck?"

"That's about the size of it," she said. She also reminded them that the so-called witness, Fran Kuyser, had been drinking, and taking heroin. Not exactly the most reliable observer they could hope for.

"When are we going to see her?"

Scully hunched her shoulders briefly. "Later, or tomorrow. From what the chief said, the condition she's in, she won't be able to tell us anything anyway."

"A hell of thing," Webber said. He shifted uneasily. "Can you tell me something?"

She nodded.

"Are the cases you work on . . . I mean, are they always this screwy? Messed up, I mean." He shook his head once, violently. "I mean—"

She laughed in spite of herself. "Yes. Sometimes."

"Brother," he said.

"Tell me about it."

Mulder rapped the trunk with a knuckle, then pried at the overlapping bark. Scully knew, however, that he saw more than just the tree. That was only the center; his focus touched it all.

"That old lady you told me about," Webber said, for some reason keeping his voice low.

Scully didn't look at him. "Ms. Lang. What about her?"

"She said . . . I mean, she was talking about goblins."

She did look then, sharply. "There are no goblins, Hank."

But she knew what he was thinking: She and Mulder were the X-Files, and that meant this case contained something well out of the ordinary. It didn't matter that the so-called paranormal had perfectly reasonable explanations, once you bothered to examine such incidents more closely. It didn't matter that the extraordinary was only the ordinary with curious trappings. They were here, goblins were mentioned, and now she wasn't sure Hank didn't believe it a little himself.

Mulder snagged his coat on a bush, yanked it free angrily, and took it off.

A hoarse cry overhead made her look up—a pair of crows flew lazily across the road, ignoring the wind.

"This place is kind of spooky," Hank said, rolling his shoulders against the damp chill.

She had no argument there. They could see barely a hundred feet into the trees now. If it was twilight out here, it was near midnight in there.

Slipping her hands into her pockets, she called Mulder's name. They would find nothing here; the trail was, for now, too cold.

He didn't hear her.

Goblins, she thought; please, Mulder, don't.

"I'll get him," Hank offered, and was off before she could respond.

He hadn't taken three steps before the first shot was fired.

Immediately, Scully yelled a warning, threw herself around the car, and pressed herself hard against the rear fender, gun in hand before she even realized she'd drawn it.

A second shot chipped the tarmac at Hank's foot, and he cried out, moving backward so rapidly he fell.

Scully eased herself up, squinting into the wind, trying to pinpoint the location of the shooter, knowing only that he was hidden somewhere in the woods east of them. She fired off a quick, blind shot, was answered by a barrage that peppered the road, forcing her back down just as Hank scrambled around the hood and squatted beside her, panting.

"You okay?" she asked.

He nodded, winced, and nodded again.

There was blood on his shoe.

He saw her look and shrugged. "Just a chip from the road on my ankle, that's all." He grinned. "I'll live."

She could see it, he was scared, but she could see the adrenaline, too.

Another barrage, this time at Mulder's position, and she rose again and fired as Hank fired over her head.

Nothing.

She could see nothing.

There was no question it was an automatic weapon, its bark suggesting something less than an Uzi. M-16, maybe. Not that it made much difference now. Bullets slammed into the trunk, walking up to and shattering the rear window.

"Mulder!" she called into the silence that followed.

No answer.

Hank tugged at her sleeve when the firing paused. "Gas tank," he warned, and on a count of three, they slipped back toward the hood. When the next round was aimed at Mulder, she took the opportunity to dart low across the pebbled verge and into the trees, pressing her shoulder against the trunk of a fat black oak. Webber found a position to her right and deeper into the woods.

"There!" he called, and fired at a point just beyond the far end of the ditch on the other side of the road.

She couldn't see anything, and then—she rubbed a hand quickly across her eyes. In the twisting leaves, a shadow. Or a figure all in black. It didn't move until Hank fired again, and then it vanished.

She looked to her left, and caught her breath.

"He's down!" she called to Webber. "Mulder's down!"

•　•　•

Mulder froze in shocked surprise at the first shot, dropped to the ground at the second, his own weapon out as he heard Scully and Hank return fire. But he couldn't see where the shooter was. The oak, the birch, the underbrush, all blinded him. Quickly, keeping low, he moved to his left, and dropped again when leaves and twigs were shredded above him, peppering his skull, stinging his cheeks.

He covered his head with one arm and waited, moving again when the firing concentrated again on the road, letting instinct take him deeper into the woods, tree to tree, searching for a muzzle flash, firing once, and once again, in hopes of diverting the shooter's attention away from Scully and Webber.

He heard glass shatter.

He heard Scully's voice.

A pine gave him cover, but he flinched anyway when the attack resumed on his original position.

It was luck, then, that the shooter hadn't seen him maneuvering deeper and around, and he used the time to search again, grunting softly when he saw the flash, and a dark figure pressed against the dark trunk of a lightning-blasted tree. He couldn't tell from this distance who it was; the figure had dressed in black from ski mask to shoes.

It didn't look like any goblin to him.

The wind quickened.

He angled inward again, and east, hoping the coming storm's thrashing branches and spinning leaves would make enough noise and present enough distraction that he'd be able to get close enough for a decent shot.

Scully's voice, and Hank's answer; he couldn't tell what they said, but the fear was there.

The black figure backed away, firing.

Mulder cursed and moved more quickly, keeping as low as he could without losing his balance. There were too many shadows now, too much movement.

He had to get there before the shooter disappeared.

At the south edge of a small clearing, he braced himself against a trunk, took several deep breaths to calm down and clear his head, and waited until the firing stopped.

There was no silence.

The wind and the woodland husked and shrieked at each other, pinwheeling debris across the clearing.

He would have to go across it; to go around would waste time.

He inhaled, blew out, and spun away from the tree in a crouch. He was halfway across, aiming, finger already squeezing the trigger, before he realized the shooter was gone.

Damn, he thought, and slowly straightened, not trusting his vision, gun still out and ready, squinting into the wind and throwing up one hand in disgust.

Something moved behind him.

He had only half-turned before something hard slammed off his temple, a glancing blow that drove him to his knees. His gun whipped out of his grip. His right arm lashed out automatically and struck something soft, but he couldn't see clearly; there were too many flares of blinding, painful light.

But he saw something, and it made him hesitate.

Then a blow to his spine almost toppled him, and he lashed out again, losing his balance as he did, landing on his shoulder before he was pinned on his chest.

A giggle in his ear, hoarse and inhuman.

Then a voice: "Mulder, watch your back," just before a foot caught him under his ribs.

TWELVE

He couldn't breathe.

"Mulder!"

Eyes watering, he tried to push himself to his hands, but he couldn't breathe.

"Mulder!"

Forget it, he told his arms, and rolled over instead, blinking furiously to clear his vision, spitting when a shard of leaf caught on his lips.

But he still couldn't breathe.

Voices, normal voices anxious and searching, until his name was called again, and he saw, or thought he saw, Scully kneeling beside him on his left, someone else on his right.

"I don't see any blood," Webber said.

"Mulder?"

He tried to smile reassurance, but it was too much trouble, and he let himself black out, to rest in the dark for a while.

By the time he regained full consciousness, there were sirens and shouts, the distant crackle of a radio. The wind had died, but the afternoon was still night. Scully was gone; Webber hovered nearby, and Mulder groaned to signal him and bring him over.

"Up," he said, stretching out an arm when the younger man leaned down.

"I don't know. Scully said—"

"Up," he insisted, and Webber brought him to his feet.

It was a mistake.

His head swelled to accommodate the fire inside, and he swayed and didn't argue when Webber eased him to a stump at the clearing's north end and made him sit. Bile burned the back of his throat; his stomach surged without delivering. He spat, and spat again, bracing an arm on his leg and resting his forehead on his palm.

"Jesus," he whispered.

Webber hunkered down beside him, concern adding too many years to his face. Mulder glanced over and smiled briefly.

"I'll live."

Webber didn't look as if he believed it. But he told him that an MP patrol, alerted by the gunfire, had arrived only moments after the shooting had stopped. Within minutes, other patrols had arrived, and Scully was advising them and their captain on a search of the woods. When Mulder looked up, he saw silver beams slashing and darting among the trees. Voices called softly. Through the trees he could see half a dozen MP Jeeps and cruisers parked on the road, and a single civilian patrol car, its roof lights still whirling.

"Chief Hawks," Webber confirmed.

Mulder nodded, and wished he hadn't—the fire rose, and fell, and his finger gingerly traced what would be a hell of a lump by nightfall. There was no blood. Then he pushed aside his jacket, opened his shirt, and tried to have a look at his ribs.

"Damn," Webber said. "What'd he use, a brick?"

"It sure felt like it." He winced as he probed the area. He

knew nothing was broken, however. How a broken rib felt was something you never forgot.

"Button up, Mulder, you'll catch pneumonia."

He smiled at Scully hurrying toward him. She seemed more annoyed at the wind slapping hair into her eyes than at him.

"You gonna examine me or what?"

"Please," she said. "I've had a bad enough day."

"What happened?" He nodded toward the search party.

"The shooter's gone. No surprise. They found a crushed area back around the bend where he probably stashed his car. No tire tracks, nothing but this." She dug into her pocket and pulled out a casing. "M-16."

"Army?"

"Maybe not," Webber said. "They're not all that hard to get outside the service anymore. Cops, bad guys, collectors." He shrugged. "Even guys leaving the service have smuggled them home."

Mulder muttered about having it easy once in a while. "Well, maybe we should check. How many can there—"

Webber groaned in anticipation. "Mulder, no kidding, it's the weekend. That means there's about eight, nine thousand reservists running all over this place. And you want to find one rifle that's been fired recently?"

"Hank, you amaze me. How did you know that?"

Webber shrugged again. "The interviews, remember? I'll bet the people in town know as much about what's going on on post as anyone who works there."

"Not quite," he muttered. He straightened slowly, hissing at the too-slow lessening pain.

"What I don't get," Scully said, "is how the shooter got to you before we did." Her expression turned sheepish. "I saw your coat on the ground, I thought it was you."

"It wasn't."

"So I see. I don't know what he hit you with, but he knew what he was doing. He could've cracked your skull wide open." She frowned. "What I don't get is how he managed to change positions so quickly. You were a good—"

"No. I mean, it wasn't the shooter."

She was startled. "What?"

"It wasn't the shooter, Scully. I saw him, the shooter, just before I got hit." He winced as he touched his head again. "From the side, Scully. I was hit from the side, right over there. The shooter was still in front of me."

Doubt was evident in her expression as she put the casing back into her pocket. "The goblin, right?"

"You got it. I just got a glimpse, but believe me, it was enough."

Webber almost laughed, but caught himself when she shook her head in exasperation. "Mulder, you'd just been clobbered, remember? Anything you saw, or thought you saw, would be suspect, you know that."

With Webber's reluctant help, he stood, looking at but not seeing the MPs' shifting lights. "It was a hand, and part of the forearm. The skin looked like bark."

Scully opened her mouth to say something, changed her mind and waited.

"I heard it, too."

She leaned away, an eyebrow cocked. "He left you a message?"

"It was like no voice I've ever heard." He closed his eyes again, to try to sharpen the memory, felt Webber's fingers lightly on his arm for balance. "I don't know. It was hoarse, whispering, as if it had a hard time saying the words." When he looked, she was scowling, arms folded across her chest. "Honest."

"I don't doubt you heard something. But I—"

"This is a joke, right?" Webber asked nervously. He looked from one to the other. "Some kind of private joke, right?"

Mulder shook his head. "Sorry, Hank, no."

"Oh, man," Webber said, almost in a moan. "Wait 'til Licia hears this one."

Carl Barelli was furious as he sped back through the woods toward Marville.

First, that sanctimonious toad, Tonero, tried to pass off the glop in the officer's mess as some kind of fancy food, instead of taking him to a decent restaurant; then tried to hand out some pious bullshit about family unity and Angie's peace of mind being more important than interfering with official investigations; and then he had the nerve to march Carl out to his car and tell him, with a smile, to go on back home and write about baseball or something.

He had fumed behind the wheel, debating the chances of his landing in jail if he went back inside and popped the toad one on the point of his spongy jaw.

Then an MP ran up, intercepted Tonero, and the two were hustled into a car. The next thing Carl knew there were sirens and men with rifles boiling out of the Provost marshal's office, and, after a suitable interval, he followed them.

To the goddamn woods.

Where another goddamn MP suggested with drawn .45 that the reporter find something else to report on, this area was sealed off to civilians.

"Bastards," he muttered, and muttered it often until suddenly he grinned.

He had seen a town cruiser at the scene, which meant the locals were involved, which meant . . .

He laughed aloud, and by the time he pulled up in front of the police station, his mood had lightened considerably. A quick check of his hair in the rearview mirror, an adjustment of his tie and jacket, and he was inside, smiling at the two men at desks near the back of the room, and the front desk sergeant, who couldn't have looked more bored if he were dead.

"I'd like to see the chief," Carl said as politely as his excitement would allow.

Sergeant Nilssen told him gruffly the chief was out, and there was no sense hanging around. He had work to do, half his people had some kind of lousy flu, and those who were around had police business to attend to.

A dispatch radio muttered static to itself while a gawky young officer flipped through a logbook.

Carl's smile didn't waver. "Then perhaps you can help me, Sergeant. I work for the *Jersey Chronicle*. My name is Carl Barelli, and I'm—"

Nilssen's boredom vanished. "Barelli? The sports guy in the paper?"

Amazing, Carl thought smugly; *absolutely amazing.*

"That's right, Sergeant. But today I'm looking into the death of a friend of mine. Corporal Frank Ulman."

"Man, yeah," the sergeant said, grinning. "So you want to hear about the goblins, right?"

The smile still didn't waver. "That's right. Can you help me?"

The policeman leaned back in his chair, hooked his thumbs into his belt. "Anything you want to know, Mr. Barelli. All you have to do is ask."

Tonero remained in the back seat of his staff car, watching as the MPs began to make their way slowly and methodically back toward the road. His driver was gone, ordered to sniff around to see what unofficial word he could pick up. It was better than talking to the captain in charge. Tonero knew the man well, and knew that the MP wouldn't give away a thing.

The car rocked a little when the wind slapped it.

He glanced warily out at what sky he could see, hoping he'd be able to get out of here before the storm broke.

This was not turning out to be one of his best days. Tymons was jumpy, and Rosemary was getting pushy; and he knew without doubt that Barelli wasn't going to leave until he had gotten some kind of crumb to fill his meager reporter's plate.

He sighed for all the injustices dropped on him since waking, and sighed again when the front passenger door opened and Tymons slipped in at the same time that Rosemary slipped into the back, beside him.

"We heard," Tymons said, agitation making his voice too high.

"What's going on?" Rosemary asked more calmly.

"I'm not sure. Someone tried to take care of the FBI, as near as I could tell."

Tymons groaned.

"It wasn't us," Rosemary snapped at him. "Jesus, Leonard, use your head."

"We should abort," was the answer. "We don't have any more control. We have no choice, we have to abort." He twisted around to look at the major. "Joseph, the FBI isn't going away now, you know that. No more just having a look around and running back to D.C. They're going to dig. And they're going to find something."

Tonero gripped Rosemary's leg briefly to keep her silent. "Leonard, I want you to pay attention."

"Joseph, we—"

"These people," and he indicated the MPs, "are looking for a shooter, okay? Not us and ours. There is no connection, and no connections can be made. Use your head, Doctor, use your head."

Tymons jumped as if slapped. "I don't know. They're going to ask questions."

"Well, that's no problem," Rosemary answered. "We'll just make sure there isn't anyone around to answer."

Tonero looked at her in astonishment.

She shrugged. "We may not have complete control, but we still have some." Her smile was cold. "Simple suggestions ought to do it."

"Jesus!" Tymons shoved his door open. "You're crazy, Rosemary. And as project director, I forbid it." He slammed the door and stalked away.

Tonero didn't look, didn't care where he was going. What he cared about was this new woman beside him. Something had changed since a few hours ago. Something drastic. He wasn't sure, but he thought he liked it.

"You better leave," he said quietly.

"And the problem?"

He gave her his best smile. "In for a penny, Rosie. In for a penny." He patted her knee. "Use your best judgment. Just be sure, all right? Whatever you do, just be sure." Then he grunted and took her arm to stop her. Ahead, he saw a man and woman helping a second, somewhat disheveled man out of the woods. *Shit*, he thought.

"Rosie, I think you'd better stick around a minute."

"You are not dead, Mulder," Scully complained. "Don't lean so hard."

She couldn't help a smile, though, at his melodramatic sigh. He might be different, but he was still a man, not above playing sick and injured to the hilt.

Someone called to them, and they stopped on the road.

"Well," Mulder whispered. "Well, well."

A man in uniform fairly marched toward them, and, when he was close enough, quietly demanded a report on Mulder's condition. When Scully balked, he ducked his head in apology. "Sorry. Major Joseph Tonero, Agent Scully. Air Force Special Projects."

His smile turned to Mulder. "This incident happened on my watch, so to speak, and I apologize for being slow getting here. A late lunch with an old friend. But I don't have to tell you how concerned I am. Is everyone all right?" Before she could answer, he rubbed his hands together. "Good, good. I'd hate to think what would happen if we lost an FBI."

His smile was intended to be warm, but Scully didn't buy it. The man was less a career soldier than a politician, she decided as she briefed him; his medical knowledge doesn't go much farther than using a bandage.

As soon as she was finished, two others came up behind him—a tall, balding civilian, too nervous for her peace of mind, and a striking, hard-edged blonde whose bearing was military, but she too was civilian. Neither spoke much save for a perfunctory mumbling of sympathies.

The major introduced them as part of his team, offering their services should the need arise. Scully assured him matters were well in hand, but thanked the officer for his concern.

"As a matter of fact," she added, "we were going to see you this afternoon, when we were done."

Mulder opened his mouth, closed it when she stepped in front of him and put a heel down on his foot to keep him silent.

"Corporal Ulman worked for you, isn't that right?"

The major grew solemn. "Yes, he did, Agent Scully. A tragic loss. He was a good man. And I've been working closely with the Provost—"

"He was going to marry your sister," Mulder said over her shoulder.

Tonero didn't miss a beat: "There was talk, yes. But just between you and me, I don't think it was going to happen." He sighed. "However, I certainly owe it to her to assist you in any way possible."

Neither made any mention of the phone call to Senator Carmen.

"Who attacked you?" Dr. Elkhart asked suddenly, sharply.

"There were two," Mulder answered before Scully could stop him.

"Really?" the major said, grabbing his hat against a gust. "I had no idea."

Scully was relieved when Mulder didn't elaborate; she watched instead as Dr. Tymons whispered something to Elkhart and hurried back down the road, one hand massaging the back of his neck.

"Major," she said, "I'm not sure, it's too soon, but if Agent Mulder here needs more assistance than I can—"

"Walson is mostly shut down," the major interrupted stiffly. "We function primarily as an outpatient clinic now, with only a few long-term patients. Cutbacks." He shrugged a *you know how it is* before the smile returned as he clapped his hands once. "However, the important thing is that you're all right, Agent Mulder." He turned to Scully. "He is all right, isn't he?"

She nodded. "But he could use some rest now, Major, so if you and Dr. Elkhart don't mind, I'd like to get him back to his room."

The major nodded, shook hands all around, and ushered Elkhart away, pausing only to have a brief animated conversation with the MP captain in charge of the search.

"What do you think?" Mulder asked when they were alone.

"I think," she said without turning around, "that there's a shooting incident, and the major brings scientists along instead of doctors."

She checked the car they'd ridden out in, the shattered glass and punctures, at the one shredded, flat tire.

"Hank," she said quietly, "get us a ride to the motel."

Then she looked at Mulder, and instantly knew what he was thinking:

You're not protected, Mr. Mulder, you're still not protected.

THIRTEEN

It took a while before Webber was finally able to get them back to the Royal Baron. Once there, as a doctor, not a partner, Scully ordered Mulder to bed with an ice pack and aspirin until she returned from a visit with Sam Junis. He didn't protest. Just a crooked smile and a phony sigh, and she knew he wouldn't sleep; he'd be too busy trying to squeeze the obvious so it ended up looking like a goblin.

Licia she found in their room, transcribing her notes from the Radnor interview. "Shorthand," the agent said apologetically. "Can't keep up otherwise, and I hate recorders." As she slipped the papers into a briefcase, Scully asked her what, if anything, she'd found out.

"It was like she didn't care," Licia complained, the insult to justice clear in her tone. "And even though she has exercise stuff—says she uses it when she remembers—in that downstairs room off the office, she still drinks like a fish." Then she smiled. "She knew the corporal, though."

"How?"

The smile became a smug grin. "It seems the engaged to the major's sister corporal enjoyed an occasional R&R. Like, nearly every weekend."

"Did she say who he was with?"

"No name, and she only got a glimpse. The corporal, it seems, was very careful. I don't know if that has anything to do with anything, though."

Scully agreed before hustling Andrews into her coat and outside. Webber would watch Mulder in case the shooter tried again, or Mulder decided to have an adventure on his own.

They took the second car, and on the way, she filled Andrews in, ignoring the comments and the outrage.

It also helped her think.

It was evident they were dealing with two different suspects. Aside from the fact that Mulder had been attacked by someone other than the shooter, she was certain the murderer of Ulman and Pierce hadn't suddenly decided to switch to a rifle as his weapon of choice. He was too good with the knife. And a knife was more personal, requiring close range; a rifle was too remote, dispassionate, requiring little or no victim contact at all.

When she had proposed this on the way back, both Mulder and Webber had agreed, but neither could find a reasonable explanation of why, suddenly, they were faced with two opponents.

"Maybe somebody's protecting the goblin," Andrews suggested.

"It's not a goblin," Scully snapped. "Please, don't you start, too. Mulder's already got Hank thinking that way."

"So what do I do? Call him Bill?"

"I don't care. Just don't call him a goblin!"

Andrews laughed and shook her head. "Boy," she said, "he really gets on your nerves, doesn't he?"

Scully didn't answer.

• • •

The doctor's bungalow was in only marginally better condition than those of his neighbors, its saving grace a large front garden whose arrangement and vivid blossoms signaled a great deal of time taken and care bestowed. The doctor himself was on the tiny front porch, sitting on the railing, smoking a cigarette. He seemed to be in his early fifties, his greying hair plastered straight back from his forehead, and despite the wind and the chill, he was in shirtsleeves and jeans. Most of him was lean, but his arms were hugely muscled, all out of proportion to the rest of him.

"Popeye," Andrews muttered as they took the narrow slate walk toward him.

Scully almost laughed aloud. She was right; all the man needed was a corncob pipe and a sailor's cap to complete the image.

"Been having a time of it, haven't you," he said by way of greeting. Then he nodded to a police scanner on a small table behind him. "It's either that or Oprah." He grinned.

Scully liked him immediately, and wasted no time getting into his reports. He took no offense at her questions, and asked no questions about the way Andrews barely took her gaze from the surrounding woodland.

The interview didn't last long—Junis agreed with her reconstruction of Pierce's murder, and actually apologized for not getting better photos. He also suggested that the knife used wasn't ordinary. "Sharp as hell, sure," he said, "but the cut of it, I think it might have been heavier than you'd find in your average kitchen."

"Like what?" Scully asked.

"I don't know. I've been thinking about it, but I still don't know."

She knew then she had to ask the next question, and for once, she was glad Mulder wasn't with her. "You had some notes in the margin."

He laughed as he flicked his cigarette onto the lawn. "Yeah. Goblin, right?"

"What does that have to do with anything? As far as your examinations went, I mean."

"Not much." He pulled another cigarette from his pocket and stuck it between his lips. He didn't light it. "Nothing. I'd just been to see Elly Lang, had to calm her down a little with a mild sedative, and that's all she talked about." A sideways glance. "You heard about it, huh?"

"We talked to her, yes."

Junis followed the wake of a pickup heading west. "Don't think she's crazy, Agent Scully. Don't write her off. I don't know who she saw, but she's no fool."

"She was drunk, Dr. Junis."

He laughed abruptly, loudly, until his eyes began to water and his face reddened alarmingly. "Sorry." He laughed again and wiped his eyes with a sleeve. "God, I'm sorry." He gripped the railing with both hands. "Drunk? Elly? You've been listening to Todd Hawks. Nope, never. She goes to that bar for the company, that's all. She's outlived her family, has no real friends to speak of. She has one drink, a Bloody Mary, that she nurses until she's ready to go home, and that's about it. That woman has never been drunk a day in her life."

"Then what about the spray paint?"

Junis watched another truck pass. "Because she believes it, Agent Scully. She believes it as sure as you believe there ain't no such thing. That doesn't mean she's certifiable."

Scully wasn't so sure about that, but she didn't know enough to pursue it. Instead she asked about the other witness.

"Fran?" Junis lowered his gaze to the garden. "I can take you to her, if you want, but she won't do you a whole lot of good."

"Why not?"

His expression hardened. "The heroin she took that night was damn close to an overdose. I brought her to a facility up near Princeton." He paused. "A mental rehab, by the way, we don't have anything like that around here. She was pretty far gone." He lit another cigarette and blew smoke into the wind. "She'll recover from the overdose most likely, but as for the other . . . she isn't going to be released for a long, long time."

Swell, she thought; just what I need—an addict who probably can't even recognize her own reflection. Interviewing Fran Kuyser quickly dropped toward the bottom of her list.

"Do you sit out here a lot?" Andrews asked then, not bothering to look at him.

He nodded to Dana, not at all fazed by the sudden change of subject. "Guess I do, come to think of it. I like to watch the world drive by, see who's going where. People around here, those that work on post or at McGuire, they have their military doctors, and the others . . ." He shrugged. "Not a lot left, but I guess you already noticed that."

Scully also noticed that he didn't seem to mind. Although he was too young to step down yet, he appeared to be resigned that this practice wasn't going to get him a retirement home in a better location, and that, for whatever reason, was all right with him.

"Oh, we have our moments," he said, startling her. "And it beats all to hell working an ER."

She wasn't inclined to disagree, thanked him for his time, and told him where she was staying in case he thought of something else.

"I already know that," he said. And grinned.

Back in the car, Andrews shook her head in disbelief. "You know, you can't breathe around here without somebody knowing it. Hardly any privacy at all." She forced herself to shudder. "That's too weird for me."

Dana grunted, but she wasn't really listening. There was something not quite right here, something she and the others had missed. She didn't think it was tied directly to the killings, but it was, somehow, important. Small, but important. She knew Mulder felt it as well. In spite of the afternoon's attack, she knew it bothered him, and maybe by the time they returned to the hotel and he had rested, he would know what it was.

As long, she added glumly, as he doesn't call it a damn goblin.

The motel lights were all on when they returned, highlighting the crown facade, flooding the parking lot with dull silver, making the clouds seem even lower and thicker than they were. After sending Andrews to fetch her interview notes, she pushed through Mulder's door just in time to hear him say, ". . . a multitude of sins."

"What sins?" she demanded. "And why aren't you in bed?"

He sat in shirtsleeves at the room's tiny table, his back to the wall, papers spread in front of him. Webber was on the bed, propped up by pillows, knees drawn up to serve as a rest for a legal pad.

"Hi, Scully," Mulder said. "I'm cured."

Webber refused to meet the rebuke in her eyes as she dropped into the chair across the table. "You're not cured, and you've been working." But the scolding was, as always, a waste of time; he would only give her one of two looks—the hurt little boy, or the sly-fox, lopsided grin—and do what he wanted anyway.

He settled for the grin. "We've been checking up on Major Tonero."

"It's weird," Webber commented from the bed. "His office confirms he's head of Air Force Special Projects, like he told us, but they wouldn't explain what that means."

"Which," Mulder continued, "covers a multitude of sins." He shook his head slowly. "Curiouser and curiouser. Why would an air force major, who isn't even medical personnel, be assigned to an air force hospital on an army post? Which, for the most part, is used as training for reservists, and a jumping-off point when troops have to get overseas in a hurry." Then he pointed at her before she could answer. "And don't tell me there's a perfectly rational explanation."

Oh, Lord, she thought; he's in one of his moods.

"And," Webber added eagerly, "why would he be so interested in the ambush? And why were his people there, too? Those two doctors, scientists, whatever."

Scully stared at him for so long, he began to look embarrassed. "Well . . . it's a good question, isn't it?" He scratched the back of his head. "I mean, isn't it?"

"Yes, Hank, it is," Mulder said when Scully didn't answer. "And I'll bet I have a possible answer."

"Mulder," Scully said, her voice low and warning. "Do not read into this more than there is."

"Oh, I'm not," he protested lightly. "I'm not even going to begin to suggest that maybe these goblins have something to do with the major." He leaned back in his chair. "I wouldn't think of it."

"Of course you wouldn't," she said. "Because you already have. Now look, we've got a—"

Andrews walked in then, smiled a not very sincere apology for being late, took a reluctant seat on the bed, and said, "So now what?"

Dana checked her watch; it was after five. "So now I think we'd better break for a while and have something to eat." A look shut Mulder up. "There's been too damn much excitement around here, and I want us to cool down for a while before we end up on horses."

"What?" Hank said.

"A definition of confusion," Mulder explained, hands clasped behind his head. "He jumped up on his horse and rode off in all directions." He winked. "Scully likes wise sayings like that. She hordes fortune cookies, you know."

Hank laughed; Andrews only snorted and shook her head.

Dana, for her part, did her best not to react, because she recognized the signs—he was high on an idea, the bits and pieces of the puzzle beginning to give him some kind of picture. The problem with him was, that picture was often one no one else saw but him.

It was what made working with him at once so fascinating and so damn exasperating.

Rather than try to derail him, however, it was better to give him his head and go along for the ride. For a while.

So she suggested they clean up and meet in the restaurant in half an hour or so for coffee. Her tone brooked no argument. When Andrews left without a word, Scully's expression sent Hank along as well, deciding it would be a good thing to take a walk around the building.

When they were alone, Mulder's expression sobered. "I saw it, Scully. I'm not kidding, I really saw it."

"Mulder, don't start."

He spread his hands on the table. "It's not like I'm the only one, you know. Even Chief Hawks admitted there were others." He held up a palm to keep her quiet. "I saw it—okay, just a glimpse—but I also touched it. It wasn't my imagination, it wasn't wishful thinking. I touched it, Scully. It was real."

She leaned away from him, thinking. Then: "I'll grant you it was real. He was real. But it wasn't any goblin, no supernatural creature."

"The skin—"

"Camouflage. Come on, Mulder, Fort Dix is a training base. That means there are personnel who are experts in all sorts of weaponry . . . and camouflage. God knows how elaborate they can be, but it's probably a lot more now than just smearing greasepaint on your face."

He tried to stand, grimaced, and sagged back. "My jacket."

123

It had been tossed on the dresser. She fetched it and looked it over.

"I hit it twice, once pretty hard." He leaned forward under the light. "There's nothing there, Scully. No paint, no oil, no nothing."

She dropped the jacket onto the bed. "A suit, that's all. Skintight, latex, who knows? No goblins, Mulder. Just people in disguise." She pointed at the bed. "Lie down."

She knew he still wasn't feeling well when he made no cracks, just nodded wearily and shifted stiffly to the mattress. As he settled down, she brought him a glass of water and aspirin and watched him drink.

"What about the major and his people?" he asked. His eyelids fluttered. "Hank's right, that's kind of fishy."

"Later," she ordered. "You're not doing anybody any good, least of all yourself, when you can't think straight." Her frown deepened. "Get some rest. I'm not kidding. I'll drop by later to see how you're doing."

"What about the others?"

She smiled prettily and headed for the door. "Oh, I think we'll manage. We'll muddle through somehow."

She opened the door and looked over her shoulder. He hadn't closed his eyes; he was staring at the ceiling.

Then his gaze shifted. "Scully, what if I'm right?"

"Rest."

"What if I'm right? What if they're out there?"

She stepped out, the door closing behind her. "They're not, Mulder. For God's sake, rest, before I—"

"How do you know they're not? You can't see them, Scully. They're out there, somewhere, and you can't see them."

FOURTEEN

X The room was empty.
Rosemary didn't really expect to find anyone there; it was too soon after the woodland incident, and it also wasn't easy for it to get away without being noticed.

What she hadn't expected, however, and what frightened her, was the destruction.

She stood on the threshold, one hand absently rubbing her arm, a faint chill slipping across her back. Although she couldn't hear it, she swore she could feel the wind pummeling the hospital, could feel the building's weight settling on her shoulders.

The notion made her angry, but she couldn't shake it off.

Damn, she thought, and passed a weary hand over her eyes.

The mattress had been sliced open in a score of places, the stuffing strewn across the floor; the desk was overturned, one leg snapped off; the chair was little more than splinters.

The Blue Boy had been yanked off the wall and shredded.

In its place, scrawled in black letters:

I'm looking for you.

•   •   •

Major Tonero sat at his desk, hands folded on the blotter, staring at the telephone.

He was neither panicked nor overconfident, but since leaving the site of the shooting, he had begun to review his options. By the time he had stopped pacing the office, he knew what had to be done. And it galled him. Not that he considered the Project a failure; too much had been learned from it, too much progress gained. No, what galled him was—

The telephone rang.

He listened to it without moving.

At the seventh ring he cleared his throat and picked up the receiver.

"Good afternoon, sir," was followed without prompting by a detailed summary of what had happened that afternoon, and what connection he suspected it had with the two incidents he had previously reported to those in charge. He spoke crisply and flatly, no emotion at all. When he finished, he listened.

He did not interrupt, speaking only when asked a question, his spine rigid, his free hand still flat on the blotter.

The voice at the other end was calm, a good sign, but he did not, could not, put himself at ease.

When the conversation arrived at the crux, thirty minutes had passed.

The last question was asked.

Tonero nodded. "Yes, sir, I do, with your permission." He inhaled slowly. "I believe it's time to explore other venues; there are several mentioned in my December report. This one, through no fault of ours, has been contaminated. I also believe the additional personnel now on site will not be put off, most especially after this afternoon's incident. That they are from the Bureau means we can neither control nor contain them with any true degree of effectiveness or guarantee of success. However, I have no doubt we can make the transfer without discovery, and then the Bureau people can investigate all they want. They won't find a thing."

He listened again, and for the first time, he smiled.

"Yes, sir, I do believe you're right—sometimes you win, sometimes you lose. But we are still light-years ahead of where we were the last time. This, I think, argues well for our eventual success."

His smile broadened.

"Thank you, sir, I appreciate that."

The smile vanished.

"Indispensable? No, sir, to be honest, he is not. His objectivity and full commitment have been lost, I believe, and, frankly, his nerves are shot. I do not believe another relocation would be in the Project's best interest. Dr. Elkhart, however, has been most helpful. It would be a severe loss if she were not to remain."

He waited.

He listened.

"Forty-eight hours, sir."

He nodded.

He replaced the receiver and for several long seconds sat without moving.

Then, as if he'd been struck across the shoulders, he sagged, and whispered, "Jesus!"

His hands began to tremble, and there was sweat on his brow.

Barelli sat at a window table in the diner, beginning to wonder if he had, in fact, wasted his time. Not that he didn't doubt his reporter's skills; that he was good was a given. But after nearly an hour with that police sergeant, with some comments from the others as they drifted in and out of the station, he had learned practically nothing he hadn't known before—Frankie was dead, the killer was still out there, and nobody had a clue what the hell was going on.

And that goblin shit—Jesus Christ, what the hell did they think he was?

A round-faced wall clock over the register ticked closer to six as he sipped at cold coffee and stared at the traffic. The weather hadn't discouraged anyone, it seemed. Men in uniform, soldiers in civilian clothes trying not to look like soldiers, strolled or drove past, filling the diner, moving into the bars that served food, lingering in front of the movie theater a block west of the police station.

Friday night in the middle of nowhere.

His stomach complained of all the caffeine he had drunk, and he popped an antacid tablet into his mouth, chewed it absently, and wondered what the hell he was going to do now. Of course, there was still that "date" with Babs Radnor to keep. If he wanted to. And right about now, it looked as if it was the only game in town.

Another antacid, another scan of the street, and he dropped a few bills onto the table and went outside.

He scowled at the overcast. He hated this kind of day. If it was going to rain, he wished it would do it and be done with it; otherwise, why the hell didn't those clouds just blow away?

He headed for the corner; his car was still parked in front of the police station.

Along the way he passed an old woman dressed in black from a heavy topcoat to a long scarf wrapped around her head. She held a large purse close to her chest, and an idle glance there made him stop and turn slowly.

What he had seen was the orange top of a spray paint can, and it didn't take a genius to figure out who she was.

He hurried after her, came abreast, and said, "Miss Lang?"

She stopped and glared up at him. "*Ms.* Lang, if you don't mind. Who are you?"

"I'm a reporter," he explained, best smile, best voice. "I'm looking into the . . ." He lowered his voice, slipping her into his confidence. "Into the goblin affair."

He waited patiently, watching her debate both the truth and the sincerity of what he had said.

A bus coughed past them.

Three young airmen on the corner broke into song.

Elly Lang eyed him suspiciously. "You think I'm a nut?"

"He killed a friend of mine. That's not crazy at all." When she didn't walk away, he touched her arm lightly. "I'd be pleased if you'd join me for dinner."

"And pump me, right?" she snapped.

The smile turned up a notch. "That, and for the company."

She shook her head. "You're full of it, mister, but I'm not going to pass up a free meal." She took his arm and led him up the street. "You going to be cheap, or are we going someplace good?"

He didn't laugh, but he wanted to; instead, he promised her the best meal this town could provide, which seemed, for the moment, to satisfy her. And as long as he didn't run into Mulder or Scully, he had a feeling this was going to be a most informative, and lucrative, night.

Tonero wasn't in his office, wasn't anywhere on post that she could tell, but Rosemary ordered herself not to panic. There was still time to make corrections. There was still time to salvage something of the years she had put in.

She returned to the hospital, nodding silently to the reception-ist and making her way down a corridor to an elevator stenciled AUTHORIZED PERSONNEL ONLY. From her pocket she took a small key ring and inserted a silver key into a vertical slot where, ordinarily, a summons button would be. When the door slid aside, she checked the hall and stepped in.

The key took her down.

She didn't bother to watch the floor indicator; the elevator only stopped at three levels—the second floor, where the major's office was, the main floor, and a subbasement.

The car stuttered to a halt and the door opened; she stared uneasily down the length of the dimly lighted corridor.

It seemed a lot longer tonight, and her heels a lot louder on the concrete floor.

The faint thrum of distant machinery was the only other sound.

As if performing for an invisible audience, she made a show of smoothing her smock over her chest, of caressing a palm over her hair as she walked. Confidence, outside and in, was the key. As long as she kept to her plan, as long as she didn't lose her head, everything would be fine.

She tested Tymons's office door; it was locked.

She opened the Project Center door and nearly screamed when she saw him bending over one of the computers.

"Jesus, Leonard," she said, stepping in. "I didn't know you'd be here. What are you—"

He turned to face her, and in his right hand was a rectangular block of black metal about six inches long. In his left hand was a gun. "Just stay where you are, Rosemary, all right? Just . . . stay where you are."

"Leonard, what the hell are you doing?"

He smiled wanly. "Correcting a few things, that's all."

She looked around the room, not seeing anything out of place until her gaze reached the first computer screen. Though the machine was on, the screen was blank. So was the second one.

He waved his right hand. "It was so easy, I don't know why I didn't think of it before." He held up the block. "Why go through the whole mess when all you need is a magnet."

"My God, Leonard!"

"One pass, and poof!" He dropped the magnet on the shelf. "Poof. All gone."

Outrage prevented her from speaking, and fear of what Joseph would do when he found out.

"The thing is," Tymons said calmly, and put a bullet through the nearest computer.

She jumped, but the gun kept her from fleeing.

"The thing is, you see, nobody's ever really going to know, are they? I mean, there's no sense going to the papers or the TV stations, because no one would ever believe it."

He shot another one, showering the floor with splintered plastic and shards of glass.

She took a step back.

He glanced at her sideways, his expression rueful. "I'm still going to try, though. Despite the odds, I'm really going to try."

"You can't," she said hoarsely, her throat lined with sand. She cleared it and tried again. "You can't." Her left hand fluttered helplessly from her chest to her throat and back again. "All those years, Leonard, all the work we've done. All the time. For God's sake, think of all the time!"

"All the failures," he said flatly. "All that time, and all those failures." He spat dryly. "Buried, Rosemary. We had to bury our failures."

He's insane, she thought; my God, he's insane.

"Listen, Leonard, if that's what . . . if you don't care about the work . . . think about—" She jerked a thumb at the ceiling. "You can't."

"Why? You mean those stupid oaths we signed?" He fired at the third and last monitor and hunched a shoulder to protect himself against flying shards. "Meaningless, Rosemary. By the time I'm through, they won't mean a thing."

"I'll deny it," she threatened. "I'll tell anyone you tell that I don't know a thing."

He straightened. "My dear doctor, I'm sorry, but you won't live long enough to have the chance."

She backed up hastily until the wall stopped her, the open door to her right. She couldn't think, could barely breathe, and a small fire in the workings of one of the destroyed computers had begun to lift feathers of smoke into the room.

"They'll come after you, Leonard," she warned, swallowing hard, fighting the nausea that roiled in her stomach. "Even if you can get off post, you won't be able to hide for long. A week, maybe a month." Sweat stung her eyes, but she didn't dare move her hands to wipe it away. "You've just signed your own death warrant."

He shrugged. "Like I care, Rosemary? Like I really give a damn?"

Without warning he emptied his clip into the shelves, the explosions deafening, damage almost total. She couldn't help but scream then, more in rage than fear, hands up to protect her face from the spinning, flaming debris. Before she could move, he had replaced the clip with a fresh one from his pocket.

And pointed the gun at her head.

Her eyes fluttered closed.

All she could think was *This is crazy, this is wrong.*

"Go away."

She didn't move, didn't understand.

"Rosemary, go away."

When she looked, the gun was at his side, but the defeat in his voice wasn't reflected in his face.

"Maybe," he said, "you'll last longer than I."

Disgust twisted her features, but she refused to say a word for fear he would change his mind. Although she wanted desperately to rail against the destruction of all their work, she wanted more desperately to get out of this alive.

"Go away," he whispered, and shook the gun at her.

Without further urging, she bolted clumsily into the corridor, and hadn't taken two steps toward the elevator when she kicked herself in the ankle and fell hard into the wall. She cried out, more in surprise than pain, and cried out again when she heard a gunshot.

Another.

At that she ran, keeping her stinging arm braced against her side, fumbling with her free hand for the keys.

At the elevator door the key slid off the control plate twice before she was able to insert it properly. "Come on, damnit," she whispered urgently, willing her nerves to settle down. "Come on, come on!"

The door opened and she virtually threw herself into the car, spun around, and inserted the key a second time.

It wasn't until the door had hissed closed that she realized she wasn't alone.

No, she thought; not after all this, no.

"You know," said a rasping voice behind her, "I'm getting pretty good at this, don't you think?"

FIFTEEN

X Andrews wasn't in the room when Dana returned, and she decided to take some of her own advice and scrub some of the afternoon away. Maybe some time alone would help her figure out the purpose of today's attack.

So little of it made any real sense.

If it had been meant as intimidation, as a warning to stay away and drop the investigation—for whatever reason—it certainly wouldn't work, and surely whoever was behind it knew that as well; if it had been meant to stop them permanently, that had failed, too, and she couldn't convince herself that the shooter hadn't been aiming to kill.

"Unless," she thought aloud, "he wasn't an expert."

She pushed a hand back through her hair and rubbed the back of her neck. There had been a lot of wind, lots of leaves and things blowing around. Branches moving, targets moving. Plus, they had been shooting back.

So maybe, she thought, just maybe, they had gotten a little lucky.

That particular idea unnerved her more than anything. Especially when she realized that the shooter really could have killed her and Webber at practically any time before they had ducked into the trees.

They had been in the open far longer than Mulder.

But he hadn't.

The more she thought about it, the more she believed he had only been trying, and succeeding, to pin them down. To take them out of the game as much as he could.

What he had actually been trying to do was put a bullet in Mulder.

The man at the Jefferson Memorial:

You have no protection, Mr. Mulder, you still have no protection.

"Oh, brother," she whispered. "Oh, brother."

Think. She needed a clear head to think this through, or she'd end up just as paranoid as her partner.

Once stripped and in the shower, however, it wasn't the shooter she concentrated on—for some reason, she couldn't stop thinking about Mulder's other assailant. The explanations she had given him were more than likely correct, or at the very least, parameters. Which did not, under any circumstances, include anything like a goblin.

And yet . . .

She made a noise much like a growl.

And yet there had been times past when she had been forced to the unwelcome conclusion that explanations could very well be only rationalizations in disguise.

She growled again and turned away from the shower head, letting the hot water slam against her back and splash over her shoulders. Her eyes half-closed. Her breathing steadied as she willed the memory of gunfire to a safer distance.

Steam rose gently around her, condensing on the narrow pebble-glass window in the white-tiled wall, running down the translucent sliding door.

She felt nothing but the water.

She heard nothing but the water.

The perfect time, she thought suddenly, for good old Norman Bates to slip into the bathroom, knife held high and at the ready. Effectively deaf and vision blurred, lulled by the comfort of steam and heat, she wouldn't know it was over until the end had begun; she wouldn't know, because all she could see was a smeared shadow on the door.

Standing there.

Watching.

Biding its time.

The shadow, of course, was the drape of bath towels over their rack by the door.

She knew that.

No; she assumed that.

Her eyes closed briefly as she damned Mulder for sparking her imagination; nevertheless, she couldn't stop herself from holding her breath to brace herself, and opening the shower door, just a little.

Just to be sure.

"Mulder, I swear I'm going to strangle you," she whispered in relief and mild anger when she saw the towels, and the rack, and not a single place in the tiny room for anyone to hide.

The steam flowed over and around her, twisting in slow spectral ribbons, creating the momentary illusion she had stepped into a light fog.

She shivered.

The room was chilly.

And the steam that should have filled it flowed and twisted, because the bathroom door was open.

He didn't want to sleep.

There was too much to do.

But the pain had finally ebbed, weariness taking its place, and he couldn't keep his thoughts in an orderly line. They drifted, fading and dancing.

Mulder, watch your back.

Patches of skin like snapshots, flashing too rapidly for him to focus on, barklike skin without the roughness of bark, without the texture, although he couldn't really be sure because contact had been so brief.

Mulder

The voice was muffled by sleep and time, yet it sounded maddeningly familiar despite the fact that it belonged to no one he knew; a roughness here, too, and forced, as if the speaker, the goblin, was either suffering low-level pain or hadn't yet gotten used to the voice that it had.

watch your back.

And if it was true, that he had to watch his back, why hadn't he been killed, like the others?

I don't know, he answered, but the voice and the nightmare wouldn't stop.

Rosemary couldn't take it anymore. Her knees buckled, and she sagged weakly to the floor, her back against the elevator wall.

"Are you all right?"

Hoarse, painful to listen to.

She nodded.

"What happened?"

Gone, all gone, she thought; everything's gone and Joseph will kill me and it's gone, damnit, all gone.

"Dr. Elkhart, what's wrong?"

She raised her head and gestured defeat.

"Dr. Elkhart, say something. You're scaring me."

"My dear," she said with a brittle bitter laugh, "you have no idea what scared is."

A shuffling, a shifting, a soft hand brushing across her ankle.

"Can I help?"

She made to shake her head, and stopped. She stared at the elevator door, seeing the two of them, reflections twisted out of recognition in the polished steel, and before long she felt her lips pull back into what might have been a smile.

"Yes," she said at last. "Yes, dear, I think you can."

Scully's purse was on the floor between the toilet and the tub. She reached through the gap and fumbled it open, pulled out her gun, and straightened, staring intently at the bathroom door, still open about an inch. Her left hand shut the water off; her right wrist slid the shower door away.

Once on the bath mat, she grabbed a towel and wrapped it hastily around her; it was no protection at all, but it made her feel less vulnerable. Her teeth chattered and her lower lip quivered as the room's chill raised a pattern of gooseflesh on her skin.

She switched off the light.

Water dripped too loudly from the shower head.

The only illumination in the outer room came from the brass lamp on the nightstand between the two beds, just as she had left it.

There was no sound or movement.

Using her left hand, she opened the door as slowly as she could, crouching low until she could slip over the threshold and duck behind the nearest bed. The gun barrel swept the room just ahead of her, but no one else was there.

Don't assume, she told herself; never assume.

Feeling like a jerk now—*never assume, Scully, never assume*—she half-crawled around the footboard to be sure her visitor wasn't hiding between the beds. Once satisfied she was indeed alone, she sat on the mattress and tried to remember if, maybe, she hadn't left the bathroom door open by mistake; or maybe she had closed it, but the latch didn't catch; or maybe Andrews had returned, heard the shower, and decided Scully didn't need to be disturbed.

But if that were true, if she had heard the shower, why had she opened the door?

A trickle of water slipped out of her hair and down her spine.

"All right," she said aloud, as much for the sound as the comfort. "All right. It's all right, you're alone."

That didn't stop her from turning on the hanging lamp over the table to help banish the room's shadows, or from drying off as fast as she could, with the bathroom door wide open. Once that was accomplished, dressing was quick and easy—blouse, skirt, matching wine jacket. By then she was almost calm, and she looked in the dresser mirror as she smoothed the blouse over her chest, deciding that one of these days, Bureau or not, she would get herself a fashion life.

Back into the bathroom, then, to wield a brush through her hair, using her reflection as a sounding board as she practiced telling Mulder what his stupid notions were doing to her. It didn't help. Her reflection just gave her the same sardonic look he would when he heard. If he heard. By the time she was finished, she had decided this was something her partner did not need to know.

A lopsided smile sent her into the front room, where she started and gasped when she spotted someone pacing her at the corner of her vision.

"Listen carefully," Rosemary said urgently. She stabbed a thumb at the door. "He's trying to destroy us. Tymons. He's afraid, and he's a coward. He doesn't care about you, me, or the Project. He wants . . . he wants us all dead."

A silence then, and she held her breath, praying.

"He didn't approve of me from the beginning, you know." Still hoarse, now with sullen rage. "He thought I was too . . . emotional."

Rosemary agreed silently.

A giggle: "He's really scared of me, you know."

"Yes. I know."

The giggling stopped. "What can I do? I'm not stupid, Dr. Elkhart. I know what'll happen if you stop helping me. What can I do?"

Rosemary tried to think, tried to set the priorities that would keep her intact.

"Do you need him? Dr. Tymons?"

There wasn't a second's hesitation: "No. No, we don't."

"Others?"

"Three," she said without having to think. Then concern made her stand when a wrenching cough made her wonder if they could pull it off. "Can you do it, dear? Are you well enough?"

"I can do it. Really. But it'll take time. A couple of days, maybe. I can't—"

The coughing increased, grinding into spasms that made Rosemary reach out a hand, grip a shoulder, and squeeze until it was over.

"It's okay," she whispered, rubbing now, soothing. "It's going to be okay."

And she believed it. It would be all right. Everything would be all right.

Then she spoke the names.

Scully's right hand was already reaching for the gun on the bed when she realized the movement was only her reflection in the dresser mirror.

Too damn many mirrors around here, she thought sourly, and pointed at it as if to order it to find someone else to scare.

She froze.

Something moved on the wall behind her. A slight movement she would have missed had she simply glanced in that direction.

She watched, waiting, thinking maybe it had only been a shadow cast by a passing car.

It moved again, and she turned and made her way between the beds.

A moth fluttered its wings slowly and began to make its way toward the ceiling.

Fascinated, licking her lips, she climbed onto the bed, balanced herself, and looked away.

Looked back, and it took a full second before she could find it again.

"Well," she whispered.

A tentative smile came and went.

Then she bounced on the mattress, just high enough to snatch the moth away in a loose fist. Feeling its wings beat against her palm. Whispering to it as she opened the door and flung it away. Standing back, rubbing her chin thoughtfully.

She needed another test, and footsteps outside made her think fast.

With the hanging lamp on again, the nightstand lamp off, she sat on the far bed and pushed herself back until she rested against the headboard, legs crossed at the ankles. She could barely see herself then, but she could see just the same.

A key turned in the lock.

She heard it but didn't move.

The door opened and Licia stepped in. "Scully?"

Dana opened her mouth, but kept silent.

Andrews headed for the bathroom. "Scully, you in there? Look, are you going to leave me with that boy all night? Damn,

THE X-FILES

you should hear—" She pushed the door open and cut herself off, sighed, turned, and yelped when she noticed Scully sitting on the bed, pointing at her.

"Jesus!" Her hand splayed across her chest. "God Almighty, Scully, I didn't see you there. Why the hell didn't you say something?"

Scully smiled. "You didn't see me."

Andrews scowled. "Of course not. It was dark. You're sitting in the dark."

Scully pushed at the hanging lamp. "Not really. But you see me now, right?"

Andrews didn't know how to answer, her lips working without a sound. Finally she said, "Well . . . yes. I guess so." She laughed at herself. "Of course I do. The light was—"

Scully pushed off the bed, shoved her gun into her purse, and reached for her coat. "Go get Hank," she said. "Meet me at Mulder's."

"Again?"

"Again." Scully pushed her gently but firmly outside. "God help me, but I have a feeling Mulder is right."

Andrews gaped. "Goblins? About the goblins?"

"Something like that." She couldn't believe she had just said it. "Yes, something like that."

SIXTEEN

Wrapped in nothing but a thin stubby towel, Mulder examined his reflection in the steam-shrouded mirror. He looked drawn, and probably a little too pale. But he certainly didn't look like a man who had almost been killed. Twice in the same afternoon. However a man like that is supposed to look, that is. He rose up on his toes and inhaled sharply when he saw the full extent of the size and shape of the bruise below his ribs. That, he knew, was going to be hell in the morning.

He toweled off slowly so as not to aggravate either the bruise or the hammer and anvil gearing up in his skull. Deliberately slowly, because, as Scully had already sensed, he had begun to feel that electric spark of anticipation, the one that signaled the true beginning of the hunt.

He suspected that right now, Webber was having fits, and Andrews was pacing whether she was standing up or not. It was only natural. A little ordinary poking around had ended up in a deadly firefight, and they probably couldn't stop the adrenaline from flowing. Action, they no doubt thought, was the key now, not methodical investigation. It didn't matter that nothing but casings had been found at the site, and nothing at all at the site of his ambush.

Action. Get moving. Keep moving. Sitting down, having coffee, talking things out, was definitely not the way things were supposed to be.

As he dressed, he glanced around the room, not really seeing the furniture or the dingy walls. Hints and whispers had come to him while he'd let the warm water and steam do their work.

Hints and whispers.

Not all of them clear.

Still, the fever dreams he had had—and there was no other way to describe them—refused to let him go. Every throb in his skull, every touch of fire below his ribs, reminded him of what he had seen.

Not what he thought he had seen.

He slipped stiffly into his jacket, stuffed his tie into one pocket, and grabbed his topcoat.

And stopped.

What he should do now was head straight for the Queen's Inn to meet the others.

Or he could slip away for a while, away from Scully's watchful doctor's eye, and—

The door opened suddenly.

He stumbled back, tripped over the edge of his bed, and fell on the mattress, his head nearly exploding.

"Jesus," he said angrily.

Scully looked down at him without any sympathy at all. "I have an idea," was all she said.

Major Tonero sat on the porch of his modest Cape Cod on the outskirts of Marville, a cigarette in one hand, a tumbler of scotch and soda in the other. Although he had been expecting the FBI to call on him since meeting those agents this afternoon, he wasn't disappointed when they hadn't. Their attention was elsewhere now. Whoever had ambushed them had unwittingly done him a great favor.

Now all he had to do was tell Rosemary about his conversation with their superiors, and they could begin the relocation procedure. By Sunday afternoon they would, with a little luck, be on their way.

He sipped, and blew a smoke ring.

It was chilly tonight, but not enough to keep him inside.

Besides, he preferred it out here. The neighborhood was small, quiet, so perfectly ordinary that there were times, both night and day, when he felt as if his superiors had dropped him into the middle of a television series, circa 1955. But it was definitely better than living with *them*, shortsighted and single-minded officers who lived and died for the service without once ever understanding what true potential there was.

He toasted that truth with another drink.

There were, now that he thought about it, only two problems remaining: what to do with Leonard Tymons, and what do with the Project's subject.

He wasn't worried, though. The answer would come. It always did.

A car sped up the block. He frowned, hating the disruption of his quiet evening, the frown deepening when the car squealed to a halt at the curb. He leaned forward—Rosemary?

After several seconds she climbed out and ran–staggered toward the house. He was up and at the steps before she reached them, taking her arms and hushing her until they were inside.

"Leonard," she gasped, and dropped heavily onto the couch.

She looked like hell; in fact, she looked like a corpse, her hair damp with perspiration, her cheeks flushed with an unnatural color that unpleasantly accentuated her already pale face.

Shit, he thought angrily; why the hell can't it be easy, just for once?

"Tell me," he said, keeping his voice low.

He didn't move when she told him what had happened at the Project lab, didn't touch her when she began to tremble so violently she had to hug herself to calm down, didn't offer a word when she finished and looked up at him, beseeching him for comfort.

He turned to the window and looked out at the lawn, hands clasped behind his back.

When he turned back, he smiled. "Are you sure he's dead?"

"He . . . he has to be by now."

"There were backups, correct?"

She passed a hand over her face, forcing herself to think. "Yes." She nodded hesitantly. "Yes, of course. Although I don't know how recent they would be. Leonard was always—"

"No matter." He took a step toward the couch. "In his office?"

"Yes."

He rubbed the side of his nose thoughtfully. "And what about our friend?" His eyes widened in slight alarm and he glanced at the front door.

"No, don't worry." She inhaled deeply, slowly, and leaned her head back wearily, closed her eyes, as her left hand unbuttoned her coat and pulled it away as if she needed room to breathe. "We were in the elevator, and then . . . I don't know where."

Another step: "I'm correct in assuming that, without the proper medication, our friend will eventually . . ." His smile flashed and vanished. "Fade away?"

"Damnit, Joseph, what's the matter with you? Haven't you listened to a word I've said?"

He held out his hands, palms up, beckoning until she took them and allowed herself to be pulled to her feet and into his arms. He kissed her ear, her cheek, her lips.

"Joseph?"

She was cold; cold with fear.

And trembling.

He whispered of the telephone call, and of the problems he had had until the problems, it seemed, had decided to take care of themselves. He whispered of the support he had given her to those in charge during that call. He suggested, in a whisper, that they take her car back to the hospital, to Dr. Tymons's office, and retrieve the backup computer disks. Although no one had access to the Project level except themselves, it seemed as if they might be leaving earlier than expected.

"Or," he whispered after she snuggled, wriggled closer, and kissed him back, hard, "we could always wait until morning."

It was her turn to whisper as she began working on his shirt: "Joseph, you can be one arrogant bastard, do you know that?"

"But for good reason, Dr. Elkhart. And don't you ever forget it."

Barelli almost felt guilty leaving the old woman alone at the Company G, but since everyone there seemed to know her, and like her, the guilt passed as soon as he was outside.

It had been, from the beginning, an evening of surprises.

The establishment itself, around the corner and halfway down the block from Barney's, was a low clapboard building outlined in soft blue neon. In its large front window a neon trooper marched guard duty around stencil-style letters that spelled out COMPANY G. A shiny black film over the glass prevented anyone from seeing inside, but once through the door he had been pleasantly surprised. The restaurant–lounge was a single large room, softly and indirectly lighted, with black plastic and glass, gleaming chrome and brass. A bar ran along the left-hand wall, and the carpeted floor held a score or more tables, about half of which were taken. A dance floor took up most of the back, with a low stage against the wall.

147

The food, too, had been more than decent, and the drinks inexpensive. Elly Lang ordered well and ate carefully, as if expecting to make the meal last all night. When he asked her about herself, she smiled and told him little except for the reputation the community had given her.

All because of the goblins.

By the time he had finished he knew he had heard all she had to say. Not ranting, exactly, but it sounded like a story she had told a hundred times, and not much different from what he had learned at the police station.

She had, pleasantly, dismissed him when his mind began to wander, and although he stopped short of kissing her on the cheek, the almost-gesture had made her laugh and shoo him away.

Now, on the street, he considered returning to the station to have a talk with the dispatcher. Because of their job, they usually knew more than anyone, and he remembered Sergeant Nilssen telling him their regular operator was a young woman, Maddy Vincent.

Which was when he remembered his date with Babs Radnor.

"Shit," he muttered. "Damn."

He would have to go back and make some kind of excuse. She had been taken with his reporting reputation, he knew that much, so maybe she wouldn't be all that unhappy when he assured her he wasn't about to head home right away. A rain check until tomorrow seemed the most likely way out.

He hurried up toward Main Street, changing his mind about driving, deciding that a phone call would do. If he played it right, sounded right, she might even be excited for him, now and later.

He shivered then and wished he had brought a topcoat with him.

True night had settled over the town, starless, feeling like rain. Houses and buildings slipped into the protection of the dark, neon and streetlamps giving the street needed color, and a semblance of life it didn't have when the sun shone. There were just enough pedestrians to make the district seem almost lively; a street cop spoke to a disgruntled knot of teens; a cruiser trolled slowly westward, not caring about the traffic it backed up behind it; several shops were open late, ghosts of customers inside.

The wind had died.

Still, he hunched his shoulders as he hurried westward, grumbling when he reached the police station without finding a public phone. He looked over, shrugged a *what the hell,* and took advantage of the first break to sprint to the other side. Once in, he had to wait for several minutes. Unlike his earlier visit, tonight the station was busy—two cops leading two lurching drunks back toward the cells, the radio in constant chatter, a man in plainclothes at a desk arguing with two women, one of whom had a bloody bandage wrapped around her hand. When he finally caught the desk sergeant's attention, he was told brusquely that Officer Vincent wasn't on this shift, he would have to wait until morning.

He couldn't.

The idea had taken hold, and now he couldn't shake it.

A handful of smiling lies inflating Vincent's importance to his story gave him an address and directions; a flourish of notebook and pen proved to the officer that Barelli wasn't about to spell his name incorrectly.

By the time he was back on the sidewalk, he realized he was out of breath.

Easy, boy, he thought; take it easy, don't blow it now.

Two blocks up, one block down, the sergeant had told him. An easy walk, and a chance for him to think of the questions he'd need to ask.

The house was easy to find—it was the only one on the street without any lights.

He knocked, rang the bell, even wandered around to the back door and knocked again, but Officer Vincent wasn't answering.

No matter, he decided, and parked himself on her front steps; she has to come home sometimes, and when she does, I'll be waiting right here to make her famous.

He sat, he smoked, he listened to the neighbors on the left have a beast of a battle. He walked around for a while to keep warm, but always within sight of the house. And when he checked his watch under a streetlamp and realized it was only a few minutes past eight, it occurred to him that Maddy Vincent might not be home for hours. It was Friday night, and she was single, and what the hell had he been thinking?

He was nearly at the corner when he stopped cursing his stupidity and trotted back across the street, pulling his notebook out of his jacket pocket. Just to be sure she'd be around, he would leave a note. Not too obvious, a little mysterious. Pique her policewoman's interest. He would save the sweet talk for when he saw her.

It took him four tries before he was satisfied and tore the page free. The next thing was a place to put it so the wind wouldn't blow it halfway to the next county.

He settled for folding it in half and sticking it between the door and the frame.

Then he turned around, dusting his hands, and saw the shadow standing on the porch.

"Who the hell are you?" he demanded.

"It doesn't make any difference," the shadow said.

Barelli didn't see the blade until it was too late, and there was nothing left to do but open his mouth and try to scream.

SEVENTEEN

X A single light over the table, barely reaching the first bed, and the second one not at all.

Scully sat with her back to the window, Mulder by the door, Webber on the edge of the dresser, Andrews on the edge of the near bed.

Mulder didn't like it. He couldn't see expressions; they were too much like spirits at the fringe of a seance, floating in and out of the dark as if they wore veils.

Scully's fingers pushed at nothing on the table's wood-grain surface. "I've been thinking about a moth I found on my wall."

She hadn't seen it right away, not only because it was too small, but also because its coloration almost blended in with the paint. That made her think of camouflage, and the goblin, who was able to hide in an alley without being seen, and hide in the woods without Mulder seeing. Despite what she had said before, she couldn't quite bring herself to believe that tactics like that were supported by an arsenal of camouflage suits and greasepaint, burnt charcoal, twigs and leaves worn as aids to blending in.

Although it was possible, it also required advance knowledge of where the target victim would be.

"And I don't think such a package could be carried on someone's back. It would be inefficient and clumsy."

There was, for example, no way the killer—the goblin, if they had to call it that—could have known that Grady Pierce would pass by that alley that night, at just that time. Webber's interview with the bartender had established that more often than not, Noel brought the ex-sergeant home himself. And they themselves hadn't decided to visit the site of Corporal Ulman's murder until they had finished lunch in the diner.

"Two questions," she said, eyes down, as if speaking to the table.

"How did it know where to be?" Webber said.

She nodded.

"Unless it knows magic," Andrews said, a smile in her voice, "how could it be ready with . . . whatever it wore to hide itself?"

Scully nodded again.

Mulder watched her fingers move, dusting, tracing circles.

"For now, let's set aside the why of it, the killing. And the who." She looked up, too pale in the light, and Mulder looked away. "The how, on the other hand . . ."

No one spoke.

A car backfired in the parking lot, and only Webber jumped.

An engine raced on the county road, another followed, and there were horns.

Mulder shifted stiffly as he watched her face. It bothered him sometimes, how smooth it was, without many lines, because it prevented him from really knowing just what she was thinking. Too often a mask. But her eyes, they were different. He could see them now, shadowed by the light over her head, and he could see that she was struggling with a reluctant decision.

He brushed a strand of hair from his brow.

The movement made her look, and when she looked, she inhaled slowly.

"Special Projects," said Webber, startling them all. "That Major Tonero and his Special Projects."

"I think so," she answered. "But exactly what, I'm not sure."

"Yes, you are," Mulder said gently. "It's not a goblin, at least not like Elly Lang says it is."

Andrews made a faint noise of derision. "So what is it? A ghost?"

"Nope. It's a chameleon."

The wind rose.

A draft slipped through the window and fluttered the curtains.

Andrews slapped her thighs. "A what? A chameleon? You mean, a human chameleon?" She waved a hand in disgust. "No offense, Mulder, really, but you're out of your mind. There's no such thing."

He didn't take offense, although he knew she wanted him to. "There are lots of things that are no such thing, Licia. Some of them aren't, some of them are." He scooted his chair closer to the table. "I think Scully's right. This is one of them that is."

Andrews appealed to Scully. "Do you have any idea what he's talking about?"

A corner of Scully's mouth pulled up. "This time, yes."

He made a sour face at her, then swiped at his hair again. "A chameleon—"

"I don't need a biology lesson," Andrews snapped. "Or zoology. Whatever. I know what they can do."

"They change colors," Webber said anyway. "To fit their background, right?" He stepped away from the dresser. "Wow. Do you really think this is what we've got?"

Mulder held up a finger. "First, you're wrong. Sort of.

153

Chameleons can't change color to fit every background. They're limited to only a few, like black, white, cream, sometimes green." He grinned. "Put him on a tartan tablecloth, he'd probably blow his brains out."

Webber laughed, and Scully smiled.

Mulder's fingers began to tap eagerly on the table. "But within certain limits, yes, he can adjust his pigmentation."

"I don't believe this," Andrews muttered. "I swear to God, I don't believe it."

Mulder ignored her; he wanted Scully to follow and watched her as he spoke, in case he made a mistake.

"Now, contrary to popular opinion, chameleons don't change at will, right?"

She nodded.

"It's things like temperature or emotion that cause the coloration to alter. When they get scared or angry. I don't think they sit down at breakfast and decide to be green for a day." He sat back, then stood.

"Careful, Mulder," Scully cautioned.

"But we can't do that," he said to Webber. "Right?"

"Change color? Hell, no. Except when we get tan or something."

"Right." He moved to the door, snapping his fingers at his side, turned and gripped the back of his chair. "But suppose our Major Tonero and his group—Tymons, right? and Elkhart—suppose they've been able—"

Around the edges of the drapes he spotted flashing lights and yanked open the door. In the parking lot below he saw a police cruiser, warning bar alit and swirling color. A patrolman looked up. "Hey, you the FBI?" he called.

Mulder winced and nodded.

The policeman beckoned sharply. "The chief wants you right away. We got another one."

• • •

Two patrol cars, parked sideways, and a quartet of orange-stained sawhorses bracketed a fifty-yard section of the street. An ambulance was parked nose-in to the curb, and two attendants leaned against it, smoking and waiting. Blue and red lights swarmed across branches and tree trunks, and the faces of two dozen onlookers gathered on the sidewalk opposite the scene. Flashlights danced in backyards, and in the distance a siren screamed.

There was very little talk.

Mulder and Scully followed their driver around the barrier; Webber and Andrews were behind them in the other car.

Hawks met them at the foot of a gravel driveway. "Man walking his dog," he said, pointing to a young man standing in the street, a terrier in his arms. "He found him." He sounded angry.

"Are you sure it's the same?" Scully asked.

Up the drive two men knelt beside a body in high grass between the gravel and the porch; one of them was Dr. Junis.

"See for yourself."

Mulder moved first, but he didn't have to go all the way before he saw the victim's face. "Damn!" He turned to block Scully. "It's Carl."

"You know him?" Hawks demanded.

Scully inhaled sharply and stepped around the two men, nodding as Junis glanced up and recognized her.

"He's a reporter," Mulder explained, disgust and sadness in his voice. "A sports reporter."

"Sports? Sports, for God's sake? So what the hell was he doing here?"

"Corporal Ulman's fiancée was his cousin. He wanted me to come up and look around. I guess . . . I guess he was doing a little looking on his own."

"Jesus." Hawks clamped his hands on his hips, glowering, breathing heavily. "Son of a bitch, what the hell's going on around here? Mulder—" He stopped and wiped a hand over his face. "Mulder, is there some shit you're not telling me?"

A man on the porch called the chief, who hesitated before telling Mulder to stay where he was. When he left, Mulder scanned the growing crowd, and the shadows the cruiser lights created between the trees, between the houses. It was bad enough when the victim was a stranger, but this . . . He crammed his hands into his pockets and stared at the ground until footsteps on the gravel made him look up.

"Come on," Scully said gently, her voice trembling slightly.

Hawks called them from the steps, and held out a piece of paper found jammed into the doorframe. It was a note from Barelli, requesting an interview which, he promised, would be paid for by a complete dinner at the best restaurant in town.

"Who lives here?" Mulder asked.

The house was rented by Maddy Vincent. The day-shift dispatcher, Hawks added. A gesture to figures moving around the inside told him the woman wasn't home, and no one knew where she was. "No surprise, it's Friday night," the chief said in disgust. "Shit, she could be in Philadelphia for all I know. Or . . ."

Mulder checked the porch, the blood on the flooring and on the door. Carl was attacked here, he thought, and the force of the attack, and his probable retreat from it, sent him over the railing. Where he bled to death without ever getting his story.

"Damnit," he said, and stomped down the steps. "Damnit!"

An hour later, Carl's body was gone and those neighbors who'd been home had all been interviewed.

No one had seen anything; no one had heard anything. A call had gone out to Officer Vincent's friends in the vain hope she hadn't left town. A check with the station told them Barelli had stopped in only a short while ago, specifically looking for the dispatcher.

"But why?" Hawks leaned heavily against his patrol car, his face drawn and tired, his voice hoarse. Most of the crowd had retreated to nearby houses; two of the cruisers had left. "What the hell did he think he knew?"

Mulder held up a small notebook. "Nothing that he wrote down." He handed it over. "He had dinner with Miss . . . Ms. Lang, and wanted to see your dispatcher. All he had were more questions."

"He's not the only one," the chief growled.

Mulder sympathized with the man's frustration, but it didn't extend to telling him about the major. That, he decided grimly, was someone he wanted to talk to himself, without the complications Hawks was bound to create.

The chief finally mumbled something about getting back to his office, and Mulder wandered over toward his car, where the others waited. They said nothing as he turned to stare at the empty house, ribboned now in yellow, a patrolman on the steps to keep the curious away. The dusting had been completed, but he doubted they would find any useful prints besides Barelli's and Vincent's.

Goblins, he thought, don't leave handy clues.

He was angry. At Carl, for playing in a game well out of his league, and at himself, for the helplessness he felt for not knowing enough. It was a waste of energy, he knew that, but there were times, like now, when he simply couldn't help it.

He walked back to the middle of the street and stared at the house, ignoring the damp wind that whipped hair into his eyes.

Carl was a big man, and definitely not soft. He had to have been surprised. A single blow, and it was over. He had to have been surprised.

"Mulder." Scully came up beside him. "We can't do any more here."

"I know." He frowned. "Damn, I know." He rubbed his forehead wearily. "Major Tonero."

Scully looked at him sternly. "In the morning. You're exhausted, you're not thinking straight, and you need rest. He's not going anywhere. We'll talk to him in the morning."

Any inclination to argue vanished when she nudged him into the car; any inclination to do some work on his own vanished as soon as he saw the bed.

But he couldn't sleep.

While Webber snored gently, and murmured once in a while, all he could do was stare at the ceiling, wondering.

Finally he got up, pulled on his trousers and shirt, and went out onto the balcony, leaning on the railing while he watched the trees across the road move slowly in the slow wind.

He thought of Carl and the times they had had; he thought of the man who had tried to kill him that afternoon, an afternoon that seemed years distant, in another lifetime; he shivered a little and rubbed his arms for warmth as he wondered why Carl had wanted to talk to Officer Vincent. Elly Lang was obvious, but what did Hawks's dispatcher have to do with the goblins?

"You're supposed to be sleeping."

He didn't jump, didn't turn his head. "The day you figure out how to turn off my brain, Scully, let me know." He shook his head, but carefully. "Amazing, isn't it."

"Your brain?" She leaned her forearms on the railing. "It's okay, but I wouldn't call it amazing."

"Chameleons," he said. He nodded toward the woods. "Somewhere out there somebody has figured out a way, maybe, to create natural protective coloration in a human being. I don't know what you'd call it. Fluid pigmentation?"

"I don't know. I'm not sure that's—"

"It was your idea."

"Yeah, but I still don't know. Do you have any idea what kind of genetic manipulation that would require? What kind of control on the cellular level that would mean?"

"Nope." He glanced at her sideways. "But if you tell me, maybe I'll be able to get some sleep after all."

She rolled her eyes as she straightened. "Go to bed, Mulder. Just go to bed."

He smiled at her back, suddenly yawned, and did as he was ordered.

Sleep, however, was still hard to come by.

Aside from the aches in his head and side, he couldn't help thinking about the possibility that there could be someone in the room right now, standing against the wall there.

Invisible, and watching him.

Waiting.

And he wouldn't know it until a knife tore out his throat.

EIGHTEEN

There was no dawn.

There was only a gradual shift from dark to shades of gray, and a falling mist just heavy enough to keep windshield wipers working, to raise the sharp smell of oil and tar from the blacktop.

Mulder was not in a good mood.

Following Scully's orders, Webber had let him oversleep, and it was close to ten before he finally opened his eyes to a note on the pillow that told him the others would be waiting in the Queen's Inn.

He was also not miraculously cured. Although his head seemed fine except for a small lump beneath his hair, his side felt as if it had been set in cement. Every time he moved, he thought his skin would rip open.

He supposed he ought to be grateful for the extra healing time, and for the concern Scully showed him, but knowing that didn't make it happen. He showered and dressed as quickly as he was able, thinking that he would eat quickly, check with Chief Hawks on the slim to none chance there had been any new developments overnight, and then . . . he smiled mirthlessly as

160

his brush fought with his hair . . . then he would have a few words with Major Joseph Tonero.

His stomach growled as he knotted his tie, and he snarled at it to hold its horses. Then he grabbed his coat, stepped outside, and was pleased to see that the weather perfectly complemented the way he felt.

I live for days like this, he thought gloomily as he descended the center staircase.

Scully recognized his mood immediately, and after a quick check to be sure he was all right, she hustled them through breakfast and outside, with a reminder that while they were heading for the post, there was also someone else out there, the shooter, they had best not forget.

Andrews still thought the so-called goblins and the shooting were related; when no one rose to the bait, she slumped into her corner and glared at the passing scenery.

There was no sound then but the rhythmic thump of the wipers and the hiss of the tires.

It wasn't until they had passed through town that Mulder remembered wanting to have a word with Hawks. He punched his leg lightly and scowled, and ordered himself to get with it, or he'd blow it all because he wasn't thinking straight.

Once this is done, he promised; I'll talk to him when we're done here.

Fifteen minutes later they passed between two simple brick pillars that marked the post entrance. No guards, no guardhouse; a stretch of woods that quickly fell away to the post's main complex—barracks, administration buildings, and on-post housing. A transport plane from McGuire lumbered and thundered overhead. A squad of troopers double-timed across an intersection, their dark green ponchos slick with water. They passed a construction site for a new federal prison twice before Scully finally gave up and made Hank ask directions. An MP gave them, and within minutes they were on New Jersey Avenue; it didn't take them long to find what they were after.

"Brother," Webber muttered as he pulled up in front of Walson Air Force Hospital.

It was a seven-story light tan brick structure, but it somehow seemed a lot smaller.

Because, Mulder realized, it was mostly empty. A lot of empty rooms and offices, a lot of space for things to happen without anyone being any the wiser.

He sat up and watched the entrance, something quickening inside when he noted that hardly anyone went in, and no one came out.

"What makes you think he'll be here?" Andrews asked, rousing herself from her sulking.

"If he's working on a project," Scully answered, "he will. Something like this doesn't often hold over weekends."

Something like this, Mulder thought.

"But do we have any authority?"

Mulder opened the door, slid out, and poked his head back in. "We've been asked in by a U.S. senator, Licia. The senator the major himself called. So if he wants to argue, he can write his congressman."

A civilian receptionist sat just inside the entrance, a multiline telephone and a logbook the only items on her small desk. Mulder wished her a good morning, showed her his ID, and asked directions to Major Tonero's office. She wasn't sure the major was in, and because of her standing orders was reluctant to give him the instructions until he insisted; then she pointed to a bank of elevators to their left.

As they moved away, he heard a noise and looked back.

Webber had his finger on the telephone's cutoff button. "I don't think so," he said politely, with a wink. "Government business, okay?"

Mulder couldn't believe it when the woman suddenly grinned. "Sure. Why not?"

Pancakes and women, he thought; the guy's got it made.

The major was in.

But it didn't look to Mulder as if he'd be there very long.

The office was a two-room suite on the second floor. When Mulder ushered the others in ahead of him, he saw a handful of packed cartons against one wall, and an empty bookcase behind what he assumed was Tonero's secretary's desk. The door to the inner office was open, and he gestured the others silent as he approached it. He could see the major standing in the middle of the room, back to the door, speaking quietly but angrily to someone seated at his desk.

"Damnit, Rosie, I don't give a damn who—" He turned and saw Mulder, and forced a smile. "My goodness, Agent Mulder, what is this, a raid?" He laughed as he shook Mulder's hand and nodded to the others.

The person behind the desk was Dr. Elkhart.

Mindful of protocol and egos, Mulder allowed Tonero to direct the conversation, politely answering questions about his health while he noticed that Dr. Elkhart, in a lab coat, was not as composed as she wanted him to think. Although she sat back in the major's chair, her legs crossed, her hands on the armrests, her cheeks were lightly flushed, and her attempt at a bland expression was nearly a total failure.

She was, he thought, royally pissed off.

What, he wondered next, is wrong with this picture?

"It's a real tragedy about Carl," Tonero said, stepping back to perch on the edge of his desk, ignoring Elkhart completely. "I want you to know that I am not going to rest until this matter is solved."

"I appreciate that, Major," Mulder said, sensing rather than seeing Scully take a chair just behind and to his left, while Webber and Andrews flanked the door. It was a large room, but their positions and attitude now made it seem much smaller. "I can assure you that we're not going to let it rest either."

He smiled quickly.

Dr. Elkhart uncrossed her legs.

"Well, good!" Tonero smiled purposefully at each of them in turn before rubbing his hands briskly together. "And what can I do to help?"

Mulder raised his eyebrows—*Gee, sir, I'm not really sure*—and glanced at Scully as if looking for guidance before facing the major again. "Well, I guess you could tell me what your project has to do with goblins."

Tonero sputtered into a laugh that proved he could appreciate a good joke when he heard one, but the laugh faded into a scowl when neither Mulder nor the others joined him. His back straightened; his expression became somber.

"I'm sorry, Agent Mulder, but what we do here is classified. I'm sure you understand."

"I do, believe me," he answered agreeably. "The DoD can be pretty tough sometimes."

"Absolutely. Now—" He waved one hand to indicate the closing and packing he had to do. "As you can see, we're being transferred—the orders came just this morning—and we're in a hell of a mess." A look over his shoulder that Dr. Elkhart ignored. "Dr. Tymons—you may recall meeting him yesterday—seems to have gone ahead without telling us, so it's kind of hectic around here at the moment."

He stepped forward, with the intention of easing the agents back into the outer room.

Mulder sidestepped around him, his right hand brushing across the edge of the desk before he leaned on it and turned his head. "Dr. Elkhart, where were you last night? I don't know, about nine?"

Elkhart started, and blinked. "What?"

"Last night," he repeated.

"Now look here, Agent Mulder," Tonero snapped. "Dr. Elkhart is one of our most—"

"Home," the woman answered, crossing her legs again. "I was home. Watching TV." Her smile was crooked. "Why, Agent Mulder? Am I a suspect?"

Mulder matched the smile, didn't answer the question as he turned his back to her. "And you, Major?"

"How—" Tonero's face darkened. "What do you think you're doing? Do you know who—"

"Chameleons," said Scully mildly from her chair.

"Lizards," Elkhart responded immediately, not quite as mildly. "Not, I'm afraid, from the goblin family."

"Goblins?" The major's voice rose. "Goblins? What are you talking about? What does some old woman's rantings have to do with my cousin's murder?"

Mulder shrugged. "I don't know, Major. But just as you have to explore all possibilities within the scope of your projects, so do we, in murder investigations." He turned to Scully. "Do you think we should come back later? I think they're in a hurry."

Scully agreed and headed for the door with the others.

Mulder, however, didn't move. "Major, can I assume you'll be around later this afternoon? Just in case?" He scanned the room. "Looks like you have a lot of work left here. And in your project office, too, I would guess."

"Absolutely, absolutely." Tonero moved again, and this time Mulder gave way. "Just call ahead, if you don't mind. I have—" He gave Mulder a brief martyred look. "Superiors, if you know what I mean. This relocation makes them nervous."

"I'll bet," Mulder said. "Nice to talk to you again, Dr. Elkhart," and was gone before the woman could reply.

Once in the silent corridor, the door closed firmly behind them, he held up a palm to keep the others from talking, then checked left, toward the elevator bank, before looking in the opposite direction, where he saw another, single elevator. A snap of his fingers sent Webber there on the silent run, and a sign that told him there was no button to push.

"Well?" Andrews demanded when they reached the lobby.

"Well," Mulder said, "they sure don't make majors like they used to." He took his left hand out of his pocket and held out his palm, showing them the key ring he'd lifted from the major's desk.

"Not a word, Scully," he said lightly when she began to object. He told Webber and Andrews to get back to town and track down Aaron Noel, Barney's bartender, to see if the man knew how close Pierce and Ulman had been, and if Barelli had been in asking questions.

"And find out where that dispatcher—"

"Vincent," Webber said.

"Right. Find out where she was last night, what time she came home. You know the drill."

"What about you?"

Mulder shrugged. "If we leave now, whatever this key takes us to will be gone before we get back. We're going to snoop around a little."

"But isn't that against—"

Mulder hushed him with a look and hurried outside with them.

The post looked deserted.

Nothing moved but a light rain that shifted now and then as a light wind passed through it.

He opened the door for Andrews, then stood back and wondered what the mighty Douglas would say when he found out that the other car was Swiss cheese and useless. He could see Webber and Licia arguing heatedly inside, but with the windows up, he couldn't hear a word.

He almost intervened, rolled his eyes, and changed his mind. That woman will be the death of me yet, he thought, and wished they'd be gone. Now. He wanted to be sure; he didn't want them suddenly turning up again.

The car jerked forward a few feet and stalled.

He smiled gamely and decided to get inside before he added pneumonia to his ills. He mimed giving the car a push with one foot, waved when Webber saw him in the rearview mirror, and trotted back to the lobby when the engine fired and held. The receptionist was clearly puzzled, but he assured her they had only forgotten something in Major Tonero's office and would be gone before she knew it.

The woman seemed to doubt it.

"Mulder," Scully said as they walked purposefully toward the elevator bank, "if we get caught . . ."

He didn't answer.

After a check over his shoulder, he took her elbow and ducked around the corner.

The corridor was empty, and only half the lights embedded in the ceiling's acoustic tiles were lit.

Whispers from the front, echoing softly.

He found the right key on the second try, and held his breath until the door opened onto an empty car. Once in, he inserted the key again and sent them down.

Scully said nothing; she had been on this road with him too many times before. The obligatory warning had been given—if we're caught; now she would be focused.

He wouldn't disturb that; it was too valuable.

He only hoped the major was still too angry to think straight, and realize what was going on.

NINETEEN

X The corridor was short, and the air not quite stale. No ceiling lights here—just a hooded bulb at the far end, and one at the entrance. The floor, like the walls, was unpainted concrete.

"Like a bunker," Scully whispered.

In and out was the order of the day. They hurried to the first door, and Mulder turned the knob. It was unlocked and, when he looked in, empty. A desk, metal shelves on the wall, a small, open safe on the floor beside the desk, and a blackboard.

Nevertheless, they searched, checking drawers and corners. Tonero had said that Tymons was already gone, but Mulder doubted it was to the relocation point. By the looks of it—the papers and pads left behind in the desk, the handful of books on the shelves—this room had been emptied in a hurry.

"I smell gunpowder," Scully said, returning to the corridor. "And smoke." She wrinkled her nose. "Something else. I'm not sure."

The middle door was unlocked as well, and open a few inches. Mulder pushed it with his foot and stood back, shaking his head.

"Jesus."

What was once on the single shelf was now on the floor, smashed and scattered, some of it scorched or charred. He counted the hulks of at least three monitors and a pair of keyboards; he counted at least a half-dozen bullet holes in the wall beneath what looked to be a one-way window.

Without speaking, they sifted through the wreckage, not knowing exactly what they were looking for, knowing only that they'd know when they saw it. Then Scully rocked back on her heels.

"Mulder."

He joined her, dusting his hands on his coat, and saw the blood. Lots of it, dry, and buried beneath plastic and blank sheets of paper.

"Not a gunshot wound, I think," she said.

"Goblin."

"I don't know. It's been here a while, though." She poked at a large stain with a forefinger. "But not that long. We're not talking about days."

He guessed that the room on the right had been Tymons's office, and Tymons's alone. It didn't have the feel of being shared with someone, like Rosemary Elkhart. This one had been the Project's heart and control center. From here . . . he stood at the shelf and looked into the next room.

"Oh, boy," he said. "Scully."

She looked, and her eyes widened.

Mulder checked his watch. "Time, Scully. Not much left."

The last room was a shambles as well, but it was the walls that fascinated him—one cream, one sand, one green, one black.

His fingers began to snap unconsciously.

This was it.

This was where the goblin was tested. One wall, one color.

Scully wasn't sure. "So what did they do, Mulder? Line him up against the wall and wait? They could have done that with a sheet on a bed."

Mulder looked at her sharply, and looked around the room

again. His lips moved as if he were talking to himself before they parted in a satisfied grin. "Training," he decided, and stood against the cream wall, unable to disguise the excitement in his voice. "Scully, it's a training room." He pointed. "Bed, desk, CD case there in the corner. Somebody lived here—no, somebody stayed here temporarily, maybe overnight, maybe for several days at a time." He spread his arms along the wall. "Somebody who—"

Scully whirled on him. "Don't say it, Mulder! I'm having a hard enough time as it is. Do not make it more complicated than it has to be."

"But it's not, Scully," he insisted, pacing now, rubbing at his chin, his cheeks, pushing a hand back through his hair. "This is where the goblin learned how to change." He turned in a slow circle. "Learned how to *will* the change, Scully, not wait for the change to happen." He took a step toward her, and was stopped by her frown. "You said it yourself, right? He can't carry every contingency around on his back. It's impossible. Even for the most basic circumstances, it would be, for him, a dangerous hindrance."

He looked to the door.

"A trained killer needs as few obstacles as possible. He needs a smooth way in, a smooth way out. No stops along the way for adjustments to a costume. No ripples. The quicker, the better."

He looked around again, closer now, searching for something, anything personal, that would give him a hint to the room's sometime occupant. But there was nothing left, and there was nothing left of the time he had hoped they would have.

On the way back to the elevator, Scully ducked into the control room and came out folding several pieces of paper she tucked into her shoulder bag. Blood samples. Not, Mulder thought, that they really needed them.

He knew who the blood belonged to.

•   •   •

On the way through the lobby, Mulder dropped the keys onto the absent receptionist's desk, then followed Scully outside, anxious to get back to town.

The light rain had grown heavier, the air darker for it.

Another squad of soldiers marched by, absolutely silent.

"Mulder," Scully said, "in case you haven't noticed, we don't have a ride."

It hadn't occurred to him, and he didn't think it mattered.

"And we don't have an umbrella, either."

She slapped him lightly on the arm and returned inside to use the phone.

He didn't follow.

He watched the rain.

A human chameleon, he thought, slipping his hands into his pockets. An effective assassin, who could theoretically slip through the tightest of cordons.

In, and out.

No ripples.

Or, more frighteningly, a small army of them, living shadows slipping through the night.

No ripples.

Only death left behind.

It wasn't a perfect disguise. It probably wasn't effective in broad daylight, and the goblin—he couldn't stop thinking of it that way—wouldn't be able to stay in the same room for very long. Even Scully had eventually spotted the moth.

Nevertheless . . . living shadows.

He shifted from foot to foot impatiently.

No question about it, Major Tonero was the project's shepherd. He knew all of it, which meant he probably knew that Tymons was dead. Killed by the goblin? If so, was the goblin under the man's direction?

But why kill the head of such a project?

Too easy—Rosemary Elkhart was second-in-command. There was no reason to believe she couldn't, or wouldn't, take over if she had to. And the best way to ensure that would be to make herself indispensable to those who were in charge. He pictured her in the major's chair, and suddenly realized that was what had bothered him earlier. *She* was in *his* chair. She was comfortable using it. She had used it before.

"Well," he whispered. "Well, well."

"Stop thinking, Mulder, and move it," Scully told him. She snapped open a large black umbrella, took his arm, and hustled down to the sidewalk.

They hadn't gone a dozen paces before he took it from her before she poked his eye out. "Where did you get this?"

"You'd be surprised what you'll find in the ladies' room on a rainy day." She hugged his arm tightly, quickly. "I called Chief Hawks, he's on his way to pick us up."

"So why—"

"The major isn't going to stay in that office, Mulder, not when he finds out his keys are gone. He'll check that setup first, using Dr. Elkhart's keys, then probably come after us. I would like to be long gone before that, if you don't mind."

"He'll follow us."

"No, I don't think so. We can't disappear, Mulder. The senator, remember?"

He almost stopped then, but her momentum pulled him along. "Carl."

"What about him?"

Mulder stared into the rain, willing Hawks to come in at speed. "According to his notes, he was asking around about the goblin." His chest tightened, his stride quickened. "Cleaning up, Scully. I think someone's scared, and the goblin's cleaning up."

• • •

The telephone rang only once before Rosemary snatched up the receiver. She listened and said, "What are you doing, calling here? Suppose *he* had answered?" Without thinking, she began to weave the cord between her fingers. "Well, you're lucky he's not. He's downstairs now. Those FBI agents were here, and he thinks they lifted his damn keys." She watched the door without seeing it. "I think, if they didn't know before, they know now."

Her gaze shifted to the window, to the trails of water almost invisible against the gray air, the gray sky.

She stiffened.

"You can't do that. No. It's bad enough, but you can't touch them."

The goblin cleared its throat painfully. "Yes, I can."

Rosemary almost rose out of the chair. "Damnit, will you listen to me? Just . . . just what we agreed, all right? Don't make it worse than it already is."

"Doctor, I can do whatever I want."

She couldn't believe it. First Tymons, now this.

"In fact, I think all that stuff you've been telling me is plain bullshit."

"Look—"

"You know, I don't think I'm affected much at all." It laughed softly, and wheezed. "And if I am, Doctor . . . whose fault is that?"

She did stand then, angrily shaking her hand until the cord fell off. "Goddamnit, listen to me, you idiot! If I have to—"

"Doctor." The voice was calm. Very calm.

Rosemary closed her eyes and took a deep breath. "What?"

"We have an agreement. I'll do what you want."

She leaned forward, bracing herself on the desk with one hand. "Thank you. It'll be fine, just fine, as long as we don't panic."

"I'll do what you want."

She nodded. "Yes."

"Are you listening?"

173

"Yes, of course."

"Then don't, Doctor. Don't *ever* talk to me like that again."

"Oh, really? And what if . . . hello? Damnit, hello?"

The line was dead.

She gaped at the receiver, then slammed it back onto its cradle. Calm again; she had to regain calm again, be the eye in the storm. It was not, yet, a disaster that those damn agents probably knew something. They could snoop around all they wanted, but they didn't know it all. As long as she made sure she, and Joseph, didn't panic, they never would.

At least not until it was too late.

But she was afraid for the goblin. Despite her assurances, she knew what little control she had was practically gone. Like all the others, those too deep in the woods to be found—here, and elsewhere—the strain and the treatment had proved too much.

This one had lasted the longest, however.

This one was the proof of her triumph.

She grabbed her purse and coat and hurried from the office. Joseph would have to come to her for a change, once he stopped blowing off pompous steam. She still had some last-minute packing to do.

Just a few more weeks, she prayed as she made for the elevators; just get me out of here in one piece, give me a couple more weeks, and it'll be over.

Really over.

The door slid open as the overhead bell chimed softly.

She took a step, and froze.

The car was empty. She could see that, but she still couldn't bring herself to go in.

With a low groan of frustration she used the fire stairs instead, yanking on her coat, cursing her own weakness, but oddly grateful for the harsh sound of her heels on the steps.

TWENTY

X Scully decided her vacation hadn't been nearly long enough, not by half.

A Marville patrol car had picked them up minutes after they left the hospital, just about the time the rain had stopped. The driver, though polite, refused to answer any of Mulder's questions.

"Talk to the chief," was all he would say.

It sounded to her as if Hawks's equanimity at having the FBI in town was being sorely tested.

Now they sped toward town, and she couldn't help feeling that everything was moving too fast. She needed time to think, and she wasn't getting it. She was reacting, rather than acting; otherwise, she never would have taken Mulder's leap from experimental camouflage to full-blown, controlled human chameleon, with no stops along the way.

It wasn't like her; not at all.

She braced herself when the car momentarily lost traction on its way around a bend, and wished she had tried to get a hold of Webber instead. And when the driver said, "Sorry, ma'am" once he regained control, she almost snapped his head off.

Not like her at all.

Then Mulder folded his arms on the back of the seat and rested his chin on them. He said nothing, but she could feel him at her shoulder. Her eyes closed briefly at a flurry of leaves across the windshield.

"Mulder, I'm sorry about Carl."

He grunted.

She realized then that that was part of her problem. She hadn't liked Barelli; he was crude, too slick, and too full of himself. But for reasons she would never understand, he had also been Mulder's friend, and she hadn't said a single word of sympathy, of commiseration. The moment she had seen the reporter's body, she had clicked into professional mode.

She hadn't let the murder touch her.

It had obviously touched her friend.

"We have to get to Elly," he said at last.

She agreed, and asked the driver to take them there instead of the station.

"I don't know," he said doubtfully. "I was told—"

"Don't worry about it," Mulder said. "We'll take the heat. You can tell him we pulled rank. FBI, pushy feds, stuff like that."

For a second, Scully thought the man would flat out refuse. Then he grinned, shrugged, and: "Whatever you say, sir."

"So punch it."

"You got it."

And it took all of Scully's self-control not to grab the dashboard.

Traffic increased as Marville began, Saturday shoppers and wanderers taking their time to make the business district last as long as they could make it. The driver took a back-road, corner-cutting shortcut to avoid the main street, and pulled up smoothly in front of the apartment building.

"You want me to wait?" He sounded hopeful.

"Yes," she told him as she opened the door.

He took the radio mike and called in: "Maddy, this is Spike. We're at the Goblin Lady's place. Maybe the chief should meet us here, huh?"

The radio hissed. "I'll tell him. Watch your back."

"You got it," he said, and hooked the mike back on its cradle.

"That's it?" Mulder asked, sounding disappointed.

"You mean, ten-four, that kind of stuff?" The driver shook his head. "The chief hates radio talk. He says it makes us sound too much like cop shows." He laughed. "Besides, half the guys keep getting the numbers wrong anyway. Maddy knows what we're saying, so . . ." He shrugged.

Scully was already outside, looking up at the bay window. The curtains were closed. She turned slowly as Mulder left the car, and clamped a hand hard against her chest.

"Mulder!"

Immediately she ran across the street without checking for traffic, heading straight for the small park and Elly Lang, sitting motionless on her bench. The old woman faced the empty ball field, bundled in a black coat, a black umbrella canted over her head.

She didn't turn when Scully called her name.

No, she thought, leaping the curb and racing across the wet grass; damnit, no.

"Elly!"

She heard Mulder behind her, drifting to her right to come up on her flank.

"Elly!"

She grabbed the bench back and propelled herself around, damning herself for not thinking of this sooner.

If they were too late, she would personally rip Tonero's medals off, one by one, and pin them back on his bare chest. One by one.

Suddenly a hand snapped out from beneath the umbrella, and she yelped as she jumped to one side when a stream of bright orange nearly caught her on the chest.

The old woman stared at her without blinking. "Oh. It's you." And she tucked the spray can back into her purse. "I must be getting slow."

Scully didn't know what to say, could only nod while she tried to catch her breath. "I thought—"

"Yes," Elly said. "I can see that." Her gaze shifted when Mulder came up beside her. "They won't hurt me, you know. Never have. I figure they figure an old lady can't do them much harm."

"Ms. Lang," Mulder said, "this one is different."

Scully dropped onto the bench and gently pushed the umbrella to one side. "It's killed at least three people that we know of, Ms. Lang. We think you could be in danger."

Elly humphed. "You don't know much about goblins, young lady." She shook a bony finger in Scully's face. "You should study more. You're a smart girl. You should learn more. Goblins," she said, "don't kill anyone. Never have."

Dana looked to Mulder for support, and he hunkered down in front of the old woman, one hand gently on her knee so he wouldn't topple. "Ms. Lang, this one is sick."

"They don't get sick."

He shook his head. "Not that kind of sick." He tapped his temple. "This kind. It isn't like the others. It's . . ." He swallowed, and let his hand slide away. "It's evil, Ms. Lang. I don't know any other way to put it."

Scully saw it then, the doubt and the birth of fear in the woman's face. Suddenly she seemed two decades older. "You shouldn't be sitting out here," she said quietly. "You should be someplace warm. It'll rain again soon."

"The children," Elly whispered.

"I don't think they'll be playing much today."

She stood, sliding her hand along the woman's coat until she grasped her hand. The fingers twitched, then curled around hers, and she pulled Elly slowly to her feet, the umbrella dropping forgotten to the ground.

Mulder retrieved it as Scully pointed to the cruiser. "See that man there? His name, if you can believe it, is Spike. I think I can talk him into staying with you for a while."

Arm in arm they walked across the grass.

"Is he married?" Elly asked.

"I don't think so."

Mulder went ahead, keeping himself between the women and the driver as he spoke. Scully blessed him for that.

"He's a nice boy," Elly said, using her chin to point at Mulder.

"Yes. I know."

In the middle of the street, Elly stopped, her lower lip trembling. "Is he right about this goblin?"

She nodded.

"I'm not ready to die yet, you know."

Dana squeezed the woman's arm. "I know. And you won't."

"Too mean, too cranky."

Dana smiled, although the woman didn't see her. "Well . . . I don't think so." She urged them forward again. "You're just tough, that's all. A good thing to be."

"Are you?"

Scully didn't know how to answer that one, and was saved from stumbling by Todd Hawks's arrival. It didn't take long to get Elly camped in her apartment, and not much longer than that, once they were outside again, to tell the chief they suspected that someone attached to, or working for, the Special Projects Office at Fort Dix was responsible for the murders. Someone, she added, who was extremely skilled at blending in.

"Disguises, you mean?" Hawks asked.

"You could say that."

"A real expert, one of the best," Mulder said, following her lead. Then he smiled so quickly she almost missed it. "You could say it gives a whole new meaning to the word wallflower."

"Son of a bitch." Hawks checked the sky as if daring the rain to add to his misery. "Damn, I don't need this. I really don't." He shook his head and looked up at Elly's apartment. The curtains were open; a lamp burned in the window. "If you don't mind telling me, you got anyone in mind?"

He sounded neither bitter nor imposed upon; he only sounded as if he wanted this to be over, so his town could get back to what passed for normal.

"Because," he added flatly, "what I've got is three goddamn corpses, and three families and some local politicians on my ass demanding explanations." He looked at Mulder then, eyes narrowed. "And would you happen to know why, while I was poking around Vincent's house this morning, a United States senator called my office?"

Oh, great, she thought; just great.

Though she could hear traffic in the distance, the neighborhood was quiet. A few lights on porches, in front windows; an old black dog trotting along the gutter; a large crow strutting across the ball field.

Like her, it seemed in a state of anticipation.

"Chief, can you patch Mulder through on your radio, to try to locate the rest of our team?"

"No problem," he said with a wry smile. "They were on their way to the station when I left, trying to find you."

When Mulder questioned her with a look, she shook her head slightly, waiting until Hawks was on the radio. "We've been sloppy," she said, matter of fact, not a scolding. "The major's ready to bolt, and all we've been able to do is run from one killing to another."

"The restaurant," he suggested.

She frowned. "Why?"

"Hank does his best thinking in front of a plate of pancakes."

"Mulder," she started, then waved herself silent. "Okay."

Then she hurried inside to be sure Elly was all right, a concern quickly allayed when she saw Spike on the stool, cap in his lap, avidly listening to the old woman describing her lifelong hunt for goblins.

Neither noticed her in the doorway; neither noticed when she left.

Hank was at the curb when she reached the sidewalk, Mulder already in the car, waving her around the back to the other door. The chief stopped her at the rear bumper.

"You'll let me know what I need to know?"

She promised, then swore when her shoulder bag slipped off and hit the ground. I have got to get control, she snapped at herself, and was grateful when Hawks crouched down to help her fetch her things. She had to kneel to grab a pen that had rolled beneath the car, only half-listening as Hawks made some lame jokes about a woman's purse.

She leaned over, saw the pen, and reached for it.

And froze.

"You need help?"

She shook her head and backed out, the pen retrieved and in her pocket. Then, as he helped her to her feet, something about the license plate puzzled her, froze her again until she saw it.

"Listen, Agent Scully, if there's something the matter—"

"No." She waved off his offered hand. "No, thank you, I'm fine. I just thought of something, that's all." She knew he didn't really believe her, but didn't know the right question to ask. "Thanks," she said, and slipped into the car.

As soon as she was settled, Andrews turned around to ask what next. As far as she was concerned, all they were doing was chasing their own tails, and widened her eyes when Scully said, "Exactly. That's why we're going to the restaurant, order a long lunch, and get things straight before we start tripping over ourselves."

"And what about our goblin?" Mulder asked quietly.

"Our goblin," she said, "won't be out again until tonight."

TWENTY-ONE

X Despite the day's gloom, the Queen's Inn's lights were kept low, giving the room an evening feel. Two diners sat at the counter, each reading a newspaper; a family of six sat in the last booth, one of the children describing the movie he had seen on TV that morning, complete with explosive sound effects and dialogue quotations. A busboy swept the already gleaming floor. In the parking lot, a trailer truck took its time making a wide U-turn, causing a minor backup and a brief flurry of angry horns.

"Another peaceful day in the country," Mulder said glumly. He sat by the window, pushed into the corner, his topcoat draped over the seatback. Although his head no longer throbbed to distraction, his side refused to give him respite. He squirmed, thought he was settled, and then a quick stitch made him shift again.

The others didn't seem to notice his discomfort.

Hank sat across from him, gleefully, for Scully's benefit, attacking a steak with all the trimmings he'd been able to think of, while Andrews and Scully settled on salads. All he could think of was pancakes and bacon, so forced himself to order just a sandwich. Two seconds later, he had forgotten what kind it was.

The truck finished its turn.

The kid finished the movie to the laughing applause of his family.

Mulder shifted again. "Do you know what W. C. Fields said about children?"

Licia asked him who W. C. Fields was.

"I'm not old, you know," he said to Scully's infuriatingly blank expression. "Really. I am not old."

"Eat, Mulder," she ordered. "We have work to do."

There was, then, mostly silence as they finished their meal. And once the table had been cleared, Scully flipped over her paper place mat and pulled out her pen, and looked to Mulder, who nodded it was her show, be my guest.

The family left.

The men at the counter paid and left as well.

"Pierce," Scully said, lightly jabbing the place mat with her pen, "was killed on a Saturday night. So was Corporal Ulman. Almost a pattern until last night." She paused, and Mulder was grateful she didn't mention Carl's name. "It's my guess Dr. Tymons is dead, too. Probably sometime yesterday." She filled them in quickly on what they had seen at Walson after the others had left, but gave neither of them a chance to comment. "The Project, whatever it is, is over."

"For now," Mulder added.

"All right. For now. And we don't have much time." She tapped the place mat again. "All the deaths are the same—throat slashed, deeply. This isn't a professional's attack. The violence . . . and the fact that each one came from the front, not behind . . ." She took a breath and shook her head. "It's almost psychotic. And the strength to do this indicates it's probably a man. Or," she added, when Mulder opened his mouth to comment, "a woman, okay. These days, there are a lot of women who go for weight training, defense training, things like that. We can't rule that out."

"Which means," Andrews said sourly, "we've narrowed it down to about eight or nine thousand people, right?"

"Wrong."

Mulder sat up, staring at the doodles Scully had drawn on the paper.

"While Pierce may have died just because he was in the wrong place at the wrong time, it's pretty obvious the others are connected. The corporal worked for Major Tonero—although we can't guarantee he knew everything that was going on, Carl Barelli was asking questions about goblins, and Dr. Tymons was the Project head."

She scribbled Tonero's name and circled it.

"I also think Mulder's right—the Project's in danger, and the goblin is cleaning house. Which is why we have someone staying with Ms. Lang." She circled Rosemary Elkhart's name. "That gives us motive. Hide the mistakes, bury the evidence. Literally."

"But if Tymons really is dead," Webber said, "won't that kill the project for good?"

"Oh, no. Not by a long shot. Dr. Elkhart, no matter what the major thinks, is in charge now. Nothing we said in that office fazed her, while the major was only partly acting. So I'm assuming she's gotten hold of the records, and I don't doubt she'd be able to have another center up and running before very long."

Andrews leaned forward eagerly. "She could have been planning it, you know. For weeks. Months, even. Something about the project, maybe it's almost ready, you know? I mean, done. Maybe she wants all the glory."

Scully tapped the name again. "I don't think there's any maybe about it, Licia."

"Then she did it!" Webber exclaimed.

Mulder blinked. "What? You think she's the goblin?"

Webber nodded, then shook his head, then threw up his

hands. "Seemed like a good idea at the time." He brightened. "But she could be directing it. I mean, wouldn't she know who was a threat and who wasn't?"

Scully smiled. "Weekend nights," she reminded them. "Only weekend nights."

"So what are you saying?" Andrews asked with a frown. "We narrow it down to only those people who are free on weekends?" She shook her head. "Give me a break, okay?" She reached out to push at the place mat. "Do you know how many troops there are at Dix, for one thing? And every one of them—"

"Damn!" Mulder said.

Scully jumped, and he apologized with a quick gesture, but he had followed her road, marked the signposts, and the more he thought about it, the more he realized he already had the answer.

"What?" Webber said anxiously.

"Louisiana," he answered, speaking to Scully.

All she could do was look.

"That guy in Louisiana, he was supposed to have disappeared in the middle of a circus ring. Walked through a crowd of people and didn't come out the other side. But he was still there, Scully. He just didn't look the same way."

"And how do you know that?"

His left arm rested along the back of the seat, forcing him to turn toward her. "You'll be happy to know that I don't think he just disappeared in a puff of sawdust. He had to be there; he was just different, that's all. The police were looking for one thing, so they didn't see anything else."

"Okay, so things weren't what they seemed. What does that have to do with this?"

"Ghosts and goblins, Scully. Ghosts and goblins."

"Meaning?" Andrews said testily.

"Meaning our field of suspects has just been made considerably smaller."

Rosemary stood his pacing, his ranting, for as long as she could. Then she came around the desk and said, "Joseph."

He ignored her. "God damn them, anyway. Did you see the way they spoke to me? Who the hell do they think they are?"

"Joseph."

He shook his head in exasperation. "This is too much. It's just too much." His face reddened, and he aimed a kick at one of the cartons. "And I even packed my damn keys away! Jesus H. Rosie, the whole world's gone nuts!"

She leaned back against the desk.

"Son of a bitch bastards are not—I repeat, are not—going to get away with it. I'll call that goddamn senator myself and—"

"Joseph!"

He whirled on her, one fist up, but she didn't flinch. She only softened her expression, and beckoned with a crooked finger. "Joseph." Her voice deep in her throat. "Joseph."

His chest rose and fell, the fist trembled and fell away.

"Joseph, there's nothing to worry about."

"What? How the hell—"

"Nothing to worry about," she repeated calmly, and beckoned him again.

This time he moved, close enough for her to place a hand on his shoulder.

"Everything we need from downstairs we already have. Everything we need from here is ready to ship."

"Yes, but—"

She hushed him with a finger on his lips. "And everything you need is right here, too."

She kissed him softly, quickly, and used all her remaining control to stop herself from slapping him.

"You have the orders?"

He leaned around her and yanked open the center drawer, pulled out a folder and handed it to her. "Signed and sealed, Rosie."

"Good." She pressed the folder against her chest. "Now we can either forget about downstairs altogether, because no one will see it for weeks, maybe even months. Or we can get Captain Whatshisname from Battalion to clean it up." She smiled. "After all, what are soldiers for?"

"I say we just leave it." The flush had receded from his cheeks and brow. He puffed a little, slipping back into his role. "And I say we don't wait for tomorrow morning."

"I don't mind."

"I can get us a flight tonight."

She considered it, and nodded. "Not too late, though. I want to get there in time to get a decent night's sleep."

His expression made her shudder. "Who says we'll get any sleep?"

"I do, you dope." She slapped his shoulder playfully and slipped around him, heading for the door. "We sleep, we see the right people, you take that leave, and then . . . who knows?"

Tonero laughed. "Okay, Rosie, okay." Then he frowned. "But what about—"

"All taken care of, darling." She picked up her coat from the chair. "All it takes is one phone call."

She waved, showed him a little chest movement, and left before he could think of anything else. There was no doubt he would make all the proper arrangements; she trusted him that much. As for the actual flight itself . . . she never had minded traveling alone.

In Elly Lang's apartment, the telephone rang.

•   •   •

Mulder knew that Scully was about to tug on the reins, haul him in before his excitement got the best of him. Nevertheless, he couldn't help the way his hands moved, darting from the notes on the place mat to his uneaten sandwich to tracing diagrams in the air only he could see.

"Civilian, first." He made sure they were listening with a look and a gesture. "Dr. Elkhart has no influence over military personnel without Major Tonero. And Tonero isn't about to use the military for project experiments. If it blew up, he'd lose his ticket to whatever election he's hoping to win when he retires."

Hank gaped, astonished. "How—"

"Us, second." He touched Scully's shoulder to keep her attention, and looked at Andrews. "It wasn't magic that told the goblin where we were yesterday. It wasn't magic that told the goblin where Carl would be last night." He scratched through his hair, then slapped it impatiently back into place. "Somebody knows us. Somebody who knows where we are most, if not all, of the time."

"Damn," Hank said. "Somebody who even knows what the hell we had for breakfast!"

It was all Mulder could do to keep the young man from jumping out of his seat.

"Right," Scully said, her eyes slowly widening. "And she was supposed to have a date with him last night. It was in his notes." She slipped out of the booth and grabbed her shoulder bag. "We talk to her now. Before—"

"Absolutely," Mulder agreed. "But not for the reason you think."

"But it has to be," Andrews protested. "God, it all fits. She's alone, so she comes and goes whenever she wants and nobody to question her, she has that equipment to keep in shape—" She grabbed Webber's arm, to pull him from the booth. Her voice began to rise. "She—"

Scully silenced her with a harsh wave and stared at Mulder. "Well?"

189

He moved more slowly, wincing when his side stabbed him again, dragging his coat along behind him. "She's not going anywhere, Scully." He tilted his head toward the window. "It's still too light."

He urged the others ahead with a nod, then tugged on Scully's coat to keep her back.

"It's not her," he said, keeping his voice low.

"How can you know that?"

He shook his head—tell you later—and gestured to Webber to cover the back, Andrews to stay outside.

"I don't know," Scully said, following him into the office.

"Three against one?" He banged the counter bell. "Come on, that's a bit much, don't you think?"

"She's psychotic," she reminded him when he hit the bell again. "And she's strong, Mulder." Her hand slipped into her purse, and didn't come out.

Mulder struck the bell once more, then rounded the counter and pushed through the beaded curtain. "Mrs. Radnor?" A staircase immediately to his left was dark. From the room at the back he heard muffled music, and hurried down the short hall.

"Mrs. Radnor!"

He stepped into the room, where the motel owner pumped furiously on a stationary bike, headphones on, listening to music from a cassette player lashed to the handlebars. She started when she saw him, her eyes wide and mouth open when she saw Scully, and the drawn gun.

"What the hell?" She held up one hand while the other very slowly pulled the headphones off and switched off the player. "Mr. Mulder, what's going on?"

"You don't seem terribly broken up about Carl Barelli," Scully said, keeping the gun at her side.

Mrs. Radnor tried to speak and couldn't; she could only look at Mulder for help, and an explanation.

He grabbed the handlebars and leaned toward her. "Mrs. Radnor, I haven't got time to explain, but I need to know something."

"Hey, I run a clean place here," she said. "You can't—"

"Frankie Ulman."

"I—what about him?"

"You told Agent Andrews you saw the corporal bring a date here every so often."

The woman nodded, her hands shifting to grip the towel draped around her neck.

"You told her you didn't know who the woman was."

"Well . . . yes."

"Why?"

"I didn't have time, for one thing." She forced a laugh. "She was in such a hurry, I don't think we talked more than five or ten minutes."

Mulder frowned, but shook it off. "You lied, Mrs. Radnor," he said carefully, and shook the bike slightly when she started to protest. "You knew who it was. You know just about everyone around here, and you knew who it was."

She mopped her face, a stalling tactic, until Scully cleared her throat and made sure she remembered the gun. "I don't want to get people in trouble, you know? It's bad for business. Word gets around and—"

"Mrs. Radnor," he snapped, "we don't have time for this, okay? I'm only going to ask you once: Who was that woman?"

When she told him, he whirled. "Scully, get the car and Webber." He turned back as Scully charged from the room. "Mrs. Radnor, I have a favor to ask."

"What?" She couldn't believe it.

He smiled, and she softened almost immediately. "I need to borrow your car."

"What?" This time she almost yelled.

Jesus, woman, he thought, would you please stop—

"Commandeer," he said quickly. "I must commandeer your car."

Her face brightened. "Wow. You mean, like in the movies."

"Exactly." He took her arm and pulled her gently from the bike. "Just like the movies."

"But you had two—"

"The other one was shot up. But you know that already, right?"

Excited, flustered, she fumbled in her purse, held out the keys, and snapped them back. "Is this one going to get shot up?"

"I sincerely hope not," he said truthfully, took the keys from her hand before she could change her mind, and ran.

"But what if it is?" she yelled after him.

"The president will buy you a new one!" he yelled back, slammed through the front door, and grabbed the edge to swing him back inside.

"Pink," Mrs. Radnor called. "It's the pink Caddy in back."

Pink, he thought as he ran out again; terrific.

And thought *terrific* again when the storm finally broke, and broke hard.

TWENTY-TWO

X "Vincent?" Scully gripped the dashboard as Mulder squealed out of the parking lot. The Caddy took a second to grip the slick tarmac and soon lost the Royal Baron in a swirling, twisting mist. "Officer Maddy Vincent?"

Webber and Andrews followed behind, their car nothing more than a smear of headlights.

Despite the storm, Mulder didn't bother to check his speed. Either what traffic there was got out of his way, or it didn't, it was their choice. He had a difficult enough time seeing through the rain.

"It's why Carl wanted to talk to her," he explained. "He wanted what he thought she knew about who was what, where, at the time of the killings." He grunted as the car threatened to fishtail. "Who else knows where all the cops will be, Scully? Who else knew where we would be yesterday?"

"Mulder, that's not enough."

He knew that. "Watch your back."

"Huh?"

"The goblin said 'Watch your back' to me, out there in the

woods. Just before I was clobbered. This morning, on the way back from Tonero's, Vincent told Spike to watch his back." He glanced at her. "The same voice, Scully. It was the same voice."

He plowed through a lane-wide puddle, sending a wave soaring over the shoulder onto someone's front lawn.

Ahead, a pickup doused the windshield with backspray, and he cursed as he set the wipers to their highest speed.

It was almost enough.

At the corner of his vision he saw her shift so she could watch him and the road at the same time. "The makeup," she said, recognition hitting home. "The calamine lotion. It's—"

He listened to her mumble to herself, then catch her breath as he pressed on the horn and rocketed past the truck.

She had caught it now; she had caught the scent.

"It's breaking down." She was thinking aloud. "Whatever treatment they were giving her is breaking down. If . . . if it works correctly, she ought to be able to revert to normal color with no residual effects. It isn't happening. Mulder, it isn't happening, and she has to hide it somehow."

He had no argument.

The Project had failed; he guessed it wasn't the first time. He also suspected that Elkhart and Tymons had come closer than they ever had before, which was why the doctor and the major were packing to leave.

They were going to try again.

And he still couldn't shake the image of shadow armies, sliding through the night.

Another car ahead, its taillights flaring red as the driver pumped his brakes. Mulder grunted and swerved quickly into the other lane without reducing speed, and frantically spun the wheel right when the blinding bright headlights of an oncoming van blurred across the windshield.

It was too late to slow down.

He swung around the leading car on its right, fighting the wheels' stubborn inclination to take them straight into the woods, ignoring the frightened, angry blare of the other car's horn. His side began to burn. The Caddy jounced through a pothole, and he was on the road again.

"Mulder," Scully said calmly, "we can't help anyone if we're dead."

He stared at her in near panic. "Jesus!" He slapped the wheel with a palm. "Elly! If she's cleaning up . . . Elly!"

"But how?"

"Vincent's the dispatcher. All she has to do is call—who cares with what excuse?—and Spike is gone on some fool's errand. And Elly is alone."

He swung to the shoulder and braked, was out with the engine still running, instantly drenched and waving his arms. The car he had just passed swept by and honked loud and long as it emptied a puddle onto his legs. But Webber saw him and pulled up, Andrews rolling down her window before the car had fully stopped.

Mulder grabbed the door and leaned in. "Get to the station, Hank. Find out where Vincent is, go there, and wait."

"Vincent?" Webber said incredulously. "You're kidding. Vincent?"

"Just do it, Hank," he ordered. He turned, and turned back. "And be careful. If Scully's right and she's gone off because something's gone wrong, she definitely won't hesitate to cut a couple of FBI throats."

There was no time for details. He jumped back into the Caddy and pushed the accelerator all the way down. The rear wheels spun, kicking pebbles and mud before they found traction and leap onto the blacktop again.

Webber's car had already vanished into the rain.

•   •   •

Elly Lang jumped when a gust of wind rattled the bay window. But she wouldn't panic. She had her spray can, she had the cane with the large ivory knob Officer Silber had found in her bedroom closet, and she had his promise he would be back in less than ten minutes.

Still, she was frightened.

The storm had come so suddenly, after so long a wait, and the light had dimmed so fast, that it was hard to believe it was only a few minutes past noon.

It wasn't, she told herself; not really.

It was midnight.

Time for the goblins to make their rounds.

Shadows snaked down the wall behind her, over her, while the rush of water in the eaves sounded too much like thunder.

She had been told to leave the lamp on, but soon after Silver left, she had turned it off. It was better this way. She could see outside better, and she hoped it would be harder for someone to see in.

The window rattled again.

The rain fell harder, and pellets of hail shotgunned against the panes.

I'm ready, she thought; I'm ready.

And then she wondered if she had locked the back door.

Rosemary Elkhart stood in the middle of her living room and decided it was hopeless. She hadn't been here five minutes, had barely taken off her coat, when Joseph had called, demanding reassurance that he wouldn't be burned, that his reputation would be intact, that no one would find Tymons's body in the woods. She had done her best, but second thoughts changed her mind after his third call.

He was hopeless.

After all this time, after all the bases and posts and installations they had been on, working through the kinks and dead ends of Leonard's discovery, Major Tonero had become, virtually on the night of their success, hopeless.

And a hell of a pain in the ass.

Worse; she had been around him long enough to know what that meant—cut your losses, cover your ass, offer the sacrifice, and start again somewhere else.

With someone else.

She looked with regret at the suitcases waiting near the door. To give him his due, he had bought her a lot of nice things, jewelry and clothes, some of which she had begun to convert to cash as soon as it became apparent that this phase of the project, while not perfect, was nearing its end.

A girl, she thought, can't be too careful.

Cover your ass.

Cut your losses.

And something else:

Travel light.

She picked up the bag at her feet, made sure Leonard's disks were inside, then zipped it closed and reached for her coat. A cab to Philly would be expensive, but she considered it an investment. God knows there were plenty of private businesses out there, not necessarily in this country, who would be more than willing to learn what she knew.

She checked the bag again, recognizing her nervousness, and reminded herself that somehow, between here and the airport, she'd have to lose the gun.

"Okay," she said, and smiled at the room. "Okay."

At the moment she didn't give a damn for Madeline Vincent. The woman would have to learn to fend for herself. For what little time she had left.

She hadn't taken two steps when someone knocked on the door.

Mulder swore and slapped the steering wheel angrily when storm-slowed traffic finally forced his speed down.

Dana didn't scold. She had been infected by his urgency as well, to the extent that she lowered her window and tried to see if there was a way he could pass again on the right. Parked cars lined the curbs, however, for as far as she could see, and she didn't see suggesting he use the sidewalk as a lane.

If she did, he'd do it.

"Two blocks," she told him. "Just two blocks."

Equally frustrating was the lack of communication between here and the others. If she had a radio, she could have called ahead to Hawks and double-checked on Webber, and on Silber's being at the apartment.

She sighed and opened her bag, to be sure her weapon was loaded and ready.

Her hand touched something else.

Oh God, she thought, and debated for nearly a full minute before making up her mind.

The drum of rain on the roof forced her to raise her voice: "Mulder—"

"I wish I could fly," he said, glaring at the windshield as if that would give his vision a better chance. As it was, the rain was so hard, with the wind blowing now, that it seemed as if the street had been invaded by drifting fog.

"Mulder, listen."

He nodded. "Okay. Sorry."

"The shooter."

"What? Now?" He shook his head, and raised his hand to use the horn, changed his mind and throttled the steering wheel instead.

"Yes. Now." She tossed a sprig of pine onto the dashboard, and waited for him to see it. When he looked, she said, "It was caught under the car. Hank's car. I found it when we were at Elly's."

He was bewildered and lifted a shoulder. "So?"

"So Mrs. Radnor only spoke with Licia for five or ten minutes. So Licia has been fighting you every inch of this investigation. So Hank and I are the only ones who have used that car, and I know damn well I didn't hit or run over any tree." She stopped. Looked outside. "Hawks said they found the spot where the shooter had backed off the road into the woods. It wasn't a clear area." Her hands danced an apology over her lap. "I didn't read her notes, Mulder. She said she had them, I even watched her put them in her briefcase . . . but I didn't read them. And she didn't bring them to your room."

"Scully—"

"I screwed up." Her hands again. "Damnit, I screwed up."

"Nope," he said, rocking back and forth, body English for the car. "If I was dead, then you would have screwed up." She saw the grin. "Then I'd have to haunt you."

"Mulder, that's not funny."

"But you don't believe in ghosts and goblins."

Hail bounced off the hood.

She jumped when a car honked behind them.

"So," he said, "what do we do?"

"We take care of business," she said without hesitation. "And when that's done, we take care of more business."

He nodded, groaned when traffic came to a complete halt, and finally unsnapped his seat belt. "Take the car."

She reached out to grab his arm, but she was too late. "Mulder!"

He stood in the middle of the street, rain dripping into his eyes. He pointed. "I can't wait, Scully. I can't. Just . . ." He flapped the hand helplessly. "Just come after me as fast as you can."

He was gone, the cars behind discovered their horns, and she slid awkwardly into the driver's seat, all the while watching him race to the sidewalk and around the next corner.

If there were any rules left in the book that he hadn't broken, she couldn't think of them.

All she could think of was, watch your back, Mulder. For God's sake, watch your back.

TWENTY-THREE

X He knew he must have looked like a fool, racing headlong through the rain, one hand held loosely over his head in feeble protection against the hail that, so far, was no larger than a pea. That didn't stop it from stinging, however, and stinging badly.

He bolted across the street, veering sharply when a minivan nearly clipped him on his blind side. He skidded, fell into a parked car, and used it to propel him onto the sidewalk again.

The hail stopped.

The rain didn't.

He didn't want to, but he had to slow up—his side had begun to pull, and he couldn't help thinking that something had torn in there.

Hang on, Elly, he thought; hang on.

At the next intersection, he paused under a tree, half bent over, hands hard on his hips, and took precious seconds to get his bearings, and his breath back. Another block west, he thought, swallowed hard, and tried to run, snarling when he couldn't do much better than a fast trot.

A winter-raised section of concrete made him swerve onto a lawn, where he slid on the wet grass and went down on his hands and knees. It felt good, not moving, and it took him a moment to get back on his feet.

He had no choice but to run now, forcing the pain in his side to another place, one that didn't bother him, one he knew would exact a great price when he couldn't concentrate any longer.

The wind pushed a curtain of water into his eyes. He slapped it away angrily without missing a step as he charged off the curb and across the tarmac to the other side. He figured Scully, with her luck, would beat him there anyway, but at least now he was moving, doing something instead of cursing traffic and feeling helpless.

Reaching the next corner seemed to take hours, and when he stopped, he almost panicked.

This wasn't right; he was on the wrong street.

Strings of mist like ghosts moved slowly through the rain; a storm drain overflowed, creating a shallow pond across the intersection.

This wasn't right, and he didn't know which way to go.

Then he saw the park across the way and up the block, the benches and ball field obscured by the rain. His lips parted—it wasn't quite a grin—and he moved on, his face turned toward the houses he passed to keep his vision clear.

The police car was gone.

The lamp was out in Elly's window.

He slowed as he approached the front walk, slipping his left hand into his pocket to wrap around his gun. Front or back? Wait for Scully, or do the stupid thing and go in on his own?

He had no realistic alternative.

He reached the front walk just as a horn honked several times in quick succession. Turning as he ran, he saw Scully bump the pink Cadillac up over the curb and practically throw herself into the street.

Sometimes you just live right, he thought, and waved her around to the back, ran up the steps, and stopped with his hand on the knob.

The wind shrieked overhead.

Something rattled down a drainpipe.

He fought his lungs into calming, then stepped into the foyer. Slowly now, knowing he wouldn't be able to give Scully enough time, he sidled to the door and put an ear to the damp wood.

Nothing; the storm made it impossible to hear a thing.

He tried the knob, and closed his eyes briefly when it turned, mouthed a *damn*, and turned it, using his shoulder to push the door inward.

The living room was dark, and empty, gray light from the bay window the only illumination. Rain shadows rippled across the furniture and carpet. An ivory-topped cane lay on the floor in front of the couch.

He could see no light in the kitchen, or in the bedroom at the front room's far side.

He chose the kitchen first.

Keeping as close to the wall as he could, he moved down the short hall. As far as he could see, no one sat at the little table, and he could see no welcome, telltale shadow in the back door window.

Water slipped from his hair and down his spine.

A shudder briefly hunched his shoulders.

Closer, gun aimed toward the ceiling, and he braced himself, counted to three, and stepped quickly into the kitchen, sweeping the barrel ahead of him.

No one was there.

He eased back toward the living room, heard a scraping, and spun around as Scully came through the back door, a sharp shake of her head letting him know there was no one outside, and no sign of Elly.

Or the goblin.

No words, then. Hand signals told her they must be in the bedroom. She nodded, once, and he took the hall again, shoulders brushing along the wallpaper.

Listening, and hearing only the wind, only the rain.

When he sensed Scully directly behind him, he stepped in and crossed the floor in four long strides. The bedroom door was open, but it was too dark for him to see much more than the shadowed outline of a brass headboard.

Time, he thought; *no time.*

Scully positioned herself opposite him at the door, and at her nod, they went in, he high, she low.

"Damn." He kicked at the bed.

The room was empty.

They were too late; Elly Lang was gone.

Rosemary adjusted the bag's strap over her shoulder, smoothed the lapels of her coat, and shook her head.

"You're an idiot, Joseph," she said, opened the door, and left.

"Maybe she's hiding," Scully said.

Mulder doubted it, but together they took less than five minutes looking into every place large enough to hold a woman Elly's size, not at all surprised when all they found was dust and cans of orange spray paint.

He stood in the middle of the living room, absently tapping the gun against his leg.

"Think," he told himself. "Think!" When Scully rejoined him, he shook his head. "She either left on her own, or she's been taken. And I don't think she—"

The front door slammed open, and they instantly dropped into defensive crouches, their guns aimed and ready to fire.

"Hey, no!" Webber cried, throwing up his hands. "Jeez, guys, it's me!"

"Hank," Mulder said, ready to strangle him. He straightened stiffly and lowered his weapon. "You are an idiot. Don't you know better than that?"

Webber tried to point in several directions at once. "I'm sorry. I saw the car, and the outside door was open, and I thought . . ." He paled. "Jesus. Oh, Jesus." Without looking at either of them, he dropped into the chair and leaned over, hands dangling between his legs. "I could have been killed, you know that? I'm so stupid, I could have been killed."

Scully offered him no sympathy. She stood in front of him, and poked his foot with her shoe. "Where's Andrews?"

"What?" He looked up, confused. "What are you talking about? She was right—"

"Here," Andrews said, standing in the doorway. Her gun was out, and it was aimed at Mulder's head. "Right here."

"How much do you charge to go to the airport?" Rosemary asked the cabbie.

"Which one?"

"Philadelphia."

"Lady, are you kidding? In this weather?"

"Whatever it is," she said, holding up her purse, "I'll double it. For the trip over. And for your trip back."

He shook his head doubtfully. "Lady, I don't know. They're saying there's flash floods—"

She took out her gun. "You either make money, or you die." She smiled. "Your choice."

Andrews shifted to her right so she could still keep Mulder in her sights while keeping the wall at her right shoulder.

He held his empty hands wide at his sides. "You're not doing an awful lot of thinking."

She shrugged. She didn't much care. "Do I have to?" She shrugged again. "You're going to die, what's there to think about?"

"One against three is pretty awful odds," Scully said.

"Oh, God," Webber moaned. "I'm gonna be sick."

"Oh, shut up," Andrews snapped. "Christ, how the hell did you ever get in the Bureau?"

Mulder's gun was on the coffee table with Scully's, and all a leap for it would get him would be a bullet in the side, or in the head. Scully, who had been ordered to sit on the couch, was in no better position.

"Look," he said, "Elly is out there somewhere, with the goblin."

Webber sagged forward, one arm across his stomach. He sounded terrified. "Oh Christ." He retched dryly.

"What do I care about an old lady?" Andrews said. "And if you think you're going to stall me long enough for the cavalry to come, forget it. I watch movies, too, Mulder. I'm not as stupid as you think."

He denied any such idea with a shake of his head, and wished Webber would stop that infernal groaning. He couldn't hear himself think, and it was only making Andrews angrier than she already was. Then he snapped his fingers, making Scully jump and Andrews steady her gun hand. "Douglas." He frowned. "You work for Douglas?" His expression hardened. "Of course you do.

Because you're not Bureau at all. Which makes me wonder who the mighty Douglas really works for?"

"Time's up," she said blandly.

"Oh, God," Webber gasped and slipped off the chair and onto one knee. "Oh, God, I'm gonna die."

With a look, Andrews dared Scully to make a move, then swung the gun back to Mulder, and smiled him a farewell.

He threw himself backward just before he heard the shot, bracing himself for the impact, landing on his back and rolling to his left when he didn't feel a thing.

He heard Andrews cry out, though, and heard her fall, her gun clattering across the hall floor.

"Nice dive," Scully told him. She was on the floor by the table, her hand around her gun.

Webber pushed himself back into the chair and closed his eyes, his gun hand dangling over the armrest. "I almost missed her," he said to the ceiling. "Christ, can you believe it? I almost missed her."

Mulder jumped to his feet, angry and relieved at the same time. But he said nothing. He picked up his weapon, tucked it into his pocket, and stood over the fallen Andrews. Webber hadn't missed; the entry wound was through her right eye.

He pointed. "You will answer questions later, Hank. Right now, you stay with her. And I mean stay with her."

He didn't argue. His face was pale, his lips trembling; the only sign that he heard was a weak flutter of his hand.

Then Scully looked out the window and said, "Mulder, the park," and he was out the door at a run, taking the three steps at a leap.

She was there, on her bench, huddled beneath her umbrella, and probably had been there the whole time. He had been so intent on getting into the apartment, he hadn't bothered with a single glance across the street once he reached the building.

"Elly, are you all right?"

He slowed when he reached the sidewalk, walked when he started across the grass.

The woman nodded, but the umbrella was loose in her grip, and it nearly fell.

"It's okay, Elly," he said when he reached the bench. He leaned down and brushed a hand over her knee, then held up a hand to shade his eyes from the rain while he looked over the muddy field to the trees on the other side.

She could be there, he thought; damn, she could be anywhere.

"Mulder," the goblin said. "I thought I told you to watch your back."

TWENTY-FOUR

X With a silent sigh he stared at the ground, at rain-
drops splashing out of the grass. Then he looked
over his shoulder as he turned without haste, blinking the rain out of his eyes.

The umbrella had been discarded.

She sat on the bench back, wearing a long black coat that
reached halfway down her shins, her bare feet on the seat, braced
to spring. Her short dark hair was matted into a skullcap, her
large dark eyes slightly crinkled, as if she were smiling.

Her left hand lay on her thigh, fingers drumming out of
rhythm; her right hand held a bayonet, and he could see the
gleam of the sharpened edge as she tapped it against her
knee.

It was odd, this meeting. Like two friends coming across each
other on a rainy day in the park. Only, one of them, before it
ended, was going to die.

She raised an eyebrow. "I don't think so, Mulder. Not me,
anyway."

"You can read minds, too?"

"No. But you have that gun in your coat, and I have—" She held up the bayonet. "It's not hard to figure out."

The water had taken most of her makeup off, and had washed the white lotion from the backs of her hands. The skin was mottled as if it were dying and ready to slough away in the rain, but it wasn't just gray and black. He could see blotches of pale green, dark green, and near her toes a smear of something almost red.

It could have been blood.

"Where's Elly?"

Maddy shrugged. "I don't know. I tried to get in the back door, and the next thing I knew I heard the front door slam." She laughed so hoarsely it made his throat ache. "I didn't know an old lady could run so damn fast. I would have gone after her, but as luck would have it, you showed up."

Her eyes shifted away, shifted back.

"Tell her to be careful, Mulder," Maddy suggested. "You may be fast, and a bullet is real fast, but it won't stop me from doing what I have to, understand?"

"I heard," Scully said from somewhere behind him.

He spread his arms. "It's silly, you know. I die, you die, it isn't going to do you any good."

Her voice deepened. "I'm already dying." She held out her hand. "It doesn't work anymore."

He couldn't believe it when her fingers *shifted*, flesh to splotchy green to smooth cream, and back. Except two of her knuckles stayed dark far longer.

She giggled. "What a bitch, huh? Instead of getting famous, I'm getting dead."

He didn't know what to say. Somehow, "You're under arrest for murder" sounded awfully stupid.

She giggled again, and that was when he saw the madness— in the tilt of her head, the movement of her eyes.

"Why?" he asked, gesturing at her skin. "Didn't you know how dangerous it was?"

"Sure." She waved the bayonet idly. "But do you know how much a cop in a burg like this makes? A dispatcher? Do you know how much that bitch gave me every month?" She laughed and rocked back, rocked forward quickly, bracing herself again. "She had pictures, I saw them, I can read, I knew the risk. Besides . . ." Her voice faded.

He waited, not moving when she began to toy with the coat's buttons, opening them, closing them, opening some and leaving them.

She wore no clothes beneath the coat, and that didn't surprise him. For what she could do, and had to do, clothes would have been a problem.

What he needed now was for Scully to get into position to cover him when he made his move. He had to. He couldn't stand here, waiting for her to decide it was time, and he wasn't about to let her go. No matter how sorry for her he felt. Which he did as she began to ramble about the tests in the room below the hospital, about the solution baths and the injections, about spying on her friends and on strangers and—

"—feeling such a sense of goddamn power, Mulder. Power." She grinned; her teeth were brown and black. She whispered, "Power."

"Maddy," he said, "don't do this."

"Oh, knock it off," she snapped, straightening, the bayonet catching silver light from the rain. "You can't appeal to my better nature. I don't have one anymore. You can't offer me a cure. You, and you," she shouted to Scully, "can't offer me a damn thing."

"How about living a while longer?"

She laughed, and brushed a strand of hair from her eyes. "Who's going to stop me, you? Her?"

"I can bet Elly's called the police by now. They take one look at you, they won't stop to talk."

"Big deal. I'll be gone." She bounced a little on her rump. "Don't you know I'm the Invisible Woman?"

Her eyes again, shifting, frowning. Scully had moved to his left and was moving to get behind her. One step at a time.

"She's not fast enough, you know."

He lifted his right hand. "Fast enough, if she has to be."

Maddy tensed.

He knew it was coming, and as soon as he recognized it, the calm finally returned.

The wind nudged her, and she hugged herself, then slipped off the coat.

He only just managed to keep his expression from reacting to the sight of her, skin rough in one place, seemingly raw in another, dark clouds of color rippling across the ridged plane of her stomach.

"You know something?" she said, licking her lips, gauging distance.

"What?" He kept his voice quiet and steady.

"I learned a lot from that bitch. I'm going to tell her that before she dies."

"Like what? What can you learn from killing people?"

She grinned. "That I like it."

He saw her toes flex.

"Please," he said, just before she giggled.

Just before she jumped.

•　　•　　•

There was no time to pull his gun from his pocket. He twisted away from the blade and, at the same time, fired through the coat, lost his footing in the slippery grass and fell on his back.

Maddy screamed when she landed on her hands and knees, spun around, and tried to stand.

"Stop!" Scully ordered, rushing up, aiming low.

Mulder couldn't stand, couldn't move; he could only watch as Maddy Vincent feinted with the blade, then tried to run-crawl at him.

"Stop!" Scully yelled.

Maddy toppled onto one shoulder as if someone had put a boot in her back, and screamed again, stabbed the ground, and slumped whimpering into the mud.

As Mulder pushed himself to his feet, as Scully braced herself behind the woman, he saw the blood seep out from under her arm.

It didn't look black at all.

It looked red, and it didn't stop.

He leaned over and took the bayonet from her hand, held it close to his eyes for a moment, and placed it on the bench. Scully pressed three fingers to the side of the woman's neck, then checked her wrist. She rose awkwardly, a hand pushing through her hair, and Mulder took off his coat and spread it over the goblin's body.

He stared at it for a long while, until he laughed once, sharply, realizing he had been waiting for her, like the Invisible Man, to return to normal, now that the adventure was finally done.

But she didn't.

She just lay there.

Mulder didn't know how long it took to answer the questions, for Scully to make sure the body would be placed in the right hands for the proper examinations, for the cold to finally leave him, for him to finally feel dry.

But it was after eleven that night before he was able to sit in the Queen's Inn and stare at the plate of pancakes in front of Hank Webber.

"Please," Hank said. "Don't say it's amazing."

"It is, but I won't."

Scully was at the counter, ordering coffee and tea, and finding out just what the cook would make this late on Saturday night. Mulder waited until her back was turned, then lifted a finger to get Hank's attention.

"Protest not," he said. "Don't insult me with denials. But how many times have you called Douglas since we've arrived, to tell him how many times I didn't follow the book."

Webber almost choked, but he managed to hold up his fork and say, "Just once."

"What?"

He looked embarrassed. "I couldn't. I mean . . . I like you. And I didn't see that you were doing anything really wrong."

Mulder grinned as he stretched his arm across the back of the seat. "Webber, I don't care—that's damn amazing." He looked out the window, but all he saw was the night and the rain. "You know that Douglas is probably a plant, don't ask me by whom, and he probably won't be there when we get back. You know you'll probably be transferred somewhere else once we get back and the paperwork is done."

"Sure. I figured. But hell, it was fun while it lasted."

Mulder laughed, a little sadly, because he knew poor old Hank probably wouldn't be with the Bureau for very long. "Fun" wasn't exactly the way to describe the way it worked.

"And by the way," he said, "in all the excitement . . . thanks."

Webber waved it away. "Not needed, Mulder. I was just doing what I had to, you know?"

And he blushed.

Scully slid in then, clucked at Webber's choice of a meal, and fussed with her napkin while she waited for her order. "You do realize, Mulder, don't you, that that was an incredibly lucky shot. By all rights, you should be dead."

He knew that. He had especially known that when he had seen the rent across the front of his coat.

The blade had come a lot closer than he'd thought; it had sliced clear through the cloth.

"Don't ever try that again."

"Believe me," he said. "I won't."

They ate, then, in companionable, weary silence, interrupted only by a phone call he took at the register. When he returned to the booth, he only said, "They found Tonero's body. Shot once. He was in Dr. Elkhart's apartment."

"And her?" Scully asked.

"Gone. Not a trace."

"They'll find her," Webber said confidently. "After this week-end, half the country'll be hunting for her. Don't sweat it, Mulder, the case is closed."

"I suppose," Mulder said. He looked out the window, through the rivulets of rain. "I suppose."

Scully touched his shoulder, light and quick. "Mulder, don't."

He didn't look. "Sure."

They both knew he was lying.

Because, he thought, looking through his dim reflection to the woodland just beyond, what if they don't find her.

What if, next year, or the year after, you're walking down the street or climbing your steps or standing on your porch or you're waiting for a bus, and an arm comes out of a wall or a tree or . . .

He stretched a finger toward the glass, watching its reflection stretch toward him.

. . . a simple pane of glass.

The lights flickered for a moment, and for a moment the reflection vanished.

He rubbed his arm absently, watching the headlights of a car he couldn't see float past and disappear.

We'll never know they're out there—
Armies of living shadows.
Slipping through the night.

WHIRLWIND

This is for Kathryn Ptacek.

For lots of reasons, but in particular, this time, because I've mangled her New Mexico homeland before, and she still hasn't shot me.

ACKNOWLEDGMENTS

My gratitude and fond appreciation to the poor folks who had to listen, advise, and humor me over the past few months:

Caitlin Blasdell, who, for reasons known only to herself, puts up with all my calls, and has never once told me to stop bugging her and get back to work;

Steve Nesheim, M.D., for the wonderfully gruesome details, and for all the possibilities therein;

Wendy Webb, R.N., M.Ed., for taking those details and actually making them fun;

Geoffrey Marsh, for graciously allowing me to borrow the Konochine Indians for my own disgusting use;

The Jersey Conspiracy, as always, this time providing me with more dead bodies than I could possibly use this time around, and one drunk;

And Robert E. Vardeman, who never stops reminding me why it's nice to have good friends in far places.

ONE

The sun was white and hot, and the wind blew ceaselessly.

Annie Hatch stood alone on her ranch house porch, one hand absently rubbing her stomach as she tried to decide what to do. The late-morning sun made her squint, the temperature already riding near ninety.

But the wind that coasted across the high desert made her wish, for the first time in a long time, that she were back in California.

It hissed softly through the brush, and whispered softly in her ear.

Of course, she thought; you could also just be a doddering old fool.

A quick smile, a quicker sigh, and she inhaled slowly, deeply, taking in the heat, and the piñon, and, so faintly she might have been imagining it, a sweet touch of juniper.

Wind or not, voices or not, this was, all in all, far better than Hollywood.

That was where she and Burt had made their money, so many

years ago it might have been a dream; here was where they had finally made their lives, no dream at all.

A breath of melancholy fluttered her eyelids closed for a moment. It wasn't easy being a widow, even after fifteen years. There were still too many times when she thought she heard him clumping back from the stable behind the house, or whistling as he fiddled with the generator, or blowing gently on the back of her neck.

The wind did that to her, too.

"Enough," she muttered, and strode impatiently to the end of the porch, leaned over the waist-high, rough-hewn rail, and looked down the side of the adobe house to the stable. She whistled twice, high, sharp, and loud, and giggled silently when she heard Nando curse, not very subtly letting her know he hadn't finished saddling Diamond yet, was she trying to get him trampled?

A second later he appeared in the open doorway, hands on his wide hips, glaring at her from under his time-beaten Stetson.

She waved gaily; he gestured sharply in disgust and vanished again.

"That's cruel," a soft voice said behind her.

She laughed as she turned. "He loves it, Sil, and you know it."

Silvia Quintodo looked at her skeptically for as long as she could. Then she grinned broadly, shaking her head as if at a child too angelic to be punished. She was a round woman, face and figure, with straight black hair forever caught in a single braid that hung down her back. Her skin was almost copper, her large eyes the color of a starlit night. Today, as always, she wore a loose, plain white dress that reached to mid-shin, and russet deerskin boots.

"You're staring," she scolded lightly.

Annie blinked. "I am? I'm sorry. My mind was wandering." She stared at the weathered floorboards. "I guess I'm just feeling my age today, dear."

Silvia rolled her eyes—*oh, please, not again*—and returned inside to prepare an early lunch.

Annie thanked her silently for not feeding the self-pity.

In truth, she knew she wasn't so bad for an old lady of sixty-one. Her face was narrow, accentuating green eyes and dark, not quite thick, lips; the lines there were more from the sun than her age. Her hair was white, but softly so, cropped short and brushed straight back over her ears. Practical, but still lovely. And her slender figure was such that, even after all these years, she was still able to turn more than a few heads whenever she drove into the city or up to Santa Fe.

It was good for her ego.

Oh brother, she thought; it's worse than I thought.

What it was, was one of those days that crept up on her now and then—when she missed Burt so much it burned. There was never any particular reason for it, no specific thing that jogged her memory. It just happened. Like today. And the only cure was to take Diamond and a canteen and ride into the desert.

Maybe, if she were brave enough, all the way to the Mesa.

Sure, she thought; and tomorrow I'll wake up and find Burt beside me in bed.

A snort behind her made her jump.

She whirled just as Diamond thrust his head over the rail, his nose catching her stomach and shoving her back a step.

"Hey!" she said with a scolding laugh. "Knock it off, you big jerk."

He was already in bridle and saddle, a short black horse with a rough diamond blaze between his eyes. Nando stood beside him, grinning, one hand on the animal's rump, his stained brown hat pushed back on his head.

"Serves you right," he told her smugly. He could have been Silvia's twin, not her husband, save for the ragged streaks of gray in his hair, and the fact that his broad blunt nose had been broken too many times for him to be rightly called handsome. Those who didn't know him figured him for an ex-boxer or an ex-Marine, not the foreman of a ranch that wasn't much of a ranch anymore.

Annie made a show of ignoring him and his rebuke. She adjusted her straw Western hat, fixed the strap under her chin, and swung her legs easily over the rail. Without pause or hesitation, she grabbed the horn and swung lightly into the saddle. Only then did she look down at him. "Not bad for an old lady, huh?"

"The day you get old, *Señora*," he answered solemnly, "is the day I stop shoveling horse shit for a living and start selling bad turquoise to the tourists up Santa Fe."

Diamond shook his mane impatiently.

A warm gust made them turn their heads, but not before she saw the expression on his face.

When he looked back, he was somber. "It talks."

"I wouldn't know."

He shook his head slowly, not quite sadly. "You know. You always know."

She grabbed the reins angrily. "I know nothing of the sort, Nando." She was prepared to cluck Diamond away when Nando tapped her leg. "Now what?"

He reached behind him and pulled out a canteen. Grinning again: "No rain, no water." He tucked it into the silver-studded saddlebag.

She thanked him with a brusque nod and guided Diamond across the side lawn to a break in the double split-rail fence she had painted white the year before. Once through, she followed it around to the front, checking the grass inside to see where it was dying.

Everywhere, she realized; everywhere.

Despite the extraordinarily expensive, undoubtedly wasteful belowground system her late husband had installed himself and had connected to one of the score of deep wells on the ranch, the grass seldom survived intact all the way through the summer. Still, she thought as the ranch drifted away behind her, wasteful or not, it was better than nothing.

At least it had color.

At least it had life.

"All right," she snapped to the shadow that rode beside her. "All right, that's enough, Annie, that's enough."

Her right hand held the reins lightly; her left hand rested on her thigh, and it trembled.

She ignored it, concentrating instead on the rolling land ahead, automatically checking for wind or flash-flood damage to the narrow wood bridges Burt and Nando had built across the several arroyos meandering across the four thousand acres, glancing to her right every so often at the high heat-brown hill that blocked the sun each morning. Like the exposed knobby root of an ancient, distant tree, it flanked the recently paved road that led east to the interstate and west to the Mesa.

To the reservation.

She couldn't see it from here.

The hill crossed the road a half-mile ahead, still high, still marked with thorned shrubs and tufts of grass sharp enough to slice through a palm, still studded with large brown rocks and partially buried boulders.

Like a wall to keep the rest of the world out.

Or to keep the Konochine in.

For some, however, it wasn't high enough or strong enough.

They left to see what the world outside looked like, to discover what the world had to offer besides life on a reservation.

For her, it was Burt, and a brief but lucrative career in Hollywood; for others, unfortunately, it was prejudice and pain, and ultimately, a grave too far from home.

Diamond shied suddenly, forcing her to pay attention, to glance quickly at the ground for signs of rattlesnakes. They'd be

out now—the sun was high and warm enough—coiled deceptively still on whatever rocks they could find.

She saw none, and frowned her puzzlement when the horse
began to prance, telling her he wasn't thrilled about approaching
the ranch side of the hill.

That's when she saw the buzzards.

Five of them circled low near the two-lane road, and she
mouthed a sharp curse as she nudged the horse in that direction.
There weren't many cattle left; she had sold most of them off not
long after Burt had died, and seldom replaced the ones she lost.
Every so often, though, one of those remaining found a way
through the barbed wire that marked their pastures. Sometimes
they tumbled into an arroyo; sometimes a rattler got them; sometimes they just couldn't find the water or the food and simply
gave up, laid down, and died.

Closer, and she saw a van parked on the sandy shoulder, on
the far side of the fence that ran along the blacktop. Vague waves
of ghostly heat shimmered up from the road, blurring the vehicle's outline.

"What do you think?" she asked Diamond. "Tourists?"

The desert beyond the Sandia Mountains was beautiful in a
stark and desolate way, with flashes of color all the more beautiful
because they were so rare. It was also a trap. It wasn't unusual for
an unthinking tourist to pull over because he wanted to walk a little, stretch his legs, check things out. It also wasn't unusual for the
heat, and deceptive distance, to combine to lose him.

One minute, you could see everything; the next, you were
alone.

Sometimes he didn't make it back.

Another twenty yards, and Diamond pulled up short.

"Hey," she said. "Come on, don't be stupid."

He shook his head violently, reaching around to nip at her
boot, a sign he wasn't moving another inch.

She glared helplessly at the top of his head, watching his ears twitch in agitation. Forcing him would serve no purpose. He was as stubborn as she, and most definitely stronger.

"Can you say 'glue'?" she muttered sourly as she swung out of the saddle and ordered him to stay put. "Idiot."

Dusting her hands on her jeans, she trudged toward the van, scanning the area for whoever it was who had been stupid enough to leave it.

She hadn't gone a dozen yards when she heard the flies.

Her stomach tightened in anticipation, but she didn't stop. A check of the fence revealed no breaks in the wire, no toppled posts. The van itself was a dusty dark green, streaked with long-dried mud.

"Hello?" she called, just in case.

The flies sounded like bees.

The wind nudged her from behind.

She stepped around a sprawling juniper, and her left hand instantly clamped tightly to her stomach.

"Oh God," she whispered. "Dear Jesus."

It wasn't a lost cow.

There were two of them, and they lay facedown, arms and legs spread, unnaturally twisted. Flies crawled in undulating waves over them, thick and black, drifting into the air and drifting down again. Not five feet away, a buzzard watched, its wings flexing slowly.

It snapped its beak once.

Annie spun away and bent over, hands on her knees, eyes shut and stomach lurching, her throat working hard to keep the bile from rising.

She knew the bodies were human.

But only by their shape.

Even with the flies, even with the sun, it was clear they had been skinned.

TWO

X The sun was white and hot, and there was no wind.

Traffic in the nation's capital moved sullenly and loudly, while pedestrians, if they moved at all, glowered absently at the ground, praying that the next building they entered had its air conditioning working. In this prolonged July heat wave, that wasn't always the case.

Tempers were short to nonexistent, crimes of passion were up, and blame for the extreme discomfort was seldom aimed at the weather.

The office in the basement of the J. Edgar Hoover Building was, according to some, a working monument to the struggle of order over chaos.

It was long, not quite narrow, and divided in half by the remains of a floor-to-ceiling glass partition from which the door had long since been removed. Posters and notices were tacked and taped to the walls, and virtually every flat surface was covered by books, folders, or low stacks of paper. The lighting was dim, but it wasn't gloomy, and as usual, the air conditioning wasn't quite working.

In the back room, two men and a woman stared at a series of red-tabbed folders lying on a waist-high shelf. Each was open to the stark black-and-white photograph of a naked corpse, each corpse lying in the center of what appeared to be a tiled bathroom floor.

"I'm telling you, it's driving us nuts," the first man complained mildly. He was tall, solid, and a close-cropped redhead. His brown suit fit too snugly for real comfort. His tie had been pulled away from his collar and the collar button undone, the only concessions he made to the barely moving air. He wiped a hand over a tanned cheek, wiped the palm on his leg. "I mean, I know it's a signature, but I'll be damned if I can read it."

"Oh, put your glasses on, Stan," the woman muttered. She was near his height, her rounded face smooth, almost bland, with thin lips, and narrow eyes under dark brows. Unlike his clothes, her cream linen suit could have been tailored. "That's no signature, it's just slashes, for crying out loud. You're the one who's driving us nuts."

Stan Bournell closed his eyes briefly, as if in prayer. He said nothing.

"It's the bathroom that's important," she continued, her voice bored. It was clear to the second man that she had been on this route a hundred times. She pulled a tissue from a pocket and dabbed at her upper lip. "It's easier to clean, it's too small for the victim to hide in or run around in, and—"

"Beth, Beth," Bournell said wearily, "I know that, okay? I've got eyes. I can see."

The second man stood between them, hands easy on his hips. His jacket was draped over a chair in the other room with his tie, and the sleeves of his white shirt were rolled back twice. His face was unlined, and his age could have been anywhere from his late twenties to his mid-thirties, depending on how generous the estimate was.

Right now, he felt more like fifty.

The bickering had begun the moment the two agents had stormed into the office; the sniping had begun once the folders had been laid out.

He took a step away from them, closer to the work shelf.

They were both right.

He had read the files several days ago, at his section head's request, but he didn't tell the agents that; their tempers were frayed enough already.

He sniffed, and rubbed a thoughtful finger alongside his nose.

All five victims—or at least, the five the FBI was thus far aware of—had first been attacked in other rooms of their respective homes. Houses, not apartments; suburbs, not cities. All signs indicated little or no struggle after the initial assault, indicating knowledge of the attacker, or near-total surprise. They had been chloroformed just enough for immobility, then dragged elsewhere. All were women, all in their early twenties, and all had been murdered in their bathrooms.

Strangled with either an unfinished belt or rawhide strap, their bodies stripped to the waist, and a razor taken to their chests.

One slice each.

None had been raped.

Beth Neuhouse groaned and plucked at her blouse. "God, doesn't the air conditioning work in here? How can you work like this? It's like a sauna."

Fox Mulder shrugged unconcern, then pushed a hand back through his hair.

He checked each black-and-white in turn, his gaze flicking over them increasingly rapidly, as though he were reading.

"Well?" Bournell asked. "You got a magic trick for us? You got a rabbit we can chase?"

Mulder held up a hand to hush him, then slid the pictures from their folders and laid them out in a line. A moment later he switched the second and fourth.

"Mulder," Neuhouse said, "we haven't got all day. Either you've got something or you don't. Don't play games, okay?"

Mulder straightened, and almost smiled. "Beth, get me a sheet of paper, please?" His left hand gestured vaguely toward the other room.

It was his tone that moved her more than the request. Those who had worked with him before had heard it at least once. One of the older agents had said it was like the first bay of a hound that had finally found the scent; you didn't argue with it, you just followed.

And you made sure your gun was loaded.

Bournell frowned. "What? I don't see it."

Mulder pushed the photographs closer together and pointed. "It's there. I think." Sudden doubt made him hesitate. "I'm—"

"Here." Neuhouse thrust a blank sheet into his hand. She stared at the bodies then, and her voice quieted. "I've been looking at those women for over a month, Mulder. I'm seeing them in my sleep."

He knew exactly what she meant.

In many ways, the black-and-whites were as bad as looking at the bodies themselves. Although the color was gone, violent death wasn't. The only thing missing was the smell, and it wouldn't take much effort to bring that up, too.

"So what do we have?" Bournell asked.

"I'm not positive. It's kind of crazy."

Neuhouse laughed quietly. "Well, this is the place for it, right?"

Mulder smiled. No offense had been meant, and he hadn't

taken any. He knew his reputation in the Bureau, and it no longer bothered him. He was a flake, a maverick, a little around the bend on the other side of the river. He worked as much from logic and reason as anyone else, but there were times when he didn't have to take every single step along the way.

There were times when abrupt intuitive leaps put him ahead of the game.

Sometimes that was far enough to have it called magic.

Or, more often than not, spooky.

He put up with it because that reputation came in handy once in a while.

"Come on, Houdini," Bournell complained. "I'm frying in here."

Beth aimed a semiplayful slap at his arm. "Will you shut up and let the man think?"

"What think? All he has to do is—"

"Here," Mulder said, slapping the paper onto the shelf, indecision gone. He grabbed a pen from his shirt pocket. "Look at this."

The others leaned over his shoulders as he pointed to the first picture, but she wasn't the first victim. "The cut runs from just over her right breast to just under the left. In the next, it's the reverse."

"So?" Bournell said.

Mulder pointed again. "It could be the killer leans over and just cuts her." He straightened suddenly, and the others jumped back when his left hand demonstrated an angry, senseless slashing. "It could be, but I don't think so. Not this time." He pointed at the third woman. "This is clearly most of a letter, right?"

"R, maybe, if you combine it with the next one over," Neuhouse answered, glancing at her partner, daring him to contradict. "I know that much."

"Damn sloppy, then," Bournell said.

"For God's sake, Stan, he's slashing her! What the hell do you expect?"

Mulder copied the slash marks onto the paper, turned, and held it up.

They stared at it, puzzled, then stared at him—Bournell in confusion, Neuhouse with a disbelief that had her lips poised for a laugh.

"He's writing his name," Mulder told them. "He's letting you know who he is." He exhaled loudly. "One piece at a time."

The luncheonette was two blocks from FBI headquarters, a narrow corner shop with a long Formica counter and a half-dozen window booths, most of the decor done in pale blues and white. The windows had been tinted to cut the sun's glare, but it still threatened Mulder with a drumming headache whenever he glanced out at the traffic.

Once done with the sparring duo, he had grabbed his tie and jacket and fled, stomach growling unmercifully, his head threatening to expand far beyond its limits. Even now he could hear them arguing, with each other and with him, telling him, and each other, that he was out of his freaking mind. Killers did not write their names on victims' bodies; at least, they sure didn't do it in classical Greek.

And when they finally, reluctantly, accepted it, they demanded to know who the killer was and why he did it.

Mulder didn't have any answers, and he told them that more than once.

When it had finally sunk in, they had stormed out as loudly as they'd stormed in, and he had stared at the door for nearly a full minute before deciding he'd better get out now, before the echoes of their bickering gave him a splitting headache.

The trouble was, stomach or not, the nattering and the heat had combined to kill his appetite. The burger and fries looked greasy enough to be delicious, but he couldn't bring himself to pick anything up, even for a taste. Dumb, perhaps, but still, he couldn't do it.

A siren screamed; a police car raced down the center of the crowded street.

In the booth ahead of him, two couples chattered about baseball while at the same time they damned the heat wave that had been sitting on Washington for nearly two weeks.

On his right, on the last counter stool, an old man in a worn cardigan and golf cap listened to a portable radio, a talk show whose callers wanted to know what the local government was going to do about the looming water shortage and constant brownouts. A handful were old enough to still want to blame the Russians.

Mulder sighed and rubbed his eyes.

In calmer times, it was nice to know his expertise was appreciated; in times like these, exacerbated by the prolonged heat, he wished the world would leave him the hell alone.

He picked up a french fry and stared at it glumly.

The radio announced a film festival on one of the cable channels. Old films from the forties and fifties. Not at all guaranteed to be good, just fun.

He grunted, and popped the fry into his mouth. All right, he thought; I can hole up at home with Bogart for a while.

He smiled to himself.

The more he thought about it, the more he liked the idea. In fact, he thought as he picked up the burger, it sounded like exactly what he needed.

He was finished before he realized he had eaten a single bite. A good sign.

He grinned more broadly when a woman slipped into the booth and stared in disgust at his plate.

"You know," his partner said, "your arteries must be a scientific wonder."

He reached for the last fry, and Dana Scully slapped the back of his hand.

"Take a break and listen. We're wanted."

She was near his age and shorter, her face slightly rounded, light auburn hair settling softly on her shoulders. More than once, the object of one of their manhunts had thought her too feminine to be an obstacle. Not a single one of them had held that thought for very long.

Mulder wiped his mouth with a napkin, the grin easing to a tentative smile. "Wanted?"

"Skinner," she told him. "First thing in the morning. No excuses."

The smile held, but there was something new in his eyes. Anticipation, and a faint glimmer of excitement.

Assistant Director Skinner asking for them now, while they were both in the midst of cases still pending, generally meant only one thing.

Somewhere out there was an X-File, waiting.

"Maybe," she said, as if reading his mind. She snatched the last fry and bit it in half. An eyebrow lifted. "Or maybe you're just in trouble again."

THREE

X Twilight promised the desert, and the city at the base of the Sandia Mountains, a pleasantly cool evening. The heat had already begun to dissipate, and a wandering breeze raised wobbly dust devils along the interstate that stretched from Albuquerque to Santa Fe. Snakes sought their dens. A roadrunner streaked through a small corral, delighting a group of children who didn't want to leave their riding lessons. A hawk danced with the thermals.

On the low bank of the Rio Grande, beneath a stretch of heavy-crowned cottonwoods, Paulie Deven snapped pebbles and stones at the shallow water, cursing each time he hit the dried mud instead.

He hated New Mexico.

The Rio Grande was supposed to be this wide awesome river, deep, with rapids and cliffs, all that good stuff.

But not here. Here, he could almost spit across it, and most of the time it hardly held any water. You could forget about the cliffs, and rapids were out of the question.

He threw another stone.

Behind him, he could hear muffled music coming from the trailer his parents had rented from the developer until their new house was finished. That was supposed to have been three months ago, when they had arrived from Chicago. But some kind of permits were wrong, and then there was some kind of strike, and . . . and . . . He snarled and threw another rock, so hard he felt a twinge in his shoulder.

He thought he was going to live in the West. Maybe not the Old West, but it was supposed to be the West.

What his folks had done was simply trade one damn city for another. Except that he had belonged back in Chicago; back there the kids didn't get on his case because of the way he looked and sounded.

A light fall of pebbles startled him, but he didn't look around. It was probably his pain-in-the-ass sister, sliding down the slope to tell him Mom and Dad wanted him back in the trailer now, before some wild animal dragged him into the desert and ate him for breakfast.

Right.

Like there was anything out there big enough to eat something built like a football player.

"Paulie?"

He glanced over his left shoulder. "You blind, or what?"

Patty sneered and plopped down beside him. She was a year younger than his seventeen, her glasses thick, her brain thicker, her hair in two clumsy braids that thumped against her chest. He wasn't exactly stupid, but he sure felt that way whenever she was around.

She pulled her legs up and hugged her knees. "Not much of a river, is it?"

"Good eyes."

"They're fighting again."

Big surprise.

Ever since they had moved into the trailer, they had been fighting—about the house, about the move, about his Dad being close to losing his job, about practically anything they could. A damn war had practically started when he'd taken some of his savings and bought himself an Indian pendant on a beaded string. His father called him a goddamn faggot hippie, his mother defended him, and Paulie had finally slammed outside before his temper forced him to start swinging.

Patty rested her chin on her knees and stared at the sluggish water. Then she turned her head. "Paulie, are you going to run away?"

He couldn't believe it. "What?"

She shrugged, looked back at the river. "The way you've been acting, I thought . . . I don't know . . . I thought maybe you were going to try to get back to Chicago."

"I wish." He threw another rock; it hit the mud on the far side. "You ever think about it?"

"All the time."

That amazed him. Patty was the brain, the one with the level head, the one who never let anything get to her, ever. He hated to admit it, but he had lost count of the number of times she had saved his ass just by talking their folks into forgetting they were mad. Running away, running back home, was his kind of no-brain plan, not hers.

The sun died.

Night slipped from the cottonwoods.

A few stray lights from the trailer, from the handful of others on the other lots and the homes on the far side, were caught in fragments in the river, just enough to let him know it was still there.

Suddenly he didn't like the idea of being alone. "You're not going to do it, are you?"

She giggled. "You nuts? Leave this paradise?" She giggled again. "Sorry, Paulie, but I've got two years till graduation. I'm not going to screw it up, no matter what." She turned her head again; all he saw was her eyes. "But then, I swear to God, I'm going to blow this town so goddamn fast, you won't even remember what I look like."

He grinned. "That won't be hard."

"And the horse you rode in on, brother."

"I hate horses, too. Their manure smells like shit."

A second passed in silence before they exploded into laughter, covering their mouths, half-closing their eyes, rocking on their buttocks until Patty got the hiccups, and Paulie took great pleasure in thumping her back until she punched his arm away.

"I'm serious," she insisted, her face flushed. "I'm not kidding."

"Yeah, well." He watched the black water, rubbed a finger under his nose. "So am I."

Angry voices rose briefly above the music.

A door slammed somewhere else, and a pickup's engine gunned to launch the squealing of tires.

Off to their left, beyond the last tree, something began to hiss.

Paulie heard it first and frowned as he looked upriver, trying to see through the dark. "Pat?"

"Huh?"

"Do snakes come out at night?"

"What are you talking about? What snakes?"

He reached over and grabbed her arm to hush her up.

Hissing, slow and steady, almost too soft to hear.

"No," she whispered, a slight tremor in her voice. "At least, I don't think so. It's too cool, you know? They like it hot, or something."

Maybe she was right, but it sure sounded like snakes to him. A whole bunch of them, over there where none of the lights reached, about a hundred feet away.

Patty touched his hand, to get him to release her and to tell him she heard it, too. Whatever it was.

They couldn't see a thing.

Overhead, the breeze coasted through the leaves, and he looked up sharply, holding his breath until he realized what it was.

That was another thing he hated about this stupid place: it made too many sounds he couldn't identify, especially after sunset.

Every one of them gave him the creeps.

The hissing moved.

Except now it sounded like rapid, hoarse whispering, and Paulie shifted up to one knee, straining to make out something, anything, that would give him a clue as to who was out there and what they were doing.

Patty crawled up behind him, a hand resting on his back. "Let's get out of here, Paulie, huh?"

He shook his head obstinately. It was bad enough he was here because his folks had had some shit-for-brains idea about starting over, when they already had a perfectly good business back up North. He definitely wasn't going to let the buttheads here frighten him off.

City boy.

They called him "city boy" at school, their lips curled, their voices sneering, unimpressed by his size or the glares that he gave them.

Yeah, sure. Like this wasn't a city, right? Like they didn't have traffic jams, right? Like people didn't shoot and stab and stomp each other here like they did in Chicago, right?

The dark moved.

The hissing moved.

"Paulie?"

He swayed to his feet, trying not to make too much noise. His hands wiped across his jeans and curled into fists. Now they had made him angry.

"Paulie, come on."

"Go back up," he ordered without turning around.

Something had definitely moved out there, probably a bunch of wiseass kids trying to creep toward him. He took a sideways step up the uneven bank; his foot nudged a short length of dead branch. Without taking his eyes off the dark, he reached down and picked it up.

"Paulie."

"Go up!" he snapped, louder than he'd intended. "Damnit, Patty."

Staring so hard made him dizzy. It was like trying to pin down the edges of a black fog.

His free hand rubbed his eyes quickly and hard, but nothing changed.

There just wasn't enough light.

This, he thought, is really dumb. Get your ass outta here before something happens.

An arm snaked over his shoulder, and he bit so hard on a yelp that he choked.

Patty's hand opened to show him the dim gleam of a gold cigarette lighter. He took it and half-turned, his expression demanding to know when she'd started smoking. He realized the ridiculous timing when she flashed him a *not now, stupid* grin and jerked her chin to turn him back around.

His own smile had no humor.

He shifted the branch club until it felt properly balanced. Then he took a bold step forward and squared his shoulders. "Listen, assholes, you want to get lost, you want to get hurt, your choice."

No one answered.

Only the hissing.

He held the lighter up and sparked it, squinting against the reach of the flame's faint yellow glow until his vision adjusted. There were shadows now that slid away and slid toward him as he raised the light over his head and moved his arm from side to side. The trees moved; the leaves turned gray; the bank took on contours that didn't exist.

"Hey!"

Another step.

"Hey!"

Another.

The breeze touched the back of his neck and twisted the flame to make the shadows writhe.

They kept coming, still whispering, and he gripped the club more tightly, angling it away from his leg, ready to swing at the first face that broke through the dark into the light. It wouldn't be the first time he smacked a homer with just one arm.

A low branch brushed leaves across his right cheek and shoulder before he could duck away.

He thought he heard Patty snap his name, but he wasn't sure. All sound had been reduced to his sneakers sliding over the ground, to the breeze tucked into the branches, and to the whispering.

He frowned.

No; it wasn't whispering.

It was, as he'd first thought, hissing. But strange. It wasn't like snakes at all, but like something . . . no, a lot of things brushing roughly over a rough surface.

Voices whispering.

He faltered, and licked his lips.

Okay, so maybe it wasn't people out there, and Patty said it probably wasn't snakes, and it sure wasn't the river.

So what the hell was it?

The breeze moved the leaves, and he looked up quickly, looked back and smiled.

That's what it was—someone dragging a branch along the ground. Leaves; the hissing was the leaves.

Growing louder.

Suddenly the lighter grew too hot to hold. He cursed soundlessly and let the flame die, whipping his hand back and forth to cool his fingers off, and the metal, so he could use it again in a hurry.

Timing now was everything.

He would wait until the asshole was close enough, then he'd turn on the light and swing at the same time. The jerk would never know what hit him.

He listened, a corner of his mouth twitching, his body adjusting slightly so that he was almost in a baseball stance.

Batter up, he thought; you goddamn freaks.

Louder.

No footsteps yet, but that didn't matter.

He checked back, but couldn't see his sister; he looked ahead, and made out a faint shadow that, because of virtually absent light, seemed taller than it ought to be.

Louder.

Very loud.

City boy, he thought angrily, and flicked on the lighter.

He didn't swing.

His sister screamed.

He couldn't swing.

His sister shrieked.

So did Paulie.

FOUR

 Assistant Director Walter Skinner sat behind his desk, hands folded loosely in his lap, and stared absently at the ceiling for several seconds before lowering his gaze. He was not smiling. On the desk, in the center of the blotter, was an open folder. He looked at it disdainfully, shook his head once, and took off his wire-rimmed glasses. Thumb and forefinger massaged the bridge of his nose.

Mulder said nothing, and in the chair beside him, Scully's expression was perfectly noncommittal.

So far, the meeting hadn't gone well.

The entire transcript of a six-month wiretap on a Mafia don in Pittsburgh had been misplaced, and Mulder, arriving first, had walked straight into the teeth of the storm Skinner directed at his secretary and several red-faced agents. Mulder had been the target of the man's temper before, and he slipped hastily into the inner office with little more than a *here I am* nod.

Then he had committed the protocol error of taking a seat without being asked. When Skinner walked in, his face flushed with exasperation, Mulder wasn't quick enough to get to his feet, and the assistant director's curt greeting wouldn't have melted in a blast furnace.

It had been all downhill from there, even after Scully arrived, with Skinner raging quietly against those whose carelessness had imperiled an important investigation.

Mulder bore it all without comment.

At least the man wasn't raging against him for a change, which had not always been the case in the past.

Then, as now, the bone of contention between them was usually the X-Files.

The FBI's law enforcement mandate covered a multitude of federal crimes, from kidnapping to extortion, political assassination to bank robbery; it also permitted them to investigate local cases when local authorities asked them for assistance and the affair was such that it might be construed to be of potential federal interest, generally involving national security.

Not always, however.

Occasionally there were some cases that defied legal, sometimes rational, definition.

Cases that seemed to include instances of the paranormal, the inexplicable and bizarre, or the allegation that UFO activity was somehow involved.

X-Files.

They were Mulder's abiding, often single-minded, concern, and the core of his conviction that, X-File or not, the truth was not always as evident as it appeared to be. Nor was it always liberating or welcome.

But it was out there, and he was determined to find it.

And expose it.

The cost was immaterial; he had his reasons.

Skinner thumped a heavy hand on the folder. "Mulder . . ." He paused, the lighting reflecting off his glasses, banishing his eyes unnervingly until his head shifted. "Mulder, how in the name of heaven do you expect me to believe that this murderer is actually writing his name on his victims' chests?"

It was the tone more than the words that told him the director was actually concerned about something else.

"I thought it was obvious, sir, once the patterns had been established."

Skinner stared at him for several seconds before he said, flatly, "Right."

A glance to Scully told Mulder he wasn't wrong about the director's focus; it also told him he had somehow stepped on someone else's toes. Again. As usual.

He was, as he had told her more than once, a lousy Bureau dancer.

There in fact were few things that frustrated him more than internal Bureau politics. He supposed he should have known, given the personalities currently involved, that it would have been more politic to let either Neuhouse or Bournell come up with the solution on their own. He should have only been the guide. Suggesting instead of declaring.

And, given the personalities involved, he should have also guessed that one of them, probably Bournell, would have complained that Mulder was trying to steal the case, and thus the credit, from under them.

"Sir?" It was Scully.

Skinner shifted his eyes; the rest of him didn't move.

"As I understand it, there's a serious time constraint here. By his already established schedule, the killer is due to strike again within the next two weeks. Possibly sooner. Anything Agent Mulder is able to give them at this stage, any guidance he can offer, despite the pressure of his own caseload, can only be helpful, not an interference."

Mulder nodded carefully; his other reaction would have been to laugh.

"Besides," Scully added blandly as the director replaced his glasses, "I doubt Mulder thinks this one is strange enough to tempt him."

Skinner looked at him, unblinking. "I can believe that, Agent Scully."

Mulder couldn't decipher the man's expression. He couldn't forget that it had been Skinner who had once shut down the X-Files on orders from higher up, from those who didn't like the way Mulder learned too much of what, from their point of view, didn't concern him; nor could he forget that it was Skinner who had ordered opened the X-Files again, and Mulder suspected the director hadn't had much support.

It was confusing.

Skinner was neither all-out enemy nor all-out ally. Despite the profile of his position, he was a shadow, and Mulder was never quite sure what the shadow was, or what cast it.

"Excuse me, sir," he said carefully. "Am I being reprimanded for lending requested assistance?"

"No, Agent Mulder," the director said wearily. "No, you're not." He rubbed the bridge again, this time without removing the glasses. "The record shows I called you in. It doesn't have to say what we talked about. But next time, do me a favor— save me some trouble and phone calls, and let someone else figure it out for a change. As Agent Scully suggested, be the guide."

He didn't smile.

Neither did the others.

Finally, he slapped the folder closed and indicated with a nod that they could leave. But as they reached the doorway, he added, "Greek, Mulder?"

"Classical Greek, sir."

The man nodded. "Of course."

Mulder resisted the temptation to salute and followed Scully into the hall, where she suggested coffee in the cafeteria, iced tea for him.

"You know," he said as they made their way down the hall, "I appreciate the support, Scully, but I don't need defending. Not really."

She looked up at him and sighed. "Oh yes you do, Mulder."

He looked back blankly.

"Trust me," she said, patting his arm. "On this one you'll have to trust me."

His temper didn't flare until later that afternoon.

He had been halfheartedly sorting through a half-dozen new cases dropped on his desk for evaluation. His Oxford-trained expertise in criminal behavior, and his natural talent for discovering patterns and traces where none seemed to exist, were natural magnets for investigations that had suddenly or inevitably run into a roadblock.

He didn't mind it; he enjoyed it.

What made him angry now was the admittedly unfounded suspicion that Bournell and Neuhouse had deliberately set him up for a reprimand. They were not incompetent. They were definitely not stupid. Given enough time, they would have undoubtedly seen what he had seen; and the Bureau was crawling with experts—either here in the city or out at Quantico—who could have reached the same conclusions.

He leaned back in his chair, stretched out his legs, and stared at the closed door.

A droplet of sweat rolled untouched down his cheek.

He couldn't help wondering if They were after him again— the unseen powers he had labeled the Shadow Government; the people who knew more than they let on about the truth he himself knew existed in the X-Files.

It wasn't paranoia.

On more than one occasion, they had tried to discredit him, and thus have him fired.

On more than one occasion, they had tried to kill him.

And Scully.

Only the fact that he had somehow attracted friends in that same gray land of shifting shadows kept him alive and functioning, and he knew it.

Now it was possible They were at it again. Nibbling at him this time. Distracting him. Possibly hoping to force him into a careless mistake on one of the cases he needed to study. He had learned the hard way that there was only so much Skinner and the unknowns could do to protect him.

"I should have told them it was Russian," he whispered to the floor.

And laughed.

Suddenly the door slammed open, nearly spilling him out of the chair. Bournell stood on the threshold, pointing at him.

"Mulder, who knows old Greek?" the agent demanded hoarsely.

Mulder shrugged. "I don't know. Old Greeks?"

Bournell blinked slowly, took a step into the office just as a hush of cold air spilled out of the vents. He made as if to close the door behind them, and changed his mind. Instead, he slipped one hand into a pocket.

"Priests, Mulder. Seminarians. Teachers in a seminary. Preachers, Mulder. Ministers." His free hand took a slow swipe of his tie. "People, Mulder, who study the Bible."

Mulder waited patiently, unmoving. He suspected it wouldn't exactly do to mention that the list might also include professors of ancient languages, archaeology, and who knew what else. Not to mention immigrants who had been schooled in Greece. Or nonacademic scholars of at least a dozen different disciplines, both scientific and otherwise. The man was excited about something, and he didn't want to throw him off.

"I got to thinking," the agent continued, a finger tapping the face of the closest filing cabinet. "You were right about the Greek part, and I've kicked myself a dozen times for not noticing it before. But I have to tell you I think you're wrong about the name."

Mulder sat up slowly, drawing in his legs, tilting his head, eyes slightly narrowed. "How?"

"I was in a fraternity in college."

"A sorority would have been more fun."

Bournell glared at him in faint disgust until he lifted a hand in apology.

"Okay. So you were in a fraternity. What does that have to do with—"

"Alpha Chi Rho, it was." He held out his right hand; on it was an impressive signet ring, a faceted dark ruby centered in gold. He took a step closer so Mulder could see it more clearly. "On the rim, Mulder. Check out the rim."

He did, saw the three raised letters, and held his breath.

The hand dropped away. "Chi Rho. The symbol for Christ, Mulder." There was glee in his voice, in the way his hand danced at his side. "That's what he carved: Chi Rho." A sharp nod, a slap of the hand against his thigh. "Those women aren't hookers, that would be too easy. But I'll bet the farm and farmhouse there's something about them, a connection, that a religious fanatic might find to be . . . I don't know, sinful."

Mulder sat back, admiration clear. "I'll be damned."

Bournell smiled, rubbed his palms together, and glanced toward the vent. "Man, it's like an icebox in here. Your thermostat busted or what?" He headed for the door, grabbed the knob, and paused before leaving.

Mulder watched his shoulders tense, and relax.

"Hey, thanks, Mulder. No kidding. To be honest, I don't know if I really ever would have seen that Greek stuff. I've had this ring forever and hardly ever looked at it. But I just had it cleaned, and when I was putting it on this morning . . . well, it got me thinking, you know? And the next thing I knew I was looking at it like I'd never seen it before."

He hesitated, about to say something else, then nodded his thanks and closed the door behind him.

Mulder didn't move for a long time.

FIVE

Sheriff Chuck Sparrow took off his hat, wiped a forearm over what was left of his hair, and slapped the hat back into place, yanking the brim down hard.

"What do you think?" the woman beside him asked, her voice tight with the effort not to lose her dinner.

Sparrow shook his head. The best he could figure, either somebody was in sore desperate need to practice his tanning skills, or there was another one of those damn cults holed up in the hills again. Either way, it didn't take a brain surgeon to see that he was in for a hell of a lot more work than his inclination wanted.

They stood side by side near the mouth of a small cave, on the west side of a solitary low hill two miles west of the Hatch ranch. Sprawled in front of it was what was left of a steer, ants and flies now vying for the right to rid the dead animal of whatever they could take.

"What do you think?"

"Donna," he said, "I wish to hell I knew."

She was a tall woman, her figure hidden in boots, baggy jeans, and a man's shirt about a size too large. Her short brown hair was brushed back over her ears, and on her right hand she wore the biggest silver ring Sparrow had ever seen. Her Cherokee was parked on the shoulder, fifty yards away; his patrol car was behind it.

She jutted her chin toward the cave. "You look in there?"

"Yes," he answered with exaggerated patience. "Yes, I looked in there."

"And?"

"And fourteen different kinds of shit is all that I found, all right? Bones. Little bones," he added hastily. "The usual crap."

"I read that they use them, you know. Kind of temporary, so to speak."

He scanned the hillside, squinted at the vehicles. "Now don't take this wrong, all right? But there hasn't been a damn mountain lion around here for nearly as long as I've been working this job. And in case you hadn't noticed, they don't generally skin their meals before they eat them."

"I don't need your sarcasm, Chuck."

No, he thought; what you need is a good swat upside the head, keep you from bothering the hell outta me.

The trouble was, this was the fourth animal he'd come across in just over a week slaughtered like this, and not a single sign, not a single print, not a single goddamn hint of what had killed them. Or rather, what had stripped off their hides. For no reason he could put a finger on, he didn't think they had been killed first. He reckoned the creatures had either died of the shock or had bled to death.

Just like he was about to die of the smell if he didn't get out of here.

He brushed a hand over his mouth as he turned and walked back to the car. Donna followed him slowly, humming to herself and snapping her fingers.

The thing of it was, Sparrow thought as he slid down the shallow ditch and took two grunting strides up the other side, if this was confined to just animals, there wouldn't be such a stink of another kind in the office.

That there were also three people dead, obviously of the same thing—whatever the hell that was—had put the fire on. So to speak. And every time someone called in with another claim, it was Sparrow who personally checked it out. It wasn't that he didn't trust any of his deputies. Thirty-five years roaming the side roads of the desert, talking to the Indians in Santo Domingo, San Felipe, and the other pueblos, getting to know the hills and mountains until he could walk them practically blindfolded, did that to a man—made him the so-called area expert, even when he didn't want to be, hadn't asked to be, and would have given his right arm just to be plain stupid.

He reached in the driver's side window and grabbed the mike, called in and told the dispatcher what he'd found and where. While Donna watched him distrustfully, he ordered a van to pick up the carcass, and a vet standing by to handle the examination. When he was finished, he dropped the mike onto the seat and leaned back against the door, arms folded across a chest nearly as broad as the stomach below it.

"You think you might go talk to Annie?" She stood in the middle of the two-lane road, sketching senseless patterns in the dust that turned the blacktop gray.

"What for?" He waved vaguely to his right. "Her place is too far away."

"Might be one of hers."

"Probably," he admitted. Then he gestured toward the hill, meaning what lay a mile or so beyond, what some of the locals called the Konochine Wall. "Might be one of theirs, too, you ever think of that?"

She didn't look, and he smiled. Donna Falkner didn't much

care for the Konochine. For years they had refused her offers to broker whatever craftwork they wanted to sell; once they had even chased her off the reservation. Literally chased her, yelling and waving whatever came to hand, as if they wanted to drag her up Sangre Viento Mesa and drop her off, just as they had done to the Spanish priests and soldiers during the Pueblo Revolt over three hundred years before.

The difference was, the Spaniards never returned to the Konochine. No one knew why.

Now there was a middleman, Nick Lanaya, who worked with her, so she never had to set foot on the reservation at all.

"Satanists," Donna suggested then, still toeing the blacktop, hands in her hip pockets.

Sparrow snorted. He had been through the entire list of the usuals, from Satanists all the way to half-assed dopeheads who thought they could bring on a better world by chopping the heads off calves and goats. None of them, as far as he knew, killed like this, or killed both animals and people quite so ruthlessly and left the bodies behind.

But then, he wasn't an expert there, and he sighed as he finally admitted that maybe it was time to bring those experts in. Pride and getting nowhere fast were getting him crucified in the papers.

Two men sat on a hillside, their loose-fitting clothes as brown and tan as the ground around them. The first was old, his straight hair dull white and touching his bony shoulders. The planes of his face were sharp, the dark skin crevassed around the mouth and deep-set eyes. There was a necklace of rattlesnake spine around his neck.

The second man was much younger, but not young. His hair was still black, pulled back into a ponytail held by a braided circlet of gold and turquoise. His knees were drawn up, and his hands dangled between them, long fingers constantly moving like reeds in a slow wind.

When they spoke, which wasn't often, it was in a combination of bastard Spanish and Konochine.

"Father," the younger man said, attitude and voice deferential and weary, "you have to stop it."

The old man shook his head.

"But you know what he's doing. He's damning us all."

No answer.

The younger man reached for a tuft of grass, stopping himself just before he grabbed it. The blades were sharp; had he pulled, they would have drawn blood. He grabbed a stone instead and flung it hard down the slope.

Below was the road that led out of the gap, past Annie Hatch's ranch to the interstate. Behind was Sangre Viento Mesa.

"People are dying, Dugan," he said at last, abandoning honorifics for first names. "He takes them as far away as Albuquerque now." He didn't turn his head; he knew the old man wasn't watching. "It's gotten too big to hide. They're going to come sooner or later, the authorities. We won't be able to keep them out."

The old man touched his necklace. "They can come, Nick. They can look. They won't find anything."

"And if they do?" the younger man persisted.

The old man almost smiled. "They won't believe it."

Donna watched the sheriff's car speed away, dust swirling into rooster tails from its rear tires. She knew his ego had taken a fierce beating because he hadn't yet been able to locate the cult behind the atrocities, but she didn't think he or the city police were looking in the right place. Haunting the downtown Albuquerque bars and sending undercover men to the university wasn't going to accomplish anything but pay out more overtime.

She squinted at the sky, saw nothing but a wisp of a cloud that looked lost amid all that washed-out blue.

The *Journal* and the *Tribune* were screaming for someone's blood, and if Sparrow didn't watch out, it was going to be his.

Not, she thought sourly as she headed back to her car, that it was any concern of hers. He was a big boy. He could take care of himself. Just because he never paid her any mind whenever she tried to give him a hand, just because he thought she was a little off-center, just because he never gave her the time of day unless she asked him right out . . .

"Shit," she said, and kicked at the Cherokee's front tire. "Idiot."

She swung herself in, hissing sharply when her fingers grabbed the hot steering wheel and snapped away. A pair of colorless work gloves lay on the passenger seat, and she slipped them on, glancing in the rearview mirror, then looked toward the hill and the cloud of flies that marked the steer's carcass. Her stomach lurched; a slow deep breath settled it.

This wasn't like her at all.

She had seen worse out in the desert, and much worse in town, after a knife fight or a shooting. She had no idea why this spooked her so much.

A quick turn of the key fired the engine, and another glance in the rearview nearly made her scream.

A pickup more rust and dust than red streaked directly toward her rear bumper, sunlight exploding from the windshield, the grill like a mouth of gleaming shark's teeth.

She braced herself for the impact, but the truck swerved at the last second, slowed abruptly, and passed her so sedately she wondered if it had really been speeding at all, if it hadn't been her imagination.

A look to her right, and the other driver stared back.

Oh God, she thought.

A gray hat pulled low, black sunglasses, long black hair in a ponytail that reached to the center of the man's back.

Leon Ciola.

She didn't realize she was holding her breath until the pickup disappeared ahead of the dust its tires raised; then she sagged against the seat, tilted her head back, and closed her eyes. Air conditioning spilled across her lap; she shivered but didn't turn it down or deflect it elsewhere. She kept her eyes closed until she couldn't stand it. When they opened, she was alone; even the dust had gone.

Go, she ordered as she swallowed dryly; go home, girl.

It took her ten minutes before she could take the wheel again without shaking, another ten minutes before she realized she wasn't moving and tromped on the accelerator, ignoring the machine gun that rattled beneath the carriage, fighting the fishtail until the vehicle straightened, and the sun made her blind to everything but the road.

Home first, and a drink. Then she would call Sparrow and tell him Ciola was back.

She had a feeling the sheriff would be royally pissed.

The younger man stood, mock-groaning as he rubbed the small of his back and stretched his legs to relieve the stiffness. He tried again:

"Dugan, we can't let this happen. It will ruin everything we've worked for."

The old man didn't rise, didn't look back. His gaze seemed to focus on the dust clouds in the distance. "We can't stop it, Nick."

"Maybe not, but we can stop him."

"We don't know for sure."

But damnit, we do, the younger man thought angrily; we know damn well it's him, and we're doing nothing about it. Nothing at all.

Asked softly: "What if you're wrong?"

Nick shook his head, though he knew the old man couldn't see it. "If I am wrong, what have we lost? The Anglos come in, they look around, they go away, we're left alone. What have we lost, Dugan?"

Answered softly: "What is ours."

Again the younger man shook his head. This was an argument as old as he, and older: let more of the world in, it can be done without loss, we have television and radio, for crying out loud; or, keep the world out because it has nothing to do with what makes us what we are.

It was the reason the young were leaving, many of them not coming back.

In a single motion so rapid and smooth it seemed like no motion at all, the old man was on his feet, dusting off his pants, checking the time by the sun. Without speaking he walked to the top of the hill, Nick following to one side and a step behind. When they reached the crest, Dugan pointed to the pale ghost of the moon.

"One more night and it will be done."

Nick said nothing, and the silence spelled his doubt.

"One more night." The old man took his arm; the way down into the valley was slippery and steep. "It takes faith these days, you know." The hint of a smile. "A lot more than it used to, I'm afraid. But it is there."

It wasn't the faith Nick worried about. He had it, too, and even during his time in the outside world, he had kept it.

It wasn't the faith.

It was the killing.

It was what the killing would bring.

SIX

Mulder strolled into his office whistling.

It was the kind of day that began with a gorgeous, unreal sunrise, Hollywood at its best, and carried that promise so well, he was half-afraid he was dreaming. The heat wave had broken three days before, bringing springlike temperatures to the capital, light showers at night to wash the streets, and a steady breeze that had thus far kept pollution from hazing the blue sky.

Leaves weren't dusty, the flowers were bright . . . it was so utterly perfect, it was damn close to sickening.

But he'd take it. He wasn't that much of a fool.

It took a second for him to notice Scully in his chair.

"Morning," he said brightly.

Since the meeting with Skinner, he had resolved two more knots in two more cases that had been bugging him for weeks. For a change, the agents involved were openly and immediately grateful; egos weren't bruised, and two more of the bad guys were on their way to capture.

He also wasn't surprised that Beth Neuhouse, unlike Bournell, hadn't come around to apologize for her behavior. In fact, he hadn't seen her for a week, another sign that life was good and maybe he'd been mistaken about the reprimand setup.

All he needed now was a generous supply of sunflower seeds, and things would be perfect.

"So what's up?" he asked, dropping his briefcase beside an overloaded desk.

Scully reached down beside her, and tossed him a plastic bag.

He caught it against his chest one-handed and held it up. It was a half-pound of sunflower seeds. He smiled. A sign; it had to be a sign. The smile turned to suspicion. "You hate it when I eat these things. It gets messy. You hate messy." He hefted the bag. "What's the catch?"

She shrugged innocently and reached down again, into her own briefcase. She wore a green suit and loose matching blouse fastened at the collar.

"What's the catch, Scully?" he repeated, tossing the bag onto his desk.

She held up a folder, waggled it, and placed it in her lap almost primly.

He stared at the folder, at her, and at the sunflower seeds. They were definitely a sign, and he had no intention of reading it.

Scully smiled faintly at his expression. "Don't worry. You'll probably like this one."

He waited.

She settled back in the chair. "So, what do you know about cattle mutilations?"

"Oh, please, Scully, not that again, please." He crossed to a wheeled office chair and dropped into it, swiveling around to face her as he crossed his legs at the knee. He wasn't going to answer what was obviously a rhetorical question, until he realized he had to. She was preparing him, preparing his mind for something "ordinary" didn't describe.

"All right." He clasped his hands loosely, elbows on the chair's arms. "Depending on who you talk to, you either have half-baked cults that demand bizarre sacrifices—cows being the animal of choice—secret government experiments in immunology based on actual and potential chemical warfare, chemical warfare tests alone, or . . ." He looked at the ceiling. "Or experiments with alleged alien-based technology." He shook his head slowly. "To name a few."

Without responding, she flipped open the folder. "The cattle are either bled, they have sections of hide and/or muscle and/or organs removed—"

"—or they're just sliced all to hell and left in the middle of a field for some poor farmer to fall over. So what? You know this isn't the sort of thing I—" He stopped, and they looked at each other.

He had almost said, "need to know."

He broke contact first, staring at the tip of his shoe. "Where?"

"New Mexico."

He barked a laugh. "Cattle mutilations? Right. Near Roswell, I suppose. Come on, Scully, give me a break. I'm not about to get into that—"

She held up a pair of photographs without comment.

After a moment he took them; after another moment, he placed both feet on the floor and leaned over, elbows now resting on his thighs. It took a while for him to understand what he was looking at, and when he did, he inhaled quickly.

At first they seemed to be little more than solid masses of stained white and gray lying on what appeared to be bare earth. Sandy, grainy, maybe desert ground. A blink to change the perspective, and their forms resolved into the carcasses of animals that had been skinned, stripped in some areas right to the bone. There was virtually nothing left of their heads but exposed skull.

"The one on the left," she told him, "hadn't been found for a couple of days."

Its eyes were gone, and a closer examination showed him

swarming ants, and a few flies the photographer hadn't been able to shoo away. Its hind legs had been twisted from their sockets; its mouth was open, the tongue still there, but it was much smaller, thinner than it ought to be, and evidently raw. Although there were shadows, and although he tried, he couldn't spot any pools or traces of blood.

He glanced up, frowning. "Blood?"

Scully nodded. "I know, I've looked, too. If it's exsanguination, it's almost too well done. Otherwise . . ." A one-shoulder shrug. "Cauterization is about the only other thing I can think of. Based on the pictures, that is. To know exactly, we'll have to talk to those who were at the scene."

At her direction, he checked the photograph on the right.

"Now that one," she explained, "was found, they think, only a few hours after it happened. The eyes are gone there as well, but I can't tell if they've been surgically removed or . . ."

She didn't finish; she didn't have to.

"The blood thing again," he said, looking from one exhibit to the other.

"Right. And again, I don't have an answer for you. Not based on what we have now. Look close at the hindquarters, though. Twisted, just like the other one. I doubt if they're still in their sockets. There was a lot of force exerted there, Mulder. A lot."

"Meaning?"

"Too soon, Mulder, you know that. Most of the hide is gone, although—" She leaned over and pointed. "—it looks as if there are still some strips around the belly. Maybe between the legs, too. With all that muscle tisssue gone or shredded, it's hard to tell."

He looked up. "This isn't just skinning. What do you figure? Flayed?"

She nodded cautiously, unwilling as always to commit until she had seen the evidence firsthand. "I think so. I won't know until I've had a good look for myself."

Then she handed him another pair.

Puzzled, he took them, looked down, and rocked back in the chair, swallowing heavily. "Jesus."

People; they were people.

He closed his eyes briefly and set the pictures aside. He had seen any number of horrors over the past several years, from dismemberment to outright butchery, but there had been nothing as vicious as this. He didn't need to look at them more than once to know this was something different. To put it mildly.

Flayed.

These people had been flayed, and he didn't need to ask if they had been alive when it happened.

"Skinner, right?" The assistant director would have flagged this for him as soon as it had arrived.

Scully nodded as she pushed absently at her hair, trying to tuck it behind one ear. "The local authorities, the county sheriff's office, called . . ." She checked a page of the file. "They called Red Garson in the Albuquerque office. Apparently it didn't take him very long to think of you."

Mulder knew Garson slightly, a weathered, rangy Westerner who had breezed through the Bureau academy at Quantico, less with considerable skill—although he had it in abundance—than with an almost frantic enthusiasm born of a man determined to get out of the East as fast as he could. Which he had done as soon as he could. He was no slouch when it came to on-site investigations, so this must have thrown him completely. It wasn't like him to ask for anyone's help.

"Mulder, whoever did this is truly sick."

Sick, deranged, or so devoid of emotion that he might as well not be human.

He grabbed a picture at random—it was a couple, and he was thankful that what was left of their faces was turned away from the camera.

"Tied? Drugged?"

Scully cleared her throat. "It's hard to tell, but initial indications are . . ." She paused, and he heard the nervousness, and the anger, in her voice. "Indications are they weren't. And Garson doesn't think they were killed somewhere else and dumped at the site."

He rubbed a hand over his mouth, bit down on his lower lip thoughtfully.

"Autopsies by the medical examiner, a woman named Helen Rios, are inconclusive on whether they were actually conscious or not at the time of death. The lack of substantial quantities of epinephrine seems to indicate it happened too fast for the chemical to form, which it usually does in abundance in cases of extreme violence."

"A victim's adrenaline rush," he said quietly.

Scully looked up from the report. "Right. Something else, too."

He didn't know what question to ask.

"They appear to have been dressed at the time of the assault."

He shifted uneasily. "Wait."

"Shards of clothing were found around each of the scenes. Not even that—no more than bits. Strips of leather from boots or shoes. Metal buttons."

"Scully, hold it."

Her hand trembling slightly, she dropped the folder back into her briefcase. "The pathologist says they either died of shock or bled to death." She inhaled slowly. "Garson, in a sidebar, seems to think they were frightened to death, that they were dead before they hit the ground."

Mulder waved her silent. "Scully, these people—forget about the animals for a minute—these people were attacked by someone, or a group of someones, flayed until their clothes were shredded and their skin was taken off." He gestured vaguely. Shook his head. "You're saying—"

"*They're* saying," she corrected.

"Okay. Okay, they're saying it happened so fast, epinephrine hadn't had time to . . ." He smiled without humor and looked blindly around the room. "Scully, you know as well as I do that's damn near impossible."

"Probably," she admitted. "I haven't had a lot of time to think about it."

He stood abruptly. "You don't have to think about it, Scully. There's nothing to think about. It's practically flat-out impossible."

"Which is why we have to be at Dulles first thing in the morning. Stopover at Dallas, we'll be in New Mexico by one their time." She raised a finger to forestall a response. "And remember: practically is the right word here, Mulder. That does not mean definitely."

He stared at her briefcase, spread his arms at all the work yet undone he could see in the office, and said, "What?" at the twitch of a smile on her lips.

She didn't have to answer.

He usually reacted this way when a clear X-File landed in his lap. A switching of gears, of mind-set, excitement of one kind changing to excitement of another. Impossible, to him, meant someone else had decided there were no explanations for whatever had happened.

But there were always explanations.

Always.

His superiors, and Scully, didn't always like them, but they were there.

Sometimes all it took was a little imagination to find them. A less hidebound way of looking at the world. A willingness to understand that the truth sometimes wore a mask.

"There's something else," she added as he reached for the sunflower seeds and his briefcase.

"What?"

She stood and brushed at her skirt. "There was a witness to one of the killings."

He felt his mouth open. "You're kidding. He saw who did it?"

"She," Scully corrected. "And she claims it wasn't a person."

He waited.

"She said it was a shadow."

Brother, he thought.

"Either that, or a ghost."

SEVEN

X A low fire burned in a shallow pit.

Smoke rose in dark trails, winding fire-reflected patterns around the large underground room before escaping through the ragged round hole in the ceiling.

Shadows on the roughly hewn rock walls cast by shadows seated on planks around the pit.

Six men, cross-legged and naked, their bodies lean and rawhide-taut, stringlike hair caught in the sweat that glittered in the firelight, their hands on their knees. Their eyes on the flames that swayed to a breeze not one of them could feel.

Over the fire, resting on a metal grate, a small, flame-blackened pot in which a colorless liquid bubbled without raising steam.

A seventh man sat on a chair carved from dull red stone, back in the shadows where the rite said he belonged. He wore no clothing save a cloth headband embedded with polished stones and gems, none of them alike, none bigger than the tip of a finger. In his right hand he held the spine of a snake; from his left hand dangled the tail of a black horse, knotted at the end and wound through with blue, red, and yellow ribbons. His black eyes were unfocused.

Eventually one of the six stirred, chest rising and falling in a long, silent sigh. He took a clay ladle from the hand of the man on his left, dipped it into the pot, and stood as best he could on scrawny legs that barely held him. A word spoken to the fire. A word spoken to the smoke-touched night sky visible through the hole. Then he carried the ladle to the man in the chair, muttered a few words, and poured the boiling liquid over the seventh man's head.

The man didn't move.

The water burned through his hair, over his shoulders, down his back and chest.

He still didn't move.

The horsetail twitched, but the hand that held it didn't move.

The old man returned to the circle, sat, and after shifting once, didn't move.

The only sound was the fire.

A lone man waiting in the middle of nowhere.

He stood in the center of a scattering of bones—coyote, mountain lion, horse, bull, ram, snake.

And from where he stood, he could see smoke rising above Sangre Viento Mesa, rising in separate trails until, a hundred feet above, it gathered itself into a single dark column that seemed to make its way to the moon.

In the center of the smoke-made basket the moonlight glowed emerald.

The man smiled, but there was no humor.

He spread his arms as if to entice the smoke toward him.

It didn't move.

He was patient.

It had moved before; it would move again.

And after tonight, when the old fools had finished, he would make it move on his own.

All he had to do was believe.

Donna rolled over in her sleep, moaning so loudly it woke her up. She blinked rapidly to dispel the nightmare, and when she was sure it was done, she swung her legs over the side of the bed and sat up, pushing hair away from her eyes, mouth open to catch the cool air that puckered her skin and made her shiver.

The house was quiet.

The neighborhood, such as it was, was quiet.

Moonlight slipped between the cracks the curtains left over the room's two windows, slants of it that trapped sparkling particles of dust.

She yawned and stood, yawned again as she scratched at her side and under her breasts. The nightmare was gone, scattered, but she knew she had had one, knew it was probably the same one she had had over the past two weeks.

She walked in the desert, wearing only a long T-shirt, bare feet feeling the night cold of the desert floor. A steady wind blew into her face. A full moon so large it seemed about to collide with the Earth, and too many stars to count.

Despite the wind's direction, she could hear something moving close behind her, but whenever she looked back, the night was empty except for her shadow.

It hissed at her.

It scraped toward her.

When she couldn't take it any longer, she woke up, knowing that if she didn't, she was going to die.

She didn't believe in omens, but she couldn't help but wonder.

Now she padded sleepily into the kitchen, opened the refrigerator, and wondered if it was too late, or too early, to have a beer. Not that it mattered. If she had one now, she'd be in the bathroom before dawn, cursing herself and wondering how she'd make it through the day with so little sleep.

She let the door swing shut with a righteous nod, yawned, and moved to the back door.

Her yard was small, ending, like all the other yards scattered along the side road, in a stone-block wall painted the color of the earth. Poplars along the back blocked her view of the other houses even though they were too far away to see even in daylight, unless she was right at the wall.

Suddenly she felt much too alone.

There was no one out there.

She was cut off, and helpless.

The panic rose, and she was helpless to stop it. Running from the room did her no good because she could see nothing from the living room window either—the rosebushes she had spent so much time training to be a hedge fragmented her view of the road, erasing sight of the field across the way.

Trapped; she was trapped.

A small cry followed her to the door. She flung it open and ran onto the stoop, stopping before she flung herself off the steps. Cold concrete made her gasp; cold wind plastered the T-shirt to her chest and stomach.

I am, she decided, moving back into town first thing in the morning.

It was the same vow she made after every nightmare, and it made her smile.

Oh boy, tough broad, she thought sarcastically; think you're so tough, and a lousy dream makes you a puddle.

She stepped back over the threshold, laughing aloud, but not loud enough that she didn't hear the hissing.

The smoke rose and coiled and swallowed the emerald
light.

Mike Ostrand was a little drunk.

Hell, he was a lot drunk, and could barely see the dashboard,
much less the interstate. The gray slash of his headlamps blurred
and sharpened, making the road swing from side to side as if the
car couldn't stay in its proper lane.

This late, though, he didn't much give a damn.

The road from Santa Fe was, aside from occasional rises not
quite hills, fairly straight all the way to Bernalillo, and into Albuquerque beyond. Just aim the damn thing and hold onto the
wheel. He'd done it hundreds of times.

He hiccuped, belched, and grimaced at the sour taste that rose
in his throat, shaking his head sharply as if to fling the taste away.

The radio muttered a little Willie Nelson.

He wiped his eyes with one hand and checked the rearview
mirror. Nothing back there but black.

Nothing ahead but more black.

The speedometer topped seventy.

If he were lucky, if he were really lucky, he'd be home by two
and asleep by two-ten, assuming he made it as far as the bedroom. Two-five if he couldn't get past the couch.

He laughed, more like a giggle, and rolled down the window
when he felt a yawn coming. Drunk or not, he knew enough to
understand that cold air blasting the side of his face was infinitely
preferable to dozing off and ending up nose-down in a ditch, his
head through the windshield.

The air smelled good.

The engine's grumble was steady.

"And so am I," he declared to the road. "Steady as a rock and twice as hard."

Another laugh, another belch.

It had been a good night. No, it had been a great night. Those pinheads in Santa Fe, thinking they knew ahead of the rest of the world what the next artsy trend would be, had decided he was it. Living collages, they called it; the desert genius, they called him.

"My God!" he yelled, half in joy, half in derision.

After a dozen years trying to sell paintings even he couldn't abide, he'd sliced a small cactus in half, glued it to a canvas, added a few tiny bird bones and a couple of beads, called it something or other, and as a lark, brought it north.

They loved it.

They fucking loved it.

He had meant it as a thumbed nose at their pretensions, and they had fallen over themselves trying to buy it.

The wind twisted through the car, tangling his long blond hair, tugging at it, threatening a headache.

Five years later, twenty-five-carefully-assembled-when-he-was-roaring-drunk canvases later, his bank account was fat, his home was new, his car was turned in every year, and the women were lined up six to the dozen, just waiting for his living desert fingers to work their magic on them.

It almost made him sick.

It didn't make him stupid.

Trends were little more than fads, and he knew full well that the next season might be his last. Which was why he needed to hole up for a while, work through an even dozen more projects, and get himself out before he ended up like the others—flat broke and saying, "I used to be someone, you know, really, I was," while they cadged another beer from a stranger in a strange bar.

The speedometer topped eighty.

The headache began.

Acid bubbled in his stomach.

The back of his hand scrubbed across his face, and when his vision cleared, he saw something to the right, just beyond the edge of the light.

He frowned as he stared at it, then yelped as the car followed his stare and angled for the shoulder. The correction was too sharp, and he swung off toward the wide empty median, swung back again, hit the accelerator instead of the brakes, and yelled soundlessly when the right-side tires bit into the earth off the blacktop.

The car shuddered.

He froze—turn into the skid? turn out of the skid?—and watched in horror as the low shrubs and deep ditch charged him and veered away at the last minute, putting him back on the road.

Sweat masked his face.

His bladder demanded immediate relief.

His left hand shook so much he thrust it between his knees and squeezed until it calmed.

"My God," he whispered. "Jesus, man, Jesus."

Twenty-five, he swore to himself; he didn't care if it took until dawn, he wouldn't go faster than twenty-five all the way home.

He wasn't sober, but he sure as hell wasn't as drunk as he had been.

The speedometer reached fifty.

He saw the needle, saw it climb again slowly, and decided it would be all right. Sixty, no more; he'd be home quicker, and that was okay because he was a menace to himself out here.

A hard swallow, a deep breath, his right hand flicking the radio off because what he didn't need now was interference with his concentration. Just watch the road, pay no attention to anything that—

He saw it again.

Just a suggestion of movement running with him on the other side of the ditch. Which was impossible. He was doing sixty-five, for God's sake, there wasn't anything except another car that could go that fast.

He squinted a stare, broke it off when the car began to drift, and licked his lips.

There wasn't anything over there.

Good God, there couldn't be anything over there. It was the headlights, that's all, running along a row of juniper maybe, or some piñon, rock, something like that. His eyes caught the strobelike reflection, and the scotch turned it into something that paced him.

That's all it was.

He wished the moon were a little brighter.

Forget the new canvases, he decided a half-mile later; the hell with it, he was done. He had enough money, the house was paid for, what the hell more could he want?

The car jumped sideways when something slammed into the passenger door.

He yelled, and watched his hands blur around the wheel, watched the road blur black to gray and black again, screamed when the car was struck a second time, and looked over to see what drunken idiot was trying to run him off the road.

There was nothing there.

When he looked back, it was too late.

The highway was gone.

All he could do was cross his arms in front of his face, close his eyes, and scream.

There was no fire, no explosion.

Mike Ostrand hung upside down in his seatbelt, listening to the engine tick, listening to the wind blow through the open window.

Listening to the hiss he thought was the tires spinning to a halt.

A few seconds later, he blacked out when something reached through the window and touched his arm.

EIGHT

X La Mosca Inn sat between the Rio Grande and a high adobe wall that fronted the road. Eight units extended left and right from a central two-story building that housed the office, a large flagstone waiting room cooled by a small sparking fountain, and a restaurant large enough to seat one hundred without elbows and voices clashing. Spanish tile on the roof, shade provided by cottonwood and mountain ash, and a single huge Russian olive in the center of the courtyard.

Scully sat on a wood bench that ringed the massive tree, facing the arched entrance whose elaborate iron gates were closed each night at, the proprietor told her, precisely midnight. She let her eyes close, and touched a finger to her forehead, to trap a droplet of sweat that had broken from her hairline.

"Feeling better?" a voice rasped beside her.

"Not really."

The day had gone wrong from minute one: she'd overslept and had to race to the airport, only to learn that the flight had been delayed. For an hour. Then two. Once airborne, she had planned to set up her laptop computer, so she and Mulder could go over what details of the case they had.

It didn't happen.

Roller-coaster turbulence rode them all the way to Dallas, making reading the computer screen a nauseating experience; she spent most of the time trying, and failing, to doze. Then a series of thunderstorms ringing the Texas city forced them to swerve wide into a holding pattern until the squall line had passed. Another hour lost, and so was their connecting flight.

"Cursed," Mulder had said at one point. "This whole thing is cursed."

By the time they landed in Albuquerque, she was ready to believe in curses; by the time Red Garson had sped them in his Jeep out of the city, north to Bernalillo, she was ready to spend the rest of her life walking.

The man beside her shifted to get her attention.

She opened her eyes and smiled at him wanly.

Red was as Mulder had told her, a tall, lean, middle-aged man whose lined face and hands spoke of time spent in the mountains and the desert. She had no idea where he'd gotten his nickname, because his blond hair was pale, his blue eyes dark; part of his left ear was missing, bitten off, he told her, in a fight with a man who had a strong aversion to spending the rest of his life in federal prison.

Hardly a stereotypical FBI agent.

When he smiled, only his lips moved; he never showed his teeth.

He jerked his thumb over his shoulder. "You think he's fallen asleep?"

"I doubt it."

A pickup chugged past the Inn, backfired twice, and left a curl of black smoke behind.

"Dana?"

She nodded to show him she was listening.

"Why does he call you Scully all the time? I mean, you do have a first name."

"Because he can," she answered simply, without sarcasm, and didn't bother to explain. Just as it would be hard to explain why Mulder was, without question, the best friend she had. It was more than just being partners, being able to rely on each other when one of them was in danger, or when one of them needed a boost when a case seemed to be going bad; and it was more than simply their contrasting styles, which, perversely to some, complemented each other perfectly.

What it was, she sometimes thought, was an indefinable instinct, a silent signal that let her know that whatever else changed, whatever else happened, Mulder would always be there when he had to be. One way or another.

At that moment she heard a footfall and grinned. "Here he comes."

Garson looked startled, looked around and saw him walking along one of the stone paths that wound through the courtyard garden. She had to admit he looked strange without his suit. Over his shoulder he carried a denim jacket, not for appearance but to hide the holster he wore on his left hip.

He also looked as frazzled as she felt.

"It's hot," he said, dropping onto the bench beside her.

"It's July, Mulder," Garson reminded him. "It's New Mexico. What did you expect?"

"Heat I can get at home. An oven I already have in my apartment." He scratched through his hair and shook his head as though trying to force himself awake.

"It isn't for everybody," Garson admitted, adding without saying so that "everybody" must be crazy if they didn't instantly fall in love with this part of the country. "And remember, you're a mile farther up than you were in Washington. Thinner air. Take it easy for a while, understand? You go shooting off in fourteen directions at once, you're going to drop."

Mulder grunted, then stood again. "Hey, look." He headed for the gate.

"Mulder," Scully called. "We haven't time—"

He turned, grinning, and pointed to a small dust devil spinning lazily in the road. "We used to get these things at home. Leaves, you know?" He moved closer; it was no higher than his shin. "We'd try to get inside." His foot inched toward the dervish's base and apparently broke some unseen barrier. The dust devil fell apart, and Mulder toed the place where it had been.

Scully, who was already feeling the effects of the altitude, let the silence settle for a few seconds before she said, "Mulder, come over here, I think we'd better not waste any more time." She checked her watch; it was just after four. "I suppose it's too late to catch Dr. Rios. What about . . . Patty? Patty Deven. Is she well enough to talk to us?"

Garson stabbed a thumb at her as Mulder rejoined them. "She always like this?"

"We have three people murdered, Red. The altitude didn't kill them."

The man nodded, accepting the point and the rebuke without taking offense. "The Devens live about a mile down the road. They're fixing to head back to Chicago as soon as this is cleared up. I'll take you over, but I'm telling you now that you won't be welcome."

He was right.

Scully caught the instant hostility as soon as Kurt Deven opened the trailer door and saw who it was. When Garson introduced his companions, the man scowled and told them to wait. Then he closed the door. Hard.

Mulder nodded toward the riverline of cottonwood sixty or seventy yards away. "Down there?"

"Yep. The bank slopes sharp right about where you're looking. It happened a little ways to the right."

Scully shaded her eyes against the low-hanging sun and tried to see it at night, with little but moon and stars for illumination. The trailer wouldn't help; it was too far away, and except for the skeleton of an unfinished house beside it, there were no other homes in the immediate area, even though she saw flagged wooden stakes in the ground, marking other lots soon to be developed. The nearest trailer was a good sixty yards away.

The door opened.

The two men stepped aside as a woman stepped down onto the cinder-block steps. She was short and slight, with straight blond hair that needed a brushing, and a lost, empty look in her eyes. When she spoke, rage and grief made her hoarse:

"She doesn't want to talk to you again, Mr. Garson."

Red told her softly he understood, and apologized for the intrusion. "But I have these folks here, Mrs. Deven. All the way from Washington." He cleared his throat, glanced at the open doorway. "They're experts in this kind of crime. If anyone can catch the—"

"Nobody has," she snapped. "It's been two weeks, and nobody has."

Scully lifted a hand to draw her attention. "Mrs. Deven?"

The woman took her time: "What?"

Scully kept her voice gentle. "Mrs. Deven, I won't lie to you. I won't pretend to know how you feel for your loss, or how your daughter feels. But Agent Mulder and I have done this more times than I ever want to tell you. And if nothing else, I can promise you that we don't quit. We're not perfect, but we do not quit."

Mary Deven's hands pressed lightly to her stomach, eyes narrowed. "Are you promising me you'll catch him?"

"No," Mulder answered, just as gently, just as firmly. "We're only promising you that we won't quit. And if you don't want us to bother you, or your family, you won't have to worry."

Mrs. Deven stared at the trees, blinking rapidly, then not at all. "Just don't take her down there," she said, barely above a whisper. "You take her down there, I'll lose her."

Scully agreed readily, and said nothing when Mulder asked Garson to show him the scene. After all this time, there wouldn't be anything left of real value—Garson and his men and the local police would have raked it over thoroughly. Mulder, however, had a knack for finding things in barren places, a knack she didn't pretend to understand as well as she wanted to.

"Agent Scully?"

Wan, painfully thin, Patty Deven was the mirror image of her mother, right down to the haunted look. A fading bruise spread across her right cheek and temple. Her eyes were too large behind her glasses.

They sat on two lawn chairs. There was no shade, and no offer of a drink.

After a long silence, with the girl staring at the knot of fingers in her lap, Scully leaned forward and said, "What did you see, Patty?" Nothing more.

Mulder stood on the bare ground, checked the branches above him, glanced at the shallow river below. "Here?"

"Just about," Garson said.

But "here" was nothing. The ground was too hard for tracks, and with no direct line of sight to the trailer, there was nothing much to work on. He asked Garson to stand approximately where Patty had been, and scowled.

Dark night, thirty or forty feet away, she wouldn't have been able to see much of anything.

Flashes of movement that accompanied her brother's attack and screams.

She saw a ghost because there was nothing true to focus on.

He hunkered down and ran a palm over the ground. "Have you had rain?"

Garson walked back, taking his time. "This is what we call the monsoon season, Mulder. You wouldn't know to look at it now, but afternoons we get storms in. Big ones. Usually from the west, and they don't fool around." He shrugged as Mulder stood. "Trouble is, rain washes the evidence away, and the ground's like rock again before noon the next day. This is a waste of time."

Maybe, Mulder thought; maybe not.

He walked north along the bank, gaze shifting slowly from side to side. Ahead, the underbrush was thick, still uncleared by the developers. He saw no signs that anyone had broken through, which meant they had either come from down below, or from the far side of the trees.

It was something, and it was nothing.

By the time he reached the other agent, he was scowling again. "Gangs?"

"Some." They headed back to the trailer. "This is no gang hit, though. Knives and guns; nothing like this."

"Cults?"

They left the trees behind, and he felt the temperature already beginning to rise. Scully was still in her lawn chair; she was alone.

"What kind of cults you want, Mulder? We have New Age swamis communing in the desert. We have the Second Coming believers who wander around the mountains and then use their cellulars when they get lost. And we have the flying saucer nuts, who figure Roswell is the key to all intergalactic understanding." A sideways glance Mulder didn't miss. "That's kind of your territory, isn't it?"

The only answer was a noncommittal grunt, and Garson was smart enough to leave it alone.

Scully stood as they approached, a brief shake of her head when he looked her a question. At that moment he couldn't help a yawn, and turned away so the pale face in the trailer window couldn't see him.

He hoped he had been quick enough.

The one thing Mary Deven didn't need now was the sight of an FBI agent yawning at the site of her only son's murder.

Garson saw it, though. "We're going back," he told them both, not giving them an option to refuse. "You two get something to eat and get some sleep, or you're going to be worthless tomorrow."

"Why? What's tomorrow?"

He touched his hat brim. "Tomorrow, my friend, you're going to meet a genuine movie star."

NINE

Mulder couldn't sleep.

After a slow, almost lethargic dinner, he listened as Scully told him about the interview with the girl, which hadn't told her anything new. Patty had seen even less than her statement had implied. Almost as soon as the attack began, the branch club her brother had been holding spiraled out of the dark and struck her on the side of the face. She had fallen, dazed, and in that state thought she might have heard someone whispering, someone else laughing.

But it was all too muddled, and she had passed out shortly afterward.

It was her father who had found the body.

"No ghosts, Scully," Mulder had said, walking her back to her room. "We're dealing with people here."

"You sound disappointed."

He hadn't answered then, and he had no answer now as he put on a jacket and left the room, glad now that he had listened to Garson—despite the day's heat, the desert was downright cold at night.

He walked through a short passageway between the rooms and the main building, and paused.

The back was a garden of cacti and now-closed desert flowers set in random circles ringed by stone, as it was in front. Stone paths wound between them and joined at the back to lead to a half-dozen benches that faced the river. Cottonwoods and willows were illuminated by miniature lanterns hanging amid their leaves, leaving patches of lazy shifting light on the ground.

He wasn't sure, but he thought he smelled honeysuckle.

When he was sure he was alone, he sat on one of the benches and watched what little water there was flow past his feet, electric lanterns on metal riverbank poles glowing just enough to turn the dark to gray.

The moon was out.

He shoved his hands into his jacket pockets and watched it for a while, thinking of nothing in particular until a slip of a cloud gave the moon a face.

Patty Deven, or her mother, adrift in a darkness they would never be able to escape. Pale, only shadows for expression, only hints of what used to be behind their smiles.

It was an all too easy, and all too painful, jump from there to his sister, gone too many years now. Taken when she was eight, by someone, or something, hiding behind the glare of a light that even now he couldn't think about without shuddering, or squinting to shut it out.

To try to see what was behind it.

That was the foundation of his pursuit of the truths buried somewhere within the X-Files.

He looked away from the moon and wiped a hand over his face, then absently rubbed the back of his neck.

He would find Samantha, there was no question about it; until then, however, the best he could do would be to find the men who had murdered Patty's brother.

Again his hand passed over his face. When it slipped into its jacket pocket, though, a brief smile was left behind.

"I'm okay," he said, shifting over to make room for Scully. "Just thinking."

"Out here, that'll get you pneumonia."

"Is that a doctor's truth thing?"

She stretched out her legs, folded her hands on her stomach. "No, it's cold, that's what it is. God, Mulder, why can't you ever have a mood someplace warm?"

They said nothing else for a long time, watching the river, listening to the rustle of the trees, once in a while listening to a dog bark or a car roar past the inn. For a while the garden filled with diners having after-dinner drinks as they strolled among the garden islands, conversation soft, laughter sometimes loud; for a while the evening breeze stopped, and they couldn't hear a thing but their own breathing.

Then Mulder said, "Scully, has it occurred to you that maybe the people who mutilated those cows weren't the ones who killed Patty's brother and that couple?"

A bird sang softly in the cottonwoods.

"No," she said at last. She looked over. "Why?"

"The history, Scully, the history. Animal mutilations of this sort aren't usually tied to murder. Particularly not brutal ones like these. The animals are assaulted, not people."

He watched her carefully as she looked away. He'd only been thinking aloud, but once the thought had been voiced, he had to make sure.

"No," she repeatd with a slow shake of her head. "Whatever was used, however it was done, the timing's too close, the similarites too great. From what we've been told." She shifted uneasily. "I'll know more when I speak to the M.E., but . . . " She shook her head again. "No." A quick smile. "Besides, aren't you the one who told me that there are coincidences, and then there are coincidences? One is real, the other only an illusion?"

He returned the smile. "Yep."

"Okay. Well, this is no real coincidence, Mulder. The brutality itself is a strong indication of that. All we need to do is find the connection."

"Right. All we need to do."

The bird sang again.

"Then think about this, Scully," he said quietly. "Why? What's so damn important out here that both cattle *and* kids have to die?"

She didn't respond; he hadn't expected her to.

But he had a strong feeling, an unpleasant one, that whatever answer they finally uncovered, it would be one neither of them would like.

In the middle of the desert, they had been dropped into a nightmare.

"I am not crazy!" Mike Ostrand insisted from his hospital bed. He glared at Sheriff Sparrow, who returned the look without expression. "I did not imagine the accident. I did not imagine this goddamn cast on my goddamn arm. I did not imagine my brand-new car flipped over and left me hanging there like a goddamn Peking duck!"

Sparrow was patient.

"Okay." Ostrand shifted uncomfortably, lips pulling away from his teeth in a grimace. "Okay. So I was a little drunk, I admit it. But that's not why I crashed."

"No, you crashed because some kind of mysterious vehicle, so low you couldn't see it out your window, deliberately forced you off the road."

Ostrand looked at him angrily. "That's right."

"And then it tried to kill you when you were hanging from your seatbelt."

The artist shrugged, winced at the pain that exploded in his shoulder, and sighed capitulation. "Okay, okay, so it was a stupid coyote, okay? So I was so damn scared it scared the hell out of me. It would have scared anybody. But it wasn't a coyote that ran me off the damn road!"

"Good." Sparrow nodded sharply. "Now we're getting somewhere." He glanced down at the small notepad he held in his left hand, chewed on the eraser end of his pencil for a moment, and said, "Now, about that invisible vehicle . . ."

The Coronado Bar was unoriginal in both name and decor. As Bernalillo inexorably changed from an outpost on the Rio Grande into an Albuquerque bedroom community, the Coronado just as stubbornly refused to change with it. A long bar on the right-hand wall, tables and booths everywhere else, and a jukebox that muttered country-western all day long. The TV on the wall in back never played anything but sports, minor league baseball tonight from Southern California. Smoke and liquor in the air, as many cigarette butts on the bare floor as in the aluminum ashtrays. It catered neither to the tourists nor the newcomers, and didn't much care that business didn't boom. It did well enough, which was well enough for its regulars.

Indian Territory was at the back.

Although there were a handful of exceptions, most of the men who drove in from the pueblos stuck to the two last booths and three last tables. There was nothing belligerent about it; it just happened that way. Even the Spanish stayed away.

Especially when the Konochine came to town.

Leon Ciola nursed a long-neck beer in the last booth. He was alone, seated under a wall lamp whose bulb he had unscrewed as soon as he'd taken his seat. He didn't like the light, didn't like the way the Anglos tried not to stare at the web of scars across his face or the scars on his knuckles.

It was better to sit in shadow.

It was also better to face the entrance, so when the man came in, Ciola would see him first and lift a hand in greeting, before a question could be asked or a voice raised. What he didn't need tonight was talk, debate—*What's the matter with your people, Leon, don't they believe in the twentieth century?* The time for that was past. The others—Nick Lanaya, Dugan Velador, fools like that—they could do their best to keep the talk alive, to deal with Anglo crooks like that Falkner woman and sell the People down the river without an ounce of guilt. Not him. He had plans.

They thought he was beaten. They thought his time away would change him.

He drank, not sipped.

It had.

It had changed him.

It had made him worse.

Just before eleven the man came in, spotted him right away, and dropped heavily into the booth.

Ciola tugged on the beak on his cap, a greeting and an adjustment. "You're late."

"Shit truck wouldn't start. Wasn't for you, I wouldn't make the effort."

Ciola watched him, hiding his distaste by emptying the bottle and waving it over his head, so the waitress, such as she was, would bring him another.

The other man didn't ask for one, and one wasn't offered.

"So?" Leon said.

The man lifted one shoulder. "So they brought in some FBI, straight from Washington. They came in this morning. One man, one woman."

Ciola coughed a laugh. "You're kidding."

"They're supposed to be experts."

"A woman?"

The man nodded, and offered a lopsided grin. "Gets better. They're Anglos."

The empty bottle was taken away, a full one left in its place. The man grabbed it before Ciola did, took a long swallow, and set it down. His fingers stayed around the neck. "Am I worried?"

"No."

"Good." The man stood and hitched up his pants. "I hate being worried. It always pisses me off."

He left without a word to anyone else.

The bartender turned up the baseball game.

Ciola wiped the bottle's mouth with his palm and drank the rest without coming up for air.

When the waitress returned for the empty, he grabbed her wrist, just strongly enough to keep her bent over the table. *"Chica,"* he said softly, "what are you doing tonight?"

"Getting a life," she answered, yanking her arm free. "Try it sometime."

He laughed. Not a sound, but he tilted his head back and laughed. Wonderful! She was wonderful! He wiped a tear from his eye and shook his head. Since she didn't want him, he would leave her the biggest tip she had ever had in her miserable life.

And to make it better, he wouldn't even kill her.

Scully massaged the back of her neck. It was hard to keep her eyes open, and she didn't bother to hide a yawn.

"The desert night air," Mulder said. "It's almost too peaceful here."

"I know." She dropped her hand into her lap. "The point is, Mulder, we haven't enough data yet to show us why they were killed, much less explain the connections in any reasonable fashion. And I don't think we're going to find them out here. Not tonight, anyway." She smiled wanly. "I think I'm a little too punchy."

"We both are." He stretched one arm at a time over his head, clasped his hands, and pushed his palms toward the sky. "I just wish I could see the connections between a handful of cows, a kid by the river, and a couple in the desert." He brought his arms down, one hand again moving to his nape.

"Mulder, relax, we just got here, remember? Besides, you have to remember that the thinner air out here slows down the intellectual process, the result of less oxygen flowing to the brain."

He grinned and looked at her sideways. "Is that a doctor thing?"

"No, that's a Scully thing." She grinned and pushed off the bench and held out her hand. When he grabbed it, she pulled him up, turned him around, pushing him lightly toward the motel. "The doctor thing is, get some sleep, like Red said, or you'll be useless in the morning."

He nodded as he waved a weary good night over his shoulder, sidestepping a garden wall just before he tripped over it. Another wave—*I'm okay, I know what I'm doing*—before he disappeared into the passageway, and she couldn't help wondering what it was like for him—seeing things other people sometimes couldn't; engaging in a pursuit with oftentimes terrifying intensity; looking so young and deceptively guileless that there had been many times when he was severely underestimated.

She wasn't surprised when, passing his room on her way to bed, she saw light slipping around the edges of the drapes.

Exhausted or not, he would be up most of the night, turning over what he knew, and setting up what he didn't know so he would know the right questions to ask, beyond the how and who and why.

She wished him luck.

Right now, she was having difficulty remembering her own name.

She fingered her key out of her pocket, moved on to the next room . . . and stopped as she inserted the key in the lock.

You're tired, Dana, that's all.

She looked anyway.

The inn gates were closed, the lanterns out. Only a faint glow from a nearby streetlamp reached over the wall.

A man stood at the gate, arms loose at his sides.

She couldn't see his face or his clothes; just his outline.

Tired, she reminded herself, and pushed into the room, flicked on the wall switch, and, as she closed the door, checked the gate again.

He was still there.

Watching.

TEN

Mulder didn't have to be outside to know it was hot and getting hotter, even though it was just past ten. Even with sunglasses, the sun's glare was almost too much, and to stare at the passing scenery too long made it jump and shimmer, showing him things he knew weren't there.

There were no clouds, no signs of rain. It was hard to believe there ever was.

He rode with Scully in the back seat of Sheriff Sparrow's dusty blue-and-white cruiser, Garson up front on the passenger side. It was evident from their conversation that the two men had known each other for a long time, using shorthand gestures and single-word answers, mostly grunts. As far as Mulder could tell, the gist of it was, there had been no further incidents since the death of the boy, except for a drunk driver who claimed to have been forced off the road by an invisible, or incredibly short, vehicle.

"It brings out the nuts, this kind of thing," the sheriff said, lifting his gaze to the rearview mirror. "You find that, too, Agent Mulder?"

He nodded. It was true. Just as it was true that Chuck Sparrow was laying on the Western sheriff routine a little thick, constantly hitching his gunbelt, chewing a wad of gum that was supposed to simulate tobacco, getting a deeper drawl in his voice every time he opened his mouth. It wasn't necessarily a bad thing, but it made him wonder why the act at all. Garson would have already filled the man in, and it was the sheriff who had finally asked the FBI for help.

It didn't sit right.

Like not wearing a suit and tie, like wearing running shoes.

He knew Garson was right—wearing his usual clothes out here would have been ludicrous as well as stupid; still, like the sheriff, it didn't sit right.

The Sandias passed them on the right as Interstate 25 left the Albuquerque suburbs behind. And although other ranges broke the horizon, there was nothing out there now but the high desert.

And the sun.

"Cult," Sparrow said then, raising his voice to be heard over the air conditioning.

"What?" Scully, startled out of a reverie, asked him to repeat it.

"Cult. You know . . . cult. One of them Satanist things, probably. Look hard enough, betcha them poor folks were all involved somehow."

"A seventeen-year-old boy?" Mulder asked skeptically.

"Hey, that ain't no rare thing, you know what I mean? You got your heavy-metal crap with all that subliminal stuff, you got your rap stuff telling kids to kill cops, shit like that . . . drugs and sex . . ." He lifted a hand off the wheel, palm up. "What more do you want?"

Mulder saw his eyes in the mirror, watching him, gauging.

"Maybe," he answered reluctantly.

"No maybe about it, son, no maybe about it."

Fifteen miles later, at a speed Mulder thought would soon launch them into orbit, the cruiser slowed, pulled onto the right shoulder, and crossed a narrow wooden bridge. A two-lane paved road led into the desert.

Sparrow pointed with a thumb. "What you got up there, them hills there about ten miles along, is what they call the Konochine Wall." He scratched under his hat. "Kind of like a jagged outline of a lightbulb lying on its side. Fat part, it's pointing toward the Sandias back there to the south. The base part, it crosses the road onto the ranch where we're going. Unless you want to climb the hills, the only way in or out is a gap where the road is."

Mulder watched a barbed-wire fence blur past on his left. Beyond it was desert, and he couldn't imagine how anyone could raise anything out here, much less cattle. When he had asked at breakfast, Garson only told him to hold onto his horses, he didn't want to spoil the surprise.

"Do the Konochine fit in here?" Scully asked. "This case, I mean."

Sparrow shrugged one broad shoulder. "Who the hell knows? Doubt it myself. Their place isn't like the other pueblos, see. It's a res and all, but they don't like tourists, they don't like Anglos, they don't like other Indians . . ." He laughed. "Hell, I don't think they much like each other a whole hell of a lot." He yanked at an earlobe, then scratched vigorously behind it. "Some of them, mostly the young ones, they've been trying for years to change things. Most of the time it don't work, though, and they leave, don't come back."

"And the ones who do?"

"Well . . ." He glanced at Garson. "Nick Lanaya, right?"

Garson nodded agreement and half-turned so he wouldn't have to yell. "Nick's a good guy. He went off to college, and came back with enough ideas to fill a canyon. Because of his family, he's on the Tribal Council, so he has to be heard. And he is, believe me. Trouble is, not a lot are listening."

"So why does he stay?"

Garson thought a moment before saying, "Because they're his people."

Sparrow chuckled, sarcasm, not humor. "Doesn't hurt he's making a few bucks, Red."

Garson sighed dramatically, a wink at Mulder to signal what was obviously a long-standing argument. "Nick," he explained, "has a deal with a local woman, an Anglo, Donna Falkner. He brings out some of the crafts the Konochine make, she sells them in town or up in Santa Fe, they each get a cut and the tribe gets the rest. Mostly jewelry," he added. "Once in a while some incredible bowls and ceremonial-style plates, things like that. Every time he brings out a load, he has a fight with the other side, who claim he's selling their heritage down the river."

"And every time he brings back the bucks to the Mesa," Sparrow said sourly, "they line up with their goddamn hands out."

"The mesa?" Scully said.

"Sangre Viento Mesa," Garson explained. "It's in the middle of the reservation. Their homes are at the base, their religious ceremonies are held up top."

"What does that mean, Sangre Viento?"

Garson faced front. "Blood Wind. It means Blood Wind."

Eventually the barbed wire gave way to a short stretch of well-maintained split rail. In its center was an open gate over which was a wide wood arch. Burned into the face was *Double-H.*

Mulder sat up as Sparrow drove under the arch onto a hard-ground road. He looked between the men in front and saw what surely had to be a mirage.

A wide expanse of impossibly green grass inside a blinding white fence; a long adobe and Spanish tile ranch house so simple in its design it looked prohibitively expensive; a stable and corral behind and to the left, with a small black horse plodding toward the shade of a tree he couldn't name; a two-car garage behind and to the right, the driveway curving around the fence to join the entrance road in front; *ristras*—strings of dried red chiles—hanging from vigas protruding from the walls beneath a porch that had to be fifty or sixty feet long.

"You want to be a millionaire and live like this, Scully?"

"I wouldn't mind."

Sparrow parked in a cleared patch of ground beside the driveway, took off his hat, and slicked his hair back. He opened the door, and paused as he leaned forward to slide out.

"I would appreciate it," he told them, "if you wouldn't bother her too much. She only found the bodies. She didn't see anything else."

From that unsubtle warning, Mulder fully expected a withered and frail woman to greet them, not the beautiful woman who came out of the double front doors and stood on the porch, shading her eyes and smiling.

Scully joined him while Sparrow fumbled with the gate latch, and as they approached the porch, a man and woman stepped out of the house and moved to one side, she in a simple white dress, he in work clothes. Their expressions were anything but friendly.

"Hey, Annie," the sheriff called, and when they were close enough, he made the introductions.

Ann Hatch, Mulder thought as he shook her cool dry hand and looked down into those incredibly green eyes; so this is Ann Hatch.

As she waved them to seats around a wrought-iron table, it was clear Scully liked her at first sight. "You know," she said, accepting a tall glass of lemonade from the woman in white, "this is like finding an oasis, it's so lovely."

Annie's eyes widened in pleasant surprise. "Why, thank you. But it's just my home."

She smiled broadly, and ten minutes later, the three of them were chatting as if they were old friends, long separated but never far from mind. Mulder didn't believe for a minute she was acting.

Another ten minutes passed before he sat back, abruptly sobered when she noted but didn't remark on the holster at his hip. She caught the change in his mood instantly, and took a deep breath.

"You want to know what I saw, and how."

"If you don't mind, Mrs. Hatch."

She rolled her eyes. "Oh, for God's sake, Agent Mulder, please call me Annie. And I don't mind at all." Her gaze shifted to the improbable lawn and the desert beyond it. "They were newly-weds, you know. They were on their honeymoon."

He knew; he had read the report so many times, he could have recited it word for word, footnote for footnote.

Doris and Matt Constella, from Kansas, twenty-five, in Albu-querque only four days, and, from all Garson could figure out, on a wandering drive around the county in a rented van. They had already stopped to visit at least two of the pueblos, and it was there, it was supposed, they had heard about the Konochine. There was no other reason why they'd be on that road. There were no signs, not for the road itself, and not for the ranch.

She explained how she had discovered their bodies, and how she had immediately ridden back to call the sheriff. "Near the gap," she said sadly. "They were right by the gap."

So much for the connection between them and the boy, Mul-der thought.

"Mrs. Hatch," Scully began, and cut herself off at the woman's chiding look. "Annie. Have you had any trouble with people from the reservation?"

Annie blinked once, slowly. "No."

She's lying, Mulder thought, and looked to his left when he sensed movement. Nando Quintodo had taken a short step for-ward, one of his hands fisted at his side. When he saw Mulder look, however, he stopped, his face bland, his hand quickly relaxed.

"Why do you ask?" Annie said.

"It's routine," Mulder answered before Scully, and grinned at her skepticism. "I know, it sounds like a line from a movie, but it's true. We've been told there's some trouble, and . . ." An apologetic gesture. "We can't afford not to ask."

Scully echoed the procedure, and apologized as she took Annie through her story again. Mulder, meanwhile, stretching as if he were too stiff to sit, rose with a muttered apology and left the table. As soon as he took a step, Quintodo walked away from him, heading for the door.

Mulder spoke his name.

When the man turned, his hand was a fist again.

Mulder leaned against the porch rail and looked out over the lawn. He didn't raise his voice; he knew the man could hear him. "Tourists ever call you Tonto?"

"Not here. No tourists here." Flat, unemotional. Careful.

"But sometimes."

There was a pause.

Mulder waited.

"Yes. In town. Sometimes." Still flat, still unemotional.

Mulder faced him, leaning back against the rail, one hand in his pocket. "You're from . . . ?"

Quintodo's eyes shifted to the table, shifted back. "The Mesa."

"Your wife, too?"

He nodded.

"So tell me, Mr. Quintodo. Why would a woman like that want to lie?"

The sheriff, mumbling something to Annie, stood.

Quintodo saw him, and Mulder couldn't miss the flare of hatred in his eyes.

"Why?" he repeated softly.

But Sparrow was already on his way over, a mirthless grin beneath dark glasses. "Why what?" he asked, rubbing a hand over his chest.

"Why would I want to visit the stable when I don't ride?" Mulder answered. "I'll tell you why—because I'm a city boy, and I'd like to be able to see manure firsthand."

"Very well, Mr. Mulder," Quintodo agreed before the sheriff could say anything. "I will show you everything. Mrs. Hatch, she has a pair of very fine horses. I think you will be impressed. Maybe you will learn something."

He nodded politely to Sparrow and went inside without looking back.

The sheriff hitched up his belt, and spat over the railing. "This is a beautiful place."

"Yes, it is."

"Annie's been alone out here for a long time, you know. Some say too long."

"I wouldn't know, Sheriff."

Sparrow spat again. "Let me give you some advice, Agent Mulder."

"Always ready to listen, Sheriff Sparrow. You're the expert around here, not me."

Sparrow nodded sharply, *damn right.*

"Okay, number one is, Nando there is a Konochine. You know that already, I assume. Don't trust him. He may live out here with Annie, but his heart's still over the Wall."

Mulder said nothing.

"Second thing is . . ." He stopped. He took off his hat, wiped sweat from his brow with a forearm, and shook his head as he walked back to the table.

Mulder watched him.

The second thing, unspoken, was a threat.

ELEVEN

The stable was gloomy, despite the open door. There were six stalls on either side, but most of them hadn't been used in a long time. A scattering of hay on the floor. Tack hung from pegs on the walls. When Mulder looked outside, all he could see was white light; the corral and the black horse were little more than ghosts.

Quintodo stood beside a chestnut, running a stiff brush over its flank. He hadn't looked up when Mulder walked in, didn't give a sign when Scully followed, unsure why Mulder had asked her to meet him out here.

Quintodo concentrated on his grooming. "You know what *tonto* means, Mr. Mulder?"

"My Spanish is—" A deprecating smile. "Lousy."

"Stupid," the man said, smoothing a palm over the horse's rump. "It means stupid." He reached into his hip pocket and pulled out a lump of sugar, handed it to Scully. "She won't bite. Just keep your hand flat, she won't take your fingers."

Scully offered the treat, and the horse snorted and snapped it up, then nuzzled her for more.

"She's a pig," Quintodo said, with a hint of smile. "She'll eat all you give her, then get sick." A loving pat to the animal's side. "Tonto."

With a look, Scully asked Mulder why they were here; he nodded a *be patient,* and put his back to the door. All he said was, "Why?"

Quintodo worked for several long seconds without speaking, the scrape of the brush the only sound. Then: "She is one, you know."

Mulder's head tilted slightly.

"Konochine. One of us. Her husband, Mr. Hatch, he met her in Old Town, in Albuquerque. She was fifteen, he was from Los Angeles. I don't know what they call it, looking for places to make a movie."

"Scouting," Scully said.

He nodded. "Yes, *gracias.* He told her about the movies, about being in them." The smile finally broke. "All hell broke loose on the Mesa. But he was very persuasive, Mr. Hatch was. Very handsome, very kind. Very young and . . ." He hesitated. "Dreamy. Before we knew it, she was gone. Making movies. Getting married." He looked at Mulder over the horse's back. "They were very happy. Always."

The smile slipped away.

"No children?" Scully asked.

"Not to be."

The horse stamped impatiently, and Quintodo murmured at it before resuming his grooming.

"She is special, Mr. Mulder," he said at last. "She hears the wind."

Scully opened her mouth to question him, and Mulder shook his head quickly.

Quintodo swallowed, second thoughts making him pause.

When he did speak again, he spoke slowly.

"We have priests, you know." The horse stamped again; a fly buzzed in the stifling heat. "Not the Catholic ones, the padres. Konochine got rid of them a long time ago. Our own. Seven, all the time. They . . . do things for us. *Comprende?* You understand? Today they are all men. It happens. Sometimes there are women, but not now. Priests are not . . ." He frowned, then scowled when he couldn't find the word. "They live like us, and then they die. When one dies, there is a ceremonial, and the dead one is replaced."

A two-tone whistle outside interrupted him. Mulder heard hoofbeats trot across the corral.

The chestnut didn't move.

"They know their call," Quintodo explained. "That was for Diamond."

"And the ceremonial?" Mulder prodded quietly.

Quintodo lowered his head, thinking.

"There was one now. Like the others, it lasted six days. No one is allowed to see it. But the wind . . . the wind carries the ceremony to the four corners. Sometimes you can hear it. It talks to itself. It carries the talk from the kiva. The songs. Prayers. Mrs. Hatch . . ." He inhaled slowly, deeply, and looked up at Mulder. "Sometimes you think you hear voices on the wind, yes? You think it's your imagination, no?" He shook his head. "No. But only some, like the kiva priests, can understand. Mrs. Hatch too can understand. We knew this recently, Silvia and I, we could tell because Mrs. Hatch was very nervous, very . . ." He gestured helplessly.

"Afraid?" Scully offered.

"I'm not . . . no. She didn't like what she heard, though." His voice hardened. "Never once since she came back from the movies has she been to the Mesa. Never once. She turned them down, you see. An old man died, and they wanted her to be in his place, and she turned them down. She had a husband, she said, and she had a way of her own. She would not go, and they never talked to her again."

"They don't have to," Mulder said, moving closer to the horse, keeping his voice low. "She hears them on the wind."

Quintodo stared at him, searching for mocking, for sarcasm, and his eyes narrowed when he didn't find it.

"These dead, Mr. Mulder, they didn't start until the ceremonial started."

Scully sidestepped nervously when the chestnut tried to nuzzle her again, upper lip momentarily curled to expose its teeth. "What are you saying, Mr. Quintodo? That these priests killed those people out there? And the cattle? For a . . . for some kind of—"

"No." He kept his gaze on Mulder. "Six days and six nights they stay in the kiva. Praying with the man who is to join them. Taking visions from the spirits to be sure they have made the right choice, and to show them the way until the next time. When they do all this, soon the wind blows." He made a rapid spinning motion with his free hand. "Whirlwind, Mr. Mulder. You know what I mean?"

Mulder didn't, and the man spat dryly in disgust at himself.

"Sangre Viento, Mr. Mulder. There are some who say they make the Sangre Viento."

A knock on the front door sounded thunderbolt-loud. Donna sat at her desk, a small secretary in the living room, working on the accounts. They added up, but not fast enough. If she was going to leave soon, on her terms, there would have to be more.

She was tempted to ignore whoever it was, pretend she wasn't home, then realized with a roll of her eyes that she could be seen through the room's picture window. With a martyred sigh, she scooped the ledger and papers into a drawer, pushed at her hair, and opened the door.

She couldn't believe it. "What are you doing here? It's practically the middle of the day."

"No. That's the wrong question. The right question is: have you been cheating me?"

A hand shoved her shoulder, hard, forcing her backward.

"Here's another one, *chica:* what do you think they would do if they found out?"

Mulder kept to himself on the way back to the inn. They had declined Annie's invitation to lunch, promised to return for a nonofficial visit, and had visited the site where the couple had been murdered. It hadn't taken long; there wasn't much left to see, and when Sparrow asked, he only said it was too soon to make any kind of determination.

Once out of the car, Garson promising to see if he could set up an appointment with the hard-to-reach medical examiner, he went straight to the front desk and arranged for a rental car to be delivered that afternoon.

"I don't like being chauffeured around," he explained to Scully, leading her into the restaurant, complaining of imminent starvation. "Especially by him. He figures, but I don't know how yet."

Scully said that was the easy part. The man was clearly fond of Annie. Just as clearly, he intended, somehow, to make sure she didn't spend the rest of her life living alone.

"He's after her money?"

"I don't know. It's been known to happen. You could see he was protective; he just wasn't loving."

They took a table in the far front corner, Scully facing the white-curtained window directly behind him. They ordered, and he watched her fuss with her silverware, fuss with her napkin before spreading it on her lap.

"What?"

She didn't hide her exasperation. "I know what you're thinking, and I'm not going to let you turn this into something it isn't."

That, he thought sourly, was the problem with working with someone who knew you that well.

Still, there was no harm trying. More than once, she had saved him from making a total fool of himself, determined to keep him at least within screaming distance of reason.

"You heard what he said."

She nodded. "And it might even be possible that that couple, the Constellas, saw something they weren't supposed to. It might even be possible they were killed for it. They wouldn't be the first to die because they'd witnessed a religious event meant to be secret." She held up a knife like a finger. "Possible, I said, Mulder. Possible."

"Okay. Possible."

And she smiled. "Likely?"

He smiled back. "Don't push it. I'm still working on possible."

She started to speak, changed her mind, then changed her mind again. "But what about Paulie Deven? Don't you think it's stretching things a little to assume he saw something, too? Which he would have had to do, if you're going to keep him with the Constellas."

"Which means?"

"Mulder, it means there's no connection between the victims and the ceremony. A horrible coincidence, nothing more."

"And the . . ." He stumbled several times, making her smile, before he managed, "Sangre Viento?"

He winced when he heard himself; his Spanish was still lousy.

The waiter brought their meal, and he stared at the strips of meat, the vegetables, the salsa in the side dish, practically feeling the heat of the spices without even getting close. He knew he would regret this later, and after his first taste, knew he would have to stock up on a supply of heavy-duty antacids if he wanted to get any sleep. The trouble was, it was so good, there was no way he wouldn't eat it.

Scully, on the other hand, popped a small jalapeño into her mouth, plucked the stem from between her teeth, and said, "Not bad, not bad."

The Sangre Viento aside for the moment, he was pleased to hear that her reaction to Sparrow was the same as his. Yet neither could think of a good reason for the act, nor could they believe the man actually thought he was fooling anyone with it. It was too broad, too born of bad movies and worse television. That led them to wondering, his feelings for Annie aside, if he was somehow involved, or just a lousy cop trying to cover his ass, make them feel sorry for him so whoever he had to answer to wouldn't take his badge.

"A little far-fetched," she judged when the table had been cleared and coffee served. "Not that we haven't seen it before."

"This isn't it. I don't know what it is, but this isn't it."

"Neither is that blood wind thing."

He opened his mouth, closed it, picked up a spoon and tapped it lightly against his thigh. "How can you be so sure?" He propped his elbows on the arms of his chair and clasped his hands in front of his mouth. "There are any number of recorded so-called unusual phenomena associated with meetings, especially religious, where the emotional intensity and concentration are abnormally high."

"All of them recorded by the people who were there, not by outside observers."

"They, these priests, were in a kiva. An underground chamber whose only exit and entrance, and source of air, is a single hole in the roof. There may have been herbal drugs, peyote maybe, something like that. Six days and six nights, Scully, and they all focus on a single thing—the man they're investing with their knowledge. Their history. With their power over the people they have to live with." He rocked forward, hands dropping to the table. "Can you imagine what it must be like? Day in and day out? All that energy building up there?"

Scully didn't answer him for a long time. She sipped her coffee, stared out the window, glanced around the otherwise empty room. She was about to reply when a woman appeared in the archway entrance. Short, stocky, in a severe summer-weight suit; her graying black hair pulled back into a bun. Her left hand held a purse tight to her side.

Mulder watched her hesitate, then march across the room toward them, no nonsense, all business. When she reached the table, she nodded a greeting.

"You are the agents from Washington?"

"Yes," Mulder answered. "And you are . . . ?"

"Dr. Rios. Helen Rios. I performed the autopsies on those poor people."

He stood immediately and offered her a chair while introducing her to Scully. When they were all seated again, he told her he was pleased to see her. Garson wouldn't have to make the appointment after all.

"He wouldn't have made it," the woman said.

"I . . . what?"

"You read my report?" she asked Scully.

"I did. To be honest, there weren't a lot of—"

"It's wrong."

Scully looked at the table, then back to Dr. Rios. "Excuse me?"

The woman opened her purse and pulled out a folded sheet of paper. "This is what I wrote first. What you read before is what I was told to write."

Mulder couldn't believe it.

Nor could he believe it when Scully opened the paper, skimmed it, and said, "Oh my God."

TWELVE

After signing for the meal, Mulder moved them immediately to his room, a precaution against eyes and ears he couldn't control.

The women sat at a small round table set by the window, covered now by dark green drapes. Mulder sat on the edge of the king-size bed.

There were four lights in the room; every one of them was on.

Dr. Rios wasted no words, or time.

"New Mexico," she said, "has been trying to upgrade its image for years; decades. People still ask if you need a passport to come here. Easterners still look for cowboys and Indians battling it out in the foothills. What the politicians and businessmen do not want most of all are the hints, the stories, the urban legend–style fables that mark the state as a place where UFOs and weird cults are not only welcome, they're encouraged. Leave that kind of nonsense," Rios said, "to Arizona, and good riddance."

Then a case like this falls into their laps.

She tapped the paper she'd taken back from Scully. "Agent Mulder, it's bad enough that these poor people died the way they did. I could tell right away how it really happened, any first-year intern could have figured it out. But for the sake of appearances, because my superiors knew it was bound to hit the papers, I was asked to file a second report. The one the public would know."

It was cool in the room, but she took a handkerchief from her purse and dabbed at her forehead.

Mulder understood the chance she had taken, and the pressure she felt. He, of all people, was no stranger to either.

"I did. For the basest of reasons—I want to keep my job." She smiled grimly across the table at Scully. "I am a woman, a Hispanic woman, in a state where the Anglos and outsiders call the tunes. I am not proud of what I've done, but I make no apologies for it."

Scully kept her expression neutral, and the doctor wiped her brow again. "The official version, Agent Mulder, is that those people were flayed. They weren't."

Mulder lifted an eyebrow. "Skinned?"

"Scoured."

He choked back a laugh of disbelief. "I'm sorry, but I don't understand."

The woman checked her watch. "I have no time. Particles of dirt, pebbles, other debris were found deeply embedded not only in the muscle tissue, but also in their mouths and the back of their throats. Other indications, such as circular striation of the exposed muscles and bone and the cauterization of most of the blood vessels, point to only one conclusion."

"Scoured."

She nodded, and stood. "Like being held up against a high-speed spinning drum covered with coarse sandpaper, Agent Mulder. Or inside a cylinder lined with the same. The only thing I can't explain is the dirt." Another grim smile, another glance at her watch. "Thank you for listening. Please don't tell anyone I have seen you. If you come to my office, if Agent Garson insists we meet, all you will hear is what you've already read in the official report." She tucked the purse under her arm. "By the way, Agent Garson knows the truth, too."

Mulder rose as she left without looking back, and stayed on his feet.

A high-speed drum covered with coarse sandpaper.

"Scully—"

"Don't say it."

"But you saw—"

"I saw the pictures, yes. I read the report, yes. But given the time frame we're working with, unless Paulie's father and sister are incredibly off-base with their sense of timing, there's no way it could happen like that."

He looked down at her, pale under the table light. "It happened, Scully. It happened."

She leaned toward him, arms resting on the table. "Then explain it to me. Explain how someone could assemble an apparatus of that size, bring it down to the river without being seen, put the boy in it, kill him, take him out, and get away. Again, without anybody seeing a thing."

"The girl—"

"Saw nothing we can substantiate. Ghosts, Mulder. She said she saw ghosts."

"And whispers," he reminded her. "She also said she heard whispers."

Scully slumped back and shook her head. "What does it mean? I don't get it."

"I don't either." He yanked open the drapes, turned off the lights, and dropped into the chair opposite her. "But so far, everyone who's talked to us has—" He stopped, closed his eyes briefly, then moved to the bed and stared for a moment at the telephone on the night table.

"Mulder?"

"Konochine," he said, and picked up the receiver. "Why do we keep bumping into the Konochine?"

"While you're at it," she said. "Give Garson a call and find out why he's so reluctant to tell us the truth."

Donna looked helplessly at the two dozen cartons stacked in her spare room. They were all ready for shipping, or for hand delivery to area shops. A permanent cold seemed to have attached itself to her spine, to her stomach. She couldn't stop shaking. She had denied cheating anyone, of course, and had even shown him the ledger to prove it. But it had been close. There had been no apology, only a lingering warning look before he left, slamming the door as he went.

She had to get out.

All the potential money in this room wasn't going to do her any good if she wasn't around to spend it.

She looked at her watch. If she hurried, she could clean out the bank account, be packed, and be out of this godforsaken state before midnight. Leave everything behind. It didn't matter. The house, her clothes . . . none of it mattered. Just take the money and get out.

But first she would have to make a phone call. She couldn't leave without saying good-bye.

Garson wasn't in his office, and no one there knew where he could be found. The secretary thought he might be at the ME's office.

The second call was to information.

When the third was finished, Mulder replaced the receiver and began to wonder.

"What?" Scully asked.

"According to his sister, Paulie picked up a piece of jewelry from one of the local shops. A silver pendant of some kind." Mulder looked up. "She thinks it was Konochine."

"And?"

"And I don't remember seeing it as being with his effects."

"Such as they were," she reminded him.

"Whatever. It wasn't there." He rose, and paced until Scully's warning groan put him back in his chair. "That woman, the one who handles the crafts."

She flipped open a notebook, paged through it, and said, "Falkner."

"You want to take a ride?"

"Mulder—"

"The connection, Scully. You can't deny we have a connection."

The rental car had been delivered, and the clerk at the front desk gave him a map and directions to the address he had found in the telephone book. The parking lot was on the north side of the inn, through a gated entry in the side wall. As he slipped behind the wheel, Mulder noted that the car seemed to have every gadget known to Detroit, except perhaps an orbital trajectory tracking system.

It took him a few seconds to get oriented, and a few seconds more before he convinced himself that he wasn't charging headlong into foolishness. The how of the murders was still beyond him, in spite of Dr. Rios's description. Concentrate on the who and the why, however, and the how would come wagging its tail behind them.

He hoped.

As he pulled out onto the street and headed north, Scully inhaled quickly.

"What?"

They passed a series of four small stores in a common one-story building. A man stood in front of one of them, not bothering to conceal his interest in the car.

"Last night," she said. "I didn't see him clearly, but there was a man at the gate, watching me."

He checked the rearview mirror.

The man, face hidden by the bill of his cap, still watched.

There was no flip of a mental coin. Mulder swung the wheel around, made a U-turn, made another to pull alongside the stores.

The man hadn't moved.

Scully lowered her window. "Do you want something?" she asked calmly.

Leon Ciola swaggered over and leaned down. "You the feds?"

With one hand still on the wheel, Mulder leaned over, curious about the fine scars that swept across the man's face. "Special Agent Mulder, Special Agent Scully. Who are you?"

"Leon Ciola."

"You've been watching us. Why?"

Ciola spread his arms wide in a mocking bow, smiling impudently. "Always like to know who's in town, *amigos*, that's all. It's very dull around here, you know? Not much to do. The sun's too hot. Not much work for a man like me."

"What is a man like you?" Scully said.

"Ex-con. They didn't tell you that?"

No, Mulder thought; there's a lot they haven't told us.

Then he spotted a faint racial resemblance to Nando Quintodo. "You're from the Mesa?"

Ciola's smile didn't falter. "Very good, *amigo*. Most people think I look Apache." Fingers fluttered across his face. "The scars. They make me look mean."

"Are you?"

The smile vanished. "I'm a son of a bitch, Agent Mulder. A good thing to know."

He's not bragging, Mulder thought; he's not warning, either.

Ciola glanced up and down the street, then placed a hand on the window well. "Sheriff Sparrow will tell you that I have killed a man. It's true. Maybe more, who knows? He'll tell you, when he gets around to it, that I probably killed those stupid tourists. I didn't, Agent Mulder. I have more important things to do."

He tipped his cap to Scully and backed away, interview over.

Mulder nodded to him, straightened, and pulled slowly away from the curb. The man chilled him. What chilled him more, however, was the fact that Sparrow hadn't said a word about him. An obvious suspect, a self-confessed killer ex-con, and the sheriff had, conveniently or otherwise, kept Ciola's name to himself.

"Scully, do you get the feeling we've dropped down the rabbit hole?"

She didn't answer.

A glance at her profile showed him lips so taut they were bloodless.

He didn't question her. Something about the man, something he hadn't caught, struck a nerve. Sooner or later, she would tell him what it was. As it was, he had to deal with street signs he could barely read because they were too small, and the vehicles impatiently lining up behind him because he was driving slow enough to try to read the damn signs.

The sun didn't help.

It flared off everything, and bleached that which wasn't already bleached.

Everywhere there were signs of a town struggling to find the right way to grow—obviously new shops, shops that had gone out of business, houses and buildings in varying stages of construction or repair. It was either very exciting to live here now, or very frightening.

"There," Scully said.

He turned left, toward the river, and found himself on a street where lots were large and vacant, spotted only once in a while by small, one-story houses in either brick or fake adobe. A drab place, made more so by the gardens and large bushes flowering violent colors. No toys in the driveways. The few cars at the curbs seemed abandoned.

He parked in front of a ranch house whose front window was buried by a tangled screen of roses. A Cherokee parked in the pitted drive faced the street. As they got out, he saw a suitcase by the driver's door.

"Somebody's going on vacation."

"I don't think so," she said, nodding toward the two other suitcases sitting on the stoop. "Not unless she's planning to stay away for six months."

He knocked on the screen door.

No one answered.

He knocked again, and the inner door was opened by a young woman with a briefcase in one hand.

"I don't want any," she said.

Scully held up her ID. "Special Agent Scully, Special Agent Mulder, FBI. Are you Donna Falkner?"

It didn't take any special instinct to realize the woman was afraid. Mulder opened the screen door carefully and said, "We'd just like to talk to you, Ms. Falkner. It won't take a minute, and then you can take your trip."

"How did you know that?" Donna demanded, her voice pitched high enough to crack. Then she followed Mulder's gesture toward the suitcases. "Oh."

"Just a few minutes," Scully assured her.

The woman's shoulders slumped. "Oh, what the hell, why not. How much worse can it get?"

THIRTEEN

The air conditioning had been shut off. The room was stifling. The woman hasn't left yet, Mulder thought, and already the house feels deserted.

Donna grabbed a ladder-back chair from in front of a small desk and turned it around. When she sat, shoulders still slumped, she held the briefcase in her lap, looking as if she wanted to hold it against her chest. Scully took a seat on a two-cushion couch, pen and notebook in hand; Mulder remained standing, leaning a shoulder against the wall just inside the room's entry.

It kept him in partial shadow; it kept the woman in full light.

"So," she said resignedly. "What do you want to know?"

"The Konochine," Mulder told her, and saw her gaze dart in his direction.

"What about them?"

"You sell their jewelry," Scully said, shifting the woman's attention back the other way. "We were told they didn't like the outside world very much."

"Hardly at all," Donna answered. Her shoulders rose a little.

"I got chased off the res once, back before I knew what I was doing." She shifted the briefcase to the floor beside her. "See, they're not the only Indians I deal with, but they give me the most trouble. Or did, anyway. There's this man—"

"Nick Lanaya?" Mulder said.

"Yeah. He's one of the out-and-backers. You know, got out, came back? Well, we met at a party once, got to talking—he's very easy to talk to, kind of like a priest, if you know what I mean. Anyway, he knew his people needed money, and after he asked around, he knew I'd be able to get them a fair price for the work."

Scully moved a hand to draw her attention again. "How mad are the ones who don't want outside contact?"

Donna frowned, the understanding of what Scully meant slow in arriving. "Oh. Oh! Hey, not that mad. God, no. You think they killed those poor people?" She dismissed the notion with a wave. "Jesus, no. They talk a lot, yell a lot, but Nick just yells right back. He's—" She stopped, frozen, as though something had just occurred to her. "Tell you, though, the guy you should be talking to is Leon Ciola."

"We've met," Mulder said dryly.

"You're kidding." Her right hand drifted down to brush at the case. "You know he was in the state pen, up by Santa Fe? Killed a man in a bar fight." Her left hand drew a line across her throat. Slowly. "Nearly cut his head off. I don't know how he got out. A good lawyer, I guess."

"Where are you going?" Scully asked.

"Vacation," Donna replied instantly.

"You take more clothes than Scully," Mulder said with a laugh.

"I'll be away for a while."

"Who takes care of the business? Nick?"

She shrugged. "Mostly, yeah."

Scully closed her notebook. "You have no control over what you receive from the Mesa? Or who buys them retail?"

"Nope. Nick chooses the pieces, I choose the shops. After that, it's the guy who has the most money."

Mulder pushed away from the wall. "What if somebody who didn't know any better just drove onto the reservation?"

"Nothing." Donna retrieved her case. "No one would talk to them, probably. Sooner or later, they'd get the hint and leave."

"And if they didn't?"

"You mean like me?" She laughed; it was false. "I'm pushy, Agent Mulder. I pushed too far. Chasing is all that would happen, believe me." She stood and looked none too subtly at the door. "I still say you should check Ciola. He has a knife and . . ." She shuddered for effect.

Scully rose as well. "Thank you, Ms. Falkner. We appreciate the time."

"No problem." She led them to the stoop. "If you don't mind, though, I have a plane to catch, okay?"

Mulder thanked her again, asked her to call Agent Garson if there was anything else she thought of before she left, and got behind the wheel, cursing himself soundly for forgetting to leave the windows down.

The sun out there, and an oven in here. He set the air conditioning to high and hurry up about it and drove off, taking his time, while Scully watched Donna Falkner in the outside mirror. When they turned the corner, Scully said, "She relaxed very quickly."

"Yeah. Because we didn't ask her about what she thought we would."

"Which was?"

"Scully, if I knew that, I would have asked her."

She grunted disbelief; he knew what she was thinking. There were times when asking questions got you answers, but not necessarily when you wanted them. There were times when it was better to spin a web and see who tried to break free.

Donna was breaking free.

Once she got on that plane, New Mexico would never see her again.

Scully looked over. "How are you going to stop her?"

He gestured toward the backseat, asking her to grab his denim jacket. When she did, his portable phone fell out of the inside pocket.

"Garson?" she said.

"Material witness to an active investigation."

"But she isn't, Mulder."

"No, maybe not. But he can delay her long enough to miss her flight. Maybe discourage her enough to wait until tomorrow."

She called, discovered Garson couldn't be reached, and demanded to speak to an agent on duty. After convincing him they weren't kidding about Falkner, she asked where the Constella van was being held.

"Right here," she said when she hung up. "A lot behind a sheriff's substation."

"Why do you want to see it?"

"You wanted to see Ann Hatch, and look what it got us. I want to see that van."

Sometimes they made her too much like him.

"And what do you mean, I take too many clothes when I go on a trip?"

The substation was little more than a double-wide on cinder blocks, only a sign on the door announcing its function. The parking area in front was only big enough for four vehicles, and the tree that cast a weak shade over the building looked about ready to collapse at any second. Beyond the tree was another lot, fenced in with chain-link and topped with concertina wire. Within were a handful of cars, a pickup, and a van.

Sheriff Sparrow was outside waiting when Mulder pulled in off the street.

"Garson works fast," Scully said when they stopped.

"Your tax dollars at work."

Sparrow waved them over to a padlocked gate in the fence. "Looking for anything in particular?" he asked as the gate swung free and they walked in.

"You never know," Mulder told him.

The van was at the back, dusty enough to ward off the sun. Mulder shaded his eyes and looked through the side and front windows, then asked Sparrow for the key.

"What for?"

"To get inside." He rapped a knuckle against the sliding side door. "You never know."

Sparrow grumbled, complained that he'd left the keys inside, and headed back to the trailer.

"Mulder?"

She was on the passenger side, and he took his time joining her. The heat was brutal, worse than the day before, and he understood now why life was so deliberate in this part of the world. Anything faster than a crawl on a day like today meant sure heatstroke, and a tub packed in ice.

"So?"

She pointed to the side.

He looked and saw the dust; then he saw what lay under the dust.

He used a palm to wipe the metal clean, and yelped when the heat scorched him. "Damn!" He shook his hand, blew on it, and pulled a handkerchief from his pocket.

"Be careful," she said. "It's hot." When he gave her a look, she only shrugged and added, "Your tax dollars at work."

There were two large tinted windows, one in the sliding door, the other at the back. He shook the handkerchief out, then folded it in quarters to form a makeshift dusting pad. Hunkering down, balancing on his toes, he swiped at the dust and dirt first, to knock off what he could before he started rubbing.

"What the hell you looking for?" Sparrow said, tossing the keys to Scully.

"This was a rental," Mulder said without looking up.

"Yep. So?"

"New, then, right?"

"Probably." The sheriff leaned over him, squinting at the panel. "So?"

"So I guess Mr. Constella wasn't much of a driver."

He didn't have to rub. When the area was clear, he rose and took a step back, waiting for Sparrow to comment. He was also waiting to hear why the man hadn't noticed it days ago. Or, if he had, why he hadn't said anything.

From the window to the bottom of the frame, the paint had been scraped off, right down to bare metal. The dust had been thick, the van having sat here for more than a week in the sheriff's custody. A glint of that bare metal was what had caught Scully's attention.

"Well, I'll be damned." Sparrow hitched his belt. "Run up against a stone wall, boulder, something like that, looks like."

"I don't think so." Mulder ran a finger lightly over the surface. "No appreciable indentation, so there was no real collision."

Scully stepped in front of them and peered at it closely, shifted and sighted along the side to the rear bumper. "If there was, it wouldn't be in just this one place." When she straightened, she leaned close to the window. Touched it with a forefinger. Took the handkerchief and wiped the glass clean. "Scrapes here, too."

"Road dirt," Sparrow said. "You get it all the time out here, dust and all, going the speeds you do."

She ignored him for the moment, using the finger to trace the damage's outline, right to the strip above the window. "Whatever it was, it was big. Man-high, at least."

322

"Like I said, a boulder."

"Come on, Sheriff," Mulder said, having had enough of his forced ignorance. "Scully's right. A collision would have produced damage wider than this, and by the force of it, at the least this window would have been cracked, if not smashed."

He scratched under his jaw, and leaned close again.

"Agent Mulder, this is—"

"Do you have a magnifying glass?"

He heard the man snort his disgust, but the expected argument didn't happen. Sparrow trudged away, muttering about how the damn feds think they know everything, just loudly enough.

Scully unlocked the passenger door and stood back to let the heat out. Then she climbed in and through the two front seats to the back. Mulder couldn't see her until she rapped on the window and beckoned.

He knelt on the passenger seat and leaned over the top. The two rows of bench seats had been taken out, leaving the holding rails behind. The floor and walls were covered with alternating swatches of vivid purple and dull brown carpeting.

"This is a love nest?" he said, wincing at the garish combination.

"Love is blind, Mulder." She was on her knees, poking at a loose section of carpet with her pen.

"In here it would have to be."

"Got it."

She rocked back on her heels and held up the pen. Dangling from it was a length of silver chain. She followed when Mulder backed out, and dropped the chain into his palm. "That's not a store chain. It's handmade." She prodded it with the pen, shifting it as he watched. "I'll bet it's not silver-plated, either."

He brought the palm closer to his eyes.

The links were longer than he would have expected, and not as delicately thin as they first appeared. Neither were they the same length.

She took the chain back, grasping each end between thumb and forefinger. Tugged once. "Strong. You couldn't yank this off someone's neck without sawing halfway through it."

"Konochine."

She gave him a *maybe* tilt of her head, and headed back to the car to fetch a plastic evidence bag from her purse.

"Bring a couple," he called after her, and glanced at his watch.

Sparrow still hadn't returned; Mulder finally lost the rest of his patience. He marched over to the trailer, yanked open the door, and stepped in. The sheriff was seated behind one of three desks in the room, his feet up, his hat off, a flask at his lips.

He looked startled when he saw Mulder, but he didn't move until he had finished his drink. "It's hot out there," he said.

"It's going to get hotter," Mulder told him, not bothering to suppress his anger. "Give me the glass, then get one of your people ready to take some evidence to Garson's technicians. I'll call him myself to tell him what to look for."

Sparrow glared as he set the flask onto the desk. "I don't believe I heard the magic word, Agent Mulder."

Mulder just looked at him, and "FBI" was all he said.

FOURTEEN

X He couldn't see Scully when he returned to the lot, slapping the magnifying glass hard against his leg. He was angry and disappointed, not nearly as much at the sheriff as at himself. Losing control like that, pulling rank, wasn't his style. Working with local law was something he had learned to do years ago, knowing that their assistance was just as vital to investigations as his own federal agents. What he had just done was a violation not only of policy, but his own code.

"Scully?"

It was dumb.

"Hey, Scully!"

It was stupid.

"Over here, Mulder."

But boy, did it feel good.

He found her standing next to what used to be a sleek Jaguar. Now most of its windows were shattered, the windshield webcracked, the racing-green paint pocked and scored from front to back, and the roof crushed as though someone had dropped a flatcar on it.

"Our drunk driver?" he asked.

"I don't know. I think so. Look at this."

He went around to the side, and saw the same pattern of scouring she had uncovered on the van, only this time it was wider.

"Invisible car," he said.

She lifted a questioning hand. "I give up, Mulder. What's going on?" A closer look at his face. "Never mind. I think I'd rather know what happened in there."

There was no chance to answer. The trailer door slammed gunshot loud, and Sparrow stomped toward them. The way his hand chopped the air, Mulder figured he was having one hell of an argument with himself. By the time he reached them, the argument was over.

He stood with one hand resting on the handle of his holstered gun, while the other folded a stick of gum into his mouth. Then he pulled off his sunglasses by pinching them at the bridge and sliding.

"I'll take the evidence in myself." It wasn't an order, it wasn't a demand. It was an offer of truce.

"That's fine with me, sir," Mulder said, accepting the offer.

"Chuck." The sheriff chewed rapidly.

Mulder grinned. "I don't think so."

"Me neither. My mother hated it. She always said it wasn't the name of anything but chopped meat." He pushed the sunglasses back on. "So, FBI, what's so important you got to rush it into the city?"

While Scully explained about the partial necklace chain, Mulder went back to the van and, with the magnifying glass and the tip of a blade on his Swiss army knife, pried loose samples of debris caught in the deep gouges on the door. He did the same to the car, sealed his findings in the bags, and handed them over.

Uneasy, but more at ease, they walked back to the office,

grateful for the cool respite. Scully tagged and numbered the bags. Mulder called Garson's office, told them what to expect and what he wanted done.

"That shouldn't take very long," the secretary said confidently.

"Have you found Agent Garson yet?"

"No sir, I sure haven't."

He gave her his number and instructed her to have Garson call as soon as he came in. When he asked whether Donna Falkner had been intercepted, he was told that she had been, by one of the other agents. Apparently she hadn't been very happy, certainly not when she was brought back to the Silver Avenue office, where she currently was giving a statement.

"A statement? About what?"

"I wouldn't know, sir. I'm only the secretary. They only tell me what I need to know."

Sure, he thought; and all the rest is magic.

He perched on the edge of the nearest empty desk and wiped his brow with a sleeve.

Sparrow was back in his chair. "You reckon it's the Konochine somehow? I figured that, what with you talking to Donna and all."

"I don't see how it can't be, now. There are too many connections."

"A lead, anyway," Scully added.

"Oh boy." The sheriff reached for his flask, changed his mind, and propped his feet up instead. "Trouble is, there's a couple hundred of them. It can't be all—" Suddenly he snapped upright, boots stamping the floor. "Son of a bitch!"

Mulder looked first to Scully before saying, "Leon Ciola."

The sheriff's jaw sagged. "Damn, Mulder, you're good." He drummed his fingers against his cheek thoughtfully, then reached for his phone. "There's somebody you should meet. He'll be able to tell you what you want know about who you need to know

327

about. Lanaya. I already told you about him. Believe it or not, he still lives on the res."

"What about Ciola?"

Sparrow held up a finger as the connection was made, winced as he made arrangements with the dealer to meet at the inn after dinner that evening, winced again and rubbed his ear as he hung up. "Storm coming," he explained. "Static'll deafen you sometimes."

Thank God, Mulder thought; at least it'll get cooler.

"Ciola," he reminded Sparrow.

"Bastard. Pure and simple bastard. Got sent up for murder, got a lawyer who found a hole and squeezed the son of a bitch through it. There's not much I can do but keep an eye out, and hope he doesn't lose his temper again."

It didn't take special intuition to figure out the man not only hated Ciola, he was afraid of him.

"You thinking he's involved with this?"

"You have to admit, he's a likely candidate."

"Nope, don't think so."

Mulder was surprised, and let the sheriff know it.

"Not his style," Sparrow explained. "He's all intimidation and reputation. The man he killed, it was over quick and dirty. These people . . . that took patience."

"But not much time, Sheriff," Scully said. "The Deven boy, remember?"

He granted her that reluctantly, but insisted it couldn't have been Ciola. "There's a reason for those people, Agent Scully. We just ain't found it yet. With Leon, there doesn't have to be one."

"Heat of the moment," Mulder suggested.

"Got it in one."

Scully seemed doubtful, but didn't argue.

The sheriff accepted her silence without comment, looked around the station, then carefully locked the plastic bags into an attache case he pulled from a bottom drawer. "Better get going. I want to get back before the storm." He walked to the back and radioed one of his men, telling him where he'd be and for how long; he called a central dispatcher with the same information, for intercepting any calls; he spat his gum into a wastebasket, opened a wardrobe on the far wall, and took down a clean, blocked hat.

When he saw Mulder staring, he pointed to the hat on the desk. "That's my comfort hat, had it for years." He flicked the brim on the one he had on. "This is my showing-up-in-the-city hat. Pretty dumb, ain't it."

Scully laughed, and Mulder could only nod as Sparrow walked with them to their car.

"Check it out, folks," he said, pointing over the trailer. "Be inside when it happens."

Mulder looked, and couldn't believe that clouds that massive, and that high, could assemble so quickly. Shaped like anvils, boiling at the edges, they had already buried most of the western blue.

"My God, Scully, we're going to drown."

He drove back to the motel as fast as he dared, which still wasn't fast enough for the others on the road. They passed him on the left, on the right, and would have driven over him if the car had been low enough.

"Calm down," Scully said when the engine died. "We've still got some work to do while we wait for Lanaya."

The bone pile stirred as the wind brushed over it, dust in tan clouds passing through ribs and eye sockets, through a gaping hole in one of the skulls.

A scorpion scuttled across the curled horn of a ram.

In the center, using the pelvic bone of a stallion for a temporary stool, a man stirred the loose earth with the point of a knife. Designs were fashioned, and erased; words were written, and vanished. He glanced up only once, to check the storm's approach, returning to his work only when he saw the lightning, and didn't hear the thunder.

It would move fast.

He would move faster.

Donna Falkner slammed into her house, slammed the door shut behind her, flung a suitcase across the living room, and began to scream her outrage. She kicked at the nearest wall, picked up the desk chair and hurled it down the hall; she grabbed the couch cushions and tried to rip them open with her nails, tossed them aside, and dropped to the floor, sobbing.

It wasn't fair.

It wasn't goddamn fair.

All she had to do was get on the goddamn plane, and she was out of here. Gone. Lost in another city, where they never heard of Indians except on TV, never bothered with Southwest crafts except in fancy boutiques that overpriced everything from a wallet to a brooch. Gone. New name, new hair, new everything.

Gone.

Now the FBI wanted her, and *he* wanted her, and there was nothing she could do about it but sit around and wait.

She punched the floor.

She screamed again, cheeks florid, teeth bared.

The sunlight began to dim, and the thorns of the rosebushes began to scratch lightly against the windows.

Suddenly she couldn't breathe, made a double fist with her hands, and pressed it against her chest. Harder. Gulping for air. Rocking on her buttocks until she thought she would faint. Tears streaming down her cheeks, dripping off her chin, coating her lips with the taste of salt.

When the attack passed, she let herself fall backward slowly, seeing nothing but tiny cracks in the plaster ceiling, forming them into images that made her weep again.

The telephone rang.

She wiped her eyes with the backs of her hands and sat up. She had no intention of answering it. Let it ring. If it was those agents who had come to see her, they could just come over on their own. The hell with them. The hell with them all.

When she stood, she swayed; when she walked down the short hall toward the bathroom, she staggered. When she reached the bathroom, she looked at her reflection, gagged . . . and giggled. Touched the tip of her reflection's nose with a finger and told it there was nothing to worry about, nothing she couldn't handle.

What she would do was, if they wouldn't let her fly, then fuck it, she would drive. By the time they realized she was gone, she would be . . . gone.

She giggled again.

Gone, but not forgotten.

Gone, and goddamn rich.

Wash up, she ordered; wash up, change your clothes, get the damn money, and be . . . gone.

What the hell are you so worried about?

She didn't know.

Suddenly, she didn't know.

She hurried into the spare room, squinted through the small window, and figured by the sky she had maybe an hour before the storm arrived. If it arrived. They had a bad habit of being all show and no action sometimes. Not that it mattered. Only a fool would tempt clouds like that on an open road.

Another giggle.

Screw 'em.

Now that she wasn't flying, she could load the Cherokee to the gills, take a little inventory to pad the mattress. The not-so-perfect plan, but better than nothing. Nothing would mean sitting around, waiting for things to happen.

She grabbed a carton and headed for the door.

Sand stirred, lifting sluggishly from the ground as if drawn by a weak magnet.

Nearby, a dead leaf quivered.

A twig shifted, rolled an inch, and stopped.

The sand settled a few seconds later.

Nothing moved.

FIFTEEN

The shower was wonderful.

After crawling around the van and automobile in the sun all that time, Scully was drenched with sweat, caked and streaked with dust, and ready to scream. In spite of the silver chain, in spite of what Mulder had dug from the vehicles' sides, they hadn't accomplished very much.

What frustrated her was a combination of the case itself, which seemed to be going nowhere fast, and the certain knowledge that she had already seen the break point and had missed it. Something small. Something so obvious she had overlooked it. The purloined letter in New Mexico.

The storm didn't help.

The clouds, frighteningly black and impossibly huge, were still out there, still in the middle distance. If they moved, she couldn't tell. They sat there, not small enough to be lurking, and too large to even be called looming. There was nothing ahead of them but a steady, hot wind.

They were also tired. The mix of altitude and heat had sapped them without their realizing it. When they reached the motel, it was a mutual decision to clean up and rest for an hour, then meet again to see what they could come up with before their meeting with Nick Lanaya.

So she used the shower to make her comfortable again, to drain the afternoon's tension from her shoulders and limbs, and to let her mind roam, seeking pathways and the places where they might possibly join into something concrete she could follow, something hopeful.

When it didn't happen immediately, she was mildly annoyed, but she didn't mind. It would come eventually; of that she was confident.

She took her time dressing, sat on the edge of her bed, and gazed at the window, scowling at the tension she could feel building again. She rolled her shoulders, massaged them one at a time, to get rid of it; it didn't work. She stretched until her joints threatened to pop or separate, deliberately groaning aloud; it didn't work.

Maybe it was just anticipation of the storm.

The clouds must have moved closer while she had been in the bathroom. The sunlight held considerably less glare, a hint of false twilight filtering into the front courtyard. By that part of the bench tree she could see, the wind had died down as well.

It seemed that the outside had decided to do nothing but wait until the storm made up its mind whether to strike or not.

"Damn," she whispered.

No wonder she was still tense. That was exactly what she was doing. Waiting, not acting. Some son of a bitch had butchered three innocent people, and all she could do was sit here like a lump and wait for the damn rain.

She snapped to her feet, grabbed her shoulder bag, decided the hell with the hat, and hurried outside.

No one in the courtyard and, when she couldn't help looking, no one standing at the gate.

The image of Ciola's face so close to her own made her pause and shudder. Those scars, and those dead eyes . . . she shuddered again and knocked hard on Mulder's door, one heel tapping impatiently. When he answered, naked to the waist and drying his hair with a towel, she said, "Get decent, Mulder. We're going out again."

The sand stirred.

The leaf quivered.

"You're the one who made the connections," Scully said as he pulled on a shirt. "So why wait?"

"Scully, we haven't been here twenty-four hours."

"That doesn't answer my question: Why wait?"

He couldn't think of a good answer, and didn't especially want to, not when she practically sparked with energy like this. It was best, always best, to go along for the ride. Besides, she was right. With too many signs pointing to the Konochine, it only made sense to pay an official visit to the reservation. The only problem was, he thought they ought to have a guide, someone who knew who they should talk to, preferably someone who knew the language.

"The sheriff."

"He's in Albuquerque, remember?"

"Falkner."

"They rode her out on a rail."

She tapped a fingernail on the table. "Lanaya would be perfect, but we don't know how to get in touch with him."

They tried the phone book, but no luck; they tried the sheriff's dispatcher, and had the same result. A call to Falkner brought no answer; Scully let the phone ring twenty times before hanging up in disgust.

Neither one of them even breathed Leon Ciola's name.

He switched on a lamp without thinking. "We could always go out to the ranch," he suggested, not really too happy with the idea.

Neither was Scully, from her reaction. At the moment, however, there was no place else to turn. And, he added, reaching for his gun and holster to clip on his belt, it didn't especially have to be Annie. In fact, it probably shouldn't be, if what the foreman had told them was true. Quintodo himself would do just as well, assuming he was willing. It wasn't a raid; they were simply looking for information.

Which, he thought glumly, they probably wouldn't get anyway. If the Indians wanted as little to do as possible with whites in general, representatives of the government in Washington, especially the law, would no doubt be treated as if they had the plague.

Then he opened the door, took a quick step back, and said, "You have an ark handy?"

The storm had finally reached them.

Scully made a wordless sound of amazement as they watched the rain pound the courtyard in dark and light streaks shot through with silver, pockets of steam rising from the ground in swirling patches that were shredded and whisked away. It was so heavy, they could barely see the wall.

Scully turned on the rest of the lights and rubbed her upper arms. "Close the door, it's cold."

Mulder didn't mind. After walking around in a furnace all day, the sensation was luxurious.

And the rain fascinated him.

"It can't last long," she said, although it sounded like a question.

He had seen downpours before, but this was more than that, this was an outright deluge; it didn't seem possible it could last for more than a few minutes. There couldn't be that much water in the sky.

Ten minutes later he closed the door and shrugged. "I guess we're stuck. Unless you want to try it anyway."

"Out there? In that?"

Looking out the window didn't do any good; the rain smothered it, completely obliterating the outside world.

He wished, however, that the wind would rise. It didn't seem natural, all that rain and no wind to whip it.

Scully moved over to the bed and picked up the receiver. "I'll try Garson again. I'd like to know what he's been doing all day."

He would, too. He had already run through a couple of scenarios, neither of which he liked. He doubted seriously that the man was upset because of their arrival; they were all supposed to be working the same territory no matter what state that territory was in. He also didn't think Garson was part of what they were looking for; it felt wrong. Nothing more; it just felt wrong.

Scully hung up. "Nothing. Sparrow's been there, but there are no results yet."

Rain slapped at the door, a little wind at last.

A constant thudding overhead, like an army marching across the roof.

"Talk to me, Mulder," Scully said then.

He sat at the table, drew invisible patterns on the surface to focus him and, at the same time, to let him think aloud without built-in restrictions.

"It's a cliché," he said slowly, "but maybe it's true here, who knows? What we know for sure is that Paulie and the Constellas had Konochine jewelry. Except for that partial chain you found, it was gone when the bodies were discovered. Destroyed or taken, we don't know yet. But it's gone.

"Maybe this Lanaya brought out the wrong kind. Maybe it has some religious or traditional significance we don't understand yet. Everyone we've talked to has made a big deal of telling us they don't want contact, minimal contact at best. So it's possible

337

that exposing those pieces to the outside could be considered a form of sacrilege. There might be some on the reservation who would do anything to get it back."

"You're right, it is a cliché." She leaned forward and rested her forearms on her thighs. "And don't forget, Lanaya is one of their own. He wouldn't make a mistake like that. Not even a careless one."

"Then maybe it's the very fact that the pieces went out at all."

"He's been doing it for years."

"He's been fighting them for years."

"But he's still been doing it."

Right, he thought; and by now, after all this time, hundreds of people must have Konochine rings and necklaces and who knew what else? Hundreds, at least, but only three had died.

A damp chill filtered into the room.

The light flickered once and settled, startling him into the realization that there was no thunder, no lightning. How could clouds like that, with all that power, not have thunder and lightning?

Scully rose and walked to the bathroom door, walked back and sat again. "I'd still like to know how it was done."

"Scoured. Dr. Rios said scoured."

"How?"

He almost said, "Sentient Brillo," but changed his mind when he saw the *don't you dare, Mulder* look on her face.

Instead, he answered, "I haven't a clue."

"Yes!" She slapped her leg angrily. "Yes, damnit, we *do* have a clue! We just don't know what it is."

There was no response to exasperation like that, so he drew patterns again, over and over, while he listened to the thunder the army made on the roof.

"Sangre Viento," he said at last.

"It has a nice ring, but what does it mean, aside from the translation?"

338

Patterns; always patterns.

He watched the finger move, trying not to control it consciously. Automatic writing that did nothing but draw senseless patterns.

Thirty minutes after the storm began, he tilted his chair back, reached over, and opened the door, squinting against a spray that dropped ice on his cheeks. "This is impossible. When the hell is it going to end?"

And the rain stopped.

He almost toppled backward at the abruptness of the cessation. One second he couldn't see an inch past the tree, the next all there was were glittering droplets falling from the leaves and eaves, and a slow runoff of water along narrow, shallow trenches set along the paths.

He looked at Scully and said, "Am I good, or what?"

Donna whispered a prayer when the rain finally ended and the sun came out. One more quick turn around the house and a check of the back yard, and she would leave. The Cherokee was packed; she had never unpacked. It had been a stupid idea anyway, thinking she could use the rain for cover. She wouldn't have made it half a mile on the interstate before she would have been forced to pull over. This way she was calmer, and had a clearer head.

She had had time to think.

Now it was time to fish or cut bait.

The bone pile had been touched by only a fringe of the storm, washed clean and gleaming.

The water had been taken by leaves and roots and the porous desert floor; there were no puddles, and there was no wind.

Nevertheless, the sand stirred.

SIXTEEN

Mulder stepped outside and inhaled deeply several times. Too many scents mingled for him to identify, but they were sweet, and he was pleased. He had caught Scully's determination, and with the dust washed away, even the prospects of success seemed more bright.

You're pushing it, he told himself, and didn't much care. It felt pretty good, and he took that where he could get it.

Scully followed, checking to be sure the door locked behind her. A detour to the front desk assured them that the clerk had Mulder's portable phone number and would relay calls or messages as soon as they were received.

Just as they were about to turn away from the desk, Scully gave a nod toward the side entrance. "I think we have company."

A tall man in denim and a ponytail walked toward them, taking off his hat as he approached. "Agent Mulder? Agent Scully?"

Mulder nodded warily.

The man held out his hand. "Nick Lanaya. We were supposed to meet later." He cocked a lean hip as he shifted his weight.

"Sorry I'm early, but I took a chance catching you. I was going to stop at a friend's first, but the storm . . ."

"Actually," Scully said, "your timing is perfect. We were about to drive out to the Mesa."

His eyes widened. "Alone?"

"No. We were hoping someone from the Double-H would go along. But," she added with a smile, "now you're here, which is exactly what we need."

"Damn right about that," he said, matching her with a smile of his own. "Today's Thursday. You go there today, they'll probably shoot you."

"What?" Mulder said.

"Well, not really shoot you, Agent Mulder, but you wouldn't have gotten in. It's a . . . call it a holy day. Kind of like Sunday, only a little more intense." He used the hat to gesture toward the restaurant. "So what do you say we have something to eat? Chuck said you had a few questions, and I answer better on a full stomach."

Not long after they were at a table, this time near the entrance. Other diners had already begun to arrive, and the room was more lively, more cheerful than last time. The contrast was startling, and it took Mulder a few minutes before he was able to concentrate on what Lanaya told him.

Anecdotes at first, as their meal arrived and they ate, trying to give them a feel for his people. They were conservative, hardworking, and surprisingly, they didn't feel at all oppressed.

"They've been at Sangre Viento since their Time began. No one has ever defeated them in war badly enough to drive them out, although the Apache gave them a hard time for a while, a hundred years or so back, and the white man hasn't seen any need to do anything but leave them pretty much alone." He seemed slightly embarrassed. "To tell you the truth, it makes them kind of smug."

Scully brushed the corner of her mouth with a napkin. "I understand you're an important person there."

Lanaya closed his eyes as he laughed, shook his head, and waved his fork. "Lord, no. Important?" He laughed again. "Not the way you mean, no. Some sort of authority figure, a position of power, something like that?"

"Something like that, yes."

"Nope. Sorry. I'm important only in that I keep their contacts with the outside healthy, that's all. They're not stupid, Agent Scully. They don't live primitively; not by their standards, anyway. They just pick and choose what they want from the white man's world, that's all. Some have TV, everybody has a radio. Schooling is important. I'm not the only one who went to college."

"But you went back."

"Yes. Yes, I went back. Often there are ties too strong to be broken." His left hand moved to his chest and away, but not before Mulder spotted a bulge there.

A medicine bag, he thought; he carries his power with him.

"Anyway, what is it, exactly, that you want to know?"

Mulder watched Scully's smile, and hid one of his own. The man was taken with her, and whether he knew it or not, Scully had already gotten more from him than he probably wanted them to know.

They.

He said *they* instead of *we*.

Scully's next question was predictable, and Mulder couldn't help feeling a faint disappointment at the answer.

"No, there's no significance to any of the things I bring out for Donna to sell. Traditional designs, that's all." He chuckled. "Once in a while, the designs are . . . borrowed, shall we say? The artisans get bored doing the same thing all the time."

"You mean they fake it? Pass their work off as someone else's?"

"I mean they get bored, Agent Scully. What they use, they make their own."

They again.

342

Mulder began to wonder.

Suddenly the man grunted and clutched at his stomach. Scully was on her feet immediately, but he waved her away. "It's okay," he said, gasping a little, his eyes watering. "Took me by surprise, is all."

Scully stood by him anyway. "What did?"

Lanaya gestured toward his plate. "Ulcer, I think."

"What? You have an ulcer and you eat this stuff?" She rolled her eyes and took her seat. "You're out of your mind."

"Maybe." He took a roll of antacid tablets from his pocket and popped one into his mouth. "No, definitely. But I keep hoping I'll get used to it before I die."

"Don't worry, you won't," she told him. "Because that stuff will end up killing you."

He laughed, and Mulder managed a polite smile in response.

He was getting damn tired of people lying to his face.

There was someone in the backyard.

She heard movement as she dropped her suitcase into the passenger seat, and swore. With hardly any neighbors to speak of, who the hell would be out there? Unless it was a stray cat, or . . . she glared. Or a goddamn coyote.

She hurried into the house, yanked open a desk drawer, and pulled out a wood-stock .38. She had never given a damn what the cautions were; it was always loaded. A single woman living alone would scarcely have the time to load if someone broke in in the middle of the night.

She hefted it, thumbed off the safety, and marched through the Pullman kitchen to the back door. As far as she could tell, the yard was empty, its grass long since given over to weeds and bare earth.

Still . . .

A low, constant hissing.

Shit, she thought; she had left the outside faucet on. That's what it was—water spilling onto the weeds beneath the damn faucet. She tried to remember when she last was out here, and couldn't. Good God, it could have been as long as a week, maybe more. Her water bill was going to be—

She laughed and shook her head.

Who cared about a stupid water bill? She wasn't going to be around to pay it anyway. Nevertheless, a twinge of guilt at all that waste made her open the door and step outside, swinging immediately to the right and crouching under the kitchen window. She already had her hand on the faucet when she realized it was dry.

No water.

"What the hell?"

The noise grew louder, and now she heard what she thought was whispering.

She rose and turned in the same move.

Too terrified to scream, she managed to fire twice before she was struck and spun away from the house, her arms flailing, her clothes shredded, strips of flesh taken and flung against the wall, her eyes blinded, her lips gone.

When it was over, she remained on her feet for as long as it took for a breeze to touch her.

When she fell, no one heard her.

Lanaya folded his napkin beside his empty plate. "If it's all right with you, I'll pick you up in the morning. The sooner we get there, the sooner we can leave."

Mulder reached for a glass of water. "You don't sound very proud of your home."

"It's for your own good, Agent Mulder. And there's not much to see." He pushed his chair back, but neither Mulder nor Scully moved. "I have to admit, I'm still not convinced you're looking in the right place. Coincidence, that's all it is."

"Maybe. Probably, if you like. But as I already said to someone, we have no choice."

"Sure, no problem. I understand."

Mulder turned around, looking for a waiter to signal so he could get the check. Who he saw was Sheriff Sparrow coming through the front door. By his attitude, the way he snapped a question at the clerk, who had walked over to greet him, it was business. Bad business.

"Scully," he said quietly, and excused himself to hurry into the lobby.

Sparrow brushed the clerk aside with a brusque nod and stared over Mulder's shoulder. "News," he said.

"What?"

"Lanaya been with you all this time?"

Mulder nodded. "What's happened?"

"You already eat?"

"Sheriff, would you mind telling me what's going on?"

Sparrow stared, shook himself without moving a muscle, and blew out a sigh. "Sorry. I didn't mean to snap like that. But I guess you're in luck, Agent Mulder. There's been another one."

Mulder beckoned to Scully automatically as he said, "Who?"

"Donna Falkner."

Shots, two, maybe three, the sheriff told them as he sped out of the parking lot. A neighbor went over to complain, couldn't get an answer at the front door and wandered around to the back. As soon as he saw the body, he called the sheriff's office. As soon as the first deputy saw the body, he called the sheriff, knowing the FBI was in on this case.

Several patrol cars were already on the scene when they

arrived, and an ambulance backed into the driveway. Yellow crime scene ribbon fluttered around the property. A handful of people stood in the lot across the street.

"How well did you know her?" Mulder asked as Sparrow led them around the garage to the back.

"She was a pain in the ass." A sharp wave. "She was okay, though."

"Did you know she was going on vacation?"

Sparrow stopped and turned at the corner. "Are you crazy? She never went on vacation. Working herself to death is what she was. Wanted to be a goddamn millionaire before she was thirty-five."

Mulder stepped around him and walked slowly through the shin-high weeds. A sheet had been placed over the body. He didn't bother to ask if the ME had been called; this report wouldn't be any different from the others.

Scully brushed by him and knelt beside the sheet. He stood behind her, holding his breath as she pulled on a pair of latex gloves, pinched a corner, and pulled it back.

Mulder looked away.

Scully braced herself on the ground with one hand, and whispered something he couldn't catch. He saw a shudder work its way down her back before she asked if someone had a camera. A deputy appeared at her side, and she directed the lens as she pulled the sheet farther back.

The mutilation here wasn't as complete as the others. There were areas where the skin was raw but still intact, and areas where a gleam of white showed through liquid red. Her face, however, was completely gone, as was most of her hair.

This had not been a swift dying.

While the sheriff barked and grumbled at his men, Mulder began a slow walk around the yard, until he realized that the color near and on the ground was actually bits of flesh. So were the splotches on the wall near an outside spigot. At the foundation just below it, he found the gun, took a pen from his pocket, and picked it up through the trigger guard. Two shots, maybe three, the neighbor had said.

At what?

"Scully."

She looked up, a little pale but recovered.

He jerked his head to tell her he would be inside when she was finished, then opened the kitchen door and went in.

It was still hot, no moving air, and no sign that she intended to return from wherever it was she'd been heading. The drawers in the tiny bedroom dresser were empty; there were a few cartons in the spare room, which looked like those he'd seen in the Cherokee outside. Nothing in the medicine cabinet. Papers and some ledgers in the desk; bills paid and unpaid, but no letters.

He didn't realize how much sunlight had slipped away until someone snapped on an overhead light.

It didn't make the place look any better.

When he took another turn around the room, he saw a briefcase against the wall beside the desk. He knelt, lifted it up, and raised an eyebrow in mild surprise. It was heavier than it looked.

When he opened it, he knew why.

"What do you know?" he said softly, closed it again, and snapped the locks. He kept it in his hand as he went through the house again, finding nothing more than tangles of dust in the corners.

Eventually he found himself by the window, staring at Nick Lanaya, who stood by a pickup parked across the street. Funny reaction, he thought as he headed for the door. The man's partner is murdered, and he just stands there.

He moved onto the stoop and waved, but Lanaya didn't see him.

He was too busy talking to Leon Ciola.

SEVENTEEN

X "Mulder."

He lifted a hand to his shoulder, bringing Scully out of the house and cautioning her at the same time. He pointed when she stood beside him.

"Well, well."

The two men were close together, sideways to the house, every so often glancing down into the truck's bed. Not once did they show any interest in the deputies bustling around the area, or in the police when they arrived, lights spinning. Mulder couldn't tell if they were arguing or not, but they certainly weren't simply passing the time.

He could see Ciola's shark smile; he couldn't read Lanaya's face at all.

Then Ciola jabbed Lanaya's chest with a stiff finger, once, twice, and leaned so close their noses almost touched.

"Do you think we should join them?" Scully asked.

"What, and disturb their grief?" He sidestepped back into the living room. "Look at this, Scully." He set the briefcase on the desk and opened it to show her the packets of money he had found, as many as could be crammed in without bursting the seams.

"A bank is safer." She picked up a packet, another, but there was no sense trying to fix the amount now. Some were in equal amounts, others were mixed. That there was thousands, however, was beyond question. She pulled back her hand and closed the briefcase with a slap. "The same as the others, Mulder." Her gloves had already been stripped off, but she scrubbed her hands anyway. "Not as complete, but the same." She looked at him, almost angry. "I'm going to do this autopsy myself. And this time the report will be right."

"What will it say, Agent Scully?" Nick Lanaya asked from the doorway.

She turned to him. "It will say, once the remains have been confirmed, that Donna Falkner was murdered by person or persons unknown, for one thing. For another, it will say that it appears to be in the same manner of death as the others you've had in this area." She turned away. "You'll have to wait for the rest."

Lanaya sagged against the door frame, head bowed. "I looked in the Cherokee."

Mulder kept the case as he walked over to Lanaya. "She was your partner. Where was she going with all that?"

Lanaya didn't look up. "I would say she was stealing it. According to the markings, they should have been sold months ago." Suddenly he kicked back at the screen door, slamming it against the house. "Goddamnit, Mulder, what the hell was she doing? All the years we worked together—" He kicked the door again and stared blindly into the room.

This time Mulder saw the pain. And something else. Maybe betrayal.

He nudged Lanaya until he went outside, and they walked

away from the house, Mulder drawing closer until the man had no conscious choice but to take him to the truck.

The bed was empty, except for a length of tarp folded near the cab.

"I didn't know you knew Leon," Mulder said, careful to keep accusation from his voice.

"There isn't an adult Konochine alive who doesn't know all the others, Agent Mulder. You can hardly avoid it the way we live."

"It seemed a bit more than just casual, from what I saw."

"Personal, okay? It was personal." Lanaya's expression couldn't decide whether to be angry or insulted. "I was with you, remember?" A one-sided, humorless smile flashed on, flashed off. "Just in case you were wondering."

"I wasn't. I have a pretty good short-term memory. Do you happen to know where Mr. Ciola was?"

"Don't know, don't give a shit." Lanaya reached into the bed and picked up a twig with long needles on it. He twirled it between his fingers before flicking it away. "Stupid woman. My God, what . . . what . . ." He gave up.

"You were lovers?"

The Indian shrugged, one shoulder. "For a while. A couple of years back. Turned out we wanted to be business partners more, so we stopped."

"That briefcase is filled with money. Would you have any idea where she got it?"

Radio chatter hung over the street.

A cop and a deputy laughed too loudly.

It should be dark, Mulder thought as he waited for an answer, there's too much light here. It should be dark.

"We haven't been doing too well lately, actually," Lanaya finally admitted. He sniffed, rubbed his nose with the back of a hand, and pushed his hat up off his forehead. "About a year ago, she said the usual stuff wasn't working anymore, that we needed a gimmick, something to distinguish our product from all the other Indian stuff getting produced around here." He laughed bitterly. "I got a bad feeling, Agent Mulder. A bad feeling I've been had." Another laugh, and he slapped the truck's side. "Son of a bitch! When they find out about this, I'll never be able to get them to trust me again."

Scully and Sparrow left the house, talking softly.

Lanaya swept a nervous hand back over his hair several times. "Will I . . . she has no relatives, I mean. Will I have to, you know, identify her?"

"That won't be necessary."

He looked, one eye nearly closed. "That bad?"

Mulder couldn't face him. "There'll have to be the usual tests."

"Tests?" He moved as if to take a run at the house. "Tests? Then how the hell do you know it's her, Mulder? My God, maybe it's someone else, a vagrant or something."

The only thing he could say was, "I know, Mr. Lanaya. I don't want to, but you'll have to trust me on this. I know it's her."

Lanaya made a growling noise in his throat, took a step around the truck, and asked with a look if he was needed. Mulder waved him on, and backed away back when the pickup barreled away, turning the corner without the brake lights flaring.

Mulder watched for a moment, then returned to the front yard, where Scully joined him.

"You all right?" he asked, seeing the expression on her face.

She nodded. "I'm just finding it a little hard to believe, that's all." She glanced toward the house. "Aside from the method, though, it's strange."

"That's not strange enough?"

She almost smiled. "Did you get a good look at the yard?"

"I saw the bare patch where she fell, if that's what you mean."

"Right. But before we leave, take another look. That bare area where the grass and weeds were cut down, that wasn't done by any kind of mower I'm aware of."

"Wait."

She passed a hand over her chin. "What I mean is, where she died isn't where she was first attacked. Whoever killed her . . . it's as if she was pushed around, and the murderer followed her."

"A force like that, I'm not surprised. When you get into a fight, you hardly ever stick to one place."

"This wasn't like a fistfight, Mulder. She wasn't punched around, falling down and getting up again. From what I can tell, given the . . . given the positions of the body, and the flesh and bone shards around the yard, she fell only once. When she died."

Mulder swallowed, but said nothing.

"The point is, Mulder—whoever attacked her, with whatever weapon, kept her on her feet."

"But the force it would take to do that much damage . . . " He gestured toward the house.

"Exactly, Mulder," she said. "Exactly. She should have fallen almost immediately. But she didn't."

That night, after the paperwork was done, interviews completed, and he and Sheriff Sparrow had finished debriefing each other, he returned to the bench in the garden. His room had grown too small, and Scully was transcribing her notes into the computer. Her mind was already on the morning autopsy—a fresh, puzzling corpse to decipher.

Oh God, he thought; you're sick, pal, you're really sick. What you need is a vacation.

He almost laughed.

Right; that's what got me into this in the first place.

The Rio Grande was higher after the downpour, but only

slightly, and the ground and paths were completely dry. There were no strolling guests tonight, either; that didn't surprise him. Word was probably out that the killer had struck again. For a night or two, people would stick close to home, the papers would editorialize about the alarming incidence of psychopathic murders in contemporary society, and someone, somewhere, would manage to reap a large or small political harvest.

Which knowledge got him exactly nowhere.

He reached down between his legs and picked up a pebble. He bounced it on his palm a few times before swatting it toward the water.

He did it a second time, swinging a little harder.

He stood for the third one, and hit it with a fist. It stung a knuckle, but he barely felt it. It was the motion that mattered. When he missed the fourth stone, he considered stopping wasting time and going back to the room. That lasted as long as it took him to find it, and miss again.

Now it was a matter of personal honor, and now he couldn't find the damn thing. Not that any of the others he spotted while on his hands and knees wouldn't have worked, but the one he had missed was the one he wanted.

He was nearly stretched out under the bench, feeling like a jackass, when he heard the rustle of something moving through the brush on the riverbank. At first he thought it might be the evening breeze, but listening for a few seconds told him it was too irregular.

Stop and start.

Just out of reach of the tree lamps and the moonlight, and the lamp poles along the bank.

He used the bench to push himself to his feet, staring upriver as he dusted off his knees. That, too, was a waste of time; the lamps in front of him blocked any chance of seeing what lay beyond.

353

The rustling stopped.

All right, so what do they have around here at night? Dogs, cats, coyotes? After that, he went blank.

When he heard it again, he took a long step off the path and picked up a small rock, aimed, and threw it as hard as he could. The crash of the missile through the brush and weeds was followed by the dull plop of its landing in shallow water. But there was no yelp, no sudden rush of an animal scurrying to get away.

Nothing at all, in fact; nothing at all.

Accepting that as a sign he was in danger of losing it, he flicked one more pebble at the water and started back to his room. He hadn't gone three steps when the noise returned.

Not a rustling now, but a barely audible hissing.

Not stop and start, but continuous and moving; slowly, very slowly.

Common sense and experience ordered him to head immediately for the inside, or, at the very least, get Scully out here with him.

What he did, for no good reason he could think of, was sidestep cautiously off the path, turning his head in short stages to try to pinpoint the source's location, whatever the source was. When he reached the lamp poles, his right hand closed around one as he slipped past, while his left instinctively slipped his gun from its holster.

He wouldn't have done that if he hadn't heard the whispering.

More than one voice, although he couldn't tell how many. Nor could he understand what they were saying. One moment it sounded like muffled laughter, the next like little children exchanging secrets in the dark.

Beyond the last pole, there was still several yards of cleared earth straight ahead, while to the left the ground sloped downward toward the river. He flexed his knees to keep his balance on the slope, to keep from sliding as he moved forward, staring, silently cursing the weak reach of the lamplight. He could barely see the brush, could only just make out a twisted branch above it, no higher than his head.

The noise was on the other side, coming toward him.

Carefully he reached behind him, fumbled for and grabbed the last square pole, a clumsy position until he put most of his weight on his right foot.

The whispering sounded more frantic, quickly blending into what sounded like a low hum.

No animal, he knew; and he couldn't see how it could be people, either. That many would make a different kind of noise, and it certainly would be louder. Which made his drawn weapon a little ludicrous.

If there was nothing to shoot at, why have it out?

But nothing didn't make a noise.

It didn't hiss.

It didn't whisper.

He released the lamp pole and eased forward, keeping low, freezing when he had a sudden image of a woman about to open a door everyone in the theater knew hid the monster. They called her stupid, they yelled at her not to do it, they threw things at the screen to get her attention, but she opened it anyway.

And she was always wrong.

And what, he asked himself, does that make you?

Hissing, climbing to a higher pitch that puzzled him because the pitch was still quite low.

It reminded him of something.

It definitely reminded him of something.

He took a step back, snapping his head around when something splashed to his left. No ripples that he could see, not even when he heard another splash, farther across the water. He could have turned then, but he didn't want to show his back to whatever was out there. He wanted to see it if he could, just in case it came into the open and could see him, too.

Then something struck the pole, taking a chip from the edge.

He didn't wait to see if it had been a shot; he fired one of his own into the dark, whirled and began to run, slipping once on the grass, flinging a hand out to stop him from falling on his chest.

When he reached the bench, he turned, trotting backward, staring at something he could finally see down by the lamps.

He never had a chance to see it clearly.

He heard a voice, heard a popping sound, and all the lamps turned red.

EIGHTEEN

Dugan Velador was tired of being old.

He didn't want to die, that would be a waste of his life. What he wanted, however, was for people to stop coming to him with questions whose answers they already knew if they would only stop to think. What he wanted was a little peace, and he didn't think that was too selfish a wish. Not at his age. Not after all he had done for his people.

He also wanted the killing to stop.

It should have ended the other night, the last night in the kiva.

For as long as he could remember, and for all that he had been taught and told, the last night should have meant the end, for it had always been before.

Not this time.

This time, from what he had heard on the portable radio he kept by his bed, another one had died. A woman. The name was familiar. He couldn't place the face or the occasion of the meeting, so he knew she wasn't Konochine *frastera,* one of those who had left.

Still, the name was familiar, and he worried at it while he ate breakfast, worried at it while, with a sitting blanket over one shoulder, he walked from his place to sleep by the Tribal Center to the Wall that overlooked the road that pointed west. When he was younger, but not young by any calculation, he used to sit there every dawn and stare at the unseen place where he knew Annie lived.

He tried to will her to return.

He prayed for her to leave the ranch and move back to her rightful home.

When that didn't work, he figured he had either really garbled the prayers so badly that the spirits hadn't recognized them, or he wasn't half as strong as he thought he was. Velador was a practical man. When one thing didn't work, there was always something else. If the spirits wouldn't listen, someone else would.

As Nick would say, what the hell.

The only thing he hadn't done, and would not do, was visit her in person. That would insult her, and demean him.

Practical, however, sometimes meant taking a bite out of pride, swallowing it, and hoping it wasn't poison.

He would have to think about it hard today. The killing of the woman he could not remember was too important. Annie would know that; maybe she already did. Maybe she would take a bite, too, and at least meet him halfway.

If she didn't, he'd be sitting in the sun for nothing.

Practical didn't always mean that what he did was smart.

When Mulder opened his eyes, he instantly allowed as how he fully deserved the booming explosion whose echoes rebounded through his skull for what seemed like forever. And when forever arrived, he still had a splitting headache.

At least he was still in his room, or would be as soon as the walls stopped shifting.

Last night, when he'd regained consciousness, he had thought he was in a hospital. A beautiful hospital with soft lights and attractive, natural decorations complete with all the appropriate scents and aromas. The bed was too hard, though, and the air conditioning had been turned up way too high. They hadn't even bothered to cover him with a blanket.

When his vision cleared an eyeblink later, he realized someone had stretched him out on one of the benches in the motel's back garden.

Scully knelt beside him, urging him to stop hiding and come all the way out. When he did, she scolded him for doing whatever he had done to get him clunked like this.

"Clunked?"

He had tried to sit up, but his head wouldn't let him; neither would his stomach. A rolling nausea engulfed him briefly, and he tightened his jaw, clenched his fits until the urge to vomit had passed.

Sparrow leaned into sight then, and between thumb and forefinger held up a stone that would fit perfectly in his palm. He turned it so Mulder could see the fresh bloodstain.

"What were you doing, Mulder?" Scully's expression was stern, but her voice was pure concern.

Again he tried to sit up, and again the dizziness was too strong. He accepted the order her hand on his shoulder gave him. "Someone was out there." He pointed vaguely, not sure of the right direction. "Maybe more than one. Definitely more than one." His eyes closed as he tried to remember.

While he did, the sheriff said, "And they knocked you out with a rock? Agent Scully said she heard a shot."

Voices had interrupted them, for which he had been grateful. He needed time for all parts of him to get back together, and when they did, reluctantly, he said, "No, never mind. I don't think it was a person."

The sheriff grunted. "Then you're the first man on record to get himself beaned by a coyote."

"Not an animal either."

"He's delirious." Sparrow sounded disgusted. "Such a little scratch, too. I'll be back in the morning, folks. There's nothing out there, Agent Scully. And if there was, he's long gone by now. Long gone."

More voices, footsteps, murmuring, then silence.

He opened his eyes.

Scully was still there, patient. "What did you shoot at, Mulder?"

"Little scratch? I thought a boulder hit me."

"Mulder, pay attention. What did you shoot at?"

He hadn't known then, and he didn't know now. Not that he could think very straight yet anyway, even if he did know. Fingers touched his forehead gingerly, skated over it until they reached the lump of a square bandage just above his left temple. He pressed, it protested, and he let the hand fall away.

What the hell was it?

Sleep on it, he ordered, and no one argued.

When he next woke up, the ache had lessened considerably, and he felt well enough to stumble into the bathroom before his bladder exploded. A double palmful of water scattered the rest of the cobwebs, allowing him to check his reflection without wanting to break the mirror.

All in all, he looked a lot better than he felt. The bandage was small, and someone, probably Scully, had already washed the blood from his face. Other than his hair poking out in all directions, he figured he looked pretty human.

A few minutes of washing, holding onto the basin while ripples of nausea and dizziness settled, and getting that hair back into place, and he felt even better. Hungry, even. He was about to give Scully a call to meet him for a late breakfast when he spotted a note taped to the mirror over the low dressing table in the front room. It was a reminder that she had an autopsy to perform, and a warning not to do anything on his own. She hoped to be back by noon, or shortly after.

Taking care to move without jarring anything loose inside his skull, he finished dressing and stepped outside.

The sky was blindingly blue, the sun simply blinding, and the heat hadn't changed, although it might have been, relatively, a bit cooler than yesterday. None of it did his head any good, and he hurried to the restaurant and the safety of the indoors.

A simple breakfast eaten in solitude allowed him to get past the muted throbbing behind his brow, to go over what had happened the night before.

Not that he needed much reminding. The humiliation of the lump was bad enough.

What had happened was, he had ignored all his instincts and had opened that damn door. What had made him do it, he couldn't figure out. It had been more than simple curiosity, and until the end of the episode, he didn't recall feeling all that threatened.

So . . . why?

He ordered a second tall glass of orange juice and sipped it while he watched the other guests come and go, wind through the courtyard, take pictures of each other beneath the cottonwood. In the white sun they had no idea what he had seen yesterday in that weed-infested yard; or if they did, they weren't going to let it ruin their day. A tale to tell when they got home, nothing more, a whole lot less.

The glass was empty when he remembered something else— that the noise he had heard by the river had reminded him of something. He concentrated, and scowled in defeat when he couldn't give it a name. He did bring back the feeling, however, and it made him put the glass down and take a deep calming breath.

Above and in that hissing was the whispering.

She is special, mr. mulder.

His spine stiffened.

She hears the wind.

He was on his feet before he realized he had even left his seat, and that he hadn't yet received his check. Luckily, the waiter spotted him and came right over. Mulder signed it, added a large tip and an effusive verbal thanks that startled the young man, and did his best not to run from the room to the lobby reception desk. There were no messages from Scully, and none from Sheriff Sparrow, who had said, Mulder recalled, that he would be back sometime this morning to ask some questions about last night.

He wondered if he could convince the man that he hadn't been delirious at all.

The wind.

Not wanting to confine himself to his room again, he strolled deliberately slowly around the courtyard, for all the world like a tourist who couldn't think of a damn thing to do. When he couldn't stand it anymore, he veered into the passageway to the back garden. Except for a woman standing near the center, he was alone.

The wind.

As he passed her, heading for the place where he'd been struck, he heard a noise. A familiar noise. One that made him stop, that made his headache return.

"Are you all right?"

The woman, a short Hispanic woman in a maid's uniform, looked up at him, not really concerned; she was only being polite because she had to. Behind her he saw a wheeled cart stacked with fresh linens and towels.

He nodded, and stared at her hands when the noise started again.

"Hey," she said, both a question and a warning.

"I'm sorry." He added a smile to the apology and moved on,

forcing himself not to look back. A moment later he heard the cart's wheels roll quickly across the stone. Obviously she thought he was nuts. Maybe he was. The sound he had just heard was an emery board being drawn across her nail. Almost like sandpaper.

At the bench where he had been last night, he looked toward the spot where he had heard the hissing, the whispers.

He didn't have to go there now to know what he would find, but he went anyway. A justification, a confirmation. He hadn't seen it on the riverbank where Paulie Deven had been killed, but he had seen it yesterday, in Donna Falkner's backyard. He just hadn't known what he had been looking at.

It didn't take long.

At the place where the grass met the underbrush, he stopped and rose up slightly on his toes. The growth wasn't so dense that he couldn't get in there; he didn't need to. He could see well enough from where he stood.

About ten feet away was an open spot, a scar. The branches of the brush at its rim were either snapped off or had their bark worn through. Stretching his neck allowed him a glimpse of the ground, and the debris that covered it.

He grinned.

"Agent Mulder!"

Sheriff Sparrow came into the garden, and Mulder answered him with a gesture that he'd be there in a second. One more scan of the area showed him everything he needed to see, and he rubbed his hands briskly as he returned to the garden path.

"Sheriff, do you think you can get hold of Nick Lanaya?"

"I suppose so. What do you need?"

Scully, he thought as he headed for the sheriff, you're going to hate what I know.

You're going to hate it a lot.

NINETEEN

There were no chairs in the lobby. The only place to sit was a thick wood bench beside the fountain. Mulder waited while Sparrow used the desk phone to reach Lanaya, hoping that Scully would return soon. He didn't want to leave without her, but he felt a need to move fast, before someone else died.

After last night, he had more than an unpleasant feeling that he knew who that target was.

Sparrow sat beside him, hat and sunglasses off, rubbing his eyes. "I left a message. There's only a couple of phones out there. Portable jobs like you have. Half the time they're left behind." He leaned back against the fountain's broad lip. "So you want to tell me what's going on, or is this going to be one of those need-to-know bullshit things?"

Mulder shook his head. "No need-to-know, Sheriff. Scully and I are going to need all the help we can get." He checked the time, wondering aloud how long his partner would be.

"She's done, and on her way," the man said wryly.

"How do you know that?"

364

"I read minds, Mulder." The jerk of a thumb toward the reception desk. "Plus, I called."

Close, Mulder thought; not quite, but close enough.

"Half an hour, maybe a little more." The sheriff rocked to nudge Mulder with a shoulder. "I can't read minds that good."

Mulder debated. No matter how many times he told it, there would be arguments and countersuggestions, especially from Scully. He decided it would be best to get it out in one session rather than have to keep repeating himself.

It would also give him time to convince himself more thoroughly that he was right.

At his hesitation, the sheriff took off his hat and dropped it beside him on the bench. He took a notepad from his breast pocket, and a pen whose tip had been chewed close to chipping. "Okay. So how about you tell me about last night? You fired a gun, Mulder. FBI or not, that needs some explanation."

Grateful for the change of subject, Mulder complied readily. He took the man through his movements step by step from the time he entered the garden until he had been struck. Sparrow asked few questions. A clarification here, a doubt there. When Mulder was done, the man put the notepad away, fixed the pen to his pocket, and scratched his forehead.

"Basically, what you're telling me is that you shot at a shadow."

"No, Sheriff. I shot at something that was definitely no shadow."

"So what was it?"

Mulder smiled and stood. "Patience is a virtue, Sheriff Sparrow."

"Patience, my friend, is a royal pain in the ass. And you gotta admit, I've been pretty damn patient with you."

Mulder agreed, and decided to take the lawman out back to show him what he had found. Sparrow reminded him that he had already been there, he and his men, but Mulder insisted gently. What he wanted the sheriff to see was something his men, good as they were, probably wouldn't have thought twice about.

"I did the same, Sheriff, the first time I saw it."

They were already at the riverbank when Scully called his name.

He made a silent wish for no surprises, no complications, then looked at the sheriff.

Sparrow was laughing.

"What?"

He pointed at Scully, then reached over and tapped a finger against Mulder's chest. "Couldn't stand it, could you?"

That was the first time Mulder realized that in dressing this morning, he had put on his tie and blue suit. It had been automatic. He had been too busy fighting his headache to think. His hands had grabbed what they knew best.

Scully, too, was the same.

For some reason, even out here, she looked more natural that way.

"Well?" he asked.

Scully greeted the sheriff almost curtly, pushed at her hair to keep the steady breeze from blinding her, and said, "Mulder, I do not want to have to do that again, ever."

"I'd think," Sparrow said, "you'd be used to it by now. Cutting them up, I mean, figuring things out."

"You don't get used to it," she told him. "You just find a way not to let it bother you for a while." She grabbed a folded paper from her shoulder bag, glanced at it, and took a deep breath. "You'll be pleased to know there are no surprises, Mulder. And Dr. Rios was right—it wasn't skinning and it wasn't flaying. Scouring, for the time being, is a pretty damn good word."

"What killed her?"

"Simply? Layman's terms? Shock. If you want the details, we

can start with the near-total destruction of a major organ—which is what the skin is—coupled with rapid fluid loss from various sources, including—"

"Never mind," the sheriff interrupted, a queasy look on his face. "I get the picture."

"No," she contradicted. "I don't think you do. Mulder, there were particles of sandy dirt lodged in the sinuses and eye sockets. And in the brain."

"What the hell could do something like that?" Sparrow demanded.

"Force," Mulder answered. "A lot of force." He started for the river. "Which is why I want you to take a look at this."

Scully looked at him quizzically. "What?"

"Just look, Scully. I'll explain on our way to the Mesa."

She didn't argue, but followed the sheriff to the brush at the edge of the grass, where Mulder pointed out the cleared area farther on. It took a while until they found a way through without ripping themselves to shreds, and when they reached the rough circle, he broke off an already damaged twig and held it up.

"The bark," he said. "Torn off."

The ground at their feet was littered with shredded leaves and shards of twigs and branches.

"If I didn't know better," Sparrow said, "I'd say a nut with a weed-whacker got roaring drunk in here."

"There's the same sort of damage done over at Donna Falkner's house," Mulder told them as they made their way back to the garden. "I saw it, but because the yard was so badly kept, it didn't hit me until this morning."

Sparrow told them to meet him in the parking lot; he'd go in to see if Lanaya had been reached. Scully walked with her head down, every few steps shaking her head. Then she stopped Mulder with a touch. "A device, maybe? Maybe the sheriff wasn't so far off with that weed-trimmer idea." She looked away, looked

367

back. "But that doesn't explain the dirt. Just falling wouldn't do it."

"No, you're right."

He started for the car, but she blocked him, a hand briefly on his chest. "What is it, Mulder? What are you up to?"

"Sangre Viento," he answered. "It's the only thing that makes sense."

"Really?" She glanced over at the sheriff, hurrying toward them. "And you think that makes sense?"

"It does to me."

"Of course it does," she said flatly. "Whatever was I thinking of."

"Nick's waiting at the res," Sparrow said, herding them toward his cruiser. A hard look at Mulder. "We'll ride together, all right? I want to hear this. Just tell me I'm gonna like it."

Mulder couldn't, and by his expression the sheriff knew it. He rolled his eyes in resignation and wondered aloud how Scully put up with it.

"Patience," Mulder said as he slid into the backseat.

"Pain in the ass," the sheriff answered.

"Maybe. But I've gotten used to it."

Scully wasn't amused.

Nick hunkered down beside the old man, hands draped across his knees. "You're going to bake out here, Dugan."

The old man only shrugged.

"The FBI is coming."

"There was a death."

"I know."

"The woman. I think I know her."

Nick shifted uneasily. "Donna Falkner, Dugan. She's . . . was my partner."

"Ah, yes. I remember her now. She ran pretty good."

Nick couldn't help but smile. "Yes, she did. And she helped us a lot. I hope you remember that, too."

The old man brushed invisible sand from his blanket, the only admission Nick was likely to get.

"There should not have been a killing, Nick."

"Yes. I know that."

"There should not have been any killings." Dugan's head turned stiffly. "The cattle sometimes. I remember a coyote once. But no people, Nick. Never any people before."

Nick nodded earnestly, leaning as close as he could without toppling into the old man's lap. "That's what I've been trying to tell you, Dugan. If we don't do something, the FBI will find out, and we won't be able to stop the news people or the police or anybody from trampling all over the Mesa." He lowered his voice. "But if we stop him now, there'll be nothing to see. Nothing to find."

A breeze stirred the grass.

"Dugan. Father. The Falkner woman won't be the last to die. You know that."

The old man's head bowed, his hands gathering in his lap. "I am hoping for—"

Nick couldn't help himself; he grabbed the man's shoulder harshly. "Damnit, she isn't coming back, Dugan. Annie isn't coming back, and she's not going to help." He felt the shoulder stiffen, and snatched his hand away. "If we're going to make it through this, we have to see that Leon is . . ."

He didn't finish.

He didn't have to.

All he could do was wait for Velador to make up his mind. As he stood, the old man began a low murmuring, and Nick walked away.

He hadn't gone ten paces when the old man said, "Nick," just loud enough to hear.

He turned to face Dugan's back, and the right hand raised, finger pointing to the sky.

"The FBI."

"What about them?"

"They must be stopped."

The breeze blew.

The sand stirred.

Imagine, Mulder said, a group of men, extremely devout men, confined for so long in a single room. The kiva. Imagine, as he had already mentioned to Scully, the energy they must create and radiate as they perform the rituals required of their faith. Suppose, then, there are moments during that time when the energy can no longer be confined, but its excess escapes through the hole in the ceiling. It can dissipate. Maybe someone nearby feels a little discomfort, but nothing more. They might blame it on the wind.

But suppose, just suppose, it doesn't scatter. Suppose it gathers instead. Suppose it concentrates.

Suppose the earliest Konochine knew this. They would also know that such a concentration would be potentially dangerous. So they come to the valley within the Wall from wherever they had been, and make it their home. It's isolated, protected by both the hills and the mountains, and nobody—not the other tribes, not the Spanish, not the whites—bothers them for very long.

But the energy is the important thing.

What happens to it?

Sangre Viento.

Blood Wind.

Nando making a spinning motion with his hand.

He called it a whirlwind.

WHIRLWIND

Not a tornado dropping from a cloud; an extraordinary dust devil, rising from the ground.

It spins alone in the desert, and when the energy is used, it falls apart, just like disturbing the plane of an ordinary dust devil will cause it to collapse. It's reasonable to suppose, then, that once in a while an animal gets caught in it, and because it spins at such high speeds, far faster than an ordinary dervish, and because it's made up of gritty, sandy earth, leaves, twigs, whatever else is on the ground . . .

Imagine, he said.

Imagine the power.

TWENTY

X He stared at the passing desert, elbow on the armrest, one hand curled lightly across his chin. Now that he had said it aloud, heard his voice, he knew he was right. There was no baroque device a murderer could cart around with him, and there was no group of whip-wielding maniacs.

Sangre Viento was all there was.

And one thing more.

"Mulder," Scully said in that voice he had heard so many times before, "assuming, and only assuming, for the moment that you're right—"

Sheriff Sparrow grumbled a few words, most of which were "bullshit."

Mulder couldn't miss the tone of disappointment and disbelief.

"—what you're talking about is . . ." She faltered. "Is a form of undirected psychic, for want of a better word, energy. Assuming it's true," she added hastily. "But how does that random activity explain four people dying? It seems to me that where and when they died indicates something else entirely."

"Premeditation," he said, still watching the desert.

"Exactly."

"Oh, sweet Jesus," Sparrow snapped. "Are you telling me there's somebody who can aim this thing? Assuming," he said sarcastically, "you're right." He yanked the cruiser so hard off the interstate, Mulder nearly fell over. "For God's sake, gimme a break."

Unfortunately, Mulder couldn't see any other answer. What he could see, however, was a couple of names who might be interested in such control. The question was, why would they feel the need to kill?

"I mean," the sheriff continued, working himself into a self-righteous rage, "how can a couple of intelligent people like you believe in such crap? Bunch of old Indians sitting around a campfire, shooting cosmic something-or-other at each other? You been nibbling at some peyote or what?" He slapped the steering wheel hard. "Scully, you're a doctor, for God's sake. You gonna tell me you actually go along with this shit?"

Mulder held his breath.

"Sheriff," she answered in her most official, neutral voice, "I have never known Mulder to be so far off-base that I would dismiss everything he says out of hand."

"Ah . . . crap."

Thank you, Scully, Mulder thought with a brief smile, I'd rather have a resounding "absolutely and how dare you," but that'll do in a pinch.

On the other hand, the day that "absolutely and how dare you" actually came, it would probably kill him with amazement.

They passed the Double-H, and he wondered if any of this had touched Annie. He wondered what she had heard on the wind. Whatever it was, he didn't believe for a second she was in any way involved.

Suddenly the sheriff braked hard, and Mulder shot his hand

out to brace himself against the seat back. In the road ahead, a pickup had been parked across the lane. Nick Lanaya lounged against the bed, arms folded across his chest.

"Stupid bastard," the sheriff muttered. "Has everyone gone nuts on me today?"

They climbed out slowly, Mulder moving around the car to join Scully. As he did, he looked up the boulder-strewn slope on his right and saw a figure sitting near the top, featureless and black against the sky.

"Dugan Velador," Lanaya said, pushing away from the truck. "He's like a priest. One of the six." A tolerant chuckle and a gesture to the hill. "He likes it up there. He says it helps him think."

"But it's so hot," Scully said, astonished. "How does he survive?"

"He's Konochine, Agent Scully. He can pretty much survive anything." He cleared his throat. "So what's up? I got Chuck's message. What can I do for you?"

The sheriff hitched his belt. "Nick, you ain't gonna—"

"We need to see the reservation, Mr. Lanaya," Mulder said, further cutting the sheriff off by standing half in front of him. "There are some questions we have to ask of the people in charge."

"The Council?"

"Are they the priests?" Scully asked.

Lanaya shrugged. "Mostly, yes. But I don't think they'll talk to you."

Mulder smiled. "That's why you're here. To convince them that cooperation in a murder investigation would be the right thing to do. Maybe save some lives."

Lanaya scuffed the ground with the toe of a boot. "Well, to be honest, Agent Mulder, I'm kind of beat today." A sour look at the sheriff. "I spent most of the morning with a police accountant, going over Donna's ledgers and bank account. It seems she was cheating me more than just a little."

"So I gathered."

"Luckily, most of the money is recoverable, so I won't lose much. But it's the shock, you know what I mean? A lot of years I trusted her, and now I'll never know why she did it."

"Your people trusted her, too," Scully said.

"No." He squinted at the hillside. "No, they trusted me. Like I said, I've got a hell of a lot of damage control ahead of me here. And you coming in like this . . . it's only going to make things worse."

Mulder walked over to the truck. "You have air conditioning, right?"

Puzzled, Lanaya nodded.

"Good." He opened the passenger door and beckoned to Scully. "Let's go." Expressionless, Scully climbed in first. "We have a job to do. Right, sheriff?"

All Sparrow could do was nod curtly, and Lanaya shrugged an *it's your funeral* before getting in behind the wheel. But his face was hard, and Mulder saw his fingers tremble as they turned the key to fire the engine. Anger, or nerves.

"Ground rules," Lanaya told them as he maneuvered the pickup around. "You don't get out unless I say it's all right. You don't speak to anyone unless I say it's all right, or they speak to you first. And you sure don't go in any building unless I say it's all right. Okay?"

"Drive, Mr. Lanaya," he said. "Neither one of us has all day."

They drove through the gap, the road curving gently to the right. When the hill was finally behind them, Mulder almost asked him to stop. He wasn't quite sure what he had expected, but it wasn't anything like this.

Off the road to the left were small fields filled with crops. Scattered gunmetal pumps resembling steel dinosaurs worked ceaselessly, pumping well water into an effective series of irrigation ditches. He didn't recognize any of the crops except, in the center and by far the largest field, corn.

It was a stark, surreal contrast to the desert land that surrounded it.

On the right, however, was Sangre Viento Mesa.

Lanaya slowed. "The Place, Agent Mulder. You'll see other mesas, but never one like that."

It rose two hundred vertical feet from the desert floor, its sides ridged and furrowed, and stark. Where sunlight washed it, faint red hinted at iron among the dark tans and browns. There was no green at all. There was no plant life that he could see from this distance. On the flat top were outlines of low buildings. Several large birds circled over it. Its shadow seemed everywhere.

At the north base was the pueblo, and again his vague expectations didn't match the reality.

"Your people weren't cliff dwellers," Scully said softly.

"No. No one has ever lived on the Mesa itself." Lanaya looked at her with a faint smile. "Every so often, maybe once a decade, I'm able to bring in an archaeologist or two and some professors who don't believe it. They insist there have to be cave homes there on several levels, with ladders and all the rest. Like at Puye and Mesa Verde. There aren't."

What there were were neat rows of small abobe houses, a single story each. One, apparently, for each family. All the doors and windows Mulder could see were outlined in pale green. As the road curved closer, he saw laundry hanging from lines on poles, orderly streets in a grid, and at the east end, two larger structures which, Lanaya explained, were a storage building for crops and a tribal center. Incongruously, to Mulder, some of the homes sported television and FM antennas; only a few had vehicles parked beside them, and most of them were pickups. He also spotted a corral where several horses munched on hay and swatted flies with their tails, a trio of black and white dogs trotting along a street, and a low pen populated by chickens whose plumage was almost garish.

It didn't occur to him to think it odd that he couldn't see any litter.

"Where do they work?" Scully asked, leaning as close to the windshield as she could.

"In the fields, in workshops in the center or in their homes. A few go outside, but not many. The Konochine have no unemployment, if that's what you're wondering. You work to eat. You don't work, you don't eat." Lanaya laughed, but not cheerfully. "I don't know of anyone who has ever chosen to starve."

"And your house?" she asked.

Flatly: "You can't see it from here."

Mulder watched a group of white-clothed children playing in front of a building near the pueblo's middle; another group chased each other through the streets, carrying hoops and switches. "What about Leon Ciola?"

Lanaya forced the truck into a tight U-turn and took a short dirt road that led them to the front of the warehouse and the tribal center. No one looked up as he passed except one small boy, whose eyes grew so wide Mulder had to smile.

When the engine stopped, metal creaking, Lanaya opened his door. "Ciola lives where he wants. I don't follow him around, Agent Mulder. He's . . . he's having a difficult time fitting back into the life."

Three steps led to double doors in the center. Lanaya pushed one open and gestured the others in. "You'll have to ask your questions here."

They were in a large meeting hall with exposed thick beams in the low ceiling. Two doors in the side walls and one in back were closed, their frames painted a pale green. The walls were white. The floor was uncovered. The only decoration was on the back wall over the door, a huge woven tapestry with a depiction of the Mesa in the center. Lightning in the sky. Symbols of sun and moon, of birds and animals. No people at all. Nothing he recognized as a language.

"No one knows how old it is," Lanaya said, his voice low. "My grandfather once told me that his grandfather knew an old woman who knew an old woman who helped with the design." He shrugged. "It doesn't matter."

Against the left wall was a long table of Spanish oak, with equally bulky chairs arranged around it. He led them over and bade them sit, Mulder with his back to the wall, Scully opposite him. "You'll want to talk to one of the Council," he said. "Dugan would be the best."

"The man on the hill?" Mulder said.

"Yes. It's time he came in out of the sun anyway. He's going to get heatstroke one of these days. Wait here. Please. It won't take me long."

The echo of his boots on the floor lingered after he had gone. And once gone, there was no other sound. The outside might as well not have existed.

Scully placed her shoulder bag on the table and folded her hands on it. "He's a strange man, Mulder. One minute you think he hates this place, and then he goes all reverent on you."

"He's been outside. How can you not have a conflict?"

She looked doubtful, but she didn't pursue it. Instead, as he expected, she launched into a perfectly reasonable explanation of why, with his belief in the Sangre Viento, he was pushing the limits of her tolerance. While she grudgingly granted him the possibility of undirected psychic energy—a phrase she nearly choked on—she was not about to grant him deliberate control.

"Do you know what that means?"

"Murder," he answered simply.

"Do you want to try to prove that in court? Do you think Skinner will buy it?"

"Right now, I don't care about Skinner. What I care about is who's doing this." He leaned forward on his arms folded on the table. "Scully, four people are dead, there's one agent missing, every connection points here, or to someone here, and unless we catch him, there's going to be more."

She stared at him for a long time.

He held the stare as long as he could, then sighed and looked down at his blurred reflection in the dark polished wood.

"Ciola," she said then.

He looked up without raising his head.

"Leon Ciola." She slipped a sheet of paper from her bag and slid it over. "You were so busy driving Sheriff Sparrow away with your story that I didn't have a chance to tell you." She tapped the paper with a finger. "Preliminary police report on Donna Falkner's house. A lot of prints were lifted. Hers, of course, and Lanaya's, no surprise, he was her partner. And Leon Ciola's." She cocked an eyebrow. "Some of them in the bedroom."

He glanced over the form and resisted the urge to shout.

"It's hard with only that one conversation," she continued, "but I don't get the feeling that she ran that embezzlement scheme on her own. Ciola could have talked her into it. It's been going on for four years. Two of those years were his last two in prison." Another tap on the paper. "She visited him there, Mulder. Often. Evidently she was the reason he lost his temper in the bar."

Mulder rested his chin on his arm. "She gets greedy. He finds out. His infamous temper."

No answer.

He looked up into a disquieting frown.

"We'll assume again, all right? For the sake of argument?"

He nodded.

"Why Paulie Deven? Why the Constellas?"

He had already thought about that; he already had an answer that disturbed him.

"Practice," he said, lowering his gaze to the table. "All they were to him was practice."

She didn't react, didn't speak. She pulled the paper back, turned it around, and skimmed it. Then she put it back into her bag and let her head rest against the chair's high back. Her lips pursed; her eyes followed an unseen trail on the ceiling.

"He's not one of the Council, Mulder. Ciola—"

"Well, well, well, *chica*," Ciola said from the entrance. "Every time I see you, you can't help but speak my name."

TWENTY-ONE

Beyond the cornfield, beyond the last of the water pumps, in the desert, the sand began to stir.

With an exaggerated swagger Ciola crossed the hall, swinging his arms, deliberately cracking his heels against the floor for the gunshot sound. His head was bare, his shirt and jeans looked stiff enough to be new, and his hair had been freed from his ponytail to sway against his back as he moved.

"You like it in here?" he asked, spreading his arms.

Neither Mulder nor Scully answered.

He made a face. "This, you know, is the place where they meet every month. They try to think of a way to banish me, you see?" He laughed and stamped a foot. "I am an embarrassment to them, FBI. I spent a lot of time in the penitentiary, and I think they think this shames them."

He reached the head of the table and dragged the chair back, dropped into it, and hooked a leg over the arm.

Scully shifted in her chair to face him, her right arm resting on the table. She said nothing; she only looked.

Ciola gestured toward the entrance. "You're all the talk out there today, Agent Scully, did you know that? It's the red in your hair, I think. I figured you were here to talk to me, is that right? So here I am. So talk."

Scully gave him a little nod. "Where were you yesterday afternoon, Mr. Ciola?"

He shook his head sadly. "You'll have to do better than that. I was telling my parole officer how wonderful it is to be outside again."

"Then how did you know about Donna Falkner? You were there."

"I have a police scanner in my truck." He grinned. "It comes in handy."

"A scanner?" She sounded doubtful.

The grin snapped off. "I'm an Indian, Agent Scully. I'm not a savage."

"You nearly cut a man's head off," Mulder said mildly. "That sounds pretty savage to me."

Ciola only glared at him, a quick glance, before he looked back to Scully. "Anything else?"

"Theft," she said.

The leg slid slowly off the arm. "I kill people, Agent Scully, I don't steal from them. You want a thief, I suggest you have a word with Saint Nick."

"What were you two arguing about? Yesterday. In the street."

"Do you know something, Agent Scully? For the life of me, I can't understand why a woman like you would—"

"Ciola," Mulder said, raising his voice.

The man sighed the sigh of a terribly put-upon man, and looked.

Mulder held up his ID. "Just for the record, the Federal Bureau of Investigation has legal authority on Indian reservations, whether we're asked in or not. That means, Mr. Ciola, that I don't need anyone's permission—not the sheriff's, not your Council's—to bring you in for questioning concerning the murder of Donna Falkner. Or Paulie

Deven. Or Matt and Doris Constella." He put the ID back in his pocket. "Why don't you just cut the crap, and answer Agent Scully."

The man looked ready to bolt, and from the corner of her eye, Scully saw Mulder tense for the chase. "He told us it was personal," she said quickly, watching them both relax as if strings had been severed.

"It is."

"How personal?"

"We hate each other, Ms. Scully. I'm an ex-con and he's a saint. I dropped out of high school, he's got degrees up his ass and out his throat." Palms down, he spread his fingers on the table. After a long moment, he said, "How confidential is this? If I tell you something, you put me back in the pen?"

"That depends," Mulder answered.

"On what?"

"On whether I say so," Scully said, holding back a grin at the astonishment on his face.

"Let . . . let me think about it."

"While you're thinking," Mulder said, "tell me how you managed not to be killed by the Sangre Viento."

Ciola gaped, his left hand moving unconsciously to his cheek to brush over the scars. "How the hell did you know that?"

Mulder didn't answer.

Scully knew, however. Now that she could examine them without fearing a knife in her throat, the pattern across his neck and face was clear; at least, clear enough to anyone who knew about the Wind.

"I had a pony," Ciola said quietly. "When I was very little, a man died, one of the six. During the ceremonial, no one leaves the Mesa, or goes into the desert. It's a foolish chance. Only people like Saint Nick do something dumb like that. I was little, and I was foolish, and I wanted my pony. She had broken out of the corral, and I chased her for nearly an hour.

"I almost had her once, but she bolted. I couldn't figure out why until I turned around, and there it was. Right behind me. I fell over backward into an arroyo, and that's what saved me."

Scully couldn't help it: "You believe in this Blood Wind?"

Ciola's fingers fluttered across his face. "That's a stupid question, *chica*. Do you want a stupid answer?"

"No, just a truthful one."

His eyes widened at her boldness, but one of the front doors opened before he had a chance to say a word. Nick Lanaya walked in, an old man trailing behind, both of them unaware of Ciola until they were halfway across the floor.

Lanaya stopped; the old man didn't. He continued on to the table and took the chair on Scully's right.

"What do you want, Leon?" Nick demanded.

"The FBI calls, I answer." He grinned at Mulder. "It's the law, don't you know that?"

"Get out, Leon. They need you in the warehouse."

"Oh, I don't know. There are many questions left to ask." He looked to Scully for support. "They want to know, for example, about Donna. How we loved, how we fought, how we—"

"*Chinga!*" Lanaya spat, face darkening with rage. "You kill, you dare to come back here as if nothing ever happened, and now you dare to talk—"

"Enough!" Mulder ordered, thumping the table with his fist. "Excuse me," he said to the old man, and turned back to the others. "Mr. Lanaya, for all our sakes, let me or Agent Scully be the ones to decide when Mr. Ciola has told us enough, okay? Mr. Ciola, I take it you're not planning a vacation or anything like that?"

Ciola laughed as he stood. "Don't leave town, eh, *gringo?* Don't worry. I won't. I still have to go to Donna's funeral."

Lanaya grabbed the man's arm as he brushed past him and whispered harshly in his ear. Scully couldn't understand what was said, but it made her wonder when Ciola swallowed heavily and left, nearly at a run. Nick made to follow, but a grunted word from the old man brought him to the table, where he sat in the chair Ciola had just used.

"I'm sorry," he said with a sheepish smile. "The man just drives me crazy." His hand waved in front of his face as if clearing the air of a foul odor. Then he introduced Dugan Velador. "He speaks very good English, so—"

"Have I left, Nick?" Velador asked quietly.

Again Lanaya's face darkened, and he lowered his head and didn't move.

Scully raised an eyebrow to Mulder at the control the old man had, then sat back so she could see both of them at once. She wasn't sure what Mulder wanted her to say, and so deferred to him when he cleared his throat, a signal that he wanted to take charge of the interview for a time.

She hoped, though, that when the Sangre Viento came up, as it surely would, Velador wouldn't be insulted. It would be easy for him to think they were mocking him, or being condescending. And although Nick had warned them of the probability, she was somewhat taken aback when the old man said, "I want you to leave the Mesa now, please. There is nothing here to discuss or tell you."

He stood, the bone necklace he wore rattling softly.

Lanaya stood as well, quickly, but Mulder only clasped his hands on the table and said, "I have reason to believe, Mr. Velador, that someone, probably one of your people, has been using either you, or the six, to establish control of the Sangre Viento." When the old man reached out to grab the edge of the table, Mulder paid him no heed. "If that's true, then this man, sir, has committed four murders, and Agent Scully and I don't intend to leave until we find him, and arrest him."

Well, Scully thought as Velador sank back into his chair, that's certainly being subtle.

A small leaf danced in a circle in the air, several inches above the ground. From a distance it looked like a butterfly searching for a blossom. Seconds later it was joined by another, this one pierced by a cactus needle.

Below them, the sand began to rise.

Mulder hoped neither the old man nor Scully noticed when he released the breath he'd been holding. Sparring with Ciola had been bad enough, but Velador, whose posture and expression told those who saw him he was meek and too dull to be considered, had given him a start as soon as he'd walked in. He may have been behind Lanaya, but he was clearly the leader.

When he sat, nothing about him moved, except for those black eyes.

Mulder had no doubt that in another time, in another culture, Dugan Velador would have been royal.

Right now, a quivering left hand covered the rattlesnake necklace, while the right hand rested on fingertips on the table. He said nothing, and Mulder kept silent. What amazed him, and puzzled him, was that Lanaya hadn't protested either. He, too, sat with one hand against his chest, the other out of sight in his lap.

It was Scully's concern that broke the silence. She leaned toward Velador, a hand out but not touching. "Mr. Velador, are you all right? I'm a doctor, sir, if you need help."

Mulder could almost hear the neck bones creaking as the old man turned his head. "I'm fine, young woman. It seems that we are not as alone as we thought."

An angry look at Lanaya forced Mulder to gesture, to regain the man's attention. "It wasn't Nick who told me, sir. He didn't . . . he didn't betray a confidence."

"What do you know?"

There was no hesitation; this wasn't the time.

"As much as I'm able without having been in the kiva with you."

"Then you know that what you say can't be true."

Mulder avoided Scully's eyes. "No, sir, I'm afraid I don't know that at all." Although he suspected the old man knew more than he gave away, Mulder told him about the four deaths, described the bodies, and used the same hand motion Nando Quintodo had. "It's the only explanation, sir. Nothing else makes any sense."

That surprised Velador. "You think it makes sense?"

Mulder shrugged—*sure, why not?*

"And you?" he asked Scully gently. "Do you think this makes sense?"

"I think I haven't heard anything else yet that . . . that covers the situation as well."

He smiled then, a broad smile that nearly broke into a laugh. "You look at things differently than your friend."

"Oh yes," she said. "Oh, yes."

Another look to Lanaya, a curious one, made Mulder frown. What had Lanaya done or said that the old man should be so annoyed?

Suddenly Lanaya bent over in a coughing fit, covering his mouth with a loose fist. "Sorry," he gasped, tears filling his eyes. "Sorry. I—" He waggled his fingers at his throat and coughed again, much harder, more harshly. Finally, when he couldn't stop it, he got up and, behind an apologetic gesture to carry on, left the hall, muttering about finding some water. Mulder could hear the awful hacking until the door swung shut behind him.

"He always gets that way when I embarrass him." Velador smiled mischievously. "One day I will have to beat it out of him. He's too old for that sort of thing."

Mulder straightened.

"Mr. Velador," Scully said, "we were told no one would speak to us. Why did you change your mind? Because of—"

"Sometimes I am not as smart as I think I am, you know. Sometimes, sitting in the sun, there is a buzzing in my head, and I don't hear the words everyone says to me very well. Sometimes the words I say are not the words others hear."

"What did you say?"

"I said the FBI must be stopped."

She tapped a knuckle lightly, thoughtfully, against her lips. "Are you saying that now we're in some kind of danger. Just because of that?"

He nodded, then shook his head. "If what this man says is true, young woman, you're in more danger than you know. But not because of what I said."

"Yes," Mulder said suddenly, getting to his feet. "I'm sorry, sir, but you're wrong." He started around the table. "Scully, we have to leave." He beckoned to her urgently, took her elbow when she stood, and nearly dragged her toward the door. "Mr. Velador, please stay inside. Scully and I aren't the only ones who have to be careful."

The old man didn't move.

The necklace rattled; he hadn't touched it.

Once they were outside, Scully pulled her arm free. "Mulder, what's going on? You're acting like a madman."

"You got it, Scully. You hit it right on the nail."

"Then what's—"

"Look."

He swept his hand through the air. Showing her the empty streets. The shuttered windows. Closed doors. No dogs, no chickens, no horses in the corral.

The pueblo was deserted.

Nothing moved but a single sheet, flapping in the wind.

TWENTY-TWO

X Lanaya's pickup was gone.

A curl of brown dust moved down the street, folding in upon itself when the wind began to pick up.

Over the flat roofs, Mulder could see another dust cloud rising and falling like the hump of a lumbering beast, until the wind shoved it against a wall and scattered it.

Scully took a step down, shading her eyes against the sun and blowing grit. A shake of her head when she couldn't find what she was looking for. When she turned toward the Mesa, the wind snapped her hair around her cheeks, momentarily blinding her until she turned again.

"How did they know?" she asked. "It's so fast. How did they know?"

"Someone told them," he answered grimly, and stepped all the way down to the ground. The few vehicles he could see were undoubtedly locked, and he didn't think pounding on doors or windows would get them any help. "We'll have to go back in."

Scully was way ahead of him. She grabbed the large door-knob and tried to turn it over.

It didn't budge.

"Mulder, he's locked us out."

They both tried, and tried using their fists and voices to get the old man to let them in. They stopped when she cursed and massaged her right wrist.

He returned to the street. "Okay, maybe we can find some-place else. A stable or something."

The first place they tried was the warehouse next door, and neither was surprised to find it locked as well. If Ciola is still in there, Mulder thought, he's probably having the time of his life.

They darted across the street and made their way between the two nearest houses to the next street over, saw nothing promising and moved on to the next. By the fourth, he knew they weren't going to find shelter. Not here. And not, he thought as he stared at the Mesa, up there. He didn't know how the Konochine got to the top, but he didn't think they'd take kindly to his trying.

Scully slumped against a house wall out of the direct push of the wind, using a forearm to mop the sweat from her forehead. "Why don't we just wait it out here, whatever it is?"

"We can't, Scully." He stepped away from the house's protec-tion and looked up and down the street. Still nothing. Shutters and doors closed against them. He stretched out a hand and beck-oned. "We have to get inside someplace."

"Mulder, it's only a dust storm. We'll need a week of showers when it's over, but it's only a dust storm."

"No. No, it isn't."

And he knew she didn't really believe in the dust storm idea, either. If it were one, they'd be offered shelter somewhere in here; if it were one, the people wouldn't have gone to ground so swiftly. Ciola had told them only a fool stayed outside when the ceremonial was in progress. But since there was no one, not now, they were obviously convinced the Sangre Viento was on its way.

He turned in a slow circle, frustrated, growing angry, beating a hand against his leg while he tried to decide what to do next. Hide, was the obvious answer, but where?

Nowhere.

At least, nowhere in the pueblo.

Apparently Scully had reached the same conclusion. She left the wall's protection and started up the street toward the road, purposeful urgency in her stride. He hesitated before following, hoping she wasn't thinking what he feared she was.

When he caught up, she said, "How far do you think it is?"

Damn, he thought.

"Too far to run. There's got to be someplace closer."

"I have no intention of running, Mulder. At least not yet." She pointed to the fields, and the desert beyond. "If it comes from out there, we'll be able to see it, right?" She gave him a tight smile. "When we see it, then we'll run and see what happens."

"What if it comes from somewhere else?"

"Then we won't have to run, will we."

More leaves, dancing.

When they were close enough, they gave the illusion of a funnel; when they separated they were butterflies again.

Until the sand joined them.

Then they become a cloud.

What Mulder desperately wished he knew, what he couldn't deduce from any of the information he had, was how long it took the whirlwind to form. If it took six men to create one only once in a while over the course of a week, surely a single man, no matter how skilled, couldn't create one with just the snap of a finger.

"Oh God," he whispered as they passed the last house and angled westward toward the road.

Not with the snap of a finger, but after sufficient preparation. Which meant—

Scully, staying on his left, unabashedly using him as a windbreak, picked up the pace as she said, "It's Lanaya, isn't it."

"Yes," he said, more convinced now than he had been that morning.

"Why? Ciola's too obvious?"

"No. Ciola didn't know we were coming today. Lanaya did. He's had time, Scully, to get ready. He took that old man literally. He's going to stop us." He held up a hand before she could interrupt. "He's going to try to stop us, okay?"

She ran a few steps, slowed, ran a few more.

The wind died abruptly.

He couldn't help glancing to the right every few feet, grateful when the fields blocked him, a little apprehensive when he could see all the way to the mountainous horizon. He had no idea what the Wind would look like, or if he'd be able to hear it coming.

He caught up with her when she paused to shake dust from her hair, and grinned when a sudden gust blew it back in her face. "It's a no-win, Scully."

"Tell me about it."

They walked on.

Ahead, above the road, curtains of shimmering heat hung in the air. He took off his tie and jammed it in a pocket. What the hell was he thinking of, wearing a suit on a day like today? And why, he thought further, turning around to walk backward a few steps, didn't he just take his gun, walk up to one of those doors, and threaten to blow the lock off if they didn't let him in?

Because, he answered, they'd probably just shoot back.

Swirls of sandy soil snaked across the blacktop when the wind returned. Rustling made him jump until he realized it was only the corn in its field. A tumbleweed rolled between them, tangling in Scully's feet until she kicked at it savagely and it broke apart, and was blown away.

"Tell me something, Mulder—if this man is so well-liked here, and he can cross successfully between this world and the one out there, why did he do it? Why risk it all?"

They had no water.

His throat was dry, his eyes felt gritty. When he breathed, it was like taking in clouds of fire to his lungs.

They weren't walking nearly as rapidly now.

"He kept saying 'they,'" Mulder answered, licking his lips to moisten them, finally giving it up as futile. "When he gave us that big speech about the Konochine and their dislike of the outside world, he kept saying 'they.'"

He had been one of them until he'd left to go to school. When he came back, he had changed. It was inevitable. And for reasons they might never know, or understand, he hadn't been able to change back, or to adapt as he had adapted to the outside. Mulder suspected it was unfocused anger that forced him to attempt to steal what belonged to the six. They were . . . Dugan Velador was the wise man, the leader. What he did, what the others did, was accepted without serious question.

How could he not want that respect, too?

What he hadn't understood was that the power the old men had came from the respect they were given, not the other way around.

Lanaya figured, have the power, have the respect. That would make him fully Konochine again.

Scully slowed a little, and he saw how her hair had begun to

393

mat to her neck and scalp. He took off his jacket and slung it over his shoulder, his shirt nearly transparent where the sweat held it against his skin. When he brushed his fingers over his hair, the hair felt hot. He would give a lot right now to look stupid in a hat.

Then he blinked, wiped his face, and blinked again.

The gap in the Wall was only a hundred yards away.

He looked back at the pueblo, and saw nothing move. Dust blew through it, and all he could think was *ghost town.*

The dust devil grew and spun in place.

It was little more than two feet high, wobbling around its axis as if ready to collapse should the wind blow again.

Butterflies and sand.

No sound at all.

Mulder stumbled, and Scully grabbed his arm to steady him. He smiled at her wanly. "Isn't that what I'm supposed to do?"

"Since when did you ever think I was helpless, Mulder?"

Never, he thought; never.

They walked into the gap, and into its shadow which was no shade at all. Ahead, the road rose and fell as if it were a narrow wave, making him rub his eyes until it steadied. In his shoes his feet burned, and his ankles promised spectacular blisters once he took the shoes off.

Something small and dark scuttled across the road.

It was tempting, very tempting, to take his shirt off. The cloth was a weight his shoulders could barely handle. The jacket on his arm already weighed a ton, and he didn't think he'd be able to carry it much longer.

"How did they do it?" Scully asked as they came out of the gap and stopped. She stared across the desert floor. They could see no interstate, no trucks, no cars, no planes overhead. There was nothing but the sky and the mountains. "How did they cross this place without killing themselves?"

"They had water, for one thing," Mulder said sourly.

"It must have been incredible," she said. She laughed. "It must have been a bitch."

He let his knees fold him into a crouch, his jacket slipping to the road. There was too much space here, too much sky; gauging distance accurately was nearly impossible, but he seemed to remember that the ranch house wasn't much more than a mile to his right. If they climbed the fence and angled overland instead of sticking to the road, they might make it faster.

He didn't realize he'd been speaking aloud until Scully said, "What if you twist an ankle?"

"Me? Why me?"

She grinned. "I'm a doctor, I know better."

It was heartening to see the smile; it wasn't good to see how her face had reddened. They were dangerously close to sunstroke; they had to be. And dehydration wasn't all that far behind. If they were going to do it, they'd better do it now.

He rose with a groan, and with a groan leaned over to pick up his jacket.

"Ciola is evil, you know," she said.

He draped the jacket over the barbed wire and held it down while she climbed awkwardly over.

"Lanaya is worse."

He didn't get it. "Why?"

"I can understand Ciola. But it'll take me a long time to understand Nick."

As tall as a man.

And now it began to whisper.

• • •

He stumbled over nothing, and commanded his limbs to knock it off. It wasn't as if they were in the middle of the desert, a hundred miles from the nearest civilization. He could already see the fences, could already make out the dim outline of the ranch house. A mile, maybe, he couldn't be sure. But he was acting as though it was ten miles, or more.

Scully sidestepped a prickly pear and nearly walked straight into another. She swiped at it with her suit coat, the move turning her in a circle.

"Do you think Sparrow is in on it?"

"What? Sparrow? No, why?"

"He didn't follow us into the reservation, and he wasn't waiting when we came out."

It was too hot to think straight, but he doubted that Sparrow was anything more than understandably skeptical about the whole thing. He was, no doubt, sitting in his office, drinking from his flask, and trying to figure out how he would charm them, or bully them, into getting some credit for the crime's solution. Even if it meant having to accept some magic.

It began to hiss.

It began to move.

"There!" Scully announced. "There it is."

They stood on the lip of a shallow arroyo, beside a hand-crafted bridge.

"Thank God, you see it too," Mulder said. "I thought it was a mirage."

They crossed the bridge single file. The vivid green of the lawn was visible now, and through the rising ghostly heat he could make out the house, if not its details.

On the other side, Scully leaned over the rail. "I think those holes in the bank down there are rattlesnake dens."

Mulder wasn't listening.

He had stopped to take a breath, a brief rest on his feet. Without much hope, he checked the gap just in case Ciola, or someone, had taken pity on them, and had followed them in a truck. He also checked the top of the hill, just in case the old man was there.

Then he said, "Scully, how fast can you run?"

TWENTY-THREE

It rose out of the arroyo a hundred yards away.

Mulder had expected it to be shaped like a minia-ture tornado, but it was conical from top to bot-tom, and cloudy with the debris that whipped around its surface, the source of the hissing it made as it left the dead river and made its way toward them.

Eight feet high; at least four wide in the middle.

Whether it was the force behind it, or the weight of the sand and grit that formed it, it wobbled as it moved, with thin dark bands rippling along its surface, snapping apart and re-forming. Every so often a gap would appear and he could see right through it; then the gap would close, swallowed whole.

Had it arrived an hour or two earlier, he didn't doubt they would have had a chance to make it to the house. Its ground speed was not much greater than that of a leisurely trot. Not now, though; not after so much time in the sun.

They ran over the uneven ground as if palsied, as if drunk, veering wildly away from each other, then having to veer again in order not to collide when they tried to rejoin. Serrated grasses slashed at their ankles; shrub and brush stabbed at their arms and legs.

The sun hadn't gone; it was still there, pressing down.

Something exploded in the dirt to Mulder's left, leaving a geyser of dust to hang in the air.

Scully cried out wordlessly in alarm when the top of a cactus shattered as she passed it.

When a third puff rose from the ground a dozen yards away, he realized it was the heavier material caught in the force of it— pebbles, perhaps large twigs; their own weight would eventually fling them out like grapeshot.

They skidded and slid down a short depression.

Mulder glanced back over his shoulder and saw the whirl-wind sweep past a small bush, shredding the branches it touched.

Scully grunted and went to one knee, her left hand crossed over to grip her right shoulder. She'd been hit. Mulder raced over and hauled her to her feet, pushed her on when he was struck behind his right knee. He dropped as she had, then launched him-self forward as if from a starting block. His right hand went around her shoulders when he reached her, and they supported each other into another depression, and up again.

The ranch house bobbed not that far ahead.

He could see the white split-rail fence, the grass, and no one on the porch.

They didn't know; they couldn't hear.

"How does it know?" Scully demanded.

It hissed along the ground, moving faster, growing taller.

Growing darker.

•   •   •

Mulder couldn't tell her. He was distracted by the sudden, guttural roar of an engine, searching wildly until he spotted a battered pickup lurch out of a boiling dust cloud to their right.

He was so startled he didn't see the rock until it was too late. His right foot slid over its smooth, flat surface, and he would have gone down had not Scully gripped him tightly and yanked him, still running, back to his feet.

The porch was still empty; what the hell were they doing in there?

Sweat ran into his eyes, blinding him, stinging.

Scully yelled, and he thought for a moment she'd been hit again, and his shoulders automatically hunched in anticipation. When she yelled a second time, he understood; she was trying to get the attention of the house.

It wouldn't do any good.

The hissing was too loud.

Something large snapped not far behind them, like the crack of a huge bullwhip.

The pickup drew closer, jouncing recklessly over the ground, slipping sideways left and right as the driver tried to keep it in line.

Scully finally noticed and waved at it frantically once, but when Mulder tried to steer them toward it, she suddenly shouldered him away. "Him," was all she was able to say.

Nick Lanaya was behind the wheel, and it didn't take long for Mulder to realize that the man wanted to herd them away from the house, to keep them in the open. It was also the answer to Scully's question: since the man hadn't known exactly where they would be, he would have had to keep them in sight once he'd set the Wind in motion.

Someone stepped out onto the porch.

"Almost there," he gasped. "Hang on, we're almost there."

The pickup aimed right for them.

400

Mulder stubbornly refused to give ground, forcing his concentration on the maddeningly slow approach of the fence and the lawn. It was Scully who threw them aside when the truck roared by, smothering them in a dust cloud that made it impossible for them to breathe.

The Blood Wind swerved.
The hiss deepened to a growling.

He couldn't see anything, but Mulder heard the Wind and urged Scully back to her feet, shoved her ahead of him and pulled out his gun. Not for the Wind, but for the truck, which had swung into a turn so Lanaya could come at them again.
Stalling them.
Dividing their attention between one death and another.
Twenty yards to the fence when Mulder swung his arm around and fired blindly, not expecting to hit anything, just hoping Lanaya would think twice before trying to close again.
The truck didn't stop.
The Wind didn't stop.
Suddenly the ground hardened, and Mulder looked down and realized they had reached the drive.
Scully had already climbed halfway over the fence.
On the porch Nando's wife screamed, and kept on screaming, her hands clutched against her chest.
The pickup charged, and Mulder fired a second time, hitting the windshield on the passenger side, causing Lanaya to swerve, and swerve again to avoid hitting the fence in front.
But the Wind didn't stop.
It hissed across the driveway, forcing him into a move he knew immediately was foolish but was too late to stop—he bolted to his

left, away from the house and lawn. But the sight of it so close and the sound of its voice had panicked him, and by the time he was able to think again, Lanaya had turned the truck around.

Scully yelled at him on her knees from the porch, where Nando was now, a rifle in his hands.

The Wind had paused; a stone, a piece of wood, smashed through one of the ranch house windows.

Mulder felt dizzy. The exertion, the heat and the dust, the sound of that thing spinning slowly in place . . . he took a step back and almost fell, staggered sideways and saw Lanaya in the cab, grinning.

Sangre Viento; it moved.

Nando fired at the truck, and a headlight exploded.

It won't make any difference, Mulder thought, sidling to his left; kill Lanaya, and the Wind will still be there. It has its target now.

He froze.

No; no, it won't.

The Wind brushed against the corner fence post, and sawdust filled the air, some of it showering into the yard, the rest sucked into the spinning.

Lanaya gunned the engine.

Mulder had no choice left but to run straight toward him. If the Wind picked up speed, he would use the truck to stop it; if it didn't, he would stop it anyway.

If he was right.

The Wind moved, and Scully shouted a warning, her own gun out and aiming.

A Wind-whipped stone glanced off Mulder's knee, and he dropped before he knew he'd lost control. He felt the blood before he felt the pain, and the pain stood him up again.

At that moment, both Scully and Nando fired; at that moment, Mulder aimed and fired.

At that moment, Sangre Viento moved, and moved fast.

• • •

If I'm right, Mulder thought as he raced as best he could to the truck.

The windshield was pocked with holes and weblike cracks, the engine still ran, and as he grabbed for the door, he saw Nick behind the wheel, his head back, his face covered with running blood.

He saw the whirlwind speeding toward him.

If I'm right, he thought, and yanked the door open, scrambled onto the seat, and reached for Lanaya's throat.

It wasn't hissing now, it was roaring.

He grabbed the rawhide thong around the man's neck and pulled, pulled again as the truck began to rock violently.

Pieces of the windshield began to fall in.

Giving up on the thong, Mulder nearly crawled into the dead man's lap and ripped his shirt open, grabbed the medicine bag and tried to rip it apart. He couldn't, and something slammed into his side, into his shoulder, throwing him against Lanaya's chest and rocking him back.

Metal shrieked.

Glass cracked and shattered.

He held the bag up, as far away as he could, and put a bullet through it, blowing it apart as he threw himself into the well and waited for one of them to die.

TWENTY-FOUR

X "They were all acting," Mulder said.

He and Scully sat at the porch table with Annie Hatch, he with a slick glass of iced tea, Scully with a glass of fresh-squeezed lemonade. They had invited themselves out on their last day, because Mulder felt the woman should know.

"Sparrow wanted us to believe he was either dumb as a post or a hick who was only around for comic relief. Ciola was the macho, I-dare-you-to-touch-me man, but he was terrified because he knew what Nick could do." He took a long drink and sighed. "And Nick didn't think we'd believe for a second in the Sangre Viento. We're trained agents, we deal with solid evidence and behavioral science and the magic we can do ourselves in the lab."

"It wasn't magic, Mulder," Scully said.

He smiled at the lawn. "Suit yourself."

Too many parts of him still stung where he had been struck by missiles hurled by the Wind, and his face was still an alarming red from his sunburn. He had also been right about the blisters.

Scully, too, was walking wounded, but over the past two days, neither of them had had much time to think about it while they filled out reports, filled out more reports, and listened as Sheriff Sparrow figured for the papers and local television news that the pickup had slammed into the fence while trying to run Scully and Mulder down.

The Sangre Viento had died when the contents of Nick's bag were scattered by the bullet.

None of the news people heard that story at all.

Annie poured herself another glass. "You know, I don't think any of my movies ever had so much excitement. I'm rather sorry I missed it."

Mulder looked at her until she had the grace to blush.

"All right, all right, I was scared out of my mind and hiding in the kitchen. And I'm not sorry at all, are you happy?"

He toasted her with his glass, emptied it, and pushed away from the table. They had a late-afternoon flight back to Washington, and driving wasn't going to be all that easy.

Scully finished as well, and as she picked up her bag and stood, he saw genuine reluctance to leave the ranch and Annie.

"Fox?" Annie said.

He didn't correct her.

"What happened to Red?"

"We don't know for sure," Scully answered for them. "We think he was trying to conduct his own investigation. From what the office tells us, he was hardly ever there once we arrived. Sparrow admitted to keeping him informed on the phone, but even he hasn't heard from Agent Garson since the night before we went to the Mesa."

"I think he went there on his own," Mulder said, slipping his sunglasses from his pocket and sliding them on. "I think he'll be found before long, but he won't be alive."

Another actor, he thought; the Easterners he couldn't stand

had come out to conduct what should have been his investigation, and he had to pretend to like it all the way.

They said their good-byes, and Mulder, if he hadn't already had the sunburn, would have blushed with pleasure when Annie kissed his cheek and made him promise to come back for a visit before she was too old to enjoy it.

They started for the car, but as Scully slid in behind the wheel, Mulder asked her to wait and hurried back to the porch. Annie leaned over the rail when he crooked a finger.

"What is it now?"

He pulled down his sunglasses. "There's a guy over there," he said, pointing toward the Wall. "He sits on that hill and fries himself practically every day. Maybe you ought to go over there sometime and have a talk with him."

Annie stared. "A talk?"

"It's a thought," he said.

"I'm not going back, Fox, if that's what you're asking."

"I'm not," he said innocently. "But there was this guy they thought was a saint, and he turned out to be a thief and a killer. The kids liked him, I understand."

She didn't respond.

"Besides," he added as he pushed the glasses back up, "who says a saint has to be a man?"

She was still on the porch as they drove toward the main road, and he suspected she would be there for some time to come.

He didn't speak until Scully pulled out onto the interstate. "Amazing, wasn't it? The Sangre Viento, I mean."

She glanced over at him, unsmiling. "I'm working on it, Mulder, I'm working on it."

"Of course you are."

Gradually the desert gave way to the first houses, which multiplied and grew taller, and the interstate grew more crowded. Scully had a silent, close to obscene altercation with a pickup that cut them off, and another with an old tail-fin Cadillac that hadn't yet discovered the speed limit was all the way up to fifty-five.

A mile later, she glanced at him and said, "Do you really think it was power he was after? Because he wasn't really part of that world?"

He didn't answer right away.

"Mulder?"

"Yes," he said at last. "Mostly. Power equals respect is an old lure for those who think they don't have either. Ciola is in the warehouse because he knew what Nick would do. And—"

"That's not respect, Mulder, it's fear."

"Sometimes people like that don't, or can't, make a distinction."

A van passed them, music blaring from its open windows.

"Acceptance," Mulder said then.

"What?"

"Acceptance. Power equals respect equals acceptance."

"Equals fear," she added quietly.

He agreed. He also agreed that murder was seldom as uncomplicated as most would believe. He and Scully could probably talk about it all the way back to Washington, and they still wouldn't have the complete answer.

The only one who did was Nick Lanaya.

"Scully," he said while she tried to follow the signs to the airport, "what do you think would happen if, for example, the man who replaces Velador in that circle gets a notion? Like Lanaya did. Lanaya didn't know exactly what went on in the kiva. He made a few guesses, got a few answers from the old man, who didn't know he was giving them, and did the rest on his own.

"What if one of the circle decided to turn mean?"

She didn't answer.

He had no answer.

What he knew was that Nick could possibly have gone on indefinitely, killing those he didn't like, killing those he took a dislike to for no reason at all. He could have, mostly because no one else believed.

He watched the city, the cars, saw an airplane drifting low toward a landing.

Those old men may be wise, but they aren't all old, and none of them is perfect.

Imagine, he thought.

Imagine the power.

For complimentary information on the official fan club, conventions, and licensed merchandise, please send a self addressed stamped envelope to:

CREATION-XF
411 North Central Ave. #300
Glendale, CA 91203

The X-Files TM & © 1996 Twentieth Century Fox Film Corporation. All Rights Reserved.